I0658032

SATAN'S LEGIONS

Book Three: Mercy

by

Philip G. Brown

Published by Swanford United Books
Please contact:
swanfordunited@aol.com

ISBN 978-0-9932461-5-9

Acknowledgements

I'd like to thank my copy-editor Jane Hammett, an Advanced Professional Member of the Society for Editors and Proofreaders, for her sterling work on my books.

There is an index of characters at the back of the book.

DI DAVID RAINS

Detective Inspector David Rains was back behind his desk after three weeks' sick leave and a further three on holiday in Marbella, paid for by Henderson Sawmills. It being Sunday, there was just him and Desk Sergeant Shawn Abbot on duty at the station. A quiet day. Time to catch up on his case files; time to plan his revenge on Justin Walker. A simple beating or arrest on a minor charge wouldn't suffice; it had to be something that would make the boy suffer, make his life a misery. The detective smiled to himself, then he remembered the needle going into his leg, and the hallucinatory journey back to the station, where a syringe of naloxone was waiting for him to counter the effects of the heroin. His smile turned to a resolute stare of loathing.

The office phone buzzed. "Yes?"

"Councillor Henderson is here to see you."

"Send him up."

The councillor's frame all but filled the doorway as he entered. Without an invitation, he picked up a chair with one hand and set it down in front of the desk. When he lowered himself onto it, the chair gave a little under his weight.

"Good holiday, David?"

The detective looked into the councillor's eyes to see if they held any irony. "Excellent, thank you."

"I've been in church for the past hour and a half, doing my Christian duty..."

David Rains nodded but did not reply, as he was certain that John Henderson had more to say.

"I prayed for our success in the election and prayed for Helms to become Prime Minister. I even prayed that you would have an excellent holiday at my expense. And all of those prayers were answered. So why is it that God has ignored my most fervent prayer, or is it because his servant in this matter is an incompetent fool?"

1

"I'm working on it," said the detective.

"Do you know how much time and money I've had to waste, paying off various public servants and covering for your botched schemes?"

"I wasn't the one responsible for letting your youngest son escape."

"If you'd not screwed up in Woolgrove Woods, the little queer would still be holed up at Folly Farm, making me twenty thousand a week in streamed video and making you a good deal in backhanders, including five-star holidays in Marbella. Do you know I had an offer of three million for him from Saudi Arabia?"

The DI looked sceptical, though his eyes glittered with avarice. "What do the Arabs see in the toerag?"

"They see a barely pubescent blond boy getting shafted, you fool, and money means nothing to them."

"What do you want me to do?"

"Think, for once in your life! The two brats are being doted on at 41 Westbury Avenue with one of my exes. She has got herself a cushy number looking after an old biddy who's lived there for donkey's years."

"Why is your ex looking after them?"

"Her name is Anne Waverley and she's Stewart's mother. I expect he persuaded her to take in the poofter, Alan."

"And you want me to..?"

"Simple. by the end of November, I want the older one dead. He could still cause me trouble with his accusations. A dreadful accident should suffice – and this time, David, no mistakes. On the other hand, I want the 'for sale' notice back round the little shirt-lifter's neck: he's still viable goods, that one, though I doubt I'll get more than a million for him now his voice has broken. But I want you to do it all in the line of duty – in other words as near to legally as you can, Detective, if you know the meaning of the word?"

"Who is this old biddy?"

"Her name is Elspeth Chambers. She's a bluestocking bitch who's got more intelligence in her little finger than all you PC plods have in your combined brains. So be careful. She's got friends in high places. And they are not supporters of UKMP, you understand."

"Can I rely on social services?"

"You can rely on Lambda Healthcare, who are the new providers of social welfare. It is a company in which my wife is a sleeping partner."

"I thought..."

"You thought my wife was a crack addict." Councillor Henderson sat back in the chair and folded his arms. "She's on almost every addictive substance known to man. Fortunately, she will be travelling to the north of Scotland to a special clinic in the very near future, where she will be spending the rest of her miserable life. The divorce will be through by December, but I shall remain her power of attorney for obvious reasons. I don't take kindly to cunts that spawn queer whelps."

"How will you explain that to the party?"

"Mr Little at the *Mail* is going to write me a heartfelt sob story. As long as I remarry by April the party will be happy, especially as my wedding will coincide nicely with the run-up to the mayoral election."

"What are we going to do about the Moseleys and that fag-lover Justin Walker?"

"I'm not interested in your personal vendettas, David. If you can't get the better of a fourteen-year-old puppy dog, that's your problem. I've told you what your job is: you just make sure it's carried out in the way I want. In the meantime, I shall bring the Moseley family to its knees and make sure that poofter boy Jack is on the next plane to Camp Queer. We won't need excuses to deal with the perverts once the new laws come into force."

The councillor had made his threats and his police flunky had soaked up his spleen, so now he could show some bonhomie and relax into his chair, which groaned under the renewed pressure. "Come on, David, aren't you going to offer me a mug of your bitter police coffee? With me as mayor and

Ken as crime commissioner, Swanford will at last get what it deserves. Who knows, if you do as you are told, you could become Chief Constable David Rains by the time you're forty!"

***

2: Monday, 29th July. 1 p.m. 15 Leighton Lane.

PAM

Pam sat on the settee in the lounge with a tray on her lap. Her lunch consisted of a bowl of thick vegetable soup and a buttered roll followed by a slice of raspberry cheesecake. Due at the post office at 2 p.m. for her afternoon shift, she intended to have forty-five minutes peace in front of the television to take her mind off her family's problems, first – and foremost – of which remained her husband Roger's redundancy and how they were going to cope if he found himself unemployed in October.

She pressed '1' on the remote controller and the studious face of Nick Oliver, Chief Political Correspondent, appeared.

"When I interviewed the Prime Minister at Chequers this morning he was in his usual robust and forthright mood. This is what he had to say about the new parliamentary session beginning on 1st September after the summer recess."

"There will be four priority bills brought before the House, as laid out at the State Opening in May. The first will be the repeal of the European Convention on Human Rights; the second, the repeal of the 2010 Equality Act. In their place we shall enact a Bill of Rights, a bill which has already been drafted by my colleague Gerard Amies at the Home Office. And finally, we shall bring to the house a Referenda Act that will ensure the British people have their say on matters most dear to them. We would anticipate that the first referendum will be held in the middle of next year."

"Do you know what questions will be asked in that first referendum?"

"Judging by my post bag, I would say it would be a toss-up between halting immigration and bringing back capital punishment for murderers, traitors, paedophiles and rapists."

"And what will be the main differences between the Bill of Rights and the two acts you intend to repeal?"

"There will be an emphasis on tradition and Christian values with protection of the family at the centre of our legislation."

"I understand that it is your intention to repeal the Marriage, Same-Sex Couples, Act 2013 at some future date."

"Not at some future date – within the first session. Tomorrow wouldn't be too soon for me."

"It wasn't in your manifesto, was it?"

"It is what the decent moral British citizen would want."

"What of same-sex couples who are already married?"

"The legislation will be retrospective. And I can tell you, and all those so-called gay rights activists, that we intend to introduce an amendment to the Criminal Justice Act 2003 in the first week of the new session too, banning the promotion and visible demonstration of homosexuality, to strike down all that paraphernalia of statistics and information that wastes so much police time when they should be fighting real crime. We want to put this aberrant behaviour back in the sewer where it belongs."

"Do you think your coalition partners will be supportive of such controversial legislation?"

"It's only controversial to wishy-washy left wing liberals, most of whom claim to be of that persuasion anyway. I can assure you that we have enough support from our partners in the Keystone Group to get a majority in excess of one hundred."

"Do you expect trouble on the streets?"

"The police know how to deal with trouble. The rank and file of decent officers have been waiting for a government that will stand up for them instead of undermining their every move. *We intend that law enforcement will mean just that: enforcement.*"

"*Was the five per cent pay increase given to the police a measure of your support?*"

"*A typical lefty-liberal question, Nick, which I will not deign to answer.*"

"*That was the Prime Minister, the Right Honourable Edward Helms, speaking to me earlier...*"

Pam picked up the tray and rose from the settee, wondering if she should say anything to Jack about what she had just seen. But what can I say to him? *Be careful, Don't tell anyone. Try to change. Hide away...* Anyway, it might never happen. A noise from the stairs interrupted her train of thought and Mikey appeared in the doorway.

"Dan just called me a *fucking* pest," he seethed.

"Because that's what you are!" shouted Dan from the top of the stairs.

Pam went into the hall. "Daniel Moseley, you will not use that sort of language in this house, and you will certainly not use it against your little brother."

Mikey smiled victoriously.

"He was hiding under my bed," exclaimed Dan.

Pam turned. "Why were you hiding under Dan's bed?"

Mikey shrugged.

"Excuse me, Mrs Moseley," called Sophie from upstairs. "I think he was eavesdropping on us."

"Pervying, more like," said Dan.

"Michael Moseley, is this true?"

The little boy's cheeks reddened and he looked askance at his mother. "I was just playing..."

"Right, you, you can spend the time until I go to work in your room and not on your games console!"

"Not fair," cried Mikey.

"Go on!"

Mikey limped upstairs, looking daggers at his brother and even Sophie.

"Pervert," mouthed Dan with a little smile as he passed.

Pam took her tray into the kitchen. So much for three-quarters of an hour's peace.

***

3: Monday, 29th July. 1.45 p.m. 35,000 feet above the Russian Federation.

<u>NOAH</u>

I thought if I ever went on a plane it would be to somewhere nice, like Spain or Greece for a holiday in the sun. Our dad is very traditional when it comes to holidays. I don't think he's even been to Scotland, never mind across the Channel. Foreign languages, foreign food, foreigners, it's just not him. I wish I knew what happened to our dad. They didn't tell me anything and when they came to take me away I was too scared to think.

I wonder if Alan came to our flat? Imagine finding it deserted like the *Marie Celeste.* I wish I was polishing the car or tickling his feet or – best of all – snuggling with him, instead of being cooped up here like a prisoner. Robert tried to come over and talk to me but he was slapped down by Madam DeVeal. That's what I call her. I won't even use the term 'nurse' to describe her; that would be an insult to all *real* nurses. Margaret Hopkins: she's on a permanent power trip, that one. I don't know who she thinks she is. Probably she's been watching too many Joan Crawford movies. Anytime we step out of line she starts ranting, and that great ape sitting in the front paws his way down the aisle.

I'm right against a porthole and I've been watching the world like I've only seen it in films before. If I didn't feel so nervous, I'd think it was brilliant. First we crossed the sea, which was all rippling in the sunlight, then there was some coast with lots of fjords, then more sea and now it's just miles and miles of practically nothing. I don't know where we're going, but there aren't many towns, not like England.

Our dad loves Joan Crawford movies on DVD. They're like little silver treasures to him. Sometimes I think he must have a gay streak in him because they're terribly camp. His favourite is *Mildred Pierce*, whereas mine is *What Ever Happened to Baby Jane?*

One of the boys, I think his name is Mark, had his hand up for so long without being noticed that he wet himself. He doesn't look older than eleven. When he started to cry, Madam DeVeal was as you'd expect – really sympathetic and called him a disgusting little shit. Charming! He's sitting two rows in front of me without his joggers or underpants on. They're hanging up in the toilet area soaking wet, because he was made to wash them.

I've been trying to lip-read what Robert says, but I'm totally hopeless. Every time our eyes meet he says something like 'rabbit hostel for gays' or something. He threw me a square of chocolate when Madam DeVeal was with little Mark. Of course, I dropped it on the floor, but I still ate it. At least that made us both smile.

Except for Robert, I don't know who any of these boys are, though I'm sure some of them went to our school. When they came to collect me from our flat, the man in charge said they were from social services; he even showed me his badge. I was driven to this big house in acres of ground where the first thing they did was cut my hair. Not like our dad does it, though. This was just a number-one clipper off. They said it had to be done for hygiene's sake. Next my photograph was taken, face and side like I was a criminal, then I was put in this really old-fashioned room and told to take a bath. That's when they took away all my clothes and gave me this T-shirt and jogging bottoms. A strange bloke who called himself Peter told me that if I came out of my room without permission my door would be locked. He took me for walks in the grounds on Saturday and Sunday and it was all God this, God that and God the other. I never saw any of the other boys until last night when we were all herded onto the minibus.

I sat next to this boy called Jamie Baker. He's quite rough and Mr Macho, but nice with it. I recognised him from school largely because he's so fit, but he's in Year Eleven. He'd been taken from his house by social services soon after his parents were arrested, same as me. I told him I didn't know why our dad had been arrested, and he replied that he didn't know either, but I'm not sure he was telling the truth. Then I asked him if he was gay and he said no, which didn't surprise me. That's when we were told to shut up, or else... I'm not sure what *or else* meant, and I didn't bother to find out. Jamie is now sitting in the front seat on the right, opposite the ape.

The seat belt light has just come on. In case we hadn't noticed, Madam DeVeal bawls out the news to us. The plane is definitely slowing down. I exchange a glance with Robert then look out of the window. The land is coming up to meet us; at least that's what it looks like. There's a lot of forest, pines I think, though I'm not good on trees. I see a river and some fields and a few wooden houses. Now there's a town coming up on the left. Actually, this is quite exciting. Oh, the airport – it's not very big. We've passed the town now. More fields and forest and the runway's just ahead. The plane's bumping around. Some of the boys are scared; they're making panicky noises and looking this way and that. I hope they don't know more than me. We're coming in very fast...

***

4: Monday, 29th July. 5.10 p.m. MSK (Moscow Standard Time), Aerodrome, Russian Federation.

ROBERT

It's late afternoon. We're being marched in single file across the concrete runway towards a couple of beat-up lorries with canvas covers. They look like old military vehicles. I can see Russian soldiers in olive-green fatigues and officers in wide-brimmed hats watching us from near the control tower.

This is not a civilian airport and it's hot out here; even Sister Hopkins is looking uncomfortable. I must stick out like a sore thumb in my button-down shirt and slacks, not to mention my backpack. The boy who wet himself hasn't been given anything else to wear, so he's marching in just his T-shirt and trainers, carrying his pants, underpants and Bible. The poor kid must be embarrassed beyond words.

I managed to get in line behind Noah and we've been able to exchange a few words without being shushed. With his hair cut short, he looks like a balloon on a stick.

"Russia? Russia? What are we doing in Russia?" he says.

"We are going to be cured of our gayness."

"Really? But I don't think all these boys are gay. That tall boy Jamie, the one carrying Madam DeVeal's case, says he's not gay."

"He's from our school, isn't he?"

"There are several."

"I'll show you the letter later," I whisper. "Try to look out for signs of where we actually are."

"Why?"

"Stop talking in line!" shouts Sister Hopkins.

"Yes, Madam DeVeal," murmurs Noah as though he's in elementary school, but loud enough for me to hear him – and some of the others, because there's a ripple of laughter. That boy is going to get into serious trouble, I'm sure.

There is a man standing by each of the trucks. Both are short and barrel-chested, both are dressed in hip-length off-white coats, more like you'd wear in a kitchen than a hospital. One is bald, the other has thick black hair. I guess they're the drivers.

Sister Hopkins steps up to the bald one and starts to talk – or, rather, shout – at him. Meanwhile we regroup into an untidy semi-circle to watch the proceedings. He stands impassively while the harangue continues, I'm pretty certain he doesn't understand a word, until a man in military uniform comes hurrying across the concrete carrying a briefcase.

This one, who has quite a few stars on his epaulettes, has

a thick Russian accent but speaks recognisable English.

"*Dobryy den', gospozha* Hopkins. Good afternoon, Mrs Hopkins," he says with a smile.

She purses her lips. "*Sister* Hopkins, if you please."

"Ooo," mutters Noah in his most effeminate voice. "Get her..."

There's another ripple of laughter, and I know this boy is going to hit the buffers sooner rather than later.

The Russian raises his eyebrows at the nurse. "Do you have the papers?"

"Is there something I can rest my case on?" she asks pointedly.

They go to the back of the truck and bald man lowers the tailgate.

"Be careful, Noah," I whisper.

He gives me a little grin, and one of the other boys turns. He's short and stocky with a mat of dark hair on his head, a fat face and narrow slits for eyes. "I'm George Eagleton, known as 'Porky'. Thanks for making us smile."

"Quiet!" roars Sister Hopkins.

Porky jumps and his double chin wobbles. "I'm shit scared," he whispers.

"So am I," answers Noah, "but I'm not going to give Madam DeVeal the satisfaction of seeing it."

It takes them a good fifteen minutes to sought the paperwork out and while they're in the shadow of the truck, we're sweltering in the heat. I pass round my bottle of Coke, everyone gets a swallow and I wonder how long it'll be before I see another. Our attention is diverted by the noise of a departing aircraft: it's the black and red Gulfstream taking off. It roars past us to our left and skims over the distant trees, heading back to the west. As it rises, my heart sinks.

"Looks like the great ape went back with it," says Noah.

"You!"

Sister Hopkins has pointed at Noah. "Come here."

He walks forward so that he's midway between our group and the truck, and puts his hand on his hip. The nurse strides up to him. They're about the same height, but she seems to tower over him.

"I thought I told you not to talk."

"Sorry, Miss," he says in that voice.

She slaps him so hard across the face that her hand leaves an imprint. Even with his back to us, I can see he's struggling not to cry or show any pain.

"I'll be watching you in particular, you insolent queer," she says, then she addresses all of us: "Six in each truck, get a move on!"

Noah turns to face us. He's shaking and his eyes are slightly moist, but he's managing to control himself better than I would ever have believed. I think all the boys are looking at him with respect, if not awe. I certainly am.

***

5: Monday, 29th July. 3 p.m. 15 Leighton Lane.

JACK

"Why do I have to look after you, pesto? You're seven, for heaven's sake." Jack was reclining on the settee while Mikey was standing in front of the fireplace wearing only his underpants. Despite his mother's attempts to wash out the colour from his hair, his blue spikes were still vibrant.

"Mummy says you have to help me exercise so that both my legs look the same."

"If both your legs were the same you'd look very strange."

"Mummy says I mustn't twist, jump or run, but I can do everything else."

Jack surveyed his brother from the waist down. The calf and thigh muscles of his right leg were a little less pronounced than those of the left. "OK, lift it up."

"Which?" asked Mikey.

"The skinny one, dumb-head."

The little boy lifted his right foot and started to overbalance. Jack groaned and reluctantly got up off the settee. "Come on, let's try doing it on the bottom step of the stair."

After twenty step-up, step-downs on the bottom tread, Mikey was bored.

"Now it's your turn," he said.

"Can I remind you that it was Mad Mike who pushed you off the stage, not me? I haven't had a broken leg, therefore I don't need to do baby exercises..."

"Jack, when is Noah coming round again?"

"I don't know – and don't ask."

"But—"

"What did I just say?" Jack gritted his teeth as he was reminded of the special edition of the *Swanford Mail* which he had delivered for Mr Ray on Saturday evening. Below the banner headline *Paedos in Swanford* were passport-sized photographs of the twelve men and three women suspected of being part of a paedophile ring. One of them was the local MP, another was her agent, and among the remainder was a picture of Alf Marshall, Noah's father. The photographs had been generously provided to the newspaper by the police, along with the names and addresses of the people in the photos. They had been taken when the individuals were at their lowest ebb and therefore were looking suitably grotesque and criminal. Since the edition of the paper came out, Marshall's barber shop had been looted, the windows smashed and graffiti spray-painted on the walls. The same had happened at 34b Savoy Flats – where, in addition, excrement had been left on the floor and urine sprayed over the furniture. The fifteen remained in custody pending further police enquiries.

"That's your phone," squeaked Mikey.

Jack had left his mobile on the desk in his bedroom. "Are you coming, then?"

"Will you carry me?"

"No, but I'll race you..." Jack ran up the stairs three at a time, then turned and looked down at his brother. "Remember what Mummy said: *don't run*."

13

"Not fair."

"That's life. Come on then, and you can lie on my bed and I'll feed you coconut mushrooms until you're as fat as Jabba the Hutt."

"He's an ugly mother," said Mikey, looking up sideways at his brother, who took no notice and went to his room. Retrieving his phone, Jack sat on the bed to read the text:

Jack, we've been flown to Russia. Noah's with me and ten other boys.

Some are from school, but not in our year.

Terrible woman – Margaret Hopkins, Lambda Healthcare – in charge.

She slapped Noah. He calls her Madam DeVeal – as in Devil, I think.

Going to some kind of clinic to 'cure' us.

We landed at a military airfield after 3.5 hour flight from E. Midlands Airport.

Now travelling in lorries thru a small town.

We've been sealed in with canvas covers, but can just see through flaps.

Crossed a railway. White blocks of flats. Statue of a rocket. Lake.

Forest. Another small town. Red and white mast.

Signal getting weaker; will keep texting.

Love you, Robert.

Jack had only read half when a second text came through.

Going south-east through woods and fields on a dirt road that's v. straight,

don't know where to. The sun is setting now.

Signal one bar.

Noah has been a m a z i n g!

He says to tell his 'Cutie Pie' he loves him and thinks about him all the time.

You will tell Alan for him, won't you?

R.

Mikey climbed onto the bed and put his arms round his brother. "Why are you sad?"

***

6: Monday, 29th July. 8.35 p.m. MSK, A road in the Russian Federation.

<u>NOAH</u>

We've been let out to stretch our legs, or take a piss if you like. We're on this long, straight, sandy road. On one side there are trees and on the other is this huge area of grass, weeds and bushes. As I said, I'm not very good at vegetation. It almost looks like it was built-on at one time, like two hundred years ago, because it's flat and almost a square. Beyond it are more and more trees, and beyond them the sun is going down. It's still warm and nearly cloudless, and if we weren't prisoners of Madam DeVeal in a strange land, it might be nice, especially if my lovely sexy Alan was with me. In fact, if he was with me, I wouldn't mind the rest. Robert's just told me that it's a mixed woodland of spruce, pine and birch. Show-off.

By the way, Madam DeVeal has done a bunk. Not literally, of course. I wish. She was riding shotgun in the other lorry, but it's nowhere to be seen. I think it was ahead of us. So there's just us and the bald Russian driver she shouted at. He's having a smoke sitting on the front bumper. He doesn't seem bothered that there are six teenagers who could easily overpower him and drive off home. I have thought about it, but there are several objections to the plan. The man is powerful and has a baton in his belt; our little group hasn't bonded; we don't know where home is; none of us can drive and we'd almost certainly get caught and punished... severely.

Robert has shared out the last of his chocolate. None of us has eaten since last night. There is a water barrel in the back of the lorry so we aren't thirsty, though whether it's clean or not is another question. There is absolutely no other sound but our voices, which sound dead out here in the wilderness. Mark's with us and Robert gave him a pair of his Fruit of the Looms to cover his embarrassment. They're miles too big as he's only ten. His own joggers and pants are still wet. I've been mothering him for most of the way because the poor little lad's in such a state. The bastards who've done this to him – to all of us – need locking up!

Porky isn't a very PC nickname, is it? But he doesn't seem to mind, and it seems more appropriate than Eagleton. Anyone less like an eagle would be difficult to find. He's another gay boy with us in the Gaz-66. *Gaz-66?* Yes, Porky's dad is a haulage driver and some of his knowledge has rubbed off. Apparently these Gazzas have been made in Russia since the year dot.

The other two in our truck are Brandon Frost, who's Robert's age and straight as a die, and Owen, his thirteen-year-old brother, who's gay – but he doesn't swish like I do. They both go to Morcross School. So why is Brandon with us? I think the clue lies in the fact that his parents are lesbians. I expect the DeVeal crowd thought that he might be 'infected', just like his brother.

The bald one calls out in Russian and by his arm signals I guess he means *all aboard!* The good thing is he doesn't bother to close the canvas flaps so we can see out of the back properly now. The bad thing is there isn't much to see anyway, and it's getting dark. Robert's just told me he's tried to send another text but there's no service. These wooden slats they call seats are pretty hard on the bum, but even they aren't going to stop me falling asleep. It's been a very long day!

***

DAN

"Where have you been?" asked Pam.

"Chill, I'm here now," said Dan.

"Sorry, Mrs Moseley, it was my fault," said Sophie. "We were seeing who could tie their laces the fastest and I got a knot in mine and didn't want to break my nail."

Pam looked at her and then at her son in silent incredulity. "I'm off," she said at last, opening the door. "There was a phone call for Jack earlier. She said she would ring again. Mikey's in the lounge."

Dan frowned. "Just for one day, can't you take him with you?"

"No," said his mother and slammed the door.

"Well, that was better than I expected," said Dan, "and that laces thing really fooled her."

"I'm hungry," said Mikey, who had just wandered into the kitchen.

"See that white thing with the door?" Dan pointed at the fridge.

"Would you like me to make you a sandwich, snookums?" Sophie asked.

"Tut," said Dan.

"Yes please, Sophie," whined Mikey. "Nobody loves me in this house."

"That's true," confirmed Dan.

"What would you like on your sandwich?" Sophie enquired.

"BLT toasty," replied Mikey, with a quick glance at his brother to see if he had heard.

"No!" stated Dan. "No cooking. Sophie and I have got things to do."

"Making out," exclaimed Mikey, "with tongues!"

"Jealous," returned Dan, "just because your *boyfriend* Noah isn't here."

"Pax, gentlemen! S'il vous plaît," called Sophie, mixing up her languages. "What about a banana and honey sandwich?"

"All right," said Mikey plaintively, "and will you make me a cup of hot chocolate too?"

The wall phone rang, forestalling further exchanges. Dan picked it up.

"Hello, Moseley House of Horror..."

"Hey, it's me."

"Hi, Just, why are you phoning on here?"

"Service is down. Just calling to see if yours is."

"I'll check." Dan took out his mobile. "Yeh, I'm down too. Where are you?"

"At 41, supposed to be helping Alan, but he's such a pain I'm thinking of jacking it in."

"You've only been doing it for a day."

"I know, but all he does is bark at me and if he's not barking, he's just as often staring into space. So I'm doing most of the work and then he tells me off for not coming up to his standard. I was unscrewing the mounting brackets for the fuel tank and he gave me an earful for not using WD40 to loosen the bolts first."

"Is that the real reason you called – to complain about Alan?"

"Sort of."

"Have you spoken to Jack about it?"

"No, he's having a high-level meeting with Elspeth."

Dan chuckled. "I don't think they have high-level meetings, Just. You sound like your grumpy old dad."

"You think it's me?"

"I think you're feeling like the newbie at the moment."

"Maybe. I'll give it another day or so and see how it goes."

"Good! See you tonight."

"See ya."

No sooner had Dan hung up than the phone rang again, but before answering he swiped one of Mikey's sandwiches from his plate. Pretending affront, Mikey turned and glowered at him. Dan grinned and took a large bite, squirting the honey and banana mix out at the sides, which he then licked off. With his mouth half full he answered the phone.

"Hello, Moseley's banana and honey sandwich bar. Can I take your order, please?"

Mikey's glower turned to a giggle.

"Oh, hello, is Jack there please?" The voice was young, precise, female and American.

Dan made a face. "I'm sorry, he's out at the moment."

"Am I talking to Daniel Moseley?"

"Yes... who's that?"

"My name is Rosa Miller, I'm a friend of Robert's. I'm calling from Tyree in Oklahoma State."

"Oh..." Suddenly Dan felt the levity drain out of him. He was fairly sure who Rosa was, and if he remembered rightly she didn't suffer fools gladly. "Sorry, I was—"

"Do you have Jack's number?"

"Our mobile service is down at the moment, but—"

"So that's why I couldn't get through to him?"

"Yes. Perhaps I can help? I'm probably not quite as stupid as I've sounded up till now."

"Do you know if Jack is aware of Robert's predicament?"

"Yes, he showed me two texts last night. He's gone to speak to someone this morning about them." Dan didn't mention that it was an eighty-three-year-old lady.

"Have you been to the police?" asked Rosa.

"The police are already involved in all this – on the wrong side."

"I see. Well, if you're in the picture, I can give you some more information which I would like you to pass on to Jack as soon as possible. You'll need to write it down."

"OK, just give me a second and I'll get a pen and paper." He looked helplessly at Sophie. "Pen?"

Mikey slipped out of his chair and dashed out of the kitchen, returning from the lounge with his monster colouring book and set of six pens.

"Thanks," said Dan, drawing out of the plastic wallet a blue felt tip and opening the book at a picture of a zombie flesh eater. "Hello Rosa, I'm ready."

"I've got some friends who think they've managed to track where Robert's cell was the last time it registered. Take this down carefully: 62° 40′ 36.6″ north, 40° 23′ 59.6″ east. These coordinates match the description given in the texts."

Dan repeated the positions back. "That's great, Rosa, thank you very much, though I don't know yet what we can do with them."

"You're welcome, Dan, and I don't think you're at all stupid for a thirteen-year-old boy."

"Robert told me you were pretty sharp."

"Take this cell number and tell Jack to give me a call sometime. Probably when little old England gets its network problems sorted out."

Dan took down the number and said goodbye to Rosa, then he looked at Sophie who smiled back at him.

"You're on a mission, aren't you?"

He nodded. "Do you mind?"

She shook her head. "I'm sure Mikey and I can find something to do."

"Have Robert and Noah gone away together?" asked the little boy.

"They've both been taken away," answered Dan.

"Who by?"

"Some bad people."

Mikey's face dissolved into tears. "I want them back!"

Dan put his arm round the little boy. "We all do, BB... and thanks for the book, I'll return it directly."

***

DAN

The garage doors were wide open and Alan was busy using a torque spanner to unbolt the cylinder head inside the engine compartment of the Humber Pullman. Beside him on a steel cabinet that could be rolled on castors were the dynamo, rocker box, hoses, clips, spark plugs, breather pipe, distributor cap and various other parts.

Dan propped his bike beside the fence and called out. "Hey, Alan..."

The boy looked round and, wiping his hands on a rag, walked over. "Got a new master brake cylinder today, cost £135."

Dan nodded. "I've got some news for Jack that I think you need to hear as well."

Alan's face immediately clouded over.

"It's OK, not bad news, just information about the two of them."

"You know Noah mentioned me in the text. Why would he be thinking about me at a time like that?"

Dan gave him a sideways look. "I would have thought that was obvious, dummy. You're special to him. Isn't he special to you?"

Alan looked helplessly at Dan. "I miss him..."

Dan wrapped his arm round the boy's shoulders and guided him towards the house. "Come on... is Jack inside?"

Alan nodded and allowed himself to be led.

"Where's your assistant?" asked Dan.

"Sorting some stuff out at the back of the garage."

"How's he getting on?"

Alan smiled. "Good – he's more mechanically minded than Noah and picks everything up straight away."

Dan stopped and turned to him. "Have you told him that?"

Alan shook his head. "No, why would I?"

"Because you're in charge, that's why! Sometimes, Alan Henderson, I think someone needs to give you a good talking-to."

***

9: Tuesday, 30th July. 3.30 p.m. 41 Westbury Avenue.

<u>ALAN</u>

Why do I always get nervous when I'm in the sitting room with Elspeth? I prefer to be out in the garage or in my room. I suppose it's because I feel more at home in those places.

Sometimes my mind drifts away, even when I'm trying to concentrate on the car, and when I snap out of it I realise I've been worrying about him. Where is Russia? I've heard of it, but I don't where it is. I know you have to cross the Atlantic to get to America, but how do you get to Russia? The fag said in that text that he loves me. He called me Cutie Pie too, which I'd normally tell him off for, but now I think it's a good thing because no one will know it's me. He says he's thinking about me, but I expect he'll find someone better in Russia anyway.

Dan Moseley wants me to admit that I'm in love with the fag, but I just said I miss him, which is true. In any case, how can I admit I'm in love with him to Dan Moseley, when I can't admit it to myself?

I think I upset Justin earlier. I forgot it was him and bawled him out for grinding the bolts on the brackets holding the petrol tank. He pushed himself out from under the car, and when I saw him, I realised it wasn't the fag. I can say anything to the fag and all he does is pucker his pouty lips at me and grin, because he knows I don't mean it. Maybe I should have said sorry to Justin, because he looked angry and a bit hurt.

Dan Moseley said I was in charge and needed a good talking-to. He called me a dummy too, but not in an unfriendly way. Maybe he's right. I don't understand very much about people. I've got to learn that side of things, but it's more difficult than cars. The petrol tank isn't in bad condition, but we're going to send it to Leeds for the Re-Nu process. That'll give it a rubberised coating and seal the inside to protect it from unleaded fuel.

"I'm not asleep, you know." That's what Elspeth said when we started talking to Jack in the sitting room. I suppose she thought we were ignoring her in her own house. If someone came to my house and started talking to a visitor instead of me I would be annoyed too. So we all sat round and Dan told us about the phone call from America. And I noticed Elspeth eye Jack, which she does sometimes, like she's boring into your mind. I go red when she does it to me, because I think she'll know I'm a fag, even though I'm not. Jack Moseley, who is a fag, just gazed back at her as if they were sharing a secret.

I got out my laptop and we all had a look at Google Maps to see where the mobile signal was last picked up. Now I know where Russia is – and I also found out that it's where those onion-domed churches come from. The funny thing is, and this proves how thick I am, it's about a hundred times bigger than England, though most of it they can keep, because it's miles and miles of nothing.

I joked that we should take the Humber and go and rescue them, but nobody laughed and I went red, as you do when a joke falls flat. But then I saw Elspeth and Jack exchange that look again and I suddenly knew that was exactly what they intended to do. Dan got it too and he looked at me as though I had read their minds. And Elspeth said it would take a lot of planning, and asked me how long it would take to prepare the car, and I thought about two months, given that we'll need an MOT before we can get insurance.

Then I went out and told Justin we were going to rescue the two fags, and he showed me this old suitcase he'd found at the back of the garage which contained the Pullman's heaters and air-conditioning unit. And I told him he was brilliant and asked if he would help me to fix it in, and he said he would, and then I told him I was sorry for shouting at him. When I told him the reason, I started to go all faggy on him and so he gave me a hug and said it was *OK, dude*. Then he asked me whether I'd like to go to karate with him on a Wednesday night. And I said yes, because I want to be able to defend myself in case they ever try to take me back to that room with the flies, and it'll help me get a six-pack and make me feel less like a wimpy fag.

I think Justin is my friend, because I like him a lot and he might even like me a bit. He's going to give me his old suit, or gi, because he is now six inches taller than when he did karate before, and he's about six inches taller than me. The reason he gave it up when he was twelve was that he had stinky feet – but Noah cured him, which I didn't know about.

I wish I could ring the fag and tell him that we're coming to rescue him. If I could ring him, it would mean he wouldn't forget me. When we get there, I bet he'll give me sad eye at first, but then he'll grin and salute me with those faggy fingers, after which – and best of all – he'll pucker those pouty lips, and I might – just might – allow myself one very quick brush of my lips against them.

***

10: Wednesday, 31st July. 6 a.m. MSK. Arkhangelsk Oblast, Gosudarstvennyi Meditsinskii Institut (gomoseksualizm).

ROBERT

Our first full day, and the PA system has woken us up playing what must be the Russian equivalent of cheerful music. The sound quality is like a teacher's megaphone on sports day. It doesn't get fully dark here, for no sooner has the sun set than it's rising again, and now it's shining through the dirty windows of our dormitory. We have fifteen minutes to make our beds then go downstairs to shower and clean our teeth before daily inspection, which takes place outside in our underwear and flip-flops.

Yesterday, our heads were shaved by the caretaker, who Noah has christened Whiskers. He's an old man and quite deaf, I think. Then they made us have a shower and took away all of our clothes except our underwear. My backpack went with the rest. In exchange, we were given green shorts, green leggings, socks and T-shirt and a black jacket with green stripes, plus a pair of rubber shoes and flip-flops. Green seems to be the favourite colour for everything. The only possessions we got back were the King James Bibles, which we found on our beds later in the day.

We live in a grey weatherboard two-storey barracks with a corrugated iron roof covered in a dull red paint, which I suppose stops it going rusty. It looks as though someone has given the front an almighty shove because the whole structure leans backwards. There's a dirt courtyard all around, enclosed by a ten-foot-high fence also made of corrugated iron, riveted together on a wooden frame. At the back there's a closed-off area and inside is a shed-like affair where the electricity generator rumbles away night and day. It is, I am informed, run on wood gas; that is, by burning wood in a sealed container. The one way in and out of the whole shebang is a gate made of wooden planks which has a castle-keep-sized mortise lock. It's not big enough to allow access for a vehicle, and so the Gaz-66s are parked outside.

Upstairs on one side of the central staircase is a landing with the door to our dormitory. On the opposite side is another landing with a corridor leading to four rooms: the first is locked and someone has nailed a crucifix to the door. Maybe it's the chapel. Then there's a school room with a blackboard, desks and chairs, and a medical room which is usually locked. Right on the end is Madam DeVeal's spacious boudoir – Noah's words, not mine. No one's ever been allowed in there, so we don't know what it's like. Downstairs are the showers, kitchen, laundry, mess room and a rest room, so called because it's where we go when there's nothing else to do. The whole place is really just a rectangular wooden box with windows and a roof, about the size of a large house.

The toilet which we all have to share is a cubicle outside in the corner of the yard. It doesn't flush; it doesn't even use water. It's a pit covered with a wooden box affair with a butt-shaped hole in the lid. Mark would easily fall in if he didn't hold on. That's where my mobile ended its life, by the way. We're expected to shower after we've been, as there's nothing to wipe your backside on. Oh, but there is a bag of quicklime beside the box: one scoop into the hole when you're done. It smells as you'd expect...

There are six beds on each side of the dormitory with a cupboard between and a stool at the end. They are of the hospital type, made of tubular steel painted green, just wide enough for me to lie flat on without overhanging the edge. The mattress is about an inch thick and we have a foam pillow and a thin duvet each. A square cast-iron stove stands on concrete blocks in the middle of the room and the flue, like something out of a fairy-tale, goes every which way until it exits through one of the side walls. There's a carpet hanging up on the wall opposite the windows – maybe they call it a tapestry – and the rest is covered in the ugliest wallpaper you'll see this side of criminality. At night the door is locked, and if we want to go to the toilet there's a bucket standing next to the stove.

As well as the two drivers, bald man and hairy man, and Madam DeVeal of course, we have picked up a gopher by the name of Valery. He's our translator and pretends to be our friend, but I wouldn't trust him even as far as I could throw him. Naturally, Noah has christened him Miss Valerie. We haven't yet met the two professors who Dad claims are going to cure me of my curse. The only other people I've seen around are Whiskers, the caretaker, and his equally bewhiskered wife. Where they actually live is a mystery to me, just like so many other things about this place.

The twelve of us are lined up in the courtyard before a rostrum by hairy man, who doesn't want any 'gay' postures, insisting that we stand up straight with our hands by our sides. He does this by gestures, words which the gopher translates as 'behave like men' and in Noah's case by holding him until he's sort of frozen into the correct pose. Fortunately the weather is mild and so standing outside in our underwear is no hardship, though I notice Noah is wearing his green shorts as well. I don't know what will happen when it gets cooler.

First up to the podium, which is actually a wooden crate, is Madam DeVeal, looking a tad more dishevelled than on her first day. She speaks as if we haven't met her before. "I am Sister Hopkins, liaison officer between Lambda Healthcare in England and the Archangel Medical Institute. You will address me as Sister, or Sister Hopkins. This treatment centre has been created by philanthropic persons in England and America in association with the Government of the Russian Federation for the sole purpose of re-educating boys who have become tainted with homosexuality. You twelve from Swanford are the first patients here, either through your own weakness and unnatural lusts, or because you have parents who are deviants. Before you are returned to England all traces of your perversion must have been eradicated, and when you get back, those unfortunate enough to have been brought up by homosexuals will find a haven with a normal family."

She pauses to let this sink in. Mark is weeping silently. Noah is rolling his eyes. The rest of us are just stunned that we could be living through this nightmare.

"Now, I should like to introduce you to the Director of the Institute, Professor Igor Rozhdestvensky, who will give a short address."

The outside gate is opened, and in walks a tall, skull-faced man in a white coat flanked by two much younger, smaller men also wearing white coats. Skull-face walks along our line as though he's inspecting a troop of soldiers. He frowns at Mark and stops by Jamie, signalling for the gopher to come to his side. Jamie is the oldest of us; he'll be sixteen in a couple of weeks, and does regular workouts with his gay dad at the gym. His muscles have obviously caught the professor's attention.

After a short exchange, our director mounts the rostrum

and begins to speak to us in Russian, which means he has to stop after each sentence so that the gopher can translate. This makes the proceedings tedious for all, but particularly for us, whose stomachs are grumbling through want of breakfast.

"You are not girls, you are boys. You do not need to be effeminate. We shall see that you grow into sturdy, normal, young men... who like girls, yes?"

Now, none of us has a gender identity problem. We're all boys who are happy to be boys, therefore we know straight away that this man is not a scientist but a quack. In addition, no one has apparently told him that half of us are straight. They just happen to have a gay parent or two. We learned this last night when the twelve of us did our own survey. Mark is in such a state of distress that he doesn't know who or what he is, he just wants to be back home with his dad, sister and pet dog. Which leaves just six of us who are actually gay: me, Noah, Porky, Owen, the African boy, whose name is Dwain Matheson, and Ryan Davis, who's in Year Eight at Swanford Community School. Noah says he must have been deep in the closet for *him* not to know about Ryan.

"You are the pioneers of this new scientific institute for the eradication of homosexuality. Your journey begins today. Each of you will receive a medical examination and then you will be given your first injection of man juice..."

As Miss Valerie makes this odd translation, Noah allows his admittedly oversize shorts to fall round his ankles, leaving him in just a pair of white briefs.

"Ooo, sorry they slipped," he says. This, combined with the *man juice* phrase, causes some giggling among us, though the thought of being injected dispels our mirth pretty darn quickly. Meanwhile, Noah pulls up his shorts and then allows himself an almost imperceptible hip sway. I never realised he was such a rebel.

***

11: Wednesday, 31st July. 6.40 a.m. MSK. Arkhangelsk
Oblast Gosudarstvennyi Meditsinskii Institut
(gomoseksualizm).

<u>NOAH</u>

We're going out at eight o'clock to chop trees down.
Apparently, we need wood for the winter. So now I'm a
lumberjack and I'm OK... Except I don't intend to be here in
the winter – or the autumn, for that matter.

All twelve of us are sitting in the canteen enjoying our
delicious breakfast of watery porridge and cold sausage
washed down with a glass – yes, a glass – of lukewarm tea.
There is no sugar. We do get two slices of bread each though,
and margarine that tastes of fish.

The floor is concrete like everywhere else downstairs,
unlike upstairs, which has floorboards, but at least wood is
warm under your feet. I have to say the furnishings aren't too
dissimilar to those in our flat back in dear old Swanford, but
the less said about that the better.

I'm sitting next to Dwain Matheson. He's from Nigeria in
West Africa, which he tells me was once part of our Empire. I
can't believe he's fifteen – though I can because I saw him in
the shower this morning. His mum brought him to England
because of the gay hate campaign in Nigeria. Well, the
cherub's so camp, he makes me look like the straightest guy
alive. I told him, out of the frying pan into the fire. His mum is
now at a detention centre in Dover awaiting export to where?

He says he's going to run away as soon as he can. I don't
know if I was stating the obvious but I told him, if you're
going to run away, you ought to have somewhere to run *to*
first. I hope he's taken that on board.

Jamie's looking hard at me across the table. He's bare-
chested and I like his muscles almost as much as Dr Death
does. That's my name for Professor Igor. I don't think there's
anything between his skin and his skull, and his hair is like
frayed rope.

"Noah, you'll get us all into trouble if you carry on the way you are doing."

Rolling my eyes has become my gesture of choice. "Jamie," I say, "I'm not going to let them inject me with *man juice*, particularly if it comes from Dr Death."

"How are you going to stop them?" asks Porky who is eating his sausage with his fingers.

"I'm going to smash whatever it comes in."

Now Robert's looking at me and I think he's going to side with Jamie, and so I try to forestall him.

"What exactly can they do to us that's worse than injecting us with some chemical that's supposed to turn us into grunting Neanderthals?" I glance along the table to see if I've got anyone on my side. Brandon and Owen look as if they might be possibilities. I point across the table at Mark, who's still struggling to force down his porridge. "And he isn't old enough to be injected with that sort of stuff."

A boy I've taken no real notice of so far – and you'll probably realise why in a second – then speaks up. His name is John Price and he's fifteen, tall and gangly with very black hair, not only on his head but also around his nipples and in a thick mat below his tummy button. He also wears Buddy Holly-type glasses – yes, I know who he is, 'Peggy Sue' – and has a disturbingly high number of zits on his face, but no beard. Seems weird to me; no beard and all that hair below.

"Noah's right. They're probably going to inject us with testosterone, something I don't need any more of for one."

"Do you know what it does?" asks Brandon.

John sees that he's the centre of attention and blushes. Suddenly, I'm finding him cute and attractive, zits and hair and specs and all, so maybe I'm the one who's weird.

"It's given to transgender kids who want to become boys, and old men who can't get it up, so you can imagine what it'll do to boys who are already boys."

"Isn't that what bodybuilders use to make them muscly?" asks Porky, who I've got a suspicion might be sliding towards favouring an injection.

"You have to use weights and exercise, Porks, to get a bodybuilder's body," says Mr Buff Jamie rather disparagingly.

Robert is looking at me now and I think he's come over to my side. Typical American; better late than never!

"I'm in," he says. "If I'm up first, I'll break as many as I can."

"Are we all going for, it then?" I ask.

Dennis and Michael Shane, eleven-year-old twins who live in their own private twin world most of the time, turn and nod simultaneously at me. I would probably find this quite creepy if they weren't so sweet, like two little pixies (though, thankfully, without the pointy ears). Their dads had them by a surrogate mother who actually lives in the same house. That piece of information was quite difficult to piece together, because twin world doesn't operate in the same space–time continuum as the world I know.

Everyone else nods their assent as well. Even Porky, who I can see still hankers after some muscle enhancement, gives a thumbs-up.

"It'll be me, then," says hunky Jamie.

"How do you mean?" I ask.

"If they call us up in alphabetical order. I'm B for Baker."

"B for butch," says Dwain, which makes us giggle.

"I'll go up in your place, if you like," I say brightly.

Jamie smiles at me. He has a nice smile. "Are you kidding? I'm not being outmanned by a little girly gay boy."

"Cheek!" But I love him.

***

12: Wednesday, 31st July. 7 a.m. MSK. Arkhangelsk Oblast Gosudarstvennyi Meditsinskii Institut (gomoseksualizm).

ROBERT

We're in the rest room. There's an old desk standing against the wall, another cast-iron stove with a fairy-tale flue, more bad wallpaper, a table, five seedy-looking dining-type chairs, a couple of wooden benches and three padded stools. As for our medical examinations, we're still waiting to be summoned. At this rate we will get less than five minutes each with the doctor if we're meant to start work at eight.

Valery has just come into the room with a piece of paper clutched in his hand. Noah's eyes light up, and I know mischief is afoot.

He assumes the pose, complete with limp wrist, and sucks in his cheeks. "Excusez-moi, Miss Valerie, before you begin can you tell me if *man juice* is a direct translation from Russian?"

Poor Valery goes very red. "I have since consulted my book and I should have said male hormone."

"You mean testosterone?" questions John.

The Russian shrugs. He is, after all, a translator, not a biologist, and is anxious to get on with the purpose of his visit. "I have your itinerary for the rest of the week, when the weather will be hot. I shall read it out to you if you wish, or I can pin it up on the wall."

"How about both?" suggests Jamie.

Valery nods and clears his throat. I've got more than a suspicion that this boy, who can't be older than sixteen, smokes like a chimney. The thumb, index and middle fingers of his right hand are stained a rich, golden brown and his voice is like Slavic phlegm. "This is your daily routine for the next five days. Reveille is at six o'clock and inspection at six fifteen. Breakfast is at seven o'clock and at eight o'clock you will assemble in the courtyard wearing your boots and summer clothing. You will be taken into the woods to cut trees under the supervision of Vasily Yegorovich Pavlov."

"Vaseline who?" enquires Noah.

"The gentleman with the bald head, *Tovarisch* Marshall. At ten o'clock you will return with your tree trunks to the compound, where you will saw and chop the wood into logs."

"What happens if we refuse?" asks Brandon.

"Come the cold, you will freeze to death." This was said

in such a matter-of-fact tone that no one doubted the truth of the statement. "At noon you will be served your meal, after which, from one until three o'clock, you will receive instruction in manly behaviours from Professor Salkorov and Sister Hopkins."

"Ooo, Madam DeVeal, how enchanting," says Noah, "and will you be translating for the professor, Valerie dear?"

"Dmitri Pyotrovich Salkorov speaks good English, Noah Marshall, therefore I would advise caution when you try to cheek him."

This drew a few chuckles, and my opinion of our gopher went up a few notches. "From three to four o'clock there will be free time, but today and on Sunday you will be expected to prepare yourself for a visit to the Church of the Transfiguration, where you will be given spiritual guidance for two hours."

"What happens on the other days?" asks Porky.

Valery smiles knowingly. "*Tovarisch* Eagleton, you will be pleased to hear that Yuri Semyonovich Bakaleinikoff will be giving you instruction in physical education."

"PE!" exclaims Owen. "For two hours!"

The only Yuri I know is Yuri Gagarin, the first man in space, and so I put the question.

He answers me. "*Tovarisch* Robert Crittenden, Yuri Semyonovich is the hirsute gentleman."

"Ooo," says Noah, waving a limp wrist, "our dad could do such a lot with Yurine's hair. A nice shave and style would do wonders for him."

If I hadn't met Noah before, I'd believe him to be the complete gay stereotype. I think laying it on so thick is his way of protesting against being here as well as entertaining us. I think he likes the way it ticks our keepers off. It seems to me, though, to be a dangerous game.

Valery looks at him with a kind of stolid amusement, then continues. "At six o'clock your education ends and at seven you will get your evening meal. At nine o'clock you will be in your dormitory, ready to sleep."

The itinerary is pinned up on the wall and Valery departs. Noah opens his mouth to speak but the words are interrupted by a familiar, though distorted, voice booming out over the PA: "Baker, J. to the surgery on the first floor." With our good wishes ringing in his ears, Jamie saunters out of the rest room.

"Where does the food come from?" asks Mark. It's the first time the little kid has spoken except when spoken to.

"I've wondered that myself," I say and everyone nods.

"Have you been in the kitchen?" asks Owen, and when most of us shake our heads, he continues. "There's a big oven in there made out of bricks with lots of metal doors, but it's not working. Another smaller one that looks like our Aga at home is used to warm things up."

"But they don't do the actual cooking?" questions John.

"Not that I've seen," answers Owen, "though the old lady makes the tea."

"Another thing," says his brother, Brandon, "Where do they all go when they've done their shift here?"

"And most important of all," says Noah, "where does Madam DeVeal do her toilette?"

"She'll be like the Queen," responds Porky, "so pure she doesn't need to go."

Our thoughts are interrupted by an alarm blaring through the PA system. We hear hurried footsteps outside the rest room. I open the door and look down the corridor to see Whiskers and his wife talking agitatedly to one another at the entrance to the kitchen, which is opposite the lobby. I walk briskly along and find Sister Hopkins standing by the open back door looking up the stairs. Her uniform is splashed with yellowy liquid. When she sees me she jumps then recovers, and sets her mouth in a grimace of hatred.

"What's going on?" I ask innocently, while the others gather behind me.

"If you know what's good for you you'll not get in the way," she answers, then she adds, "You'll all pay for this outrage, you can be sure."

34

"Oh, Sister, what have we done?" cries Noah in his most whiny voice.

Madam DeVeal has begun to back away from us, probably realising her vulnerability as there's no one to defend her if we choose to attack.

"Where's Jamie?" asks Brandon.

I look over my shoulder at him and signal that we should maybe go and find out. He nods in agreement and we move towards the stairs.

"Where do you think you're going?" Sister Hopkins shouts from the open doorway through which she's ready to take flight if necessary.

I ignore her and the two of us ascend the single flight to the first-floor landing. At the top of the stairs, we do a quick recon. All is quiet, and so we proceed down the corridor. We pass the door with the crucifix and then the open doorway to the classroom, but the door to the surgery is locked. We listen for any sound, but hear nothing. Then Brandon notices shards of glass and traces of an oily liquid seeping into the corridor from under the door.

A commotion draws us to the window of the classroom. The outside gate is open, and marching across the courtyard are four men in blue camouflage fatigues. They look tough, like either military or prison guards, and are armed with side-handle batons. We squat down to make sure we're not seen, but still have a view. Sister Hopkins goes out to meet them and points up towards the medical room. They barely take any notice of her and disappear from view.

We hear their heavy boots thudding on the stairs and hide behind the door, hoping they don't enter the classroom. They pass by and there's a rapping of a baton on wood. There follows a confusion of activity and harsh voices, and shortly we glimpse through the crack in the door the guards going back the way they had come, followed by the flash of a white coat. They speak to each other in such terse sentences that, even though we can't understand the words, it's obvious what they're saying.

Once again, we go to the window. Jamie is being hauled across the courtyard between two of the guards, his hands secured behind him by plastic cuffs. We can't tell if he's been hurt or not. The rear of a jeep type vehicle is visible through the open gate. Jamie is bundled inside with a guard on each side of him. The vehicle roars away in a cloud of diesel, meaning that a driver was already in situ and that two of the military types are still in the compound.

We go back to the medical room, which is now open. The floor is covered in small pools of oily liquid spilled from broken ampoules, some of which have been crushed underfoot. In among this debris are scattered hypodermic syringes, most still in their wraps. Jamie has done a good job. I see one of the sealed vials is not broken, and pick it up. Sustamed 250 is written in English and below it there is a list of four testosterone compounds and the supplier, Balkan Chemicals. Brandon shows me one of the boxes the ampoules came in and taps the expiry date, which is one month ago.

I smash the ampoule, then we crush all the syringes. It doesn't mean there won't be any more, but it makes us feel better.

***

13: Wednesday, 31st July. 10 a.m. MSK. Arkhangelsk Oblast Gosudarstvennyi Meditsinskii Institut (gomoseksualizm).

NOAH

We were locked in the dormitory for an hour while our Russian friends sorted themselves out. I think they thought gays would be a pushover and wouldn't need proper guards. Now we've got two, and they're standing to our rear in their blue uniforms, their legs apart and hands behind their backs like real tough men. Once more, we're lined up in the courtyard wearing just our underwear and flip-flops, as if the past three hours have never happened. Except there's only eleven of us now, and we don't know where Jamie's been taken or how he is.

First up is Miss Valerie, who has some interesting news. Our spiritual guidance counsellor has not arrived in town yet, and so our twice-weekly visit to the Church of the Transfiguration has been cancelled until further notice. Instead we will be outside doing press-ups. I expect that's why the door with the cross on it is still locked. Oh yes, I try them all as often as I can.

After Miss Valerie's profuse apology comes Madam DeVeal, marching towards the rostrum in a freshly starched uniform and with a face like fury. No doubt we are about to be torn off a strip. She's got hairy man Yurine on guard beside her, and he has a bandaged hand – way to go, Jamie!

I put up my hand. "Excuse me, Miss..." I say in my best whiny voice.

"No questions!" she shouts without looking at me, so I moan a bit and think nice thoughts about my Cutie Pie back home working on the Humber in his sexy dungarees.

She gets up on the box and begins her tirade. "You children have been taught that you have an inalienable right to be homosexual. To display your perversions and to be the sons of perverts..."

Robert interrupts. "Can you tell us why we were going to be injected with testosterone that is out of date?"

One of the guards steps forward and hits him from behind on the shoulder with his baton, making him stagger.

Brandon takes the box out of his boxers and throws it at Madam DeVeal. "Motherfucking bitch!" he shouts, and it sounds really butch coming from him.

He gets the same baton treatment, only he's slightly more prepared. His brother, Owen rushes at the rostrum like a little tiger, but Yurine gets in his way and he is dragged kicking and screaming back into line.

"Moon time," I shout, and those of us who are still able to turn, bend and drop our shorts. We've left our underwear in the dormitory.

37

Madam DeVeal retreats while our guards lay into us with their batons. I try to think more nice thoughts about my Cutie Pie...

***

14: Thursday, 1st August. 11.45 a.m. 10 Beckwith Close, Swanford.

<u>JACK</u>

Mr Colt was surprised when two bedraggled figures wheeling their bikes turned up on his doorstep, but he had to admit agreeably so. The day had promised fair, but had turned out quite miserable, with one shower after another blown in on a blustery southwester. This had scuppered his plan to cut the privet hedge that bordered his and his neighbour's lengthy back garden, a task which they shared and complained about in equal measure.

"Do come in, boys, but please take off your shoes and outer garments, lest my wife has a fit."

A smiling Muriel Colt came into the hall to greet her unexpected guests. "I'll get you a towel to dry your hair."

"My socks are wet too," said Dan, seeing a damp footprint on the polished oak floorboards.

"Well, if you remove them, I can find a place where they might dry out sufficiently before your return journey. Meanwhile, you can use the towel to dry both ends of your bodies."

"Sorry about this," said Jack.

"It is of no consequence, my dear chap, and it's very nice to see you both."

A few minutes later they were settled on the sofa in the front room. With its large south- facing bay window covered in whiter-than-white net curtains, the room was light and airy, despite the lowering clouds outside.

"If you find the cushions a burden, like I do," said Mr

Colt, settling down into an armchair, "do cast them aside."

Jack made the effort to relax into the sofa. "That's your son, isn't it?" he said, noticing the large colour photograph on the dresser. It showed a smiling young man and, behind him, her arms folded on his shoulders an equally happy-looking young woman. "He's got the same shape of head as you."

Mr Colt chuckled. "He wouldn't thank you for saying that, but yes, that's Roy, he's twenty-one this year. He's doing a PhD at Yale University in America."

"And is that his girlfriend?" asked Dan, shyly. "She looks American."

"You are both astute observers," said Mr Colt. "That's Shandra. They met at Yale last year. Another case of hands across the sea, Jack, though without the complications of your union with Robert..."

"Would you boys like to stay for lunch?" asked Muriel, coming into the room. "It should be ready about one o'clock."

"Ooo," said Jack, and the brothers exchanged glances.

"We're having cottage pie, one of Ralph's favourites."

Jack found himself quite discomfited hearing the use of Mr Colt's Christian name, but not discomfited enough to refuse the offer of homemade cottage pie. "That would be very nice, thank you, but we don't want to put you to any trouble."

Mr Colt chuckled. "I think that means yes, dear."

Muriel left the room and the boys looked at each other again, not quite knowing where to begin. Absent-mindedly, Jack pushed his unloved toes under the rug in front of the fireplace.

In the end it was Mr Colt who broke the silence. "Well, unless you tell me, I won't ever know."

Jack decided to plunge in. "We need an adult, preferably a teacher, to go to Russia with us to rescue Robert and Noah."

"I see..." Although Mr Colt did not see, yet.

"We're going to travel by car – five of us there, seven back," said Dan.

"We plan to go on Wednesday 2nd October," added Jack, "that's when Alan says the Humber will be ready. He and

Justin are fixing it up now. We go from Harwich to the Hook of Holland then drive through Europe to Estonia and cross the border at a town called Narva."

"A Humber?" queried Mr Colt.

"It's brilliant," said Dan, "like really classy."

The explanations followed thick and fast, though it took over half an hour for the schoolmaster to tease out every fact and explore every nook and cranny of the plan.

"We thought because you're retired you'd be the ideal person to come with us," rounded off Jack.

"But," said Mr Colt carefully, "there are two fundamental objections to my presence in the party."

The boys faces fell. They had already put hours of their time into the venture, and had been banking on him accepting their invitation. "What are they, sir?" asked Jack.

"The first, and probably the most important, is that I don't drive."

"Oh!" the boys chorused.

"I am rather ashamed to admit that I have to rely on my wife for transportation," continued Mr Colt. "But my other objection, which is more abstract in nature, is that I don't speak Russian, and though I can see merit in your enterprise and admire your usual esprit de coeur, without someone who can speak the language I think you will have great difficulty in achieving your objective." He regarded them while they mulled over this line of reasoning.

Eventually Jack nodded. "I see your point, sir. Is there anyone else you know of who speaks Russian and can drive and who might be willing to go with us?"

"Well, it's very strange you should mention that, Jack. If you would excuse me for five minutes, I should like to make a telephone call."

***

After an agreeable lunch cottage pie, carrots and peas followed by blackberry and apple pie with cream, the boys volunteered to wash up, an offer which was taken up.

"That's very kind of you," said Muriel. "Just leave everything in the drainer when you've finished. And I suggest you leave the cottage pie dish to soak. Ralph will put them away later. I play bridge on Thursday afternoons and I must go and put my face on."

"I'm trying to become more domesticated now that I am in my dotage," said Mr Colt, "but I have yet to fully adjust."

The double sink made it easier for the boys, as one could wash and the other rinse. Jack filled the pie dish with cold water and left it to one side, so that by the time the plates and cutlery were in the drainer the grilled-on cheese came off quite easily with a sponge scourer. They had almost finished when the front door bell rang. Mr Colt went to answer it.

Moments later he was back in the kitchen. "Our visitor has arrived and so I shall make us all a pot of tea."

Jack slid off the rubber washing-up gloves and rinsed his hands. Dan handed him a towel. "Do you think it's someone we know?" he asked quietly.

Jack shrugged. "I can't think who, but we'll soon see."

Mr Colt spooned loose tea into the teapot and smiled benignly at them. "You go on through; I shall be along shortly."

As soon as they entered the front room they were greeted by their Russian speaker. "*Privet mal'chiki* – hello boys."

"Ms Lane!"

In her trademark pink and purple chiffon, their old equality counsellor sat in the second armchair with a sceptical look on her face. "Now, what is all this nonsense about? And you better make it good, dragging me out in this rain."

An hour later the two boys were hoarse with answering questions, and without the tea to lubricate their larynxes would probably have been voiceless. Ms Lane looked across at her fellow teacher. "Do you think this sounds as completely madcap as I do, Mr Colt?"

"Oh, completely..." he said without hesitation.

She turned to the boys. "Well, I've got nothing else to

do..."

"Great," said Jack, uncertain whether he meant it or not.

"And who will be accompanying us on this journey?"

"Alan Henderson is our chief mechanic and co-driver..."

Jack saw Ms Lane frown.

"Don't worry, he's a natural born driver."

"Brilliant," added Dan, "like the car's part of him..."

The frown lessened somewhat, but did not disappear.

"Justin Walker is deputy mechanic and in charge of security," continued Jack. "Dan is our chief medical officer; I'm communications officer and then there's yourself, supervisor and driver-in-chief. All this subject to parental approval, of course."

"But we don't see a problem there," said Dan quickly, "not with you on board."

"And what about your schooling?" asked Mr Colt. "How do you intend to get the time off?"

"I'm going to get myself suspended."

"Now Jack, that sounds like foolishness."

"I'm not going to fit in there, anyway, am I, sir? Sooner or later, someone somewhere will take action against me, just like they did Noah."

His teacher grunted. "Maybe, and I know that quite a few parents wish to withdraw their pupils from the Community School because of the new regime there."

Ms Lane responded. "The difficulty for them will be finding a school that doesn't have the same problems, given the intentions of our new Secretary of State."

Mr Colt shook his head sadly. "Nadine Collins, a borderline sociopath with no experience of education and a third-class degree in home economics."

"Justin and I will be moving to Dumbleton Boys' School," said Dan.

There was an audible intake of breath from the two teachers. Ms Lane frowned again. "A public school!"

"I don't wish to be rude," said Mr Colt, "but aren't the fees somewhat prohibitive?"

42

"Elspeth is funding us for at least a term. We'll only be day boys, of course," answered Dan.

"And the school has promised to waive part of the fees for the period they'll be on their educational trip to Russia," added Jack.

"Mrs Chambers is truly a Lady Bountiful," said Ms Lane. "I can't wait to meet her."

It was Jack's turn to frown. He wasn't sure that the two women would get on. Something about an irresistible force and an immovable object...

Mr Colt smiled at him. "I think you and I were probably thinking the same thing there, Jack."

Ms Lane began to scribble down her contact details. "There is one thing I must insist upon," she said.

"What's that?" asked Jack.

"You two boys will have to be given instruction in basic Russian, and I shall be your tutor. Three days a week for two hours during the holiday and two nights a week thereafter. And I shall expect you to practise together between lessons."

Mr Colt chuckled at the consternation on their faces. "A very worthwhile exercise, especially if some unforeseen circumstance should occur that verbally incapacitates Ms Lane."

The logic did not escape the boys, and they agreed, if somewhat reluctantly.

"Time for me to make tracks," said Ms Lane, rising to her feet. "First lesson for you two, Sunday morning, nine until eleven at my house. Don't be late."

Dan nodded and Jack slumped back into the sofa. "OK"

"Though I am aware of your gentlemanly proclivities, Mr Colt, I shall see myself out. I think these boys still have something to ask you."

After saying their goodbyes to her, the boys turned to the old teacher. "Ms Lane was right, sir. We were going to ask if you would help us with the administration, particularly the visas?"

"I would be happy to, boys. I have a personal computer

which is upstairs in the office, and so if you could supply contact details, such as an email address for all the relevant parties, we can stay in touch and report progress."

At four o'clock, in good spirits and wearing dry socks, the boys left their old form tutor's house and made for home. The rain had passed, the wind had eased and the evening promised to be warm and settled.

***

15: Saturday, 3rd August. 10 a.m. 15 Leighton Lane.

ROGER

In the lounge, Roger and Pam stood before their three sons, who were lined up on the settee, waiting expectantly. To be called to a family meeting like this was not usual for a Saturday morning, especially as they had been forewarned by their mother the previous evening to make themselves available between ten and eleven o'clock. It had meant Dan had to rearrange his work schedule.

Roger took a deep breath. "I have some bad news for you, boys. I have been made redundant from my job with the council, and I have not been re-employed by the firm taking over Environmental Services. That means, at the end of September, I will get my last salary."

"So, we'll be poor," observed Dan.

"Yes, we'll have to tighten our belts," said Pam.

"I shall begin looking for another job, but it is unlikely that any new employment will pay as much as I am getting now."

Jack looked up at his father. "I bet the firm taking over your jobs is either a subsidiary of Burnoco Oil or a company belonging to the likes of Councillor Henderson."

His mother sighed. "Why must you see a conspiracy in everything?"

"Mike's getting a bike for his birthday," stated Mikey

with a scowl.

"That doesn't mean you're entitled to one," answered Pam.

"Anyway, you've got a bike," said Dan with a smirk.

"Have not!" fumed Mikey, locking eyes with his brother.

"Yes, you have. You've got your little thwee wheeler, baby Mikey, twikey bikey."

Roger put his hand over his mouth to hide his smile.

"Bugger!" cried Mikey.

"That's enough!" said Pam. "Daniel Moseley, you will not wind up your little brother. Michael Moseley, do not swear in this house. We shan't have enough money to buy expensive presents, especially bikes which you'll grow out of in ten minutes."

"S'pose I won't even be able to have a proper haircut any more," responded Mikey sulkily.

"There is a silver lining to every situation," said Pam.

"We'll see," said Roger, pacifically.

Dan looked across Mikey to his elder brother. "Well, now we've got that over with, shall we give them our news?"

Jack shrugged nonchalantly. "Go on, LB, see if they can take it as well as we've taken theirs." He gave Mikey a squeeze. "Excepting my skinny tiny tot of a brother, of course."

"I'll fetch the letters then," said Dan, getting up and leaving the room.

"What's this?" said Pam, already on edge.

"Sit down, Mum and Dad," advised Jack. "LB won't be a minute."

"Oh lord!" said Roger, backing towards the armchair nearest the window. "What have you two been up to now?"

Dan returned carrying two envelopes, one brown manila and the other a white one. Before handing them out he sat down again and spoke. "Justin Walker and I have been offered places at Dumbleton Boys' School, probably for just one term. And Jack and I are intending to go on a trip to Russia in October with our equality counsellor, Ms Lane."

45

"Nicely put, LB," said his brother. "Just the right amount of information and no histrionics."

"Can I go too?" asked Mikey.

"Yes, there's a special one-way ticket for pests to Siberia," said Jack, giving his little brother another squeeze.

Dan handed the manila envelope to his mother and the white one to his father, who opened his first.

Dear Mr and Mrs Moseley,

I am currently organising a trip to the Russian Federation for several pupils at my old school. Both your elder sons have expressed an interest in the project, of which I wholeheartedly approve. The venture will be under the leadership of our esteemed Mrs Edith Lane, who is a fluent Russian speaker. It will commence on 2nd October and last for circa three weeks.

I require a letter of parental permission, plus passports of the relevant individuals, in order to proceed with their visa applications, and I should be very much obliged if you could forward them to me as soon as possible.

Needless to say, there will be no financial burden placed upon you, as all costs have been offset by a generous benefactor.

I remain,
Yours very sincerely,
R. E. F. Colt.

Roger narrowed his eyes at his sons before passing the letter to his wife. Meanwhile, Pam was sorting through the envelope from Dumbleton Boys' School, which also held a covering letter.

Dear Daniel,

I am very pleased to inform you that you have been granted a place as a day pupil at Dumbleton Boys' School commencing on Tuesday, 3rd September.

Therefore I should like to invite you and your parents to

an open day on Thursday 22nd August at 11 am, during which you will be given a tour of the school. Luncheon will be served between 1 and 2 pm.

I enclose the school prospectus and a pro-forma acceptance letter for your mother or father to sign. I understand that congratulations are in order, as you have obtained a scholarship from a private individual that will cover the whole cost of your tuition for the winter term.

Incidentally, I have heard of your upcoming educational visit to Russia, which I'm sure will be a positive addition to your knowledge base.

We look forward to you becoming a valued member of our School, and wish you all the very best for the coming academic year.

Yours sincerely,
I.A. Forster
Headmaster

Roger examined his fingernails before looking over them at his wife. She gazed back at him. In time, he spoke. "I think your mother and I would like to discuss this together in detail, and we'll talk to you both afterwards," he said.

"OK," said Jack. "Now LB and I have got work and swimming, so we'll see you tonight."

"Can I go?" asked Mikey.

"Only if you can hold your breath for ten minutes underwater," said Dan.

"No problemo," answered the little boy, who ran out to get his kit.

"See what you did?" said Jack.

"Chill, man," Dan replied. "He can play with Stewy on the slides."

***

Roger watched the boys from the kitchen window as they walked down the garden path towards the gate. Then he turned to Pam, who was writing the shopping list for their weekly supermarket expedition.

"Yes!" he exclaimed, punching the air with both fists. "We can send Mikey off to my mother's and have three whole weeks to ourselves! Where do you fancy; what about Tenerife?"

"Roger, be serious, we'll have no money."

"We can spend a little of my redundancy pay."

Pam paused to consider the possibility of a relaxing holiday in the sun away from her children. "It would be nice," she conceded, "but this is too fishy for words. A trip to Russia! What is that about, and how is Jack supposed to get time off school? They'll never allow it."

"I very much doubt that's a factor they've overlooked. And don't you think they've done really well, organising this all by themselves?"

"But it's not by themselves, is it? It's that dreadful old witch at 41 Westbury Avenue. Mikey was right about her. She's cast a spell on all of them. I know it, you know it, they know it."

"If Elspeth is an old witch, what do you call that silly old buffer of a headmaster and those barmy new teachers at Jack's school?"

"I hear in the post office quite a few parents want to pull their children out."

"I'm not surprised. I would do the same for ours if there was anywhere else for them to go."

Pam put down her pen. "Except Dan, who has got somewhere else to go, at least for a term. An upmarket public school. There's something not right about it, but I can't think of a reason to stop him going."

"I wonder how he'll take to that kind of life."

"I think he'll do very well; he's that kind of boy."

"I can't see Justin adjustin' so easily," said Roger. "He hasn't quite got the academic reach."

"You'll have to get a day off work."

"Well, that won't be difficult. I'm owed over a month's

holiday, most of which I'll also get paid for. Here we come, Tenerife!"

"Was Jack right about the new company taking over your department?"

"Of course he was. Burnoco have a 40% holding in Green Acres Environmental Services. The union was on to it straight away, but the council don't give a fig."

"I don't like any of this. It makes me feel powerless, Roger. And another thing: have you noticed that we haven't seen or heard from Robert for nearly a week?"

"Let's not..." Roger stopped mid-sentence and did a double take, having glanced out of the kitchen window. "Oh lord!"

"What's wrong?" asked Pam, rising to her feet.

"We have a visitor," he said.

There was a knock and Roger took a deep breath before answering. Alf Marshall, Noah's dad, stood on the doorstep, dishevelled, exhausted, with at least three days' growth of beard, wearing an old raincoat that had a belt but no buttons and which looked like a relic from the Second World War.

"I didn't know where else to come," he gasped.

Roger looked out in case anyone had seen them. "You'd better come in."

Pam frowned, as if to say, what about the children?

"Sit down – you look..." Roger was going to say 'dreadful', but thought better of it. "A cup of tea? I'll put the kettle on."

"I'll do it," said Pam, not taking her eyes off their visitor.

Alf collapsed into one of the kitchen chairs and put his head in his hands. "Where's my best boy?" he cried. "What have they done with him?"

Roger sat opposite. "When did they let you out?"

"They let me out today. The copper said they'd sent away my boy for treatment and when I asked him what for, he said for being a little nonce."

Roger frowned. "What's that supposed to mean?"

"My old shop... there's nothing left. I'm ruined."

49

"Have you been home?"

Alf clasped his forehead. "They've used it as a toilet. My boy mustn't see it like that. His room, all his little bits and pieces..."

"Do you take sugar?" asked Pam, banging down the mug in front of him, her face set in a frosty scowl.

"Hmm?" said Alf and looked up at her. He blinked rapidly and rose from his chair. "Sorry, I shouldn't have come. Iris is frightened of me too, and even Ken doesn't want to know me. I've got to go... I've got to find my boy."

He half-staggered to the door, pulled it open and loped off down the path, his open raincoat billowing behind him.

"What did you do that for?" asked Roger. "The man's in a terrible state."

"Why did he have to come here, of all places? Is it because we have children? We can't take any chances, Roger."

***

16: Sunday, 4th August. 8.45 a.m. 41 Westbury Avenue.

<u>ALAN</u>

Why don't they leave me alone? I'm going to lie here on my bed, in my room and do what I like, not what they want me to do. They can't force me, so there! I doubt whether I shall work on the car any more. What's the point? Why should I care about them? They're just fags. Let them rot in Russia!

Stewart gave me a memory stick with all the pictures of the fag on it. They're mostly taken in the garage and he's wearing that ridiculous white coat. But here's one of us on the sun loungers in our dungarees, which I didn't give permission for. I can't remember him taking it. He probably sneaked up when I had my eyes closed. Why is the fag holding my hand and looking at me in that faggy, luvvy-duvvy way? If anyone sees this they'll think I'm a fag too. I'm definitely going to

50

delete it. I'm definitely going to delete them all and take that picture down from above my bed as well.

They want me to go to my old house, to speak to my mum. To ask her for my passport and a covering letter for my visa. But if I go there, I'm likely to get caught, and then they'll take me back to the room with the flies, and Derek will chain me to the bed and force things up inside me again. Then he'll laugh and show me the blood. I'd rather die!

That's why I'm shit scared. That's why I don't want to go.

Someone's knocking on my bedroom door. It's Stewart. I'd better close the lid of my laptop in case he sees what I've been looking at, but it's too late; he's standing right by my bed.

"You're lucky," he says with a smile that's not cheerful at all.

"What does that mean?" I ask.

"To have someone special who loves you. I can do a print of that if you like, and put it in a frame."

I don't know what to say. "I'll think about it."

He nods. "We're just about to go. Jack's at the church and he's going to text us when they arrive. Dan's phoned Justin and he's coming down to help, so we should be OK without you."

"I'm coming," I say and then I have to force myself to get the extra words out, "...but I might get scared."

"Might!" says Stewart. "I've been shitting bricks all night."

He shows me his hand. It's shaking. Of course it's because the same thing happened to him, only he doesn't show it like I do.

"You must think I'm the faggiest coward ever."

He shakes his head. "It was far worse for you, Alan. You're a year and a half younger than me. They were your brothers; you respected them. You cared what they thought about you. I never did. I never felt part of that family like you.

They betrayed you. Just as bad, you thought that nobody cared about you, whereas I knew I had people looking out for me."

"Jack Moseley..."

"I owe Jack, just like you owe Noah, which is why you have to help him get back home." He looks at me hard. "You've got to go and get tested, you know."

He's brought that up. Something else I don't want to think about. He means tested for AIDS. We all have to have a certificate saying we don't have AIDS if we're to be let into Russia. I don't want to be tested. It's not my fault if I've got AIDS. In any case, they've got more of it over there than we have, but they don't talk about it.

"All right."

"When you go, I think I may as well have it done too."

I know why he's said that. It's because of what they did to him. The same as they did to me. We both might have it. Still, it can be treated now, so it's probably best to know. "We could all go together."

He smiles at me. We've never spoken like this, and I want to talk some more, but we haven't got time now. Maybe later... But only if we succeed, so I'd better get this over with before I back out again like a complete fag.

***

17: Sunday, 4th August. 9.05 a.m. Edwards Lane.

<u>JUSTIN</u>

It's about a month and a half since I was waiting in this same spot for Jack, and a lot has happened since then. When I showed my dad the letters from Mr Colt and Dumbleton Boys' School and told him that Dan was going too, he got straight on to Mr Moseley and asked his opinion. That seemed to do the trick because Mum and Dad are looking forward to going to the open day and are even considering a holiday in October.

Now that I'm not going to the Academy, Dad keeps saying that being a pupil at this posh school might make me sit up and work. He's even dropped hints about me staying on. I think if he knew how much it cost even for a non-boarder, that would be a non-starter. After all, he is a self-employed plumber, not a doctor or a teacher. In any case, it's a boys-only school and I want to be around girls too.

I'm getting to like Alan quite a bit now. He still goes off on one every so often, but I no longer take offence because I know it's not aimed at me personally. I think he appreciates my being calm because he can let his anger out without fear that I'll storm off. Sometimes, and it's really quite scary, he goes into this depressed state and I'll find him just stopped, like he's been switched off, and he'll have this blank expression on as if he's gone far, far away. I know he misses Noah something awful – it's almost like he's lost part of himself, not that he'll admit it. He still calls him 'the fag'. It's really cruel that they've been separated like that just when they were getting really close. I hope we can find Noah in Russia and they can be reunited.

I admit I'm not the brightest bulb on the Christmas tree, so it's not a complete insult to say that if you meet Alan casually, he does seem pretty thick. His lack of basic knowledge and the weird view he has of people, including himself, is quite comical. But of course when it comes to cars he's an absolute wiz. The way he soaks up the knowledge and is able to put it into practice is gob-smacking. I think he's pretty well memorised all the Humber Pullman manuals and knows where every nut, bolt and washer goes. The only downside is that he's a complete perfectionist and expects me to be as well.

For instance, seat belts: he hates the idea of them anyway, because they spoil the lines of the interior, and, worse, we're having to drill into the coachwork as well as the chassis. Anyway, he's rabbited on endlessly about them and when they were finally delivered this week, the colour of the belt material didn't quite match the interior trim, and when I say 'didn't quite match' I mean a casual observer would never notice the difference. I was marched down into the cellar to compare them, and got torn off a strip when I suggested it wasn't worth bothering about. They've been returned now and Alan has sent a tiny piece of the West of England cloth with them, plus a note. What they're going to make of his scrawly, thirteen-year-old, handwritten diatribe is another matter.

I have been able to get my own back a bit, because last week was our first night of Kyokushin karate. I don't think he expected it to be quite so physical, and let's just say he's got more enthusiasm than technique – he did spend a lot of time falling over. Still, when he's not in one of his moods, he can laugh at himself, which is no bad thing. I've invited him back to do some weight training as well, which means that what with swimming and the car we spend a lot of time together. We're both determined to get a sixer like Dan, and having someone to motivate you is a definite advantage – even if I do catch him checking me out sometimes.

Anne's just arrived in her Honda Civic, so it's time to get things started. She's our getaway driver – ha! ha! Oh, and Alan's with them too.

***

18: Sunday, 4th August. 9.15 a.m. 14 Edwards Lane.

ALAN

Jack Moseley texted ten minutes ago to say Dad, Derek and John have arrived at church in the Volvo. He also said he was going to let their tyres down. Good! I hate them. I wish they were dead, and all of those people in that anti-fag church. I hope it burns down with them inside!

Stewart and I are standing outside the house. It doesn't seem like my home any more. I don't ever want to live here again. Dan and Justin are sitting on the wall just inside the driveway. Near enough if there's trouble.

"Ready?" says Stewart.

"Do you know where the passports are kept?" I ask, probably just to delay.

"In the wall safe, I think."

"I don't know the combination."

Stewart smiles. "That's because you were a good boy." He rings the bell and then rings it again. At length a large shape appears behind the frosted window panels and the door is opened by my brother, Ben, dressed in jogging pants and black socks. He looks surprised to see us – why wouldn't he? But then we get his usual sneer.

"Good job I put some clothes on. Don't want to be arsed by a couple of queers," he laughs. "Are you two collecting for the Society of Shirt-lifters' legal funds, because you're going to need them."

"Mum in?" asks Stewart.

"Indisposed."

I try to adopt Stewart's even tone. "Aren't you going to invite us in, Ben?"

"So the baby homo's voice has finally broken. You sound almost like a man." The sixteen-year-old notices Dan and Justin up the driveway. "Hey, Moseley! How's your fag brother? Haven't seen his boyfriend round for a while... Why is that?" He laughs even louder than before.

"Jack's at church," calls Dan, "just like your paedo brothers."

"You what?" shouts Ben, colouring up.

Justin stands on the low wall. "Your tits are tremendous, lard-man. What size bra do you wear?"

My brother's beady eyes scan us in turn, and he appears to be deciding if he can take on all four of us, but his deliberations are interrupted by a voice from inside the house.

"Benny, whatchu doin'? Come on, I'm getting bored." A girl aged about fifteen appears in the hallway dressed in an oversize dressing gown and nothing else.

Ben looks round at her. "All right, Kim, I'll be there in a minute. You go back to bed."

55

"Who are they?" she questions, pointing beyond him.

"They're nobodies. They're just leaving."

"Not till we've seen Mum," says Stewart, sticking his foot in the door just as it's being shut in our faces.

Ben opens it wider still, meaning to slam it on Stewart's foot, but I jam mine in nearer the hinge, and though I'm only a size six, I'm wearing work boots. "She's got Mum's dressing gown on," I say.

"I just borrowed it," the girl says.

"Let them in, Ben," says Dan, who's now standing right behind us with Justin. Neither of them are quite as tall as my brother, and they certainly haven't got his bulk, but they're fitter, more agile and between them more than strong enough to deal with him.

"Wot's the problem if they want to see their mum, Benny? Just let them in, why don't you?"

My brother puffs out his chest, still not wanting to lose face. Then a solution comes to him. "Right, just you two, not them..."

"Fine by us," says Justin. "Just leave the door ajar."

Dan gazes at the girl. "You're Kimberley Robinson, aren't you? Louis's sister? I've seen you at some of our matches."

She smiles at him and Ben doesn't like it.

"Oh, yeh!" says Justin, and his mouth grows a broad smile. "I recognise you now. Do you come to see our fancy footwork or is the main attraction our muscular young bodies?" He actually winks at her, and even I know this is so corny.

"Shut your poncey mouth, Walker," says Ben. "And you two, make it snappy and then clear off and don't come back." He takes Kimberley's arm and together they ascend the stairs, though she glances back at Justin and, if I'm not mistaken, winks at him.

"You go up," whispers Stewart. "I'll get the safe."

I get up to the landing. Her bedroom door is closed. I look back down the stairs and see my friends in the doorway.

Justin gives me a thumbs-up, which gives me courage. I knock, but there's no reply so I open the door quietly and enter.

The smell almost knocks me back. It's like sour perfume. The curtains are drawn and the bedside lamp is on. It reminds me a bit of the room with the flies, and makes me feel weak and faint. Mum is sitting up on the bed, propped against pillows. She's wearing her best canary-yellow dress suit and black high-heeled shoes. But the dress is crumpled and stained. Her hair is like straw, and instead of being styled in a neat bob it sticks out in a frizz. Her face is thin and covered in sores, and I can see needle marks in her arms. I don't want to look any closer.

"Mum..."

She points a finger at me, and her nail is broken. "You're not real," she says, and laughs from deep down inside her throat. I've got the taste of sick in my mouth.

"Mum, it is me, Alan."

She gives another hoarse chuckle and glances over at the bedside cabinet. There are two lines of cocaine on the glass top and a straw. I can see her nose twitch. It's red and puffy.

"What do you want?" she asks, still not quite believing I'm real.

I hate myself for doing this, but I take out the letter which I want her to sign. "I need your signature for a school trip."

She smiles at me, and she's almost like the mother I once knew. "That's nice. Where are you going?"

"Russia," I say.

"Russia!" she exclaims. "That's a long way. When are you going?"

"October."

"Oh! The October revolution, *Dr Zhivago*, Omar Sharif, the Winter Palace. How wonderful it will be. But you must be careful of the cold, Alan or you'll catch a chill. Now, where are my glasses?"

I look round and see them on the dressing table. They're covered in dust and I wipe them on my T-shirt. When I return to her, I see she's already taken one of the lines. She sniffs and gives me a curious smile. "Clears the head," she says, positioning the glasses carefully on her nose. "Do you have something to rest the letter on, and my pen? Can you get my pen?"

The pen is also on the dressing table, a green and black *Pelikan Souveran*. I just hope there's ink in it.

"You look very well, Alan. You're growing into such a beautiful young man."

On the floor by the bed is a BBC *Countryfile* magazine dated March. When I pick it up I see a hypodermic syringe just sticking out from under the base. I kick it all the way under. I'm so depressed I feel like crying, but I carefully wipe the magazine and lay the letter on it. Now I have to get close enough to show her where to put the signature. I try to hold my breath.

She signs the paper carefully and looks up at me.

"It's the fourth of August," I say, and she smiles because I have anticipated her question.

The pen scratches the paper again, then she screws the cap on and hands everything back to me. "I shouldn't come again, Alan," she says matter-of-factly. "It's not good here."

I want to give her a kiss, but I'm too grossed out, too afraid of being sick. "Do you need anything?" I ask.

She looks at me in surprise. "Need anything?" She spreads her thin arms wide and smiles gaily. "Why would I? I've got everything I want right here."

"Goodbye, Mum, and thank you."

She settles down and closes her eyes. "Goodbye, Alan, be a good boy now," she says and her expression is one of contentment.

When I get back downstairs, I feel sad, but I'm not going to cry. Stewart has the passport and gives me a hug, but he doesn't ask about Mum. He's good like that.

***

19: Wednesday, 7th August. 11.30 a.m. MSK. Arkhangelsk Oblast, Ketozero, a lake.

<u>NOAH</u>

I'm sitting in a wooden hut by the edge of a lake. That sounds nice, doesn't it? A late summer's day by a beautiful stretch of water surrounded by bountiful nature or whatever. Except that it's raining and has been raining for two days. Not a heavy downpour, not drizzle, just normal rain coming out of a grey sky for forty-eight hours non-stop, with no end in sight. At night when it beats on our tin roof some of the boys, particularly Owen, John and the twins, can't get to sleep, but I find it quite restful.

I now know why not many people live around here. It's a bog in a forest, and you can take that any way you want. Every footstep squelches. No wonder we were given these rubber boots and waterproofs. The trouble is, they're nylon, which makes you hot and sweaty, especially when the weather's warm. Oh, and this hut; it's not a hut, it's more like a kiosk with an open front and half-walled sides. Except it doesn't sell ice cream and it's wrecked. One of the corner uprights has rotted away so the roof hangs down and will probably collapse on us shortly. What do I care if it does?

Since it started to rain, early morning inspection has been in our dormitory, standing to attention by our beds dressed in our *new* underwear. We've each been given two pairs of *Pound Shop*, floral, Russian boxer shorts. I don't know what's happened to our own. One minute they were in the laundry, the next I expect they were on sale in the local flea market. Miss Valerie translates the day's orders as usual, but since our *contretemps* with the man juice, these now come from Ivan the Terrible, as we've nicknamed the senior guard. Unfortunately, he has a smattering of English so it won't be so easy to pull the wool over his eyes. We don't see much of Dr Death any more and, as for Madam DeVeal, she's definitely on the slide, that one – at least I hope so.

Today our itinerary for the morning was slightly different, because instead of working round the camp we were driven in the Gazzas along a track in the forest, little more than a path actually, and at intervals we were pushed out in pairs with an axe and a saw. Our orders were to cut down a tree, remove the branches and return with the trunk to our pick-up point within two hours. The pair with the largest tree get extra rations; the pair with the smallest get half-rations; the pair with no tree get no rations. If you are not at the pick-up point at the right time, you spend the night in the forest and when you're found, you spend the corresponding amount of time in solitary on bread and water. Our blue-uniformed guards, or thugs as I like to call them, think this is very funny and encourage us in hearty masculine competitiveness.

'Solitary' is a rusty metal cage newly installed in the courtyard right next door to the bog. Obviously a lot of cunning thought went into that placement. The current occupant – and there always seems to be someone in residence – is Brandon, who told Dr Death to 'go fuck himself' when he received an unsympathetic hearing about a broken tooth, broken by biting down on what appears to have been an air-rifle pellet found in our delicious breakfast sausage.

Yeh, the meals are pretty much the same tasteless, colourless mush every day. Dinner last night was a soupy stew made of cabbage with some type of stringy meat in it, a slice of bread and fishy margarine, and a glass of tea. I eat everything and I always make sure that Mark does as well, otherwise he'd waste away. Maybe my diet at home wasn't so good, which is why the look and taste of the food here doesn't bother me as much as it does some of the others. Funny, do you know what I fancy the most? Not chocolate, not cake, not Coke, but an orange; a big fat juicy orange.

My fellow lumberjack today is Ryan Davis. He's not the most talkative person I've ever met. Not that he's unfriendly or anything, I think it's the way he's been brought up. *Don't speak unless you're spoken to*. Here he is, a gay boy who's been right under my nose at school for nearly two years, and I can't remember ever having noticed him. Admittedly, he is Year Eight and eight months younger than me, but he's easy on the eye, with a nice trim body and a chipped front tooth, which makes him look a bit of a lad, so where was my gaydar when it was needed?

We were the last pair out of the Gazza, which meant under normal circumstances we'd have the least time to cut down our tree. Fortunately there was already one keeled over by the lake, practically rootless and, now we've hacked off just about all the branches, it's light enough for us to carry back up to the track.

Shortly I'm going to try to get Ryan to speak, because we're going to be in this hole for at least another half hour and I'd prefer to share our miseries rather than keeping them to ourselves. My main misery at the moment, besides pining for my Cutie Pie, is the dreaded eczema. My hands are itchy, red, scaly and scabby. But I'm one of the lucky ones. Robert still hasn't recovered from the baton beating he received. I think he's got a cracked collar bone. It looks inflamed and swollen and he's in a lot of pain, but they're still making him work.

John Price and Porky have got the shits. They do their best, but it is so gross. Poor old Brandon in the chokey with a sore tooth is having to put up with that all day. So far we've been spared it at night, but they've each got an extra bucket just in case. I expect we'll all get it at some point. I'm just glad that John and Porks were paired off this morning and were first out of the truck. I'm pretty certain it's the water, not the food. There's probably a tank in the roof or something which collects rainwater. Maybe it'll be better now that it's rained properly, because it might have flushed out all the germs, but I'm only going to drink the water if I'm forced to.

Talking of which, I've made a friend: the caretaker's wife. I know she's got warts and whiskers, and whiskers coming out of her warts, but I think she's actually quite decent. Not all that hygienic, I grant you, but I helped her with some logs she was having to carry because her hubby is a lazy dog, and when I set them down by the oven she gave me a nod and a smile, and I pointed at myself and said *Noah*. And she smiled and nodded and pointed at herself and said *Babooshka*. Miss Valerie told me that word means *grandma* and also told me that *hi* in Russian is *privet*, like in the hedge. So now every morning I say, *Privet, Babooshka, yest' li u vas kakikh-libo rabot?* Do you have any jobs? This gets me free access to the teapot.

Dennis and Michael Shane have got colds, and are sniffing and sneezing in unison. They keep apologising for keeping us awake at night and spreading the virus to all and sundry. Fortunately I'm in the corner furthest away from them, but I'm waiting to see which of us gets the shits and a cold simultaneously.

There's still no sign of our spiritual guidance counsellor, and the door with the cross is still locked. Miss Valerie says there has been a delay in getting a visa, for reasons he doesn't know about, but he should be here next week. I can't wait. Meanwhile, our pile of logs is getting ever higher. The trouble is, chopping logs into firewood isn't easy. None of us has mastered the technique yet, though Porky, when he hasn't got the squits, is the best of the worst.

Jamie came back to us on Monday with a very interesting story of where he'd been taken after he was dragged into that jeep by the guards. He said a couple of miles to the north-west is a village called Puksa, cut out of the forest. In the centre there isn't a green for playing cricket matches or a duck pond, but a prison camp for teenage boys. Inside a pair of perimeter fences there are four two-storey barracks, separated by fencing to keep the different categories of prisoners apart. The staff either live in wooden houses around the camp or a new block of flats, and there is a small market, shops, a meeting hall and a railway station, but he didn't see any trains.

When we quizzed Miss Valerie about it, he said there are terrorists, murderers, sex offenders and petty criminals housed in the different blocks, and that we English pussies should think ourselves lucky we weren't imprisoned with the macho Russian boys because we would become their bitches in ten seconds. If you ask me, Miss Valerie seems to have a mighty high opinion of his criminal countrymen, and for a respectable translator knows just a little bit too much about them. As to the railway station, he said, that is a narrow gauge track mostly for ferrying supplies, and it belongs to the prison authorities. Miss Valerie said that the trains are few and far between, and so perhaps that explains why we haven't had any fresh 'man juice' offered to us. I was keeping an eye on Dwain during this little chat, in case it put fresh ideas into his head about running away now that we know there's a town not too far from us.

Jamie was put in with the petty criminals for five days, but came out no worse than he went in – that is, with cuts and bruises from when he was restrained. He said that most of the inmates kept themselves to themselves and only a few spoke English anyway. I think there was probably another reason why he wasn't bothered by them: he's the biggest and strongest of us. One thing he did learn was that most of the Russian boys know about the new camp for the 'Gay Brits' and think we're getting all sorts of privileges and cushy treatment. We should be so lucky.

"Ryan..."

I've got his attention.

"Why are you here?"

Shrug... It must have been too broad a question. Uh-oh, he's looked away again.

"Ryan..."

I've got his attention again.

"Who sent you here?"

"Social."

Quick, before I lose him. "Who told social services about you?"

"Priest."

"How did a priest find out you were gay?"

"Parents."

I've got to be careful with the next question, or I might just get a shrug. "Did your parents send you to a priest because they found out you were gay?"

He nods.

"How did your parents find out you were gay?"

Oh, he's gone red, and do I detect a guilty little smile?

"Go on Ryan, spill the beans."

"Porn," he murmurs.

"Oh my God!" I screech. "They didn't catch you at it, did they? If our dad caught me I'd die of embarrassment!"

I can tell he's not going to provide any more information on that subject, so I let him off the hook. "Do your parents know you were being sent to Russia?"

He gives me a quick nod then picks up the axe and walks out of our shelter. Moments later he's hacking at one of the side branches that's still left on our tree.

***

20: Friday, 9th August. 11.45 a.m. 15 Leighton Lane.

JACK

Only when Jack realised that they'd be travelling through seven countries, each with slightly different requirements, did he understand that compiling a list of essential items for their journey was not as straightforward as he had first imagined. Now after two hours of concentrated mental activity, he'd thought of thirty items they would need, including snow chains, two warning triangles and a pair of wheel chocks for parking in Estonia. At this rate there wouldn't be any room for luggage, Jack thought, and smiled to himself as he imagined Alan's reaction at being asked to put a roof rack on the Humber.

On Monday they were going to collect their HIV certificates from the clinic and on Tuesday all the crew would meet at number 41 for the first time, including Ms Lane and Mr Colt. Stewart would take his camera, to take the remaining passport photographs they needed for their visas. Dan was preparing the route that would take them from Swanford all the way to St Petersburg with mileages, timings and probable fuel consumption, given the Pullman's thirsty reputation. Alan and Justin would report progress on the car itself and have a list of items still required. Meanwhile, Anne was ruminating on what the boys' clothing needs would be, given that they would be heading towards a Russian winter. Everyone was expected to have costed their part of the arrangements so that Elspeth would have some idea of the total outlay.

For the first time, Jack felt some excitement over the project, even though they were not due to depart for another eight weeks. He couldn't wait to see Robert's face when they turned up outside the clinic in their limousine ready to whisk him back to England.

"Jack, why are you happy?"

He swivelled his chair round until he was facing the doorway and folded his arms. "Who said you could come into my room, pesto?"

"What is pesto?" asked Mikey.

"It's nutty and cheesy just like you..." Jack picked up his bag of coconut mushrooms and held it out. "Well, now you're here, you may as well come in and entertain me."

The little boy picked out a sweet and went and sat on the bed. "Can I go to Russia with you?"

"Seven-year-olds aren't allowed, especially ones with blue hair and a skinny leg."

"Will you learn me some Russian words?"

"Teach me!"

"Will you teach me some Russian words?"

"Nyet."

"What does knee-et mean?"

"Nyet means no and da means yes."

"Russian is easy," said Mikey.

"It is if you have a two-word vocabulary."

"Jack, will Daddy have enough money to send me to Dan's new school when I'm old enough?"

"Only if we win the lottery, which we don't do, so no."

"Oh," said Mikey. "I'd like to go. Wouldn't you?"

"I'm not bothered," said Jack, stretching. "And why do you want to go so badly?"

Mikey smiled. "I like the blazer."

"Ahh, I see. Would that be because it's bright red?"

The little boy nodded. "And the blue and yellow badge. Dan says the motto is in Latin and means virtue is the only nobility. He's learned that in case."

"In case of what?"

"In case he's asked, silly."

"Oh, I get you."

"Jack, I won't be able to have my hair cut and coloured blue at the barber's any more, will I?"

"Not for a while at least, and if Mum has anything to do with it, 'a while' will mean forever."

"The man who cut my hair was Noah's dad, wasn't he?"

"That's right."

"He's died."

Jack sat up. "What do you mean?"

"I just saw it on the telly. They showed his picture."

"When was this?"

"Just now."

"Jesus!" said Jack and began to mouse into his computer. "What channel?"

"SLTV."

Quickly he brought up the iPlayer screen for the TV station, launched the catch-up news and scrolled quickly through the time bar.

...the by-election for the Woolgrove Constituency will be held on Thursday 12th September, following the resignation of Sarah Heath, who has been the MP for ten years. A party spokesperson said that Ms Heath could no longer serve her constituents in the manner they were accustomed to while this shadow was hanging over her, but she was determined to refute the allegations made against her, which were totally without foundation.

Meanwhile, a woman out walking her dog early this morning found the body of a man floating in the River Teme. An ambulance was called, but the victim was pronounced dead at the scene. The body is thought to be that of local hairdresser Alfred Marshall, who was recently in police custody following investigations into a paedophile ring in the town.

In a statement, Detective Inspector David Rains of Swanford police said that the death is not being treated as suspicious, but an enquiry has been launched into the circumstances surrounding this tragic incident. He appealed to anyone with information to contact the station.

"Jesus Christ, poor Noah," said Jack. "I'd better tell them at number 41."

***

20: Wednesday 14th August. 12.30 p.m. MSK. Arkhangelsk Oblast, Gosudarstvennyi Meditsinskii Institut (gomoseksualizm).

ROBERT

We've been here just over two weeks, or a fortnight as the Brits would say. Noah says I now have a mid-Atlantic accent, but I guess he's kidding me, like he always does. At inspection this morning, Ivan told us that from tomorrow we'll start to cook our own food, the reason being that transporting meals every day as the weather deteriorates will not be practical. "Your time of living in hotel conditions is drawing to an end," he said – at least, that's how Valery translated it. It seemed like a bad joke to me.

The other announcement he made was that this afternoon will be our first visit to the Church of the Transfiguration, wherever and whatever that is. Apparently our spiritual guidance counsellor arrived earlier in the week and has been preparing for our session. Noah says the door with the crucifix is still locked. I'm not sure what that means.

The days are still long, but getting noticeably shorter. The sun is above the trees when we get up, but there is a definite period of darkness now instead of a night-time twilight. We had three days of rain and several that were overcast, but at the moment we're in another period of fine weather, which Valery says should last till the weekend at least. This means that inspection has been outside again.

I think we have all lost some weight, but it's most noticeable in those who've had stomach upsets, particularly Porky. He's the one person who actually looks healthier now; certainly his double chin and most of his gut are gone. But it may not have done him any good to lose so much so rapidly. He certainly complains enough of feeling weak and hungry, though the food is so bad that weak and hungry has become the natural state for all of us.

Dwain spent two nights in the forest after not returning from the tree-felling expedition, even though his partner Jamie tried to talk him out of it. He wasn't exactly recaptured, because he turned up at the wood-chopping session outside the compound, exhausted and hungry, on the third day. We tried to smuggle him in but being the only black person among us put him at a disadvantage. Hairy man, Yuri, spotted him, which meant two days in solitary. I know that Noah managed to sneak him a hard-boiled egg and some extra bread during the time, but he still isn't back to anything like his full strength, though he's one of these people who remains cheerful whatever the circumstances.

It was Jamie's sixteenth birthday on Monday, and Brandon talked Vaseline into giving us a sheet of A4 paper and a pen to make him a card. Mark designed a nice 16 on the front – I guess he's still doing that kind of thing at his school – then got us all to sign it. Maybe the little fella is coming out of his shell. At breakfast Jamie was presented with the card and we all sang Happy Birthday, which actually made him cry. I think we were all affected by that. It's surprising what you learn about people when you live with them every day.

Professor Rozhdestvensky has had a brass name plate made and screwed onto the wall by the front door. It's in Russian and English and has his name at the bottom as the founder. As if that was the only thing needed to make this place a legitimate medical facility! If Mom and Dad knew what this 'institute' was actually like, would they have sent me here? Noah says that there are none so blind as those that don't see, which I guess means he thinks they would have.

I'm playing a cat and mouse game with Sister Margaret Hopkins and Professor Dmitri Salkorov – that's Madam DeVeal and Dr Sex in Noah speak. They want me to undergo a radical new sex therapy which they believe will cure me of my perversion. That is, they want me to sign a paper agreeing to this new therapy without telling me what it is. I'm not even sixteen until November, and so signing a bit of paper would have no legality. What I think they need is to make me compliant first, so that later I accept anything they throw at me.

Once I agree to their demands I'll be transferred to the hospital for my shoulder. It is very painful and if it's jolted I feel sick. I'm not sure how much longer I can hold out against them, though Noah says I should start faking how bad it is, because he thinks Madam DeVeal is bluffing and will get my shoulder seen to anyway.

I believe I am the one they are most anxious to get results with; the others are bystanders in comparison. I am the son of one of the sponsors of the project, and if they don't 'succeed' with me the cash may not be so forthcoming in future. I don't think any of the Russians have any conviction about what they are doing. This is a sham operation, done on the cheap in order to line as many official pockets as possible.

Perhaps for the sake of the others I should let them do their 'therapy' and pretend it's worked. Maybe then we'll all be sent home. The problem with that is, of course, it will mean more unfortunate people will be forced to follow in our wake.

I'll have to discuss this with the others in the dormitory tonight.

Noah hopes they've all but given up on converting him to 'normality'. He has the advantage of taking nothing they do to him seriously, but pretending the opposite. In one of our afternoon 'manly behaviour' lessons, Dr Sex gave him a folder containing six photographs of naked people and asked him to choose which one gave him the most 'stimulation'. This folder must have been in use fifty years ago, judging by the quality of the pictures. Three showed females probably aged between puberty and thirty and three showed males, all of whom were older than my dad! Noah spent as much time as possible studying each one before choosing the saggiest, baldest, most wrinkled and pot-bellied man. Of course he did it with a completely straight face for the professor, but always managed to give Madam DeVeal a knowing look, which infuriates her. The point is, she clearly wants to be boss in these sessions but Dr Sex pretty well ignores her.

When Noah holds up the picture, making sure we can all see it, he says: "This is a real turn-on, Professor. Do you think I need help?"

"Do you wish to have this daddy figure force himself upon you, or do you want to force yourself upon the daddy figure?" asks Dmitri in his halting English.

Noah looks up at the ceiling. "Er... both, I think. Yes, both... at the same time, with two daddies."

"Ooo, go for it, Noah," shrieks Dwain, entering into the spirit of the exchange.

"Noah Marshall, your perversion is very deep-seated," the professor says. "It is a good job you are a willing student."

"Ooo, yes Professor, I am really trying," says Noah, in his whiniest voice, at which point Sister Hopkins is tight-lipped and silently seething.

We've just eaten our lunch – a bowl of porridge with sweetcorn in it, a slice of bread and margarine, the usual glass of tea and an apple. Whoa! Fresh fruit, where did that come from? I had to leave some of the porridge, though, it was just too disgusting. I wasn't the only one. John Price, Brandon and Owen Frost left most of theirs as well. That was after seeing who could do the grossest vomiting impressions.

However, two of our number always have clean plates – the two that are only skin and bone anyway. Noah keeps his beady eye on Mark, and if it looks like the little fellow isn't going to eat something, he taps the table with his finger then points and says, Every scrap. I think the two of them enjoy this meal time ritual, and it encourages them both to eat the uneatable. The only time you see Mark smile is when he's with Noah.

***

21: Wednesday, 14th August. 4 p.m. MSK. Arkhangelsk Oblast, Gosudarstvennyi Meditsinskii Institut (gomoseksualizm).

NOAH

The order's just been given over the PA for us to assemble in the yard. I'm still in the dormitory saying goodbye to the twins, who are in bed. Their colds have settled on their chests and Madam DeVeal keeps coming in and taking their temperatures. I think she's worried about them, which means they must be really ill. They're both feverish, off their food and have sore backs. I got Babooshka to make them some tea, so at least they'll be drinking boiled water.

I was going to be naughty and go out in my undies and flip-flops, pretending I'd forgotten we were going to church, but I'm too interested in where we're going to bother. Maybe on Sunday. Before I go out, though, I'm going to have a quick shufty down the corridor to see if the door with the cross is still locked.

I'm halfway along and I've got my ear against the door of the medical room. Dr Death and Madam DeVeal are having a heated argument. What fun! Wait till I tell the others. Of course, poor old Miss Valerie is in there too as the translator.

"Why does the nigger only do two sessions a week and gets an apartment in the village and I have to live in this slum with the buggers twenty-four hours a day, seven days a week?"

Ooo, she's used the N word, not to mention the B word, even though I don't think any of us gay boys has done the B word yet. I doubt if my beautiful Cutie Pie will be up for that for a long, long time. Oh, my poor heart's just done a flip thinking about a little Thrupp and Maberly session.

"Sister, the arrangements were made by your people. The money from Burnoco for the Reverend Akinola and his retinue was far in excess of that given by Lambda Healthcare for you."

"Retinue? What retinue?"

"The Reverend has a small support staff."

"So the nigger gets staff as well? Disgraceful!"

"That may be so, but it is a fact of life. Now you say these twin boys, Dennis and Michael Shane, need antibiotics."

"They may have contracted pneumonia. They need amoxicillin."

Pneumonia! That's serious, isn't it?

"We do not carry such medications at the Institute, Sister, but I shall order some from the pharmacy in Puksa."

"And make sure it's not out of date!"

"There will of course be a cost."

"There'll be a cost if we have fatalities, I can tell you that."

"Only if the word gets out, Sister. Homosexuals are expendable in Russia."

"But word will get out, Professor. If one of them dies, the others will report it."

"Then it is your job to see that it doesn't happen, Sister Hopkins."

Ooo! I think I'll head down to the yard sharpish now. At least I know why the room with the cross is unoccupied, and I don't want to hang about listening to those two psychos any longer. That was a bit of an eye-opener.

We've formed a crocodile and are lined up at the gate, just like in primary school. Vaseline is leading us and Yurine is bringing up the rear, if you know what I mean. We also have one of the blue uniforms with us, twirling his baton in that menacing guard sort of way.

I thought we'd be going in the Gazzas, but no, we've walked right past them onto a track. My sense of direction is hopeless, but Jamie says we're going due east. We've never been taken this way before. It's quite nice in the forest this afternoon, with hazy sunshine filtering through the branches. The squelch has gone from underfoot too. Robert's suffering with his shoulder, but he's bearing up for the moment. I haven't told anyone yet about Madam DeVeal and Dr Death's conversation; I think I'll save it until dinner tonight. What I don't get is why there's a church in a forest when no one lives here.

Owen claims to have seen a red squirrel, but Brandon said it was grey. A typical argument between brothers over nothing. I didn't see anything and wouldn't know the difference anyway. I can just about recognise the flock of sparrows that've take up residence in our compound. When it's dry they like to dust-bathe in the courtyard, but the main reason they've decided to stay is because Babooshka feeds them on the stuff we leave. I'm expecting a mass extinction.

I didn't expect this. We've come out of the forest onto some kind of sloping field which is really overgrown with grass and white flowers. But up on the top of the rise is the Church of the Transfiguration, standing all alone in the middle of nowhere, silhouetted against the sky. It's made of wood and has five onion domes, one on each corner of the central tower and the fifth and largest in the middle, raised up on a spire. They're all topped off with giant crosses, but they're not normal crosses like in England because they've each got three cross-pieces and the bottom one, which is the shortest, is at a slightly different angle.

As we get nearer, the church seems to get smaller until at the doors we can see that the top of the spire is about thirty feet above us, still tall enough for something made entirely of wood. It's not in tip-top condition; it looks to have been painted many times, but even I can tell that it's due for a fresh coat of creosote. Our dad loves creosote, especially the smell, and is really anti all the modern wood preservatives, which he believes are just watery paints. I expect he's thinking back to his childhood, because we haven't got a shed or a fence to our name.

There's a mud-spattered pick-up truck parked by the side of the church with giant tyres and a canvas hood over the back. I can see the tyre marks on the grass where it came up the slope.

Someone has removed the padlock and chain from the doors and hung them over one of the handles. Vaseline takes us inside. We're in a space about the size of a large shed, only twice as high. It smells musty and some of the floorboards have either rotted away or been filched. Until our eyes get used to the dark, we can't see much. Then in the half-light I look up, and there's a false ceiling covered in painted angels against a blue background. Strangely, they've all got black halos round their heads. Brainbox John Price says these religious figures are called icons, which is a word I only know from computing.

We proceed through a short passage into the main body of the church where there are three rectangular windows high up in the north and south walls, each with four panels of yellow glass in them. Before us there are candles burning in small glass globes arranged around a slightly raised semi-circular platform on which a man is standing. He's wearing a fancy gold medallion with a cross on it and a maroon silk robe which glitters in the candlelight. Behind him there are more decorated panels with religious figures in them.

Robert gives me a light dig with his elbow. "I've seen him before," he whispers. "He was at my dad's house one evening and he had a chauffeur-driven car."

I feel a draught from above and look up through the semi-darkness to the onion dome at the top of the tower. The walls right up to the spire are covered in more icons connected by the flowing branches of a painted tree. Here the figures have golden halos and many have crowns and rich costumes. My view is only obstructed by two cross beams at the intersection, from which hangs a metal chandelier.

"Come sit at my feet," the man says. "For you are in God's house."

We obey, for the lack of something better to do.

There is a folder in his hand which he opens, and the way he is looking at us means he probably has a file and a photograph of each of us. It is some time before he speaks.

"I am the Reverend Joseph Akinola of the Baptist fellowship of Nigeria. It is my duty and my privilege to bring you into the Fellowship of the Holy Spirit. To redeem your souls. To save you from everlasting torment. From this day forth, we shall work together to rid you of the demon, the agent of Satan, that has possessed your corporeal bodies.

Seven of you have the mark of the beast already upon you. The rest are in mortal danger from the transference of one of his legions."

This man is scary. I think he actually believes this nonsense. On the other hand, he could be a very good actor, but his eyes have a kind of madness in them. Maybe he is possessed by a demon!

The Reverend closes his folder and stares at each of us in turn. "The Bible teaches us that homosexuality is an atrocious and unnatural act." He pauses, to let this sink in. "The Law of Moses is against it and stipulates capital punishment for the offender. It is classified among the most offensive crimes, such as idolatry involving the sacrifice of children, having intercourse with animals, or marrying a woman and her mother."

I'm watching the others while this performance is going on and I can see that Ryan and Mark are listening with more than a passing interest. In fact, they seem quite riveted. Is it because they are the youngest and most impressionable among us? Stories by candlelight. I'm wondering, as he said seven of us have the mark of the beast upon us, whether he's included

Mark in his list of gay boys. Now, I know I'm no judge and I admit he's only ten, but I don't get any impression of gayness in him, so where does Reverend Joe get his information from?

"Do you believe we should be put to death, Reverend Akinola?"

Ooo, that was Robert being very forward.

"If you do not repent, your immortal souls will be lost in the fires of hell."

"You didn't answer the question," says Jamie.

"Almighty God has given me a mission to save your souls, my young friend."

"Can't you just tell us, Reverend, what are your personal thoughts on killing us gay boys?" That's me putting my twopenn'orth in.

"The demons within you have spoken, and I have no truck with the words of Satan."

Our three Russian friends are not sure what is going on, but I think they sense rebellion and are getting restless. The baton is definitely being twirled a fraction faster.

"Have we really got to listen to you for two hours at a time?" asks Brandon.

The Reverend raises his hand as a policeman might to stop traffic. "I rejoice and praise God that I am saved and that the mocking clamour of the demon has no effect upon me. It is my intention over the coming weeks to fight with every breath against the legions of Satan that inhabit your bodies, and by the grace of Our Saviour the Lord Jesus Christ I shall root out these blasphemies and free your souls."

"I've seen and read a lot about your kind in my country, Reverend," says Dwain. "You are interested in only two things: money and power."

The Reverend Joe gives a sign with his upraised fingers, and the blue-uniformed thug hits Dwain across the back with his baton, causing him to cry out in pain.

"The demon speaks and has God's answer."

"Does your God like hitting young boys?" I ask.

The swipe I get isn't that painful, but it made me shut up. So I sit there on the plank floor and after a time, as the Reverend drones on, I drift off into my own private world of me and my beautiful Cutie Pie, though every so often he'll raise his voice to such a pitch that I'm brought back to his reality, which in its madness seems less real than my daydream.

***

22: Friday, 23rd August. 8.15 a.m. 15 Leighton Lane.

PAM

Pam put a second slice of toast on Roger's plate, joining the half-eaten one already there.

"Thank you," said Roger. "I suppose we could consider buying a new toaster tomorrow."

"If we bought a four-slice one, we might be able to enjoy breakfast together."

Roger, who had his head buried in the latest copy of the *Swanford Mail*, looked up at his wife. "We're being a bit ambitious there, aren't we? From a toaster that only toasts one slice and won't eject automatically to an all-singing, all-dancing four-slicer seems too much like a quantum leap to me."

"I used to like that TV series," said Pam, sitting down to her first slice.

"Have you been reading this story about Alf Marshall too?"

"I glanced at it," she said, spreading a thin layer of butter over the toast.

"Do you think we could have made a difference?"

"It's no good speculating on what might have been, because undoing the past only occurs in science fiction."

"What past do you want to undo?" asked Jack, coming into the kitchen in T-shirt and boxer shorts.

"Nothing important," answered Roger.

"Does nothing important mean you just don't want to talk about it in front of me?"

"Yes," said Pam. "Now get some breakfast."

"It's a private matter between me and your mum," added Roger.

Jack dropped a piece of bread into the toaster. "So you're going to buy a four-slice toaster, even though we're on the skids?"

"Haven't we taught you that eavesdropping is a very rude habit?"

"Actually, no, you've always taught us to keep our eyes and ears open." He glanced down at the article his father had been reading on page five, under the heading *Drunk's Funeral*:

A pauper's funeral took place last Monday for Alfred Marshall, 41, of Savoy Flats, Swanford. This followed a post-mortem carried out on the Coroner's instruction, during which the cause of death was found to be drowning by the aspiration of water into the lungs. The victim was said to have had 454 milligrams of alcohol in his blood. The limit for driving is 80 milligrams. A verdict of accidental death was recorded.

The body was cremated and the ashes scattered in the Garden of Rest at the town cemetery on the Malton Road.

"And doubtless nobody was there to see him off – certainly not his son."

"A shame," said Roger.

"Is that what you'll say when they come for me and arrest you for being paedophiles?"

"Don't talk such nonsense," said Pam.

"I wonder how many other people in Swanford have got their heads buried in the sand."

"Look," said Roger. "I know that things are not easy in the world for people like you, Jack, but it's only a phase, you'll see."

Pam smelled burning and looked towards the toaster, where a plume of smoke was rising from the interior. "Jack!" she shouted.

He turned to the decrepit machine and ejected the blackened bread, picking it out between thumb and forefinger. "Ah well, I'm not so hungry now anyway." He threw the offending slice into the bin and wandered out of the kitchen and back towards the stairs.

"That was a close one," said Roger in a quiet voice.

"Do you mean the toast catching fire?"

"You know exactly what I mean."

Pam swallowed the last of her toast and had a drink of tea. "I think there's a bit of a hate campaign against gays at the moment since the new government was elected."

"You voted for them," said Roger.

"I didn't expect things to work out like this."

"The trouble is, you didn't read the manifesto small print."

"Did you?"

"No, but I wasn't going to vote for the fascist bastards in the first place."

"Oh Roger, it's not that bad. Things will settle down once the papers find something new to talk about."

"This is tabloid heaven, Pam. It was a terrible blow to the newsprint moguls when homosexuality was decriminalised in the sixties. Just think how many cheap and juicy sex and blackmail stories they lost through it."

"I wonder how many other people are regretting their decision."

"I know one thing: I don't fancy our kids' chances in the modern world if they start teaching Biblical truths."

Pam frowned. "If we relied only on books that were written a couple of thousand years ago, where would we be now?"

"Probably somewhere in the Middle East," chuckled Roger.

"Well, I say it's a shame people can't live and let live."

"You weren't exactly pro-Noah yourself."

"Noah was a bad influence on Mikey."

"So you say, but I believe our little lad is more astute than you give him credit for."

"I think the newspaper headline was a bit much: *Drunk's Funeral.* I wonder if we'll ever learn the truth about Noah's father and all those other people who were accused of being child molesters? I can't believe our MP was one. She always seemed like a decent person to me."

"I think we already know the truth."

"I hope Jack doesn't go out of his way to cause trouble. Once someone comes out, as they say, they can easily become a target."

Roger folded the paper and stood up. "Time I was off. It's going to happen at school if anywhere. It's a pity Jack wasn't given the opportunity to go to Dumbleton like Dan."

"I remember what Mr Colt said to us on parents evening too."

"It's good that he's got this trip coming up. It'll give us all a bit of breathing space."

"We have to stand up and fight for our boys, Roger, whatever..."

"I know, dear wife, and fight we will."

***

23: Thursday, 29th August. 11.30 a.m. MSK. Arkhangelsk Oblast, Gosudarstvennyi Meditsinskii Institut (gomoseksualizm).

NOAH

Our little band of twelve is falling apart. No longer united against the common enemy. The twins Dennis and Michael were moved out after Madam DeVeal got medication for them, but found that the tablets weren't making them any better. We've had no news of them for days. Robert has finally given in and agreed to undergo 'therapy' in exchange for treatment to his shoulder, and leaves for the hospital tomorrow. I don't blame him; he can't move his right arm, and he's very drawn and listless.

Last Sunday Dwain got into a second argument with Reverend Joe and received another beating from the baton-wielder. After that, he told us he was never going back to that church, ever. Yesterday, I thought he'd changed his mind as he started off with us from the compound as usual. But as our crocodile wound along the track through the forest, Dwain suddenly wasn't there. He'd positioned himself right in the middle of our group and on a bend dashed off into the trees. It took the baton thug a moment to realise what had happened, and by the time he started off in pursuit Dwain was nowhere in sight. We all started shouting, Way to go, Dwain! Meanwhile, Vaseline and Yurine were exchanging dark looks from each end of the crocodile and seemed relieved when the thug came back empty-handed.

The only ones not to join in shouting for Dwain were Mark and Ryan. They seem to have fallen hook, line and sinker for the Reverend Akinola's poison, and think we are all possessed by demons. They've isolated themselves from the group and they're especially anti-me for some reason. Ryan was never especially communicative, but Mark seemed to be coming along after his miserable start, but now he isn't feeding himself properly and neither of them is washing. Let's put it this way: no one wants them on the cooking rota.

What else has deteriorated? Oh, yes, the weather. We're still made to go out in our boxers for inspection when it's fine, even though on some days we're all shivering with cold. The sun has been risen an hour when we get up, but by the time we've finished dinner at night, it's getting dark. There's no electricity in our dormitory either, just a hurricane lamp which is filled once a fortnight with paraffin by Whiskers the caretaker.

We made a cooking rota and even got it approved by Madam DeVeal. Jamie flashed his muscles and sweet-talked her into it; at least, that's what happened according to him. So each day, two of us, instead of chopping wood and doing other manly things, become head cooks and bottle washers. Now I'm not exactly a masterchef, but compared to George 'Porky' Eagleton or Brandon Frost I come pretty close. Their meals are worse than the standard fare we used to get. I don't believe they're faking it either, because working in the kitchen by our newly lit stove is a pretty cushy number, and one I'd do every day given the choice.

Babooshka helps when we get stuck but mostly she sits in the corner and smokes a pipe, which isn't as bad as it sounds because the amount of tobacco she uses is pretty small. Mostly she's just sucking. I tried to find out how old she is by holding up a number of fingers, but she wouldn't play ball. Jamie, my co-worker today, thinks she's older than his grandma and she is seventy-four, but it might be that she's just had a harder life.

This brick Russian stove is a really neat idea because not only does it cook food, it also warms the room much better than our dad's New World gas cooker. It's a cube-shaped affair with a chimney going right up through the roof. The heat is channelled through a maze of brickwork which keeps the warmth constant throughout. In the morning first thing before inspection, we put the cut logs in the firebox low down at the front, filling it right up. Then, with the damper open we light it with some twists of Whiskers' newspaper, though if we're lucky we might still have the embers from the previous day to start us off, and that's it. Once the wood has burned to a layer of hot coals we close the damper and all systems are go. The wood only needs replenishing once a day. This stove has got two ovens with cast-iron doors, a large one located above the firebox and another smaller one at shoulder height in the side.

Every Wednesday we get our weekly supplies from Puksa. Usually they come early in the morning but yesterday they didn't arrive till after six. Babooshka was livid and tore the delivery man off a strip. Our consignment consists of a large bag of bread-making flour, a couple of sachets of dried yeast, a box of oats, a sack of potatoes, a small sack of other vegetables, which are likely to be onions, cabbages or carrots, a packet of leaf tea, and – if we're lucky – a dozen eggs and – luckier still – thirty-two small apples. The rest comes in tins, normally ten big silver tins per week, with small labels in Russian. Oh, and once a month we get a big bottle of oil and a tub of the multi-purpose fishy margarine.

Now, I know teenage boys have a reputation for being thick, but generally speaking I don't find this to be the case at all. It's just a way for adults and teenage girls to keep us in our place. However, there are exceptions and not mentioning any names – Brandon and Owen Frost – when our first delivery came, without consulting Babooshka, they opened all the tins at once. That's one each of pickled cabbage, pickled beetroot, pickled cucumbers and sweetcorn, two of a meat product – I can be no more certain about what it is than that – and last and probably least, four of our favourite pink breakfast sausage.

There's a small room beneath the kitchen reached by a flight of steps which serves as a larder. But even storing the opened tins in there only gave us two days to use up the meat products and no one really wanted to trust the rest after four, especially with our recent bout of tummy upsets. So by the end of the week we were on a bread, potato and water diet, though we did keep back the apples and eggs. Now thanks to me, John Price and Babooshka we've had the labels translated into English, so we know what's what.

Jamie is getting the vegetables ready for today's lunch, which will be pickled beetroot and onion broth, while I am in charge of the bread-making. I soak the dried yeast in warm water for a while then add it to the flour with salt and more water. Babooshka showed me how first, and I've passed the knowledge on to my sous chefs. Then, when it's all mixed you have to knead it with your knuckles. Jamie looks at me sideways while I'm doing this, obviously thinking this is gay boy heaven. So I smile and bat my eyelashes at him, because he is very nice and quite handsome, especially without his shirt, and he rolls his eyes and goes back to work on his vegetables. Once it's been kneaded, I flop the dough into a bowl and cover it with a cloth to let it rise. It takes about an hour, so in the meantime I make Jamie, Babooshka, Whiskers and me a pot of tea from the kettle.

After the first rise, the dough is kneaded again and then I cut, shape and score it. Then it's allowed to rise for a second time before I put it into the oven using a wooden paddle. Professional or what? There's enough flour to make three loaves a day, and if it comes off right it's the best-tasting food we have, especially if I make it!

We're hoping that Dwain comes back to the compound shortly. It might be fine out now, but the nights are getting chilly, especially for someone who's more used to an African climate. None of the adults seem in the least bit concerned about him. I expect they think he's even more expendable than the rest of us. I've got a feeling that the Reverend is going to start some exorcism baloney shortly, now that he's got two willing disciples. Then he'll be able to proclaim a triumph with Mark, for no other reason than the boy's not gay, so getting rid of his gay demon will be quite easy. On the other hand, I don't know what he'll do with Ryan, though you can be sure he won't have his best interests at heart.

***

24: Monday, 2nd September. 10 a.m. 41 Westbury Avenue.

ALAN

It's Justin Walker's last full day working on the car before he starts at that posh school tomorrow. School is out as far as I'm concerned, forever. I've had enough of places like that. When I told Anne I was never going to school again, she gave me a look that I didn't understand. Then she asked me whether I thought I knew enough to get me through the rest of my life, and she sort of smiled. I expect she thinks I'm thick, like most people do.

I'm not sure I want to go on this Russian trip any more. We're only going to rescue a couple of fags who nobody cares about. Well, Jack Moseley cares, but he's the only one. The car's supposed to be ready in a fortnight for its MOT and then it's got to be licensed and insured and prepared for the journey. But why should I put myself out? They'll only want me to tell him, I know that. Get Alan to do the dirty work, that's what they'll say!

That second picture of me and the fag lying on the sun loungers is hanging on my bedroom wall now. Stewart did a 20×16 print so you can see everything! His stupid big feet sticking out of those dungarees, and his scrawny chest with his pin-head-sized nipples. And his fat head with the ridiculous blue fringe and his pouty lips which are smiling in that faggy way at me and, worst of all, his diseased fingers holding my hand. No, that's not the worst. The worst thing is I'm smiling back at him, like I'm in love with him or something!

So, I'm not going, and that's an end to it. He can stay there and rot as far as I'm concerned. And I'm not going to do any more work on the Humber. I've been checking the contact points in the distributor with a 0.4mm gap gauge, but that's it now. I'm going to my bedroom and I'm going to smash those two pictures of me and the fag and then I'm never going to think of him again.

"Alan..."

That's Justin Walker. What does he want?

"Alan?"

He's close by now, but I don't want to talk to him.

"Alan?"

He's put his hand on my shoulder so I'd better answer. "What?"

"You've stopped again."

I can't answer.

"What's the matter?" He's put his arm round my shoulder, which means he knows I'm being all faggy.

"I don't want to go to Russia," I say.

"OK, why not?" he asks in his usual level way.

"They're going to make me tell him, aren't they?" And I feel even stupider now because I've just wiped my nose on the back of my oily PVC glove – oily because a while ago I was checking to see if there was any fluid in the differential.

"Who's going to make you tell who what?"

"I'm going to have to tell the fag that his dad is dead and I didn't go to the funeral and he'll hate me."

"Time to have a sit down and talk," says Justin, and he leads me to the bench in the front garden, which Dan has renovated and made a really good job of. He leaves me for a while and I try to relax, for a start by taking off my gloves because they're all wet and sweaty.

He comes back with two cans of Coke. I take one and he sits down and hands me a baby wipe. "That's for your nose," he says and grins at me and I feel better.

"I wish you didn't have to go back to school," I say, wiping my hands and face.

"You and me both," he replies, then he becomes serious. "OK, I've been giving it some thought, and here's how it is. Tuesday evening, I can't come at all because it's football practice. Wednesday, you come to my house for six-pack work and then it's karate. Thursday after homework I'll be here. Friday is a no-go because me and Kate are going out on the town. Saturday morning is match day, but Saturday afternoon I'll be here..."

"What about swimming?"

"Well, I've talked it over with Dan, and because it's football on Saturday we could swap swimming to early Sunday afternoon, which will then give us the late afternoon and evening to work on the car."

I nod as he's obviously got it all worked out. "What about Monday?"

He wraps his arm round my shoulder and squeezes. "On Monday after homework I'll be here working with my co-best buddy Alan Henderson."

Why do I like Justin so much? Is it because he's kind and patient and doesn't mind if I go all faggy on him, and he calls me his co-best buddy?

"The oil in the differential was never drained and it's gone sludgy. I suppose we ought to strip it out and check it for wear."

"Is that our next job?"

I nod and I've almost forgotten what I was worrying about now. Maybe I won't have to tell the fag about his dad. Maybe when we get to Russia he'll be pleased to see me. That means I'll have to be especially firm with him because I know he'll want a cuddle and possibly even a kiss.

"Hey, smiley, what were you just thinking about?"

That's Justin calling me smiley and I've gone red.

"Well, look who's here," he says, which means I'm saved from having to explain.

I look out between the trees and see Jack Moseley propping his bike up against the fence. Justin calls to him and he walks over. "So this is what hard work looks like, is it?" he says, which if you ask me is typical fag sarcasm.

Justin hands him his can and he takes a swig and hands it back. "Thanks." He pauses and gives me a hard look. "Alan..."

My heart starts to beat faster. I knot my brow, not knowing what he's going to say, and for some reason he looks shifty and nervous, despite being two years older and a head taller than me. There must be some sort of tricksy fag behaviour going on.

"Alan, I've come to ask you a favour."

A favour! Why would he want a favour from me? I'm stroking my chin with my hand, which I didn't realise I was doing. "What favour?"

"It's about the car and our luggage."

I know what he means, so I give him a hard stare. "You're talking about a roof rack, aren't you?"

"Er, yes." He takes a step back as if I'm going to bite his head off, and for some reason Justin is chuckling to himself.

"I've got one on order. Do you want to come upstairs and see it on screen? Oh, and by the way, we don't need to buy wheel chocks for Estonia; they're standard issue in the toolboxes."

He gazes down at me and blinks several times, and I don't think I'll ever understand fags because his face breaks out into a stupid grin.

***

25: Saturday, 7th September. 11 a.m. MSK. Arkhangelsk Oblast, Ketozero, a lake.

<u>NOAH</u>

Now that we're doing our own cooking, Dr Death has put out a general order saying we're not cutting enough wood. So today we're on a double shift starting with lumberjacking in the morning and ending up with a nice pile of firewood in the afternoon. Some hope. I got my wish to be at the lakeside again because I knew there was another fallen tree only a stone's throw from our kiosk. My partner this morning is John Price, him of the hairy tummy and zits. He's a year and a few days older than me and I've really got to like him. There's no side to him and he's a lot brainier than me, though not so practical. In fact, Ryan was a better branch-stripper than he is, as I watch him hacking away with an axe to very little effect. He pauses and grins breathlessly at me and I ask him if he'd like me to have ago, and he readily agrees. That's probably one of the reasons why I think he's clever.

It's a nice day today; sunny but there's an autumn chill in the air, which is why I'm happy to warm myself up by swinging the axe. The trees around the lake are turning fast to shades of gold and brown, and the water already has a layer of leaves floating around the edges. Miss Valerie told us that next week we'll be issued with thicker winter wear, and inspection will be transferred permanently to the dormitory because by the end of the month it'll be dark when the muzak starts and our door is unlocked at six o'clock.

It was Owen's fourteenth birthday last Monday, and I actually baked him a cake. It wasn't much of one, mind you; I used two eggs and some of the margarine, under Babooshka's supervision, and from somewhere she found some sugar, a wax taper which I cut in half, and even a pot of jam. I wonder if she brought them from home for us?

We made Owen a card, only this time his brother Brandon did the design, which was a football with a fourteen in it – quite simple, really. So there he was in the rest room smiling away, having been given his card, and probably thinking I'm not going to cry like soppy straight Jamie, even if they do sing Happy Birthday. Only this time when they started to sing, I came in with the cake, on which was one little white candle burning brightly, and that really started him off. Sob, sob, sob. "You're supposed to be happy, bro," said Brandon, rubbing it in. Sob, sob, sob. Fortunately the jam mostly masked the fishy margarine taste of the sponge, and all nine of us got a slice. Even Ryan and Mark couldn't resist the lure of cake, and against my better judgement I gave the last bit to Miss Valerie who, as usual, was hovering in the background. You'd think he'd never been fed, the way he wolfed it down.

Our twelve-year-old twins, Dennis and Michael, came back on Wednesday with our delivery driver, looking extremely frail, but at least they are up and about. They're still on tablets and both have coughs, therefore it seems a mite strange that they've been put on kitchen duty for the next week – to spread their germs, lucky us. I showed them how to make the bread on Thursday because everyone agrees that mine is best. Well, everyone who matters anyway, and that doesn't include Mark and Ryan, who both accused me of being Satan's chief disciple at Reverend Jo's bi-weekly gathering. Neither have been near the shower for a week or more, because they think they're going to be gang-raped by us, not to mention have several demons inserted into their orifices. Personally, given the current state of their hygiene, if I was a demon I'd be wanting out fast.

I'm hoping that the twins' meals will be more like mine and Jamie's and a lot less like Brandon and Owen's, but we'll see. I told them about fifty times not to cough on our food, but the trouble is, they're so cute, the way they look at each other, smile and then both turn to look at you that you just can't tell them off properly, especially now that they've both lost about a stone in weight and look like little skeletons in the shower. I instructed them not to drink tap water, and only to drink tea or water that's been boiled. I think Babooshka's on the job, so even if twin world hasn't quite got the message, it should be all right.

Robert's been gone exactly one week and a day, and I miss him. He was solid and dependable and always willing to help out. His opinion always counted with the group too, because he thought things through first and never gave in to the loudest voice. Most important of all to me, he was my friend from the old life, which seems to be getting further and further away in my memory. I hope the so-called 'therapy' doesn't dull his spirits or lessen his character. If he's got any sense he'll pretend he's gone straight and get out of there as quickly as possible.

"Do you fancy a swim?" calls John from the edge of the lake.

Did I say he was clever?

"No, it's freezing, probably full of dangerous bacteria and is almost certainly radioactive."

"You can't swim," he says.

"I can, actually." But I don't say how badly.

In a flash he's stripped down to his boxers and half-waded, half-dived in and is doing a fast crawl out into the lake. I'm horrified. He's still got his glasses on! About thirty feet out he stops, turns and starts to tread water. "It's great!" he shouts. "Warmer than the air."

I very much doubt that. "We're supposed to be chopping wood," I shout back, knowing that I sound like Mr Boring Killjoy, but that's how I feel.

He laughs and starts off again, going further out. I don't really want to watch, because if he gets into trouble I'm not going to be able to do anything to help.

Suddenly I hear another voice nearby. I look round, thinking I'm probably losing my marbles, whereupon Dwain steps out from behind a tree. He looks pretty healthy, and I'm still not one hundred per cent sure I'm not hallucinating.

"Noah, come with me. I need your help."

"What about the tree?" I say, whereas I suppose if I was thinking straight I should have said, *What about John?*

"This is important; you need to see this."

I look out across the lake, but can't see a sign of a hairy tummy. "All right as long as we're not too long."

We walk together through the forest and he seems to know where he's going.

"How have you managed to survive out here?" I ask.

"I have been a guest of the Reverend Akinola," he says and smiles brightly at me.

I hope I'm not being led by a mad boy. "What does that mean?"

"I smuggled myself into the back of his pick-up and he took me all the way into Puksa, where he has an apartment in the best block in town."

"Did you know he has staff as well?"

Dwain laughed. "The Reverend Snake Oil is a very holy man who has brought two pious African lady missionaries with him from Nigeria."

I narrow my eyes. "Which bits of pious African lady missionaries are untrue?"

"The first and the fourth."

"So they are ladies, then?"

"Of the night, yes."

"You've spoken to them, haven't you?"

"When the Reverend is away, Dwain Matheson will play. I went and begged at their door. I told them that I was a Russian street boy who had been abandoned by my parents because I was black and I had seen them shopping in the market. They are very nice, kind prostitutes who speak excellent English. They gave me food and a few roubles."

"You're a right one, Dwain," I say.

We trudge through the forest for about ten minutes before coming out at the top of the rise where stands the Church of the Transfiguration. There's no sign of the Reverend's truck. Despite admiring his sense of direction, I'm getting anxious about having left John swimming in the lake, not to mention the 'no tree, no rations' deal and getting locked in solitary for going AWOL.

"I was here three days ago, Dwain," I say tetchily, "and nothing's different."

"Noah, the Reverend and his ladies came to the church this morning to prepare for tomorrow. When I stowed away in the back of the pick-up I could hardly move because of the amount of equipment they were carrying."

"What's special about tomorrow?"

"The two boys, Mark and Ryan, they're going to be exorcised of their demons. Come on, this is what I wanted to show you."

We walk to the double front doors of the church. The handles have a chain wrapped around them several times. It is securely padlocked. I let out a sigh of exasperation.

Dwain isn't fazed by this. "No matter. You can look through the window."

We walk round the north side and I gaze up at the windows, which are a foot above my head with no sills. "This is ridiculous," I say.

"You can stand on my shoulders." He points to the third window along.

Dwain's shoulders are as narrow and scrawny as my own; nevertheless, he kneels down and somehow I balance myself on him with my hands against the wooden wall.

"How much do you weigh?" he asks.

"I was a seven-stone weakling, but I'm probably even less now."

"How much is that in kilos?"

"God knows. Stop asking questions and get on with it."

"Right, I'm going to lift you," he says, and actually with surprising ease he does, which annoys me for some reason.

My eyes are now level with the bottom two panes of cheap yellow glass and I peer in, cupping my hand against my face to get rid of the reflection. What I hadn't realised was that behind the raised area where Reverend Jo stood there is a door into another small room, also covered in paintings connected by the branches of a tree.

"Can you see?" asks Dwain, and I can tell he's tiring because I'm beginning to teeter.

As my eyes become accustomed to the gloom, I seem to be looking down into a medical room in a hospital rather than a church. There's an examination table similar to those used when a woman is going to give birth, with gas cylinders and a stand next to it carrying bags of what look like blood. There is also a table with bottles and medical instruments.

"What is it all about?" I ask.

"I'm going to lower you now."

Getting down doesn't go as smoothly as the lift, and we crash into a heap on the grass which, fortunately, is fairly giving.

We get up and brush ourselves off, then he cocks his head at me. "Well?"

"I don't get it. It looks like they're ready to give someone a blood transfusion."

"Like all religious people, the Reverend Joseph Akinola is at heart a showman and so when he performs an exorcism he must be seen to be performing an exorcism."

"Just tell me straight, Dwain, please."

He smiles condescendingly at me, which is really irritating. "Tomorrow, while he is preaching at you and getting you into an hysterical state, his lady friends will be preparing

Mark Wright and Ryan Davis for the casting out of demons. First they will be asked to remove their clothing, then on the examination table each will be given enough gas to make them feel sleepy. Then, by means of a tube up the bottom and another down the throat their guts will be filled with salt water, coloured red for effect. At the Reverend's signal they will be brought forth to face you, whereupon he will loudly incant some religious verse over them and press a special cross to their lips. Only this cross will in fact be a bottle of amyl nitrite, which he will make sure they breathe in. Cue vomiting, shitting and general mayhem from the two boys while you look on in horror as the demons are expelled and the Reverend goes into ecstatic communion with the Almighty." Dwain looks at me. "Do you get the picture?"

My jaw has dropped to the floor. I can't think of anything to say except, "I must warn them."

He nods approvingly. "You see now what your colonialist Anglican religion has done for my country?"

I'm sure he's having a dig. "I don't think they do exorcisms in England,; they just sing hymns and pray..."

"Only because you keep the dog on a leash, Noah, my friend. In Nigeria the dog is a wolf and is encouraged to run wild."

He sounds bitter, probably with good reason. "Well, don't blame me. Our dad's family were all Catholics."

"That is like saying I'm not a killer; I'm a murderer."

This boy isn't just bitter; he's twisted too. "You'll be pleased to know I'm not either, and I don't go to church anyway."

"Don't they say once a Catholic always a Catholic?"

Now I know he's just trying to get a rise out of me. "Actually, our dad is lapsed as well. He fell out with our local priest over his best boy's sexuality."

"He keeps a boy?" questions Dwain in amazement.

"Yes, me, you fool!" At least I got one over on him there.

He smiles at me. "It's been nice, Noah. I hope you are successful in persuading Mark and Ryan that a tube up the arse is not something they should gladly receive. Meanwhile, I'll do my best to thwart the good Reverend's theatrical intentions."

I get the impression he's saying goodbye. "Aren't you coming back?"

"What for? I'm better off on the streets of Puksa."

"But Dwain, we'll be returning to England soon."

"England isn't my country, Noah. They won't let me in – or if they do, they will then deport me back to Nigeria where I'll probably end up being killed and probably getting my mother killed as well."

"But what will you do? Where will you go?"

"Maybe I'll find a nice Russian daddy to look after me, like in Dr Sex's photographs."

"Dwain, you're not being serious. Russia is a dangerous place for gays."

"The way the world is going, everywhere is dangerous for gays, including England. Which is why, when you get back, you and your Cutie Pie are going to have to fight for your rights."

I look at him and he looks at me. We give each other a little hug and I'm sad now that he's going his own way, even if he is annoying. I watch him walk across the open field until he reaches the forest edge, where he turns and waves. I can see his teeth flashing their bright smile. I wave back and then he's gone.

I hurry down the field to the track that should take me back to the compound. I don't know how long I've been away, but my main concern is for John Price. I don't exactly run, but I hurry through the forest. When I look up, I can see that the sun is well past its highest point, which means I've missed the deadline to be picked up from the lakeside.

When I come in sight of the corrugated iron fence, I see people aimlessly milling around and there's only one Gazza parked out on the grass. Now I'm beginning to fear the worst. The gate's open and no one seems to be in charge. The first person I recognise is Porky, who is sitting with his back to me on the stump of a tree.

I go up to him. "Porky, where's John?"

He turns and gazes vacantly up at me. His face is thin and pale and there are tear streaks on his cheeks. "John? I don't know."

I'm about to ask him what's happened when a voice hails me. I look over to the compound and see John Price standing in the gateway. His hair is damp, but otherwise there's nothing different about him. He beckons me over.

"What's going on?" I ask. "What's the matter with Porky?"

"There was an accident. They've taken Brandon away."

"Brandon? What sort of accident?"

"Porky says that Brandon was swinging the axe and caught his own leg with it."

"Jesus! How is he?"

"Noah, we think he's dead. Porky said the blood just spurted out of him..."

I hold my head. It feels like it's going to burst. John's voice comes to me as if from a distance.

"You need to sit down, Noah."

John takes me into the compound and guides me to the rostrum.

"Are you sure?" I ask.

He sits down beside me. "Pretty much. Porky ran all the way up the track to where the guards were. I think he managed to sign to them what had happened. They went for Brandon and have taken him to Puksa."

"But..."

"From Porky's description, Brandon must have cut the femoral artery in his leg. He'd have about thirty seconds until he lost consciousness and four minutes to live. It might have been a bit longer with a tourniquet, but I don't think Porks was thinking straight enough."

I fold my arms and close my eyes. "Jesus Christ, what a nightmare..." It takes me a while to collect my thoughts. "I thought it was you, you know."

"Me?"

"I thought you'd drowned in the lake."

John snorts. "And where did you get to?"

"That's a long story..."

Before I can say any more, Brandon's brother Owen runs out of the barracks, screaming. He crosses the courtyard, making for the gate. Jamie follows and as he passes us he glances over and shakes his head desolately.

"Oh God!" exclaims John. "Why can't they just send us home?"

"Money," I reply. "While there's loot to be made out of us, they'll keep us here. And where is Madam? Shouldn't she be offering us comfort?"

"Noah, I'm going to see what I can do for Porky. I'll talk to you later."

I nod and John heads out of the compound while I continue to sit and think about all that's happened today, and wonder how I'm going to stop Mark and Ryan going through the Reverend Akinola's exorcism. It all seems just too much for one little gay boy, and I wish I had my Cutie Pie with me to give me a mega-Maberly hug, or even our dad to draw me into him by my big head and ask how his best boy is getting on...

***

26: Saturday, 7th September. 9 p.m. 15 Leighton Lane.

PAM

There now follows a statement by the Prime Minister, the Right Honourable Edward Helms MP.

"What!" exclaimed Roger, about to throw a cushion at the TV screen.

"Hush," said Pam, "and put that cushion down. This might be important."

"What can be more important than—"

"Roger!"

Good evening. I am speaking to you from the Cabinet Room at 10 Downing Street. As I am sure you are aware, last night a terrible fire severely damaged the Chapter House of York Minster. If it weren't for the brave men and women of the emergency services, the whole cathedral could have gone up in flames and one of the great architectural masterpieces of our civilisation would have been lost forever.

This morning, I asked the fire investigators for a preliminary report into the cause of the fire and was told that incendiary material had been found within the building, characteristic of an arson attack. Since then, my colleague Mr Ronald Bartram, the Police and Crime Commissioner for North Yorkshire, has informed me that the police have arrested a well-known homosexual activist in connection with the blaze...

Roger turned to his wife. "You know where this is leading, don't you?"

"Shush, I'm trying to listen," said Pam.

Possibly the most forthright and well-argued Christian perspective on homosexuality has come from the York Diocese. A champion of morality has seen his spiritual home burning because he dared to challenge a powerful and vociferous minority.

Our bill to stop the spread of this perverted creed is likely to be blocked in the House of Lords by a minority of their Lordships by devious methods of parliamentary procedure. I cannot allow this to happen. This legislation is of paramount importance to the health of the nation. Therefore, to speed the processing of this bill, I intend to invoke the Parliament Act immediately to counter this group of fifth columnists who are working against us.

Unfortunately, this country has recently become the laughing stock of the world because we have allowed the travesty of so-called gay marriage and the promotion of sodomy as a normal lifestyle. We owe it to our children to make certain that this type of behaviour does not prevail over traditional family values and the sacred communion of one man and one woman.

I'm sure all good Christians and our brothers in other faiths will unite with me against this plot to undermine our centuries-old way of life.

The good news is that tomorrow my good friend and colleague at the Home Office, Mr Gerard Amies, will be strengthening the bill to ban the promotion of homosexuality by reintroducing the prohibition of homosexuals in the armed forces and preventing these people and their sympathisers from working in any capacity with children. This will include adoption, fostering and surrogacy. We shall also seek to give businesses the right to refuse services to people who adhere to this aberrant lifestyle and to make it grounds for the termination of employment.

Of course, we cannot be punitive on a personal level to our citizens, therefore we shall offer the hand of Christian fellowship and counselling to those who wish to change their behaviour. We know that this unnatural predilection is mostly as a result of aggressive grooming by older males, and therefore we shall open centres for children who have become victims of this criminal activity.

Our symbol for these new powers will be that great religious building engulfed in flame, under an assault from the forces of darkness. It is time to call a halt to the tide of immorality which has swept our country for the past thirty years and which has led directly to last night's near catastrophe. I ask you, ladies and gentlemen, to join me on *this great crusade. With your help we shall stamp out this menace to our society!*

Thank you. Goodnight and God bless you all.

That was a statement by the Prime Minister, the Right Honourable Edward Helms MP. Our scheduled programmes are now running approximately ten minutes late.

"Tell me, Mrs Moseley, will you be voting for Edward's party next Thursday, like you did last time?" asked Roger.

"Don't be flippant," answered Pam, pressing the off button on the remote.

"Hey, I was watching that!"

"Roger, this is serious. You're going for an interview on Monday for a job at that school."

"As a groundsman, not a teacher."

"Even so..."

"I know," conceded Roger, "it is a dicey situation for me, but far more so for Jack. He's got to live his life in our brave new world."

"He'll end up leaving the UK and going abroad," said Pam flatly.

"And who will blame him? I thought the UKMP were trying to take us back to the 1950s, now I realise it's the 1350s."

"The trouble is there's no one to vote for on Thursday who has a hope of winning against them."

"Maybe you should stand," said Roger. "Well, next time round anyway."

"If I could afford it and had the time I probably would," stated Pam.

"Quite ruined the evening, hasn't it?" said Roger.

"How do these small-minded, bigoted people get into such positions of power?" exclaimed Pam.

Roger made an exasperated noise. "Because people like us put them there, dear. At least we do in this country, at least for the time being..."

"What do you mean at least for the time being?"

"The burning of York Minster allegedly by a so-called homosexual activist and the Prime Minister taking extra powers immediately afterwards? UKMP have been reading their Ladybird book of History. Berlin, 1933, the burning of the Reichstag by a boy from Holland, supposedly a Communist..."

"Roger, I don't want to hear any more of that..."

"Strangely, he was guillotined for his crime ... shades of Madame Defarge and la Terreur, except in moderate, civilised Germany."

"Horrible," said Pam.

Roger smiled at his wife and put his arm round her. "Do you fancy a bit of sacred communing tonight then, old girl? It'll make a change from the telly and take our minds off Mr Helms and his gang."

***

27: Sunday, 8th September. 8.05 a.m. MSK, Arkhangelsk Oblast, Gosudarstvennyi Meditsinskii Institut (gomoseksualizm).

NOAH

Vaseline has lined us up in the courtyard and Madam DeVeal is expected to waft over and address us at any moment. I can only guess it's about Brandon, and I hardly need to guess what's she's going to say. How I have come to hate that woman. Two guards are already standing ready, one each side of the podium, tapping their batons on their hands. Clearly they're expecting trouble in the ranks. We are all doing our best to stand like men, though my hand just won't come off my hip today.

Owen is squeezed between John and Jamie. This is deliberate in case he tries to run at her. He was babbling in his sleep last night, and won't eat. He says if Brandon's dead, he's going to kill himself because there's nothing worth living for any more. There's not much I can say to him about that because if it wasn't for my Cutie Pie and our dad, I'd probably be thinking the same.

Porky didn't have any breakfast either. I think he's still traumatised by what he saw – and who wouldn't be? He also feels guilty because he couldn't help. Though Jamie has tried to talk to him, I think he needs a professional counsellor, which isn't going to happen in this godforsaken hole.

I had another failure last night when I tried to convince Mark and Ryan that the Reverend Joe was a snake oil salesman, to use Dwain's expression, whose lady friends are going to make intrusions into their most private entry points. Mark called me a queer and a liar and told me that it was the demon inside me that wants to get at his butt, not Pastor Akinola. I never realised how easy it is to brainwash some people. Ryan said he didn't care what the Rev and his holy ladies did to him, because he deserved it for allowing the demon to get inside him in the first place. You can't reason with such a mindset.

I tried to get John to talk some sense into them then, but since he hadn't been lectured to by Dwain or seen the evidence with his own eyes, not to mention that he was still dealing with the fallout from Brandon's accident, he was even less convincing than me. Afterwards, I was more than a bit unfair to him when I claimed that if he hadn't gone on his stupid swim, things would be different. I could see that really cut him up, and hurting someone's feelings is not something I pride myself on, especially when they've done nothing to deserve it. Even so, it wasn't till we were all in bed that I apologised to John for being such an arsehole.

I grovelled to him again in the shower this morning, and he said we were all under strain and to forget about it. Then, when we got back into the changing area, he gave me a manly hug and told me that I was a good friend and the best wood-chopper he knew, which made me both smile and start to blub at the same time. I know Cutie Pie would frown and call it my faggy way of getting round him, but there we are.

Oh my God! She's got a fur coat on. It's not even that cold today. I bet she was out last night skinning the furry animals and eating their entrails. Red lipstick as well. Who is she trying to impress? Our dad would call that mutton dressed as lamb – not that he was averse to the occasional bit of mutton.

"What a baggage," murmured Porky.

Madam DeVeal has mounted the podium and is looking across the top of our heads. "The Reverend Akinola will not be ministering to you today, and so you will do extra forestry duties. This will make up for the lack of effort you put in yesterday, when barely any logs were stacked."

Three things there. First, Jamie had to hold on to Owen hard to prevent an incident. It looked like he was going to explode. Second, I am certain that Dwain has had something to do with the lack of our Sunday service, and third, you should have seen the look of hate I got from my ex-little friend, Mark. I assume he blames my demon for the Reverend's absence.

Oh, she's off again. "As from Wednesday next the delivery of rations will be cut by forty per cent. This takes into account the revised numbers relative to your ages."

I assume she's talking about Robert, Brandon and Dwain which in my book makes: "Twenty-five per cent," I say out loud.

"Relative," whispers John Price. "That's American for we've lost three of our oldest who eat more."

Madam drones on for another five minutes, listing all our shortcomings, but when she appears to be on the point of winding up, still hasn't mentioned anything about yesterday's incident. Time for little Noah to take the plunge. I raise my hand, noticing its tendency to flap in a rather gay way.

"Why have you got your hand up, you egregious boy?"

It seems Madam's been eating the dictionary.

"Ooo, Sister Hopkins," I whine, "do you know what's happened to Brandon and Robert?" I don't mention Dwain, as the less said about our agent provocateur the better.

Her red lips curl into a look of distaste, but there's a sort of unpleasant relish in her expression as well. She takes out a notebook from the recesses of her fur, as if she needs an aide-memoire to prompt her. "Robert Crittenden is still undergoing treatment for his disorder. Once this is completed, the results will be scientifically analysed and then each of you will be offered the hope of a normal life."

Scientifically and offered! Who is she trying to kid? I scratch my head. I'm about to ask a supplementary question when she continues.

"Brandon Frost was taken to the prison hospital in Puksa, where he was pronounced dead on arrival."

Jamie and John hold on to Owen, who has started to scream and struggle. Madam signals to one of the guards, who strides over to the distraught boy and clubs him on the head. This does quieten him, but Jamie and John are so shocked they let go of him and he slumps to the ground. The guard walks back to his position and Madam continues as if nothing has happened.

"His body has been cremated and the ashes scattered in the prison yard." She pauses to let this information sink in. "Brandon Frost had been weakened by his association with homosexuals. That's what caused his death, and the same fate is likely to befall you unless you seize the opportunities being given to you here."

Her lips reform into something of a smile and she leaves the podium in a cloud of venom, followed by her two goons. Vasily Yegorovich Pavlov rubs the stubble on his chin, yawns, then tells us to Uvolen! Which means we're dismissed.

***

JUSTIN

Justin straightened up and stretched to ease his back muscles. He had been bending over the engine compartment of the Humber Pullman, filling the glass bowl filter on the fuel pump with the hand priming lever.

"Is it full?" questioned Alan from behind the wheel.

Justin gently closed the bonnet and came to stand by the open window of the driver's door. "To the brim," he replied.

Alan gritted his teeth. In the next few seconds he'd know if two months' work had gone according to plan. The Humber was standing on its own Dunlop whitewall tyres, looking pristine except for the lack of seats and upholstery in the back, which were still stacked neatly in the cellar. They had an MOT booked at the Wayside Garage on Weymouth Road for late on Monday afternoon so that Alan could attend without arousing suspicion about his absence from school.

"Nervous?" asked Justin.

"No!" snapped Alan, knotting his brow angrily. Then he looked apologetically up at his friend, who was smiling down at him. "Maybe..."

"Maybe a little, or maybe to the max?" continued Justin, unabashed.

"Maybe the second," confessed Alan.

Justin reached through the window and hugged him. "My anxious buddy."

Alan gripped the wheel with his right hand, made sure the gear shift was in neutral, depressed the accelerator pedal to trip the fast idle mechanism, turned the ignition key, noting the red warning glow of the generator and ignition lamp in the centre of the dash, then pressed the starter.

For a moment, after the initial turnover, Justin thought nothing was happening, then he realised the engine was purring away gently to itself. Alan had pressed the accelerator again immediately after starting, to automatically reduce the idling speed.

The two boys looked at each other, grinning from ear to ear. "You are one hell of a mechanic," said Justin. "Russia, look out, because here we come!"

"There's a lot more to do yet."

"Are you going to roll it out onto the drive?" suggested Justin.

Alan nodded, depressed the clutch and put the car into first gear. There was barely a change in the note of the engine as he slowly brought his foot off the clutch, and with a light touch on the accelerator moved the limousine at a stately pace out of the garage where it had been confined for the best part of fifty years. The black paintwork gleamed in the late summer sunshine.

Alan switched off the ignition and emerged from the car to a round of applause from the front porch where Elspeth, Anne and Stewart had gathered discreetly to watch. Alex was pressed between his mother and brother, wondering what all the fuss was about.

"What a beautiful sight," said Elspeth. "This calls for a celebration."

"You boys have done marvels," said Anne.

"Alan has done marvels," said Justin, modestly.

"I'll get the camera," said Stewart. "Hey, why don't we get Jack and Dan over to join in?"

"By rights we should also invite your teacher, Ms Lane, as well," asserted Elspeth.

"Hmm, you can go too far," replied Justin, who already had his mobile out to phone his friends.

Twenty minutes later, five boys were clustered around the front of the Humber. The bonnet was open again and they were watching the six-cylinder engine gently vibrating while Alan fielded questions from his excited audience.

"Two gallons of oil and four gallons of water?" questioned Jack sceptically.

"Actually, seventeen pints of oil in the engine and five in the gearbox."

"And it only does sixteen miles to the gallon," commented Dan. "Our Mondeo does nearly forty."

"The Pullman's a real car, not a poxy toy!" retorted Alan, getting annoyed at the assumed negativity.

Dan smiled, wondering whether to wind up his friend some more. Jack noticed and pressed his palm down onto the wing then moved away, leaving a greasy imprint. Alan came over with his cloth and wiped over the area. The two brothers looked at each other and grinned.

"You're being mean," said Stewart, who was watching them through the viewfinder of his camera.

Elspeth came out onto the drive, followed by Anne, who was carrying a tray on which was a bottle of champagne and seven crystal glass flutes.

"A toast to our chief mechanic, his deputy and to that wonderful old machine," said Elspeth.

"Maybe we should have smashed the bottle over the radiator," said Dan, watching Alan's reaction out of the corner of his eye. "I name this ship..."

Justin put his arm round the chief mechanic's shoulders. "Take no notice. He's teasing you."

They raised their glasses and sipped their drinks, all except Dan, who snorted as the bubbles caught in his nose, having downed half the contents in one go.

"Serves you right," said Stewart, snapping a picture, "trying to wind up my little brother."

"And now another toast," said Elspeth, holding up her glass in a shaky hand. "To absent friends."

Jack and Alan exchanged glances and Justin tipped both their glasses. "To Noah and Robert," he said. "We're coming for you, buddies."

***

29: A day in September. 1.30 p.m. MSK. Arkhangelsk Oblast, Juvenile Prison for Boys, Puksa.

ROBERT

When Robert first awoke, he thought he was back in the dormitory at the Institute. The bed felt the same, with the thin mattress on top of unforgiving springs. It was the smell of Lysol that made him first realise that he was somewhere different. He opened his eyes to see a sky-blue wash on the ceiling and a pair of fluorescent strip lights. Without moving, he scanned as much of the room as he could. He was in a corner and there was another bed to his right and a pair of unpainted swing doors immediately opposite. The walls were a lighter blue than the ceiling and covered in black-and-white portraits of bearded and moustachioed Russian leaders and intellectuals of a bygone age. And there was a clock; something he had not seen in a long time.

He moved his position slightly. His right shoulder and upper arm were tightly bandaged and though it was uncomfortable, the gnawing pain that had made him feel so ill was absent. Then he remembered a doctor telling him in broken English about his cracked clavicle and the infection which needed an operation. So, he was in a ward in the prison hospital.

"Hey!"

The voice came from nearby. Gently, he turned his head. It wasn't too painful. A man was sitting up in the next bed, wearing a neck brace, both arms in slings. His face was angular, with prominent cheekbones and a dagger tattooed on his forehead. Like himself, he was wearing a thin blue smock and nothing else. His mouth smiled but his eyes were empty.

"You gay Brit, yes?"

"American," answered Robert.

"I Sergei," the man said.

"Robert..."

"You famous. Boys in here don't like you. You get..." The man couldn't think of the word.

To show he didn't understand, Robert tried to shake his head, but just the small effort tired him out. He closed his eyes and drifted back to sleep.

When he woke again it was because the end of his bed was being shaken. Robert's eyes focused on two men, orderlies by the look of them, wearing semi-transparent white coats with heavy stubble on their chins. One of them nudged the other and pointed at him. "Pedik bodrstvuyet."

The other chuckled. "Pidaryuga."

They guffawed and the first orderly made a stroking motion over his genitals. "Sosi moi hui, sooka!"

Their conversation and laughter continued until a female nurse appeared, wearing a shapeless, creased white coat and fez-style hat. She barked an order and the two men retreated through the swing doors. The nurse came over and examined Robert. She said nothing but motioned with her hand that he should sit up. It took some effort but eventually he had heaved himself into a position that satisfied her. She pulled the pillow out from under him and propped it on the bedhead then pushed him back into it. Then, after a cursory look at his bandages and a toss of her head, she left.

"You better now, gay?" asked Sergei.

Robert looked at him and realised that the man was not a man at all, but a boy like himself, only aged beyond his years. "I'm awake. Where did you learn English?"

"I speak good, yes?"

"Not bad."

"I learn at Moscow elementary school."

"What did those two men say?"

Sergei smirked. "They insult. Ask you to suck their cocks."

"I guessed it was something like that."

"How old you, gay?"

"Fifteen."

"I seventeen."

109

"What happened to your arms?"

"I was..." Sergei tried to think of the word. "Att..."

"Attacked?" suggested Robert.

The boy nodded. "Attacked, a word I remember from now on. Three of them in rest room while I was writing letter."

"Why?"

"I same as you, gay, only I fiddle with little girls, not boys." Sergei winked.

Robert was about to open his mouth to protest, but the sudden rush of blood made him feel faint.

"You go back to sleep, gay, you not look well..."

The next time he awoke, another orderly was squeezing his arm.

"Tualet!" the man barked in the manner that some English people adopt when talking to foreigners. "Vy idete tualet!"

That was fairly easy to understand, and Robert swung himself carefully out of bed. Planting his feet on the cold floor, he hoisted himself up. The man didn't seem particularly anxious to assist and so he took a few tottering steps in the general direction of the swing doors, keeping the fingers of his left hand lightly on the bed for balance.

"You go careful, gay," called Sergei.

The American paused. He was about to head out onto the open floor. It was only six steps to the exit, but there was nothing to hold on to. He noted that, of the twenty or so beds spaced haphazardly around the walls, less than half were occupied. Most of the patients were lying prone, but in the three beds adjacent to the doors bare-chested youths with star tattoos on their shoulders were sitting upright, gazing with interest at him. Robert was pretty certain that, like Sergei, life had aged them beyond their years, and that the eldest was no more than a couple of years older than himself. He had a second tattoo of a rose encased in barbed wire on his arm and, judging by his facial features, was almost certainly the elder brother of the youngest member of the trio. There didn't appear to be much wrong with any of them.

The orderly took him by the arm and propelled him forward. He managed to keep his balance and once through the doors found himself in a short corridor with rooms leading off to left and right. One of these rooms was a toilet with five open cubicles. It was relatively clean, but there were no seats and no toilet paper. The orderly left him and he lowered himself onto the least offensive-looking of the bowls. He managed to pee but nothing more, so he just sat, for want of anything else to do. In his mind's eye, he tried to conjure images from better times. It was difficult, for even Jack's face could only be brought to mind in a hazy impression.

A boy shuffled in, saw Robert and moved away to the furthest bowl. He was a walking corpse, desperately thin, his skin sticking to his ribs, sores and spots all over his body. A groan came from him as he sat and relieved himself. The stench of diarrhoea made Robert want to gag, and he got out as quickly as he could. Once more in the corridor he momentarily forgot which way he had come. Then to his left, he saw the brown swing doors with the round windows and trod slowly towards them.

Immediately on entering the ward, the voices he had heard fell silent. Suspicious, he looked round. The three youths watched him through shifty eyes. Sergei too had his gaze on him. Robert moved slowly across to his bed, only to be accosted by a similar smell to the one in the toilet. He drew back the bed covers to find two piles of faeces lying on the mattress. The three youths burst into wild laughter. He swallowed but remained outwardly calm.

"Yankee gay. You like shit, yes?" the youth with the rose tattoo called to more hysterical laughter.

"Homo, you go home to Yankee land," said his young brother.

Robert imagined his fist punching the boy with the rose tattoo in his self-satisfied mouth. He looked for a buzzer to call the nurse, but there was nothing. In any event, there was no doubt in his mind what would happen when the nurse or orderly came in. The boys would blame him for shitting in his own bed, and since he couldn't defend himself, they would be believed. Even if they weren't, the orderlies would still take their word for it.

If his physical condition had allowed him to, he would have taken action, but as it was he made for the first vacant bed two down from Sergei and parked himself there. He was pleased to see that they had not planned for that, and he gave them what he hoped was a contemptuous smile.

Not long afterwards, the three youths got up from their beds and left, no doubt partly driven by the smell that was filling the ward.

"Welcome to Russia, gay," said Sergei immediately after they had left.

"Who were they?" asked Robert, turning to him.

"They are the boss boys, gay. If guards no like a prisoner, they get those three to beat him up in dark corner. They get many privilege. Drink, smoke, even allowed out."

"They can speak English," the American observed.

"Probably learned selling their bodies in Moscow subway," said Sergei dismissively.

Robert blinked, mulling over this statement for a while before speaking again.

"Did they break your arms?"

"No, gay! No one like kiddy fiddler. He get beaten up by everyone."

The nurse came in and immediately caught the smell and marched over to the bed. She let out a bellow and moments later the two stubbly orderlies entered. Her gaze fell upon Robert and her jaw tightened, but Sergei spoke softly to her and she turned on her heel and marched out.

***

112

30: Tuesday, 17th September. 9.15 a.m. Swanford Police Station.

DI DAVID RAINS

The DI drummed his fingernails on his keyboard. "I hear you've joined UKMP."

Constable Richard Masefield stood ramrod straight before his superior officer. "There's no law against it, guv."

"We can't be too careful in these days of political correctness, can we?"

"That's why I joined UKMP."

"I've got a job you might be interested in. A bit of undercover work."

"I'm just a beat constable, sir."

"You can drive, can't you?"

"Yes, I enjoy motoring. Got a caravan. Me, the wife and the lad go touring. Yorkshire Dales, the Lake District... God's own country, guv."

"Ever been on the Continent, Constable?"

"Not much. Went to France twice in my twenties. Didn't fancy it much."

DI Rains smiled. "Too many foreigners, I suppose."

"You could say that, sir. I couldn't possibly comment."

"Heard of Operation Q-Tip?"

"Only recently, guv; the ink's still not dry on that law."

"We're working on a pre-emptive strike. There's a homosexual cell which has been recruiting in Swanford. The sad part is, they're mostly young teenage boys, led astray by the sodomites in charge. Not all of them have been corrupted yet. Our job is to gather evidence which will lead to the prosecution of the ringleaders, and counselling for those who have been brainwashed into supporting this dirty lifestyle."

"My son calls the poofs batty boys; that's the lingo used by the bongo bongo jungle bunnies. They hate queers as much as we do."

113

"It would be good to set one lot off against the other, then we could stand back and watch, but as it is we've got to make sure there's no hiding place for these shit-shovers; not on my patch, at any rate."

"Sounds like a worthwhile operation. But what's this got to do with driving and the Continent?"

"My sources tell me that a party of queers and their supporters are organising a trip across Europe and into Russia."

"Why can't we let the Ruskies deal with them? They're good at that sort of thing."

"Special reasons, Constable. The comrades might not get our nuanced approach. Some of this is very hush-hush, and I'm not at liberty to divulge all the details."

"I get you, guv."

"Good! At last this country is waking up to the fact that these perverts are a menace to our society. So then, Constable Masefield, are you up for it?"

"Oh, I'm up for it. Is it a freebie?"

"Of course. All expenses paid. This is important work."

"When are we travelling, and how long will I be away?"

"Couple of weeks, probably, maybe a bit more. Sometime in the early part of October we'll be flying to St Petersburg, which is where we'll pick up their trail. They've made a provisional booking at a hotel there for two nights, but I haven't got the specific dates. You need to be able to travel at a moment's notice."

"Shouldn't be a problem, guv. Have you any idea where these homos are going after their stay in the hotel?"

"One of the objects of this exercise is to answer that very question. Earlier this year, a shipment of teenage homos was sent from this country into the Russian Federation for correctional training. I only have my copper's instinct to go on, but I believe they may well be trying to find the location of this facility."

"That'll be like looking for a needle in a haystack without any prior knowledge."

"Yes it will, and no doubt this place will be well off the beaten track."

"Do you think that they might be intending to spring these homos, guv?"

"You may well have hit the nail on the head there, Constable. I can tell you're just the quality of officer I need on this case. Our job will be first to gather evidence and then step in, when the time is right, to put a stop to their shenanigans."

Constable Masefield nodded enthusiastically.

"A blow for the moral majority," he said.

"Too right!" agreed the DI. "A blow for the moral majority. I like that. I like that a lot. But remember, we'll be working without the knowledge of the Russian government and so there maybe consequences if we're caught. Comprenez?"

"I get you good, guv."

"Excellent! You know, there's a whole underground conspiracy grown up around these perverts over the years, and we've got to put a stop to it for our children's sake."

"I second that, guv. My son says there's a homosexual mafia even at the Community School, working against the Christian ethos we're trying to bring in."

"They'll stop at nothing, these people," reflected David. "You're a governor there, aren't you?"

"That's right, and there's a lot of opposition to what we're trying to do," declared Dickie. "Fortunately, we've now got the local authority and the government on our side."

"Not to mention God," said the DI.

"I'm not a man to take the Lord's name in vain, sir."

David Rains drew out a folder from his top drawer. "You're a good man, Constable, the perfect person to have on my team when moral questions are involved. It'll be civvies, of course; we'll be tourists to all intents and purposes. You'll be moving into this office for the time being, on secondment to the CID, as acting Detective Constable. You're to study this folder and familiarise yourself with all aspects of the case.

Don't forget, this is an undercover operation and it is not to be spoken of outside these four walls, not even to your family."

"They'll know something's up when I tell them I'm going away."

"Police business, Constable, that's all you need say. If the mission is a success there'll probably be a permanent position here for you."

"I'm looking forward to working with you, sir."

"There'll be one other joining us, a special constable specifically sworn in for this job."

"Do I know him, guv?"

"You might, as he's one of Councillor Henderson's boys, Derek. He's young and a bit of a rough diamond, but just the sort of person we may need if we get into a tight corner."

"I don't think we've met, but if he's built like the councillor he's sure to be an asset."

"And from now on, Constable, or should I say Detective Constable, it has to be first name terms. I am David and you're Richard, right?"

"Dickie is what my friends call me, sir... David."

"Dickie it is, then. At last this country is trying to get back to the moral high ground, and we shall be a small but important part in the process. Bring in your passport tomorrow. We'll need to get you a visa."

***

31: Wednesday, 18th September. 8.30 a.m. MSK. Arkhangelsk Oblast, Juvenile Prison for Boys, Puksa.

ROBERT

Robert opened his eyes. It was the fifth day after the operation on his shoulder. He had eaten breakfast – porridge with a hunk of bread and margarine and a tin mug of strong tea – an hour ago. Now two orderlies were standing by his bed. Without speaking, they removed the bedclothes and not bothering to straighten his hospital gown, lifted him bodily onto a gurney. He didn't resist. The move made his shoulder ache and he still felt weak and listless.

He watched the ceiling rush by, then closed his eyes and listened to the squeak of the trolley wheels as he was pushed along. Then there was a bump and a rattle as if he were on a train going over points. A sliding door was closed with a snick. There was a sudden lurch and his stomach turned over. He opened his eyes. They were in a lift, going up. Two floors, he guessed, before it stopped. The concertina gate was drawn aside and he was pushed out into a windowless corridor with a green linoleum floor and cream-emulsioned brick walls. Shortly the trolley was manoeuvred sharp left through a pair of double doors, and Robert found himself in a small darkened room.

A face came into view, looking down on him. It was Professor Dmitri Pyotrovich Salkorov: Dr Sex.

"You have recovered sufficient health for you to begin treatment for your disorder," he said. brightly. "We're going to give you a subcutaneous injection in your thigh and then you will be placed in a chair. Just lie still."

Before he could protest, he felt the prick of the needle and discomfort as the liquid spread out beneath his skin. Madam DeVeal's bonnet of blonde hair came into view and his face became a rigid mask.

"What have you injected?" he asked.

"You don't need to know that," she answered.

Two orderlies lifted him bodily and sat him in a restraint chair, strapping him in by his wrists and ankles. A cabinet containing a cathode ray television and other apparatus was wheeled in front of him.

"Excellent," said the professor. "We are now going to attach electrodes to your extremities."

The nurse's long fingernails scratched as she pressed the pads into position above each of the straps. Then he felt her hand snake under his gown and attach a loop of wire over his penis.

117

"Keep still!" she ordered, tightening the ligature until it was firmly fixed.

"What are you doing to me?" he asked, pulling at the restraints, though the effort made him feel dizzy.

"If you struggle you will only be here longer," she said, as if that was what she wanted.

The professor put a switch in his hand, then began to attach the wires from the electrodes to a control panel in the cabinet. "Each time you feel a shock, you can relieve it by pressing the button. We shall monitor the state of your arousal throughout these procedures." He smiled at Robert as if he was doing him the greatest favour. "I shall now leave you in the capable hands of Sister Hopkins." He turned to her. "I shall be back in about fifteen minutes to begin the second part of the operation and to evaluate progress."

The orderlies left with the professor and Madam DeVeal turned to him. "Now, you disgusting queer, we've had enough of you people shoving your perversions down our throats for the past twenty years. We had hoped you'd all die out with AIDS, but unfortunately that didn't happen." She adjusted two of the knobs on the control panel then slipped a CD into a player in the rack.

A picture of a naked man appeared on the screen and Robert felt a jolt of electricity in his ankles, which spread uncomfortably up his legs. He pressed the button, the electric current was shut off, and the screen went blank for a moment before an image of a fully dressed woman was shown. The American tried to calm himself. He knew what was going to happen now. A feeling of nausea was building inside him. Half a minute elapsed before the image of the woman was replaced by a naked youth sitting with his legs apart, fully aroused. The shock to his wrists was more pronounced. He pressed the button, then closed his eyes.

Madam DeVeal slapped him across the face. "Watch the screen!"

He blinked several times. "I feel sick."

"That's because of your perversion."

118

Robert couldn't have thought of a less erotic scenario if he'd tried. "I'm going..."

Another jolt of electricity to his ankles emptied his mouth of words. He pressed the button then retched again and again. The third time he emptied the contents of his stomach into his lap.

"You disgusting pig!" exclaimed the nurse.

She rang a bell and shortly the professor reappeared.

"The apomorphine worked too quickly. I told you we should not combine these sessions."

"New science, new techniques, Sister Hopkins," he replied calmly, getting a hypodermic needle from the bottom shelf of the cabinet. "I'll give him a shot of metoclopramide, which should stop the vomiting, and we'll recommence tomorrow."

"I'm not clearing any of this mess up, Professor Salkorov."

"Of course not, dear Sister; the orderlies will take care of the patient."

***

32: Thursday, 19th September. 7.45 p.m. 15 Leighton Lane.

ROGER

"'One more step, Mr Hands,' said I, 'and I'll blow your brains out! Dead men don't bite, you know,' I added with a chuckle."

"Read that bit again," said Mikey, eyeing the illustration a bit further down the page of Israel Hands plunging to his doom from the mizzen.

Roger put down the book and repositioned himself on his son's bed. "Actually, there's something I want to talk to you about."

"I'm not in trouble, am I?"

"Not as far as I know."

"Why can't I have a bike like Mike? I'm nearly eight."

"You're not eight for six months."

"Five..."

"A long time, anyway," amended Roger, "and you know why – I might not have a job."

"Jack will pay some; he's rich."

"Mikey, we're getting off-piste here. I want to talk to you about when your brothers are away on their European tour."

"How can they go on holiday in school time?"

"We've told you a hundred times. It's special... a school trip. Mikey, how would you like to spend a fortnight or so at Nana Moseley's?"

"No, she's a battleaxe."

"Mikey!"

"That's what Mummy calls her."

"Mummy calls people lots of things she doesn't mean, and you shouldn't be listening in to private conversations."

"I don't want to go, it's boring..."

"Look, Nana's a better cook than your mother, and in any case it'll be boring here without your brothers."

"Why do you want to get rid of me?"

"We don't want to get rid of you. It's just that for once Mummy and I would like to spend a little time together."

"You mean sexing each other, don't you? Jack says that old people shouldn't be allowed to have sex."

"Jack will be old one day, and so will you, and by then I expect you'll have changed your tune. In any case, Mummy and I aren't old."

"Where are you going?"

"Ah well, we haven't quite decided that yet."

"You're having a holiday, aren't you? You're all having a holiday except me!"

"All right, you can have a bike for your birthday in February."

"Christmas."

"OK, Christmas."

"Eighteen gears..?"

"Eighteen gears, if that's what you want."

"Can Mike come for Friday and Saturday night sleepovers at Nana Moseley's?"

"Don't push it, Mikey. We'll see..."

Roger picked up Treasure Island, intending to get to the end of Chapter 26, but Pam called to him from the bottom of the stairs.

"Rog, there's some people here to see us."

He frowned, then looked solicitously at his youngest son. "Sorry sport, duty calls."

"I can read it myself," said Mikey.

"You can have dreams about it instead," said Roger, tucking him in. "Jim and Israel will still be in the rigging tomorrow."

He kissed his son on the forehead and squeezed his shoulder. "Night, night, my little pirate."

"Night, night, Daddy," said Mikey, sleepily, feeling quite satisfied with his night's work.

At the bedroom door, Roger turned, smiled and flicked the light switch off.

***

Downstairs, in the lounge a man and a woman were standing silently, waiting for him. Pam was already seated. Roger thought he recognised the man, but the woman was a stranger to him. When she spoke, she had an American accent.

"Mr Moseley, I am Helen Allingham and this is Thomas Roberts. We're from the Swanford social services department." She stuck out a hand which Roger shook doubtfully, then did the same with her colleague.

Thomas Roberts was a middle-aged man with unkempt hair, dyed black, wearing a rumpled battleship-grey business suit. On the other hand, Helen Allingham was impeccably turned out in a calf-length green pleated skirt and jacket. She had bobbed auburn hair and discreetly applied makeup.

"Please take a seat," said Roger, waving towards the settee while exchanging suspicious glances out of the corner of his eye with Pam. "To what do we owe the pleasure? I thought the department closed at half past five."

"Not any more," the woman said briskly. She took a folder from her briefcase and opened it, scanning the pages methodically before speaking. "I'm here to talk to you about your eldest son, Jack Moseley."

"Oh yes," answered Roger.

"I'm sure you know that Jack has been in quite a lot of trouble recently. He was suspended from school and has now said he is a homosexual."

"Where did you get this personal information from?" asked Pam.

"It's not personal information when it becomes public knowledge, is it?" answered Thomas.

Helen gave a professional smile. "We're here to offer your son counselling, so that he may be set back on the right course."

"I'm afraid my son is at the gym tonight," said Roger, "so we can't actually ask him if he wants to be counselled."

"Your son is fifteen, and so we only require your consent."

"You want to force him?" questioned Pam.

"Mrs Moseley, we want what is in your child's best interests. Homosexuality is a crime and to go down that path at such a young age is going to ruin Jack's life."

"Actually," said Roger, "homosexuality isn't a crime. Promotion of homosexuality is going to become a crime now we have the UKMP running the country, but at the moment that bill is still stuck in the committee stage."

"We are trying to pre-empt trouble for our young people before it's too late," said Thomas.

Roger squinted at Thomas Roberts as memories of the man began to surface. "Weren't you dismissed from the department last year after you were found to be sending homophobic emails from your office about clients?"

"There is no such thing as homophobia, Mr Moseley," said Helen sharply. She delved into her briefcase again and withdrew several differently coloured papers. "These pamphlets will describe the new laws and how it will affect certain families and pretended families. I suggest you pay close attention to them."

Pam rose from her chair. "I think we've heard enough of this, thank you, and you can keep your pamphlets. Roger, will you see this lady and gentleman out?"

"I'm sorry you're not being cooperative, Mrs Moseley," said Helen. "If your son does not repent, I can assure you he will suffer the consequences."

Roger began to usher the pair towards the front door. "I'll see hell freeze over before I hear any more about repentance, Ms Allingham."

Helen turned to him. "It's Mrs Allingham actually, Mr Moseley. I know you are about to lose your livelihood and if you're not careful, your children too."

"You will not return to this house, *Ms* Allingham, nor your guard dog," said Pam.

Roger opened the kitchen door and waved his hand dismissively. "Remember to close the garden gate behind you."

A minute later, husband and wife fell into each other's arms. "Oh Roger, that was awful. How could I have been so stupid as to vote for those people?"

"You're trembling, Pam," he replied. "No one is going to frighten my family and get away with it."

"We must be careful, Rog, for the children's sake."

"What we need is a stiff drink," he answered, moving to the fridge.

"Are we going to tell Jack about this?"

"Whisky on the rocks," said Roger, tossing ice cubes into two glasses and pouring a generous measure of Glenlivet over them.

They took their drinks into the lounge and sat close together on the settee.

"I don't think we've got a choice; he's got to be told –
and Dan too, for that matter. Anyway, if you tell one the other
will learn it soon enough."

"They'll both be home soon," said Pam, eyeing the
pamphlets on the arm of the settee. The top one printed in a
green pastel on a grey background was entitled 'Christian
Values in Modern Britain'.

The lounge door was pushed open and a small figure
entered in his glow-in-the-dark skeleton pyjamas. "I can't
sleep, I'm worried," Mikey said in a whiny voice.

Roger sighed and held up his arm. "Come on then, sit
between me and your mum. Let's have a bit of family
solidarity."

Quickly, Pam shovelled the pamphlets out of sight and
made room for him.

***

33: Sunday, 22nd September. 6.02 a.m. MSK, Arkhangelsk
Oblast, Gosudarstvennyi Meditsinskii Institut
(gomoseksualizm).

NOAH

Lukewarm water trickled from the shower heads. High on
the wall opposite, a single fluorescent tube gave off a pasty
flickering light. Three naked boys stared disconsolately at one
another.

"Maybe the tank's frozen," said Jamie, his voice echoing
off the concrete.

"Or there's a rat caught in the downpipe," responded
John.

"What would Madam DeVeal be doing in the water
tank?" asked Noah, hugging himself and shivering.

His companions smiled.

"You know, you're a very strange shape, Noah," said
John, who had decided to wear his glasses in the shower today.

"You sort of go straight up and down. And you've got really small ears but a big nose and mouth, and your feet and hands are huge compared to your body."

"Has it really taken you nearly two months to come to that conclusion?" asked Jamie, wiping droplets of water from his face.

"I'm not in the habit of staring at my fellow prisoners in the showers," said John. "It's just that there's nothing else to do today."

"So because you're bored you draw attention to all my physical shortcomings," responded Noah, who didn't really mind because it enabled him to gaze at the tangle of black hair on John's tummy, which he found endlessly fascinating.

"You're not short in one department anyway," observed Jamie, with a chuckle, "at least relative to your height."

"Thanks," said Noah, "but I know I'm not exactly Donkey Kong down there either, especially in here – it's freezing."

"Shall we give this up as a bad job and see what's happening in the kitchen before we go up for inspection?" suggested John. "At least it should be warm in there."

They retired to the changing area where they dried themselves on their scraps of towel and put on their boxers. On their way out, they met Porky coming in. Only by now his nickname was hardly appropriate, because he was a gaunt and hollow-cheeked figure with only some folds of skin on his abdomen to show where the fat had been.

"Don't bother, Porks," said John, "there's no hot water."

"No water full stop," added Noah.

Porky nodded without saying anything. Since the accident in the woods with Brandon, he had remained morose, despite attempts by the others to jolly him along.

"Is Owen up?" asked Jamie.

Porky's eyes lost a little of their vacant look. "Yeh, he hasn't topped himself yet."

125

"We're just off to the kitchen to get a sneak preview of breakfast," said Jamie. "I expect the twins will be in full flight by now."

When they got to the kitchen, however, they found it locked, which was unheard of. Down the short passage opposite, cold air was seeping in through the half-open door, where a misty dawn light could be seen.

"Ooo, who left that open?" said Noah, and padded off to close it.

"It's only the middle of September and it's freezing already," said Jamie. "God knows what it's going to be like by Bonfire Night."

This reference brought a smile to John's lips as he thought of happier times. "Not the middle of September," he corrected, "we're very near the autumn equinox, but you're right, from now on the nights will be longer than the days and it follows that it's going to get a whole lot colder."

"Cheer us all up, why don't you?" said Jamie.

A guard entered the passageway from the outside, almost knocking over Noah, who gave a screech. The nameless, faceless man pushed by, taking no notice. Then, pointing and shouting and waving his baton, he ordered the boys to leave the corridor and go back upstairs to the dormitory.

"Something's happened," said John.

"More trouble," agreed Jamie.

"Where have Dennis and Michael got to?" asked Noah.

That question was answered immediately when they entered the dormitory because the twins were standing around the stove warming themselves with the other three boxer-clad boys.

"Have you been in the kitchen this morning?" demanded John.

The twins turned in unison and smiled, then they exchanged glances which somehow cued one of them to speak. This time it was Michael.

"John, it's not our fault we couldn't light the oven. The door was locked." He started to cough, which was immediately taken up by his brother.

"Will you two ever stop barking?" complained Jamie.

Dennis rubbed his chest, which appeared to have only a thin layer of skin covering the ribcage. "Hurts," he said.

Michael nodded in agreement and the twins smiled at each other. Jamie looked away guiltily.

The dormitory door opened and Valery Fyodorovich Khrennikov entered, along with the guard who had shouted at them earlier.

"Ooo, it's Miss Valerie," murmured Noah, loud enough for their translator to hear.

"Please to stand by your beds," said the sixteen-year-old Russian.

The English boys obediently lined up and were ceremonially counted.

"Mistress Valerie," whined Noah, "there's no water and we can't get in the kitchen so we'll starve."

"*Tovarisch* Marshall, listen and learn," said Valery and produced notes from a pocket in his jacket. "Sister Hopkins is indisposed and will not be in attendance today..."

"Something fatal, I hope," said John.

"Fucking bitch," exclaimed Porky, abandoning his silence for a moment.

"I believe she has a chill. She will return on Tuesday or Wednesday."

Valery looked up at them and Noah noticed a slight tremor in his hands.

"Someone has been stealing from the kitchen," he continued, "and until that person or persons comes forward and admits their guilt, the kitchen remains closed."

"Who in their right mind would steal that junk?" said John.

"What about water?" questioned Jamie. "You can't deny us water..."

127

"I am not denying you anything, *Tovarisch* Baker. The ball is in your court, so to speak. Find the culprit and the kitchen will be opened for business as usual, and so will the main stopcock."

"What's been stolen, Mistress?" asked Noah.

Valery shook his head. "That is not a matter I can discuss. Yevgeni Borisovich Mravinsky has the details."

"Which one is that?" asked John.

"I believe you call him Ivan the Terrible. Hardly an appropriate name for the Lieutenant Guard, *Tovarisch* Price."

"Nothing's too good for you lot," commented Jamie.

"Penultimately," went on Valery, proud that he had been able to use that word at last. "Penultimately, your rota for today will consist of tree felling this morning and log shaping in the afternoon. Still you soft, pussy Brits do not realise that without wood to burn you will not survive a Russian winter."

"Maybe we don't want to," said Owen, speaking for the first time since he got up.

"That is your choice, *Tovarisch* Frost, but your brother would probably wish you to survive."

Noah gasped, but then held his breath, expecting Owen to react, while Jamie and John braced themselves, ready for a tussle with the fourteen-year-old, but the boy did nothing but stare straight ahead, his jaw set. The moment passed and the tension eased.

"You want us soft, pussy Brits to chop wood on an empty stomach with no water?" asked John.

"You have until ten o'clock to find the guilty party before you need to assemble in the yard to begin your duties."

"Generous," muttered Jamie.

"Finally, I have some good news for you..."

"We're going home!" proclaimed the twins in unison, clapping their bony hands.

Valery shook his head. "No, I cannot offer you that, but what I can tell you is that on Wednesday, M. Wright and R. Davis will attend a service of absolution with the Reverend

Akinola before they are exorcised next Sunday, when you will all attend a service at the Church of the Transfiguration."

"Yes!" cried Mark.

"At last!" responded Ryan and the two boys shook hands and embraced.

"That's the good news, is it?" said Noah.

"Fuck me backwards," said Porky.

Valery looked at the once rotund figure with a blank expression, then he pulled out a roll of paper from the inside pocket of his jacket and walked the length of the room to where Noah was standing. "Sister Hopkins said you might be interested in this, *Tovarisch* Marshall."

"Ooo," exclaimed Noah, recoiling slightly. "What is it? Is it poisonous?"

Valery thrust it into his hand. "I do not know. It looks like an English language newspaper, but it has been bound with sticky tape, which made it impenetrable to me." He walked back to the door of the dormitory and turned. "If you find the guilty person, bring him to the school room. If not, you will assemble in the yard at ten wearing your winter suits and boots."

The guard followed Valery out into the corridor and closed the door behind him. Most of the nine boys began to dress but Jamie stood with his hands on hips looking round at them. "So which of you dumbasses has been taking stuff from the kitchen?"

Noah had started to pick at the cellotape that bound the newspaper, but his fingernails had begun to peel, and it was proving difficult. He looked up at Jamie, noticing that the sixteen-year-old was still more toned and muscular than he had ever been.

"Not me," he called, wanting to add 'gorgeous' but thinking better of it.

"Nor me," said John in a much deeper voice.

Porky shook his head and the twins looked at each other, smiled and turned to Jamie. "Not us," they chorused.

"I don't want any of their rubbish," growled Owen.

Jamie frowned. "That just leaves you two," he said, staring accusingly at Mark and Ryan.

Ryan shrugged. "We're going to be exorcised next week then we'll be going home."

"You think," said John.

"What's that got to do with anything?" demanded Jamie.

"We don't care what happens," answered Mark.

"You can't go without food and water for a week," pointed out Noah.

"The Reverend Akinola will feed us on Wednesday," replied Ryan.

"Yeh, feed tubes up your stupid arses," said Porky.

"We don't listen to queers and their demons, Pork Chop," said Mark.

"Brandon would still be alive if you weren't queer," claimed Ryan.

Porky moved more quickly than one might have been expected, and managed to land a punch on Ryan before John and Jamie could restrain him. Ryan held his nose and screamed while blood trickled between his fingers, but it wasn't over for him as Owen crossed the floor and slapped him round the head. "What did you say about my brother?"

Mark retreated towards the door. Ryan's screams were now punctuated by sobs as Owen stood over him, threatening to repeat the punishment. Noah threw the newspaper onto the bed and went over to them.

"Owen, don't hurt him any more. Honestly, he's not worth it. He doesn't know what he's talking about."

Owen eyeballed Noah for a good few seconds, then jabbed his finger at Ryan. "Don't ever talk about my brother again!" And with that he turned on his heel and stalked away.

Noah exchanged miserable looks with John and Jamie while they continued to hold on to Porky who was still shaking with emotion.

"You're a stupid, dozy gay boy prick, Ryan," said Noah, manoeuvring him over to one of the spare beds and sitting him down. "So it's a good job I got to know you a bit before that freaking preacher got his claws into you." Noah stripped the case off the pillow and stuck it to Ryan's face, bending his head down as he did so. "Hold it there," he ordered.

"Are you OK now, Porks, if we let you go?" asked John, who was tiring fast.

Porky nodded curtly and was released. Immediately, Jamie made his way over to the spare bed.

"Ryan, what did you take from the kitchen?"

Red-eyed, the boy looked up at him. "I think my nose is broken," he wailed through the pillow case.

"Answer the question, Ryan, or I might start getting mad myself."

"Vodka," said the boy, though it sounded more like 'wodka'.

Jamie glanced at Noah, who raised his eyebrows.

"Where do they keep vodka in the kitchen?"

"The old granny and Whiskers bring in six bottles every Monday and sell them for 1500 roubles each. They keep them under the sink and they're usually gone by nine."

"To who?" asked Jamie.

"To whom?" corrected John, who had joined them at the bedside.

"Not to us, that's for sure," said Noah.

"Madam DeVeal, hairy man, bald man, the guards, anyone who wants to buy," said Ryan.

"How many did you steal?"

"Three, one every week." Ryan removed the pillow case from his nose to see if the bleeding had stopped.

"This reminds me of one of our dad's favourite films," said Noah. "The Roaring Twenties with James Cagney and Humphrey—"

Jamie frowned. "Noah that is irrelevant."

"Sorry, it's a really good film, though, one of the best gang—"

"Noah!"

After silence had fallen, Jamie turned his attention back to Ryan. "You drank three bottles of vodka and you never thought (a) to share them with your friends, or (b) what might happen if you were found out?"

Ryan shrugged. "It was only half a bottle each for three weeks."

"And where are the empties?"

"We threw them down the crapper."

John scratched his forehead, making one of his spots bleed. "So you and Mark have been bullshitting us these past three weeks with your holier-than-thou demon crap, while you've been getting yourselves secretly pissed on vodka?"

"When we've been exorcised, they'll send us home," said Ryan.

"What happens when your parents find out your exorcism, which may kill you by the way, hasn't changed you one jot?" asked Jamie.

"I'm going to live with Mark."

"Durr!" said John, wiping his forehead and finding a trace of blood on his fingers.

"What a div you are, Ryan," said Noah. "You especially, because you're three years older than Mark."

"You won't say that when we've gone home and you're still stuck in this mouldy dump."

"Time for you to face the music, Ryan," said John.

"You're going to grass on me, aren't you?"

"No," said Jamie. "You're going to the classroom to grass on yourself."

"I'm not!"

Jamie smiled menacingly. "On your own or with me holding you by the collar – your choice."

Ryan could see no way out. "What about Mark? It was his idea."

"There's no loyalty among thieves, is there?" commented John. "Noah and I will collect Mark from his bolt hole and make sure you both share whatever comeuppance is on offer."

"Me?" screeched Noah.

"You three are no different to my dad," said Ryan.

"I didn't think I'd ever have any sympathy for your dad," said Noah, "but I was wrong..."

***

34: Sunday, 22nd September. 5 p.m. MSK, Arkhangelsk Oblast, Juvenile Prison for Boys, Puksa.

ROBERT

They've moved me out of the ward and put me in a holding cell in the hospital. I know it's not the prison proper because I can still smell the Lysol. There are no windows for me to look out of, just blank brick walls, painted green, a hospital bed, chair and a bucket. Not very fancy; there's no cupboard, not even a shelf, for my non-existent worldly goods.

I had another injection to make me feel sick yesterday, and then had to watch three hours of cheap gay porn in which all the actors pretended to be in their early twenties but most were thirty-five if they were a day, and the majority had their body hair shaved off, leaving stubble, a rash, spots or a combination of all three. I didn't need an injection to be turned off by the sheer tackiness of it.

For the two days preceding that episode, I had electric shock 'treatment' but I started to get burn marks round my wrists so they cut the Friday session short. I assume the smell of burning flesh put Madam off her dinner.

Earlier today, I had an equally unpleasant and embarrassing encounter in my cell when I was given my breakfast. I was lying curled up on the bed because I was still feeling nauseous from yesterday. The woman who brought the mush in on a tray announced, with a big forced smile, that her name was Irina and she would be my servant for the day.

Even before she said this, I thought there was something strange about her because she was wearing a hospital gown and obviously nothing else. Her feet were bare and her cracked toenails were painted pink.

Irina put the tray on the chair and came and sat on the bed. "You like me?" she asked.

Oh joy, I thought, and she smells like the margarine back at the encampment. And I really was feeling quite sick by this point. My stomach began to heave, I could taste bile in my mouth and feel the blood draining from my face. Whatever orders Irina was under to pursue my heterosexualisation, she had enough sense not to wait around to be sicked on. She sprinted for the door and made her exit just in time before everything that was in my stomach ended up on the floor.

What I hadn't realised was that this holding cell had a hidden camera which had spied on our aborted encounter. Not long after, two orderlies appeared carrying mops and buckets filled with hot water containing liberal amounts of disinfectant.

They made it clear that I was to clean up my own mess, which I was more than happy to do. Much happier, in fact, than sampling the delights of Irina who, like the porn actors, had long since passed into her fourth decade, although whether she had a shaving rash or not will I hope remain a mystery to me forever.

Having been sick I actually felt better, and the floor of the cell was soon cleaner than it had been in years. I even managed to eat some breakfast.

About mid-morning, the good Dr Sex and Madam DeVeal entered, she two steps behind him and as usual looking daggers both at me and him. These two so-called medical practitioners were in their full dress uniforms and he had a clipboard.

"Robert, you displayed an unnatural paroxysm when you were presented with the opportunity for a normal sexual encounter." The professor tapped his pen on the clipboard, but couldn't help taking a sneaky peek up into the corner of the cell. When I followed his gaze, I notice a small black box with a lens.

I wanted to ask him whether voyeurism turns him on as much as Irina and this whole stupid farce turns me off, but I clammed up.

"Dumb insolence," said Madam. "Look at him. He needs a short, sharp shock to bring him to his senses!"

"And what do you suggest, Sister Hopkins?" asked Professor Salkorov with a smile, though his tone bordered on the sarcastic.

"Maybe we should show him the body of that boy who was in the bed next to him. That would teach him what happens to perverts if they don't change their ways."

She's talking about Sergei, the boy who was beaten up for being a child molester. I assume they've finally killed him.

"These unfortunate incidents are not a good advertisement for the Russian prison service, Sister," says the professor, and I believe he means it.

"Who killed him?" I ask.

"No one killed him," said Madam. "They cut off his testicles and he bled to death."

I think the lady walks a fine line between torture and murder, and may not know the difference. "Was anyone held responsible?" I ask.

The professor shrugged. "The three boys were drunk on vodka that had been illegally smuggled into the prison. They couldn't remember the incident so they were not responsible for their actions. They spent a night in solitary."

A night in solitary together with another bottle of vodka, a pack of cards and a carton of Winstons no doubt, and no doubt the same three youths who were responsible for the shit in my bed.

"They were sensible enough to write 'pervert' across his chest with a knife," smiled Sister Hopkins. "I think this young man should spend a day with the Russian boys in Block Two; perhaps that would have a salutary effect on his American arrogance."

So that's where I'm due to go tomorrow. A gay, ginger-haired American to share living accommodation with the finest juvenile criminals Russia has to offer. I expect a message will have got through to the three stooges to be on the lookout for me as well. That being the case, I can expect a really fun day.

I wonder if I'll survive, or will I end up like Sergei? I suppose my life must have some value to them, given the money they're getting from Burnoco Oil and the church, courtesy of my loving parents. If I ever get back home to Tyree, I promise to go to Pastor Dunn's Sunday service and in front of the whole goddam congregation, do exactly the same to him as those boys are going to do to me tomorrow.

***

35: Sunday, 22nd September. 7.45 p.m. MSK, Arkhangelsk Oblast, Gosudarstvennyi Meditsinskii Institut (gomoseksualizm).

<u>NOAH</u>

Noah peered through the window of the dormitory into the darkness. There was nothing to see: no stars, no tops of trees against the night sky, not even the sheet metal walls of the compound. It was pitch black, as if the world ended a few feet in front of him. Then he shifted his gaze to the reflection in the glass, seeing John Price sprawled on his bed reading the sports pages of the Swanford Mail by the light of a hurricane lamp. Everyone else was downstairs in the rest room.

"There probably won't be a frost tonight," said Noah.

"Hmm," responded John, turning from the back page to the inside back page.

"I said..."

"I heard what you said, and I'm not bothered if Ryan and Mark freeze to death out there. They deserve to."

"They're only little," said Noah.

"You're only little," answered John, "but you aren't a totally selfish, objectionable piece of shit who would sell his grandmother for a bottle of vodka."

"No one in England would lock a ten-year-old boy in a cage outside all night in the cold."

"More's the pity," said John distractedly.

136

"I took them some tea," admitted Noah, sitting on the bed worrying.

"I saw. You're an idiot."

"That's pretty much what Porky said too, only he added the word fucking."

"He has tended to overuse that word of late, but in this instance he was quite correct."

"Mark said he wasn't going to drink it because I was a demon."

"Did they drink it?"

"Of course they did. Ryan gulped his down and when Mark saw him, he drank his too."

"And did they thank you?"

"No."

"Little shits."

Noah looked over to their stove in the centre of the room, which was emitting enough heat to keep them comfortably warm. "Miss Valerie thinks we're not chopping enough wood for the winter."

John sighed, folded the paper and sat up. "Noah Marshall, has it ever occurred to you that our ever-diminishing wood supply is the result of Miss Valerie and the rest of the comrades filching it for their own use?"

Noah blinked in disbelief at John. "Never!"

"A Gazza full of wood goes into Puksa every week, in my estimation." John said and he laughed at his friend's expression. "Noah, when was the last time we had any PE with the hairy man? When was the last time we had any lessons in manly behaviour from Dr Sex? When was the last time you saw Dr Death?"

"But they're doing unspeakable things to Robert, aren't they?"

"OK. What about Madam DeVeal's so-called chill?"

"Her door's locked. I tried it," admitted Noah, smiling sheepishly. "I was going to wish her a speedy recovery."

"Ten to one she's actually out on the razz in her furs in Puksa."

"Oh!"

"We've become the fag end, if you'll pardon the expression, of a timber industry run by our guards. They've given up on any pretence of 'curing' us here."

"Holy Joe hasn't."

"You said yourself that the Reverend Akinola's main interest is being in the missionary position with his two lady friends."

"That's what Dwain told me."

"You are just too nice, Noah."

"You make 'nice' sound as big an insult as 'paedo'."

"What's that?" enquired Jamie, entering the dormitory.

"Noah thinks I've just called him a paedo," answered John.

"Oh well, there are worse things you can call a person," stated Jamie, "like 'nice', for instance." He sat facing them on the adjacent bed. "Have you found it yet?"

"No," said Noah.

"He's too busy worrying about Wright and Wrong in solitary."

"Jamie, do you think the Russians steal our wood?"

"Yes, except it's not our wood."

"I've been telling him a few home truths about our lives in the forest," explained John.

Jamie picked up the newspaper and turned to the back page. "You made a good job of removing the cellotape without tearing the pages. How are Swanford Firsts getting on so far this season?"

"As of 21st August, played four, won one, drawn three. Position fourth," answered John.

"Well memorised," said Jamie. "I see they drew with those dossers in Supermarine on Saturday."

"Yeh, Saturday a month ago. They could be bottom of the table by now."

"Or top..."

Noah yawned.

"Not a fan of the beautiful game, then?" enquired Jamie.

"Strange you should say that," chipped in John, "because this effeminate gay boy, who would prefer to be baking cupcakes than supporting his local football team..."

"Oi!" interrupted Noah.

"As I was saying," continued John, "this little fairy from the bottom of the garden claims to number among his friends Moseley and Walker, only he calls them Dan and Justin, if you know who I'm talking about?"

"I've never met them personally, but I've seen them play," remarked Jamie. "They're in the Under 15s now, or should I say they are the Under 15s?"

"They're my friends," drawled Noah. "We hang out."

"I think it's all part of some sweaty, gay, erotic fantasy of his," said John, pressing his glasses into the bridge of his nose with the tip of his index finger.

"They're not sweaty!" admonished Noah. "Well, Justin's feet used to smell a bit, but I cured him of that."

Jamie shook his head and sighed. "You're right, John, this boy is one log short of a tree. I wouldn't be surprised if we found a bottle of vodka under his pillow."

"What's going on downstairs?" enquired John.

"The twins are coughing, Porky's moaning and Owen's asleep. That's why I came up here," Jamie replied, starting to divide up the newspaper.

"What are you doing?" asked Noah.

"Let's have one last go at finding the secret entry that Madam left for you," Jamie said, handing out a section each.

John frowned. "How is it that you've got the sports pages, and I've been given the property section and interesting news like toddler group plants a tree?"

"The privilege of being the eldest, strongest and best-looking," replied Jamie.

The first indication that Noah had discovered why Sister Margaret Hopkins had given him the newspaper was when he gave out a barely audible gasp. The others paid no attention. It was only when he began to sob that they took notice.

"Noah," said John quietly. "What is it?"

"Our dad," cried Noah. "He wasn't a drunk... He was the best dad..."

When John put his arm round him, Noah buried his face in his shoulder and began to cry in earnest.

Carefully, Jamie relieved Noah of the newspaper and looked for what had caused his distress.

"Jesus," he murmured. "Jesus Christ! That evil, evil woman..."

"What is it?" asked John quietly, holding Noah firmly in his arms.

Jamie held up the bottom half of page five so that John could read the column headed *Drunk's Funeral* for himself. After he finished, he squeezed Noah gently. "He must have been a really great dad for you to have turned out the way you are."

Jamie moved over to the bed so that Noah was sandwiched between them both. "We're here for you, buddy," he said, putting his arms round them both. "We'll fight these people to the end."

***

36: Thursday, 26th September. 7.30 a.m. 15 Leighton Lane.

DAN

Dan dozed contentedly, knowing that first period at Dumbleton Boys' School on a Thursday wasn't until ten o'clock. Maths was not his favourite subject by any means, but was a subject in which he was quite capable of holding his own against the boarders. On Mondays and Fridays he had to be there by eight, as that was when compulsory assembly began, but thankfully there were only two more of those earlys before the expedition to Russia.

His bedroom door was flung wide and a smiley face loomed over him and planted a kiss somewhere between his right eye and his nose.

"Happy birthday," said Mikey, thrusting a creased and bulky envelope at him.

Dan groaned, though it wasn't as if this ritual was unexpected, having been going on annually for at least the past three years; only the weight pressing down on him had increased significantly. He yawned and stretched, then focused on his brother. "You... are... a... pest..." he said.

"Open it," said Mikey, rolling off his brother and reclining on the bed, supporting his chin in his hand.

Dan hoisted himself up into a sitting position and slit the envelope as best he could with his finger. A 200-gram bar of Cadbury's Dairy Milk Turkish Delight fell out onto the duvet.

"I didn't expect a present," said Dan.

Mikey smiled. "Do you like it?"

"Very much, thank you," said his older brother, "but probably not quite as much as you do."

"It's my favourite," admitted Mikey and as he spoke, a little drool escaped from his mouth.

"Not before breakfast," said Dan.

The little boy seemed to accept this. "I made you a card as well."

Dan pulled the folded A4 sheet out of the envelope and opened it out. "'Happy 14th birthday Dan, love from Mikey'. That's good, and you've even spelled 'birthday' right this time."

"Jack helped me."

Dan looked at the picture on the front. "I take it this is me and Justin in our football kit, though my legs are a bit more muscular than these twigs..."

"Yes, and that's me, Mummy, Daddy and Jack cheering you on from the stand."

"Oh, I get it, though by their expressions I thought it might be a hold-up at the bank. But who is this figure in goal with the large blue head? He's saving my shot, I notice."

Mikey giggled. "That's my style guru, Noah. You're going to bring him back from the nasty place, aren't you?"

"Have you been hiding under people's beds again, listening in to private conversations?"

"No," said Mikey. "In any case, I can keep a secret."

"You'd better, or you'll never ever see us again, never mind Noah."

Mikey's face clouded for a moment as the words sank in. "I'll never tell anyone," he said.

***

Fifteen minutes later Dan came down for breakfast, finding three packages and a stack of cards in his place.

"Happy birthday, dear," said his mum, giving him the obligatory kiss.

"You've entered the fifteenth year of your life on this planet," said Roger, looking up from his newspaper. "A heavy responsibility."

"Many happy returns of the day," said Jack, "whatever that means."

"Open them," said Mikey.

"OK, give me a chance to sit down."

Dan picked up the oddest-shaped package wrapped in black paper with silver edging. "To Comrade Daniil Rogerovich Moseley from Джек..." He grinned at his brother. "So some of Ms Lane's teaching has stuck?"

"Like fly-paper," said Jack.

Dan tore off the wrapping and his grin grew wider. "This is so QL."

"It's called a ushanka," explained Jack, "a genuine Russian army surplus hat complete with hammer-and-sickle badge."

"That'll keep your ears toasty," said Roger.

"To be honest, I've bought one for myself as well," admitted Jack.

"Maybe we should all get one," suggested Dan.

"Can I try it on?" asked Mikey.

"No! I don't want nits..."

"Daniel, your brother has not got nits," said Pam.

Dan took off the hat and plonked it on Mikey's head.

"Can't see," said the little boy.

The blue paper that the next package was neatly wrapped in was quickly despatched. "Oh, pants and socks," said Dan, "er... great!"

"We thought you needed some nice Marks and Spencer's white pants and black socks for your new school, dear," said his mother.

"Not many people see my pants," observed Dan.

"No, but you might have an accident and we wouldn't like to be shown up, and I'm afraid most of your boxers are rather cheap and common."

"Well, you bought them!"

"I know, but we didn't anticipate you going to a posh school."

Dan looked askance at his mother. "Thanks anyway; they're lovely."

"There's a music voucher in there too," said Roger with a paternal smile, "which is probably of more interest."

Dan brightened. "Now that's more like it!" The thin white envelope was tucked into one of the packs of seamless trunks – which, if truth be told, he did actually prefer to boxers.

"Who's that from?" asked Mikey impatiently, eyeing the rectangular box wrapped in red paper dotted with stars and tied with fancy gold ribbon, surmounted by a bow.

Dan coloured slightly as he read the label. "It's from Sophie."

"Oh!" said his older brother. "I hope she's got you the XXL size condoms this time; we don't want any more of those embarrassing splits."

"Ah! A chip off the old block, eh, son?" said his dad proudly.

"Tsk," said Pam. "Roger Moseley, why are you encouraging Jack's vulgarity, especially when a certain person is around?"

143

Mikey pulled off the ushanka which was making him feel hot, and frowned at his mother. "I know what a condo is!"

Dan took out a spray can and plastic bottle from the box. Both were turquoise with silver stripes. "Deodorant and shower gel," he said.

"Jean-Paul Gaultier," said his mother, impressed. "Sophie's splashing out on you."

"There's only one reason why girls buy deodorant and shower gel for boys," said Jack.

Dan's colour deepened. "Are you serious?"

"Take no notice of him," said Pam, firmly. "You hardly ever smell."

Roger chuckled. "Hardly ever... that's not exactly a ringing rebuttal."

"Are you saying that I do smell?" challenged Dan.

"I'm saying, dear, that all boys smell to some extent. That's why you must always be careful with your personal grooming. Girls notice these things."

"Especially when you're having sex with them," added Jack.

"It's my fourteenth birthday and you happen to tell me on this day, for the first time in my life, that I smell!" exclaimed Dan, folding his arms and putting his chin on his chest. "Well, thanks very much!"

"Dan stinks," said Mikey with a phoney look of disgust. "Gross!"

"Shut up, you," laughed Jack. He turned to Dan. "LB, you are without doubt the least hygienically challenged boy, or girl for that matter, that I know, and don't forget, I live with you."

"There you are," said his dad. "Come on, Dan, buck up, open your cards or I'll be late for the office."

The boy glanced at his older brother and relented, picking up the first envelope. "It's from Justin," he said.

"Well, I'd never have guessed," said Roger, holding out his hand and taking the card which showed an aerial view of Wembley Stadium. "To Dan from Justin Walker." He shook his head and chuckled. "I wonder how long it took him to think up that snappy line. That boy has about as much imagination as a snail."

"Dad!" exclaimed Dan.

"I think we can all agree Justin is a nice young man, but quite limited," said Pam.

"No we can't," said Jack, vehemently. "Justin is someone you can trust with your life, which is rather more important than being able to write unfunny crap in a birthday card."

Roger exchanged a surprised look with Pam. "Well, where did that come from?" he said.

"You tell 'em like it is, Jack," murmured Dan.

Pam narrowed her eyes at her two sons. "So, why do we have to wait for bad-tempered outbursts to learn what you really think?"

"Because parents should only be able to view their teenage sons through a glass darkly," replied Jack, who had been wanting to use that phrase since the last school year when Mr Colt had quoted it humorously in relation to one of Max Seddon's impenetrable essays.

"Time for me to go to work," said Roger, getting up and folding his newspaper. "An enlightening breakfast. Not quite what I expected. I do hope the conversation at tonight's dinner is as intellectually stimulating. I assume it is booked, dear?"

Pam looked at her husband. "Don't I always?"

"But I haven't opened all my cards," said Dan.

"Don't worry, at the rate you're going, I'll be back home before you've finished."

"Can I have my piece of Turkish Delight chocolate now?" enquired Mikey with a sweet smile.

***

37: Sunday, 29th September. 10.45 a.m. 'Fouracres', off the Retford Road.

JACK

Fouracres was an old gamekeeper's cottage which had been spruced up and modernised, just over a mile from the Moseley residence on the south-west side of town. Here, Helen Edith Lane lived with her husband and a pair of yellow parakeets called Ethel and Iris. In the last quarter hour of their tutorial, Jack and Dan were supposed to be practising their Russian speech while Ms Lane got her two nieces ready for their riding lesson. The Friday night through Sunday afternoon stay by the girls had become a regular duty which she undertook for her sister, who lived in Woolgrove. Ms Lane claimed that these weekends with her family were being sacrificed on the altar of male ego, meaning the coming trip to Russia.

As soon as their tutor was out of earshot, Dan took out his mobile and began to text his girlfriend, Sophie, while Jack gazed misty-eyed out of the sitting-room window across a field, where a tractor was ploughing in the wheat stubble ready for sowing the winter crop. His thoughts were back on a day in July when Robert had come round to his house and they had shared a couple of blissful hours alone together. Well, they seemed blissful in retrospect, but they were probably fraught with the danger of discovery at the time.

Jack's mobile rang which brought him back to the present with a start.

"Good morning Jack, I hope I haven't disturbed your tuition?"

"Hello Mr Colt, we're supposed to be practising but Dan's busy texting his girlfriend."

"Shut up, you," said Dan. "I wasn't the one staring into space like a lovesick puppy."

"I trust the redoubtable Ms Lane is not with you at this moment," guessed Mr Colt.

146

"No, sir, she's getting her nieces' jodhpurs on."

"Ah!" His form teacher paused, then spoke again. "Jack, I don't know if you have kept up with the news of late, but my wife drew my attention to a piece on the radio an hour ago. It seems that our friends in the Kremlin are closing the borders to Western traffic for a fortnight starting on the first of October. The great leader says this is in retaliation for the West's aggressive stance against the legitimate rights of the Russian peoples."

It took a moment for Jack to comprehend the full significance of this. "Oh, this is very bad news, sir. Does Elspeth know at number 41?"

"I can't answer that question, as you are the first person I have phoned on the matter. I think we should probably have a meeting as soon as possible."

"I'll get on to it, sir. Are you free later on this afternoon?"

"Yes, I am. I suggest about four o'clock."

"Unless you hear otherwise, that sounds fine."

***

The whole crew gathered in the lounge at number 41 to decide on their next move.

"The people rejoice and the cathedral bells of the Kremlin peal out over Moscow as the Russian bear once more asserts its power and influence over the illegitimate claims of the decadent West." Elspeth sighed. "And I thought those days were over."

"*Plus ça change, plus c'est la même chose,*" added Ms Lane.

Stewart swivelled his eyes at their old equality counsellor and took a drink of Coke.

"I don't see what they gain from this," said Jack.

"I'm afraid that is not the point," said Mr Colt. "If you are a gangster surrounded by gangsters in a gangster state, then face and machismo come well before logic and the well-being of the people."

"It's strange when our government wants to be more friendly with the Russians and less friendly with Europe," observed Anne.

"I think that just tells you how far our star has fallen," answered Elspeth.

Justin fidgeted in his seat and exchanged weary glances with Dan and Alan.

"It seems politics has become the province of the old and fusty," commented Mr Colt with a teacher's eye on the boys, "judging by the fact that some of the younger natives are getting restless."

"Yes, let us come to the matter in hand," said Elspeth. "What implications does this delay have on our expedition?"

"The car is ready now," said Alan, as if that was the be-all and end-all, "but we may have to adjust the amount of antifreeze and use a lighter oil."

"Because it's going to be colder?" questioned Jack.

Alan nodded. "We've renovated the heater and air conditioner and they work fine."

"Assuming the mission is still on, we should consider an alternative date for departure," said Mr Colt. "I fear I shall have to reapply for visas."

"Are we all agreed that this is a delay and not a cancellation?" asked Elspeth. "No, let me rephrase that. Is there anyone here who has doubts about us going ahead?"

"How cold does it get in late October or early November?" enquired Anne.

Dan opened the folder he'd brought. "Usually around freezing most of the time in that part of Russia, but the journey out will just be like late autumn here."

"I don't like the cold," said Ms Lane.

"I expect Robert and Noah like it even less," pointed out Jack, "and they are the reason we're going."

Elspeth smiled at the mild rebuke for his former teacher. "So when, then?" she said.

"If the borders are closed for two weeks won't there be thousands of cars and lorries piled up waiting to get through?" asked Justin.

"The young man makes a very good point," said Mr Colt, which caused Dan to dig his friend in the ribs. "I suggest a three-week delay to our original plan, which will bring us up to just before the half-term holiday. The advantage of this will be clear to Jack, I'm sure."

Jack nodded. "Fewer questions, for certain. But it'll mean holiday rearrangements for our parents."

"Lastminute.com," said Justin with a smile.

"It's a blow," said Dan. "Think about it, Just, yet more early starts on Mondays and Fridays."

Mr Colt studied his diary. "Thursday the twenty-fourth of October would seem an appropriate date, and I should be able to get the revised paperwork by then. And I have to say that fits in very nicely with my own plans. Muriel and I have been invited over to Boston by the Oppenheims – that's Shandra's parents – for Thanksgiving. It sounds like it's getting serious if the prospective in-laws have to meet."

"Maybe it will be a Christmas wedding," said Anne.

"Good lord! I never thought of that. I'd better pack an extra pair of long johns."

The boys smirked at each other.

"Tut tut," admonished Ms Lane. "You young men would do well to follow Mr Colt's example. Russia isn't going to be a picnic in November."

"Let's hope the great leader doesn't extend the closure," said Dan, "whoever he is."

Elspeth pulled a face. "I think you're right, Mr Colt, young people today are sorely lacking in political education."

***

149

<u>JACK</u>

"You're a very devious little boy."

Mikey sat on Jack's bed swinging his legs to and fro and smiling seraphically.

"What's devious?" he asked.

"It's what you are," said Dan, "a crafty little shit."

"Dan swore!" exclaimed Mikey. "Bugger, bloody hell!"

"Watch it!" warned Jack, "or I'll record what you say and play it back to Nana Moseley, then you'll never get sleepovers with Mad Mike."

Mikey pouted for a second then smiled again. His parents had agreed to persuade Roger's mother to allow Mikey at least two sleepovers with his friend Mike Huntley because he was so disappointed that he wouldn't be going to stay on the original date.

"I was never as two-faced at his age, was I?" asked Dan.

"I don't know about that," answered Jack. "You always managed to twist Dad around your little finger over anything football. Which reminds me, have you told Coach Brennan about the revised dates for the trip?"

"Justin did. He's better at that sort of thing than me."

"You mean he doesn't mind being seriously bollocked?"

Dan smiled. "Coach called us a pair of pantyhose slackers who would have to earn our place back in the team."

"In other words, he's pissing himself because he knows the Under 15s are going to lose two or three games in a row."

"Jack said piss," said Mikey.

"No I didn't, I said 'pissing'. That's different; you ask Mum."

The little boy looked sceptically at his brother, but didn't pursue it. "What is Grand Canyon?"

"*Gran Canaria*, stupid," corrected Dan. "The hotel they liked in Tenerife was booked up."

"It's an island off Africa," explained Jack.

Mikey frowned. "Do a lot of old people go there for sexing holidays?"

"Loads," said Dan.

"Definitely a place for young people to avoid during the old people's rutting season; you can hear the bellows for miles," added Jack.

"They do a lot of sex swapping as well," said Dan blithely. "Mum will probably come back with Justin's dad."

Mikey's eyes went wide.

"Yes, it's not just coincidence that they're going to the same place," said Jack, handing round the bag of coconut mushrooms. "Would you prefer it if Dad came back with Justin's mum?"

Mikey took a mushroom and popped it into his mouth. "You're liars," he said, folding his arms across his chest.

"You're quite smart for a snotty-nosed seven-year-old," said Jack.

"Do you think the parents will get on, just because Justin and I are friends?" mused Dan.

"I'm not sure, ours are always sniffy about Justin for some reason."

"It's because they think I dominate him."

"You are the boss, though."

"It's not like that," argued Dan. "It's because we fit together like two pieces of a jigsaw. Just look at him and Alan as well."

"Yes, but he's always second in command. I'm sure part of the reason he gave up on the Academy is because you weren't there."

"I rely on him and so does Alan."

"Yeh, I know, Justin is number one in my book too, I'm just playing devil's advocate... And talking of devils, shall we tickle this cheeky little sprogette to death?"

Mikey screamed, leaped off the bed and ran to the door, where he turned and stuck his tongue out at them. "You've got to catch me first, suckers!" he said.

39: Sunday, 29th September. 9 a.m. MSK, Arkhangelsk Oblast, Gosudarstvennyi Meditsinskii Institut (gomoseksualizm).

NOAH

Noah opened his eyes and tried to focus on the figure standing over him.

"Robert?"

The figure smiled and sat on the edge of the bed. "It's me."

"I think I've had a nasty turn," said Noah as his vision cleared at last.

"I think you've had two or three nasty turns over the past week, according to your friends."

"Our dad..."

Robert took Noah's hand. "I heard, I'm sorry. Sorry for your loss and sorry for the way you learned about it."

Tears ran out of Noah's eyes. "He wasn't like they said. He only ever had a couple of pints on a Friday..."

"I wish my dad was half as good as yours," said Robert.

The gangly figure of John Price came into view. "Hey, it's time you were up, Marshall, lazing around in bed."

"I've had a nasty turn," repeated Noah.

"I know. You gave us all a fright, as the last one was on the stairs."

"Which is why you've got a bandage on your head," added Robert.

Noah felt with his fingers. "Who did it?"

John smiled. "Your lady friend Babooshka. She's been very concerned about you."

"Is he hungry?" called Jamie from the other side of the room.

"You can actually ask the patient directly without the need for an intermediary," retorted John.

"Shut up, Price," said Jamie. "Are you hungry, Noah?"

Noah thought about this for a while, then nodded. "I'm on empty," he said.

"We've got something special for you, if you'd like, but it'll take about ten to fifteen minutes to prepare."

"What is it?"

"Surprise."

"Oh..." Noah directed his attention at Robert, who was thin and pale like the rest of them, but also had cuts on his face, a swollen cheek and the remnants of a black eye.

"Who hit you?"

"The professor and Madam decided I wasn't being cooperative enough in my 'treatment' so I spent a day in the prison."

"They beat you up?"

"There are three boys who run the show for the guards. They look about thirty but are probably seventeen or eighteen. We'd crossed swords once already inside the hospital. They shit in my bed."

"Ooo, Robert, they don't sound very nice."

The American chuckled. "No, but they're only doing what those higher up want them to do. The point is, after they laid into me, I had to go back to the hospital ward to have my injuries attended to."

With Robert's help, Noah pulled himself up into a sitting position.

"They're not going to send you back for more 'treatment', are they?"

"Who knows? John thinks I'm only here for the exorcism, then it'll be back to Madam's tender mercies."

"You ought to run away, like Dwain did," whispered Noah.

"We've all got to go to church this afternoon, including you," said Robert seriously. "Do you think you can manage?"

"Jamie can give him a piggy-back," said John, returning to the bedside. "I think Noah would enjoy that..."

153

"Oi... cheek!" But inwardly Noah smiled at the thought of snuggling up to Jamie.

The dormitory door opened and a small procession entered, led by the twins and followed by Porky and Owen. Michael was carrying a plate and Dennis a mug. Both were trembling slightly as they passed down the centre of the room and came to stand before Noah's bed.

"Twins!" said Noah. "What you got for me?"

The two boys smiled at each other, then Michael put the plate down carefully on Noah's lap. "We made it special for you and we haven't coughed on it."

"Ooo, egg and chips. Thank you. I love egg an' chips. Is there any sauce?"

"'Fraid not," said Porky.

"He's saucy enough," said John.

Owen handed Noah a spoon.

"What you got me, Dennis?"

"Tea," he replied, placing the mug at an angle on the bedside cupboard, "with sugar."

"Ooo, lovely. Have a chip, Robert, you need building up."

"No need to give yours away, Noah," called Jamie, striding towards them. "Here's a spare plate of chips for everyone." He put the plate down at the foot of the bed and they all tucked in.

After the meal, Owen was the only one left hovering beside Noah. In the two months since their arrival at the camp, there had not been a great deal of personal interaction between them, despite only a five-month difference in their ages and both being gay. Owen was less of a stereotype than Noah, without the mannerisms, voice or penchant for fabrics and bread-making. His most androgynous feature was his wide hips, otherwise he was just as masculine as any heterosexual boy.

Noah, assuming Owen had something to say, smiled and patted the edge of his bed. The boy hesitated and then sat.

"Owen, where are Mark and Ryan?"

"Don't you remember?" he answered. "They went to holy Joe's service on Wednesday and haven't been back."

"Oh, that's strange, isn't it?"

"That's what you said on Wednesday night when they didn't return for dinner. That's why you asked Valery where they'd got to on Thursday morning."

"I don't remember that. Forgetting must be part of my nasty turn. What did Miss Valerie say?"

"He said the Reverend wanted to keep them safe from the demonic influences of the soft, pussy Brits until the exorcism today. You said that Valery was at his most ironic. The next thing I heard was that you'd fainted and fallen down the stairs."

"This fainting, it must have been in the mind, because I don't feel ill. 'Specially since having the egg and chips and tea."

A silence fell. Owen's shoulders slumped and he looked down at the floor. "It's only been two weeks," he murmured, "and I've started to forget about Brandon already."

So that's what he wanted to talk about, thought Noah. "You don't forget, Owen, it's just that life moves on and what's gone before becomes memories. Our dad still talked about his mum and dad, even though they died before I was born. His favourite was the one about the holiday he had in Cornwall when he was twelve. They got cut off by the tide and all had to hold hands and run through the waves to the next cove where there was a path up. Each time he told that story, the waves got higher, but there it was lodged in his easy-access memory bank." He paused to see if his words were having any affect. "Owen, if I say 'Brandon' to you, what's the first picture that comes into your mind?"

The boy looked up and his eyes gazed at something only he could see. "A couple of summers ago, we were out on our bikes in Woolgrove Woods and I hit a tree root and fell off and twisted my ankle. He carried me all the way home on his back, then he went out again to collect my bike."

"Well, there you are – what better way to remember him?"

"What about your dad, Noah?"

"Oh, that's easy. He's in the shop in his white coat and he's got his scissors and comb in his hands, but he's not clipping or snipping at the old geezer in the chair but holding forth on some topic of interest. I walk in and he puts down his scissors and comb and puts his arms round my fat head and draws me into him, and he smells of brilliantine, and he asks me how his best boy is doing and even though I feel a fool and say *gerroff* me, I still snuggle into him because he makes me feel safe and I know he does it because he loves me..."

"I've made you cry, Noah."

"Not *you*, Owen – the memory made me cry because I'm sad at the moment. I hope one day I'll be able to remember and be happy."

***

40: Sunday, 29th September. 2.30 p.m. MSK, Arkhangelsk Oblast, the forest.

ROBERT

Robert walked – or, rather, shambled – along the wide path through the deep woods east of their encampment. He was last in the single file of eight boys. Immediately in front of him, Dennis followed Michael, their laboured breathing punctuated by rusty coughs. For a late autumn day in the Russian north it was not cold, eight degrees, and the air was clear and dry. A gloomy half-light endured beneath the spruce and pine trees, but occasionally a fleeting glimpse of watery sunlight filtered through the leafless boughs of a stand of birch.

From the front of the crocodile came the sound of Noah's high-pitched squeak, and John's deeper baritone wafted on the light breeze, which stirred the dead and decaying undergrowth.

Robert smiled to himself at Noah's resilience. He had not told him half of what he had suffered at the hands of the three Russian youths – the taunting, the crude sexual humiliation and physical pain – but he knew the boy was wise enough to read between the lines anyway.

The relative peace was disturbed when one of the baton-wielding guards shouted at them, presumably to stop talking. The two blue uniforms were to left and right while Vasily Yegorovich Pavlov and Yuri Semyonovich Bakaleinikoff, bald man and hairy man, came up front and rear. It did seem like overkill now to have four guards supervising such a small group of increasingly infirm boys.

Robert pondered what he would do if he was sent back to the prison in Puksa for more 'treatment'. An image of Jack came into his mind, telling him to be resolute and not to give in. And then Rosa was there too from home in Tyree, giving him a stern lecture on the same topic, particularly on how the likes of her sister Tammy must never be allowed to win!

They reached the edge of the forest where the first indication that something was amiss came with the faint smell of fuel oil.

"Oh!" cried Noah.

"Jeez!" exclaimed Jamie.

The members of the crocodile broke ranks and rushed out onto the slope where they took up positions to stare at the Church of the Transfiguration, which was ablaze.

"That didn't start by accident," said John. "Smell the petrol and look at those flames!"

The Reverend Akinola's pick-up truck with the giant tyres was parked beside the building but as yet had not been affected by the fire, which seemed more interested in the oil-painted timbers of the old church.

"What about Mark and Ryan?" said Noah.

Jamie and John began to run up the field. The billowing flames had completely encircled the base of the building and were creeping steadily upwards towards the onion domes at the corners. Now the guards started to run too, but whether it was in pursuit of Jamie and John or from a desire to help those inside the building was not clear. The other boys began to move up the slope at varying speeds. Robert passed the twins and caught up with Noah, who was panting for breath. Though they were still thirty yards away, they could already feel the heat on their hands and faces. They stopped.

"Robert, someone's put the chain through the handles," said Noah in distress.

They watched as Jamie and John tried to get near the doors, but each time the livid orange flames forced them back. It was as though the fire was alive and aware of what they were trying to do. The Reverend's truck began to move slowly towards them, away from the conflagration. Three of the guards were pushing while the fourth, Vasily, was in the driver's seat. Shortly, it started to roll down the hill of its own accord. One of the guards didn't let go soon enough, and sprawled onto the ground, much to the amusement of the others. The pick-up came to rest on the lower part of the hill and, when Vasily emerged, the others whooped in triumph and ran towards him.

Suddenly Noah clapped his hands over his ears and shut his eyes. "Oh, Robert, I can hear them screaming!"

The American listened but could hear nothing above the roar of the flames. He wondered if Noah was imagining the horror inside the church. Then a new sound filled the air as the blaze lapped over the plank sides of the building and took a greedy hold on the tar-soaked wooden roof shingles. Two of the smaller domes caught immediately, and flames were soon racing up the spire towards the large central dome.

It was then that Robert noticed out of the corner of his eye a movement across the top of the rise at the edge of the forest. A figure was jumping up and down and dancing round, his arms raised high in the air.

"Noah!" shouted Robert. "Look up there!"

Noah opened his eyes but his hands remained over his ears. The American pointed. "That's Dwain, isn't it?"

Noah peered through the haze of heat and smoke to where the Nigerian was still dancing round in triumph. "I knew he was a mad boy, but I didn't expect him to go this far."

After their fruitless attempts to rescue those inside, Jamie and John saw their own danger and ran back towards the other boys, just as the first of the domes began to tilt and then crash inwards, producing a volcanic-like shower of flame and sparks.

"Couldn't get near," exclaimed Jamie above the roar. "That chain on the door was red-hot!"

The two boys turned to watch, wiping away smoke-induced tears that left their faces streaked.

"We should get further back," said Robert, and as if in answer there was an explosion from deep inside the building, sending up a fresh plume of flame and burning timber.

They ran – just in time, because another, much louder report came from inside, showering a wide area around the church with blazing embers and broken glass.

"What was that?" cried John as the boys turned once more to look.

"They had oxygen cylinders in there," said Noah.

Inexorably, the whole structure began to collapse in on itself. Once more, Noah shut his eyes and covered his ears, but he couldn't entirely blot out the thunderous reverberation, as if some enraged monster had been unleashed from the depths of the inferno.

"I hope Ryan and Mark had been drugged already," said John.

In three-quarters of an hour the Church of the Transfiguration was reduced to a burning pile of white-hot ash and cinders. The boys milled around the periphery for a while but the heat remained intense and none had any desire to get closer.

"It'll smoulder for days," said Jamie.

Robert looked to where the guards were still standing around the pick-up truck engaged in conversation.

"Probably deciding which of them is the new owner," said Jamie.

"They weren't very interested in the church, that's for sure," remarked Porky.

"Nor the people inside it..." added John.

"I didn't like either Ryan or Mark, but I wouldn't have had that happen to them," said Owen.

"I wish we could go home," said Dennis, and he began to cough. "Smoke..." he spluttered.

Michael joined in and the hoarse, hacking sound came from deep inside his lungs.

"They'll never let us go now," predicted Noah in a small voice. "Not after this..."

John slung his arm over his friend's shoulder. "Don't you start being a pessimist."

Robert made no comment, because he was fast coming to the same conclusion as Noah.

Soon, they were lined up ready for the march back to the compound. Yuri appeared to have won the vehicle, because it was he who was in the driver's seat, steering a steady course behind the procession, a grin of satisfaction on his normally dour, stubbled face.

***

41: Tuesday, 8th October. 6.15 a.m. MSK, Arkhangelsk Oblast, Gosudarstvennyi Meditsinskii Institut (gomoseksualizm).

NOAH

Robert came up behind Noah and clapped him lightly on his bare shoulder.

"So what has got you so deep in thought?"

"Another day, another log," replied Noah.

The American put his arm protectively around the small figure and they both stared out of the window as a grey light

160

broke over the encampment, revealing another rain-sodden dawn. Water poured off the corrugated roof, dousing the saturated ground like a battery of unattended hosepipes.

After a week of dry fine weather, three days of heavy rain had turned their compound into a shallow lake and the surrounding forest into swamp. Still, they had been out each day felling trees and bringing them back in the afternoon to be sawn and chopped into manageable logs. It was tiring, dispiriting and boring work, especially as later they would see much of the fruits of their labours spirited away for no benefit to themselves.

"Funny, I've got so used to the rain, I no longer hear it pattering on the roof," said Robert.

Noah nestled into his friend. "Don't tell John Price, but I quite like it. It drives him up the wall."

"Are you two gossiping about me?" asked John, walking over.

"Yes, we were just talking about your hairy tummy," said Noah. "I call it the wedge of darkness."

John pushed the elasticated top of his boxers down and stroked the furry mat.

"Ooo, can I do that?" asked Noah.

"I would like to say that I allow only members of the opposite sex access to those areas of my body, but sadly that would be a flagrant distortion of reality. I think I will die a virgin."

"What you need," said Noah, "is a style guru."

"And do you have someone in mind for this position?" asked John.

"Well, I can give you a few tips..."

Robert frowned. "Is this going to be excruciatingly embarrassing? Because if it is I can make myself scarce."

"Oh, no!" exclaimed Noah, "anyway, you're nice and warm."

"Go on, then," said John.

"Well, first we'll get rid of the zits and the Buddy Hollys, then troll down to Specsavers for contacts or a pair of designer glasses: nice silver metals would suit your lovely, dark blue eyes. And having that deep black hair which, if I remember rightly from before we were all shorn, had a natural wave, I recommend a short back and sides, kind of messy on top with a floppy fringe."

Robert nodded his approval. "I have to say, I'm quite impressed."

"I'm not just a pretty face, you know," said Noah.

"OK! If we ever get back home, will you help me to become a babe magnet?"

"Er... let's take things one step at a time, shall we?" advised Noah. "The new you isn't going to happen overnight."

"How far can you see without glasses, John?" enquired the American.

"To the end of my nose. After that, everything becomes a colossal blur. I'm already on minus five dioptres and sinking fast."

Jamie came over, his hair still damp from the shower. "Whiskers and Babooshka aren't in and I've only seen the hairy man on site this morning."

"Is the stove working?" asked John.

Jamie gave him a look. "If you mean, have I made up the fire, yes."

The dormitory door slammed and a fur-clad Sister Hopkins stood before them with her entourage of one.

"Why are you not ready for your inspection?" she shouted, while beside her Yuri Semyonovich Bakaleinikoff beat the palm of his free hand with the baton.

The boys scurried to their beds and stood more or less to attention. It was noticeable to everyone that Valery Fyodorovich Khrennikov wasn't present either.

Madam DeVeal pointed at Michael and Dennis. "Get dressed and go to the kitchen now. I want breakfast over and done with in good time this morning."

The two boys looked at each other like a pair of startled rabbits then sat on their respective beds and began to pull on their socks.

"Sister," called Noah, "where is everyone this morning? Has rain stopped play?"

"Did I give you permission to speak?"

"No, Sister."

"Then keep your mouth shut."

"Very sorry, Sister," whined Noah.

Madam DeVeal drew herself up to her full height of five foot five. "After breakfast you will all assemble in the compound. Today you will start to earn your keep. The bridge over the river has been washed away during the night, and you will help to restore it."

***

A bedraggled line of eight boys filed listlessly through the main gate towards the Gaz-66 which was parked just outside the compound. Expending little energy, Jamie lifted Dennis and Michael into the back then hoisted himself up. Yuri closed the tailgate then went round to the cab.

"So, welcome to the bridge-builders club," said John.

"That bloody cheeky cow," exclaimed Porky, "telling us that we have to start earning our keep when we've been supplying them with firewood for months."

"Say we overpower hairy man and head for freedom," suggested Robert, none too seriously.

"Good idea," said Porky. "Let's get out of this shit-hole."

"Let's get out of this shit-hole and drive straight into the river," retorted John.

"We could go the other way," said Owen.

Robert gave him a sideways look. "Isn't Siberia the other way?"

"Can't be worse than here," rejoined Porky.

"Ooo, it's too cold in Siberia," said Noah. "My little toes wouldn't stand it."

"At least we could refuse to work. Go on strike," proposed Porky.

"Remember, if the bridge isn't there we can't get supplies from Puksa," said Jamie.

"Oh! I don't like that idea," exclaimed Noah. "Having no pink sausages would take all the fun out of breakfast."

"I don't understand what we have to do," rasped Michael, patting his chest.

"There's only one thing you and your brother should be doing," declared Jamie, "staying in here out of the rain."

"Some hope that they'll allow that," said Owen.

The truck's V8 petrol engine chugged into life and they moved out onto the sodden track of hard-packed sand, gradually gathering speed, the tyres throwing up sheets of water to left and right as they entered dips.

"I can't remember crossing a bridge on this road," said Robert.

"It's not a proper bridge and this isn't a road," said Jamie, looking round at the pale faces as if he was a teacher about to begin a lesson.

"Come on then, Professor Baker, tell us what you know," scoffed John.

"Can anyone guess?" asked Jamie.

Noah smiled, remembering the time in the garage at number 41 when Alan had operated the Humber's indicator signal. "Choo, choo, choo," he mimicked, pumping his arms like pistons.

Michael and Dennis looked at each other and their faces lit up with amusement.

"Give that man a coconut," said Jamie. "This was a single track railway line."

"Noah, you're a div, even if you are right," said Porky.

"How do you know, Jamie?" asked Owen.

"My great-granddad worked on the railways and he went out to Russia in the 1960s as a member of the National Union of Railwaymen. I think it was one of the highlights of his life. He said that except for the main lines out of Moscow and Leningrad, the track beds were built mostly of sand, just like what's under us now, and some of the branches didn't go anywhere, just like this one."

"How did you guess, Noah?" enquired Robert.

"Er... I don't know. Maybe because it's straight and flat and has no side roads."

"Smart cookie," stated Robert.

"He's still a div," said Porky.

The journey ended abruptly after a mile or so, when the lorry came to a shuddering halt. They could hear the sound of rushing water. The tailgate opened and they were ushered out onto the old railway track. They lined up in front of the vehicle, looking across a three metre gap in the carriageway where, during the night, a torrent of water had swept away the rotten beams of a flat trestle bridge. These beams were now piling up in pools and eddies downstream.

On the other side of the breach, the second Gaz-66 was parked on the narrow strip of vegetation between the road and the forest. Valery Fyodorovich Khrennikov stood by, partially hidden under a black umbrella which had one broken spoke, causing the rain to gush over his left shoulder. Vasily Yegorovich Pavlov, whose short, stocky frame was emphasised by his new waterproof puffer jacket, leaned back against the radiator grille, shielding his cigarette from most of the wet in a mittened hand.

Yuri called out to his colleagues and they had a brief conversation in Russian before he clambered back into the cab and began to roll a cigarette for himself.

Michael broke into a hacking cough and Dennis soon joined in, both shivering as water soaked their hair and ran down their thin faces.

"You two, all you do is cough, cough, cough!" exclaimed Owen, without hostility.

"Sorry," gasped Michael. "I'll try to stop... won't we?" He smiled wanly at Dennis, who smiled back.

Noah called out to Valery, who was looking as miserable as they were. "Mistress Valerie, what are we supposed to be doing?"

A wry smile crossed the Russian's lips. "Watching and awaiting instruction, *Tovarisch* Marshall."

Noah lifted his chin in acknowledgement. "Do you think it would be possible to allow the twins to watch and wait for instruction inside the Gazza, Mistress? They're not very well."

The translator considered this for a few moments, spoke briefly to Vasily, then nodded his permission. Quickly, before there was a change of mind or Yuri could object, Jamie helped the two boys back onto the truck. "Keep close and stay warm," he ordered them and, once he was back out, gave Noah a pat on the back.

Shortly, a team of four Russian navvies and their foreman arrived in a lorry and immediately started to unload a stack of two-and-a-half-metre-long railway sleepers from the back.

"That's a Ural-4320 eight-cylinder diesel," said Porky, displaying his knowledge of transport vehicles once more to no one in particular.

The workmen brought out the first of two leg-angle five-metre steel girders which were to support the sleepers. They tied a rope to the leading edge then hoisted it into the vertical position, before manoeuvring it close to the divide.

The boys stood back as the girder was lowered over the breach, leaving overlaps at both ends of a metre. The process was repeated with the second girder, and then the foreman and one of the men walked easily across the gap, balancing two spades in each hand like experienced tightrope walkers.

The men put the spades down in front of the boys and went straight to the cab, where they spoke to Yuri. It was clear that the three men were on friendly terms: cigarettes were exchanged, and they laughed and joked for a short while, leaving the boys to endure the downpour.

The foreman and his worker re-crossed the girder and went into a deep conversation with Valery who eventually came to the edge of the gap, carrying the umbrella on his shoulder like a rifle.

166

"You will dig an abutment two and a half metres in breadth, point six of a metre front to back, and one hundred and fifty millimetres deep," he shouted.

"I get it, so that the bridge and the track form as level a surface as possible," said Jamie.

John pointed doubtfully at the concrete buttresses which had been constructed at some earlier date to strengthen each end of the bridge. "We're not going to be able to dig through those."

"Do your best," said Valery, after a brief consultation with the navvies. "Three of you must now cross to work on this side."

"Ooo, I don't like it!" cried Noah, looking at the others. "We'll fall in and be *drownded*."

Jamie, Robert and Owen volunteered to ford the river by way of the fifteen centimetre-wide girder, and one at a time they gingerly picked their way across. Noah turned his back and shut his eyes tight. "I can't look, tell me when!"

John waited for longer than was strictly necessary before clapping him on the shoulder. "It's all right, windy, they've made it."

Meanwhile, Valery had shaken out his umbrella and retired to the Gaz-66, joining Vasily, who was already licking a pair of roll-ups.

The boys scraped away the sand as best they could, finding the concrete some two inches below the surface. Despite the ambient temperature of only five degrees, it was hot, sticky work inside their nylon jackets, and there was the added discomfort of rainwater running down their necks, soaking their shirts and their backs.

The unaccustomed use of a spade, together with the wet conditions, soon irritated Noah's eczema and his fingers became swollen and painful. Eventually, he went to the door of the cab. "Excuse me, sire," he whined, "do you have any gloves?" He held up his hands.

Yuri wound down the window and looked at him through a haze of cigarette smoke. "Fuck off!" he said.

"Ooo!" exclaimed Noah, stepping back in surprise: surprise at the rebuff and even more surprised that it was in English.

Yuri wound the window back up and went back to smoking and reading a magazine.

By noon, it had stopped raining, the girders were in place and had been bolted into the concrete. Now it was a matter of hauling the railway sleepers one by one into position. Porky volunteered to join the boys on the other side in order to help lift the ninety-kilo weights. For the fun of it, he decided to stop halfway across the girder and gently bounce up and down, watching Noah's disquiet with a contemptuous smile.

"You're being horrid, Porky!" Noah cried and turned his back.

It took them two hours to lay the new bridge, moving fifteen sleepers into an orderly row between the two girders. Early on, one was sent crashing into the water below when they let go too soon, but they learned from that mistake. While the boys worked the navvies erected speed restriction signs of five kilometres per hour on each side. Finally the sleepers at both ends were bolted into the concrete and a pair of four-metre steel plates were laid adjacent to the girders to join them together. As soon as the last screw was in place, the navvies took off in their Ural-4320, driving a straight course in reverse towards Puksa.

Valery Fyodorovich Khrennikov walked nonchalantly across the bridge, carrying his folded umbrella. "I shall accompany you and Yuri Semyonovich Bakaleinikoff in testing your bridge- building skills," he said. "Will you now please get into this vehicle?"

Noah held his hands out to the Russian. "Look at my poorly paws, Mistress."

Valery frowned. "Why are your fingers in such a mess, *Tovarisch* Marshall? Does not the good Sister see to your chiropody?"

Noah looked at his cracked and broken fingernails and scaly red knuckles, then at the Russian as if questioning his

168

sanity. "I don't think Madam DeVeal would touch me with a barge pole."

A bellow came from inside the cab and the windscreen got a thump.

"I believe Yuri Semyonovich Bakaleinikoff wishes us to get aboard," said Valery blandly.

"Must have got out of the wrong side of the bed today," said John.

"He gets out that side every day," retorted Porky.

They climbed into the back, finding the twins huddled together asleep under a piece of tarpaulin which they had discovered beneath the bench seat.

"Aah," said Noah, "two little angels."

The Gazza moved forward slowly and they felt the bump as the front tyres met the first sleeper, which was four inches higher than the road surface. There was just under three inches of bridge to spare on each side.

Once the railway sleepers were cleared, they sped off down the track until they found a suitable turning point, and then the procedure was repeated at the head of the bridge on the return journey. When they got back to the encampment the other Gazza was already parked up. It was nearly dusk and they had not eaten since breakfast. There was no sign of Madam DeVeal, and so the boys hung up their wet jackets on a makeshift clothesline in the kitchen and made for the showers, which stayed hot for a good five minutes. The twins were then ordered back to the kitchen to prepare their evening meal while the rest went to the dormitory to relax or sleep off the effects of their labours.

***

42: Wednesday, 9th October. 11.30 a.m. MSK, Arkhangelsk Oblast, the forest.

<u>ROBERT</u>

Noah was in trouble again this morning. Straight after breakfast he was summoned to the medical room, and the next thing we knew, he was being frogmarched to the sin-bin in the compound. I hope he's OK. It's not raining today but it's a lot colder. If he's not out when I get back, I will make such a ruckus.

I'm with Owen in the woods, which means I'm doing all the work. It's not his fault and it's my own choice. After his brother's accident, he just can't deal with axes and saws. Even watching me terrifies him. He doesn't make a noise, but he starts to shake and even his knees knock together. If he was at home, he would be sent for psychiatric counselling. Not unnaturally, the more I see of his reaction the more nervous I become and therefore the more likely I am to have an accident. So I suggested he go to reconnoitre a good spot for next time we're out – not a brilliant excuse to get him as far away from me as possible, but he accepted it without comment.

I've cut down a pine – it was practically dead anyway – and stripped off the side branches and crown. Now I've got to saw it in half to make it a manageable weight to carry, which means two trips up to the track. I expect most of it will end up in someone's stove in Puksa.

"You've got a boyfriend back home, haven't you?"

The traumatic part is over and he's back, right on cue. I signal for him to grab the narrower end of the trunk, which he does.

"Yes, his name's Jack."

"Is he ginger like you?"

"No, he's dark, though his skin is pale, almost translucent."

"Ugh! You mean you can see his veins?"

"No, it just appears that way. My mom said it was like porcelain."

"I thought your mum hated gays."

"It was before she knew."

"If I had a boyfriend I would expect him to be trying to get me out of here."

I'm not sure what he means by that. Is it just wishful thinking on his part, or is he inferring that Jack isn't a good boyfriend because he hasn't dashed to my rescue on a milk-white charger? Either way, I don't reply and we carry the trunk for the rest of the way in silence.

Now we're tramping back through the dead and dying undergrowth to get the other half. I just hope we can remember where we left it. The ground is absolutely saturated from the rain and water bubbles up around our boots at every step.

"If we're still here at the end of the month, I'm going to run away," he says.

"Where to?"

"Anywhere! I can't stand this place. I have to get out."

I don't know what to say to him. I suppose we're all near the end of our tethers, but Owen may be well past his. I suppose I ought to discourage him because at the beginning of November it'll be too cold to get very far outside. Even this early in October, on most days there is a chill in the air, and the nights can be frosty.

"You need to think long and hard about that."

He looks at me. "Don't you want to get away too?"

"More than anything, but I want to live to be able to tell people what sort of hell this place has been." I kind of just made that up on the spur of the moment. It sounds OK, but I'm really scared they'll send me back to the prison hospital in Puksa for more 'treatment'. If that looks like it's going to happen, I may have the same notion as Owen.

***

171

When we get back, Noah is out of the cage and looking more cheerful than at any time since the news about his dad. Not only that, he's in the kitchen sharing a glass of tea with Babooshka, the little creeper.

"So, while we've been working, you've been lazing."

"Oh, Robert, don't scold me," he says and his full lips break into a smile. "I've got something to show you."

John Price and the twins, who have just taken the bread out of the oven, join us and we go upstairs to the dormitory where Owen and Porky are already lying on their beds. Noah takes us to his corner and feels under the pillow.

"Look what was left for me by the good fairy," he says and holds up a pair of nail clippers.

"Wow!" I say not at all sarcastically.

"What, who, how?" says John, as impressed as if it were a new iPhone.

"Can I borrow them sometime?" asks Owen, like a polite little English boy.

"They're to share," says Noah seriously. "Our dad was really pleased once at Christmas-time when we got a pair of these out of a Lidl cracker. *Crackin' value,* he said. That was one of his little jokes. I used to love Christmases with our dad, even though it was just the two of us..."

The twins, like two miniature skeletons – though I can't talk, being all skin and bone myself – look at each other and splutter and smile, then clamber onto the bed, one each side of Noah. "Mind your germs on me!" he shrieks and they giggle and snuggle up to him.

Jamie comes in and puts two halves of a freshly cut pine log into the stove. "At least that's one they won't be stealing," he says, then looks round at us. "What's going on?"

"Noah's going to tell us a story about his morning's adventure," I say.

"It's even got a happy ending," adds Porky.

"Come and park your muscles next to me, Jamie," calls Noah, batting his eyelids at him like the flirt he is. "Make room, twins..."

***

43: Wednesday, 9th October. 2 p.m. Arkhangelsk Oblast, Gosudarstvennyi Meditsinskii Institut (gomoseksualizm).

NOAH

When I got to the medical room, I found Madam DeVeal in full starched white uniform with a nurse's cap parked on top of her head. The big boss, Ivan the Terrible, was there too and standing in the corner with a real hangdog expression on his face was Mistress Valerie.

Straight away she starts on at me, telling me that my homosexual perversions had stunted my growth and made me into the mongrel I am. I wanted to say 'woof, woof, bitch' but I thought better of it as Ivan was there. Meanwhile, my little mind was wondering what all this was about because I couldn't think of anything I'd done particularly wrong, and thought they might be planning to send me away for 'treatment'. Which if they did, I was going to throw the biggest hissy fit they'd ever seen.

Madam brings her face so close to mine I can smell her hairspray. "Did you ask permission for Dennis and Michael Shane to be excused from work yesterday, and was it granted – against my express orders?"

So that's why the Mistress is here looking so miserable. Madam wants her pound of flesh by having him hauled over the coals by Ivan for disobedience, and maybe even hankers after a pound and a half by getting him sacked. Two ways to go here: drop Mistress V. right in it, or try to think up some lie to thwart Nursey's dastardly plan. It occurs to me that the snake in the grass in all this is Yuri Semyonovich Bakaleinikoff, hairy man, who must have grassed on his mates. And lo! I have a revelation as to why Madam is able to disappear from the compound with comparative ease and why Yurine has suddenly developed a smattering of English. They must be whispering sweet nothings to each other in the boudoir. Yuk, the thought of it!

"Ooo, no Sister. I did ask Mr Yuri Guard if he had a pair of gloves hanging about to protect my poor little fingers from all that spade work..." I hold up my red and scaly hands with the cracked and peeling talons. "But he told me to fuck off, in English! Then he blew cigarette smoke in my face and suggested, if I wanted gloves, to ask the navvies if they had any spares. Strange, isn't it, Sister, that the macho Russian men were all wearing hats and gloves, and all the pussy Brit homos had to work in the rain without any protection?"

I'm just getting into my stride with my lies, when Ivan makes a surprise interjection in his basic English.

"Where are your winter clothings?" he asks.

"We've got boots, trousers and jackets, but no hats or gloves, sire," I say in my most grovelling voice.

He nods slowly and takes a notebook out of the top pocket of his uniform and pencils in a little note to himself. Then he turns to Madam. "Do you have any more questions for this boy, Sister Hopkins?"

She stares at him as if he's just belched garlic breath on her. "I most certainly do! This homosexual is a born liar, and we must tease out the truth about this flagrant violation of my orders."

Madam isn't going to let it go so easily. Damn! I glance at Mistress V in the corner, who is still in the slough of despond, and I imagine him with a big dunce's cap on.

"I know you are an incorrigible, conniving, little pansy, always stirring up unrest and at the centre of every disorder." She wags her finger at me. "You will tell me how those two boys managed to evade work by sleeping in the back of the lorry, or you will spend the rest of the day and night in solitary."

Out of the corner of my eye, I catch the Mistress's look of consternation. He thinks I'm going to fold.

"I don't know, Sister Hopkins, really I don't. My hands were so sore, I asked the foreman if there were any spare gloves, and when he said no, I went to each of the workmen in turn and offered them a BJ if they lent me their gloves. But none of them would because they're all macho Russian men who don't accept BJs from little English homo boys..."

Madam has gone red and I think she's going to blow a gasket. Meanwhile, Mistress Valerie's mood has suddenly improved and he's trying not to laugh.

"What is this BJ?" asks Ivan, who obviously only has a grasp of formal English.

Madam shakes her head, as if she either doesn't know or is too shocked to say. Personally, I'm sure she's more familiar with BJs than she is with nursing, probably from experience with old businessmen in hotel bedrooms. He turns to Mistress Valerie and they have a short conversation in Russian, after which I see a glimmer of a smile on his usually impassive Siberian lips.

"I have heard enough," he says to me. "You will spend three hours in the cooler." And I'm quick-marched out before Madam can react. And I feel quite victorious, happy and glorious, just like a queen should.

And that is why, dear audience, we now have a box full of assorted hats and gloves in the rest room, courtesy of Ivan the Terrible, and a pair of nail clippers from a grateful Mistress Valerie...

***

44: Sunday, 13th October. 6.30 a.m. MSK, Arkhangelsk Oblast, Gosudarstvennyi Meditsinskii Institut (gomoseksualizm).

ROBERT

The electricity has gone off downstairs and John Price and Porky Eagleton are on a mission to investigate with our lamp. That means that Noah, Jamie and Owen are standing around in the showers waiting for hot water and the light to come back on, while the twins are in the kitchen, trying to stoke up the fire with Babooshka by candlelight. Meantime, here I am, standing in the dark at the window on my lonesome, which is a pity because I'm watching something interesting.

When Noah told us that he thought Madam DeVeal and Yuri the guard were 'intimate', as he put it, I thought it was just another of his gossips which he does to amuse us. Now, it seems that he was right because they've just come in through the compound gate, she in her furs and him being very attentive. They probably think they're safe from prying eyes, but the sky is clear and there's a frost on the ground so, even though it's not quite dawn, there's light enough to see them by.

"Told you!" squeals Noah, creeping up behind me and making me jump.

"Hush up or they'll hear us."

Noah peers down into the yard, following their progress towards the front door.

"She's half-cut," he says.

"Meaning?"

"She's been at the vodka and limes. Look at her – she's been out on the tiles and can't put one stiletto in front of the other."

"We'll soon know; they'll be up shortly."

Noah turns as the room is suddenly bathed in light. "Ooo, the lady with the lamp," he says.

"Watch it!" warns John Price, who's wearing only a pair of boxer shorts.

"You weren't outside dressed like that, were you?" I ask.

"I had a quick shower to warm me up," he replies.

"Was it the circuit-breaker?"

John hangs the lamp from its hook near the stove, then gives me a derisive look. "Circuit-breaker! This is feudal Russia, man. There's a Second World War diesel engine outback housed in a little shed, but it's been converted to run off gas produced from our logs. The gasifier is under an awning next to it, and pipes run from that into the shed. Whiskers is in charge of the whole contraption and, reading between the lines, I don't think he's been keeping it up to scratch. He showed us one of the pipes, which was choked with black tar. It's OK for now, though..."

He grabs Noah and puts him in a headlock. "Who are you calling a lady?"

"Oh, John, don't! Give me a cuddle instead."

"Say you're sorry, then."

"I'm sorry, John, for calling you a ladyboy, when everyone knows you're a virile hunk of manliness with a lovely wedge which I've currently got a big close-up of. Can I stroke it, please?"

John scoops Noah up, takes him over to his bed and drops him onto the duvet. "You're a wanton strumpet, Marshall," he says. "And either you're a lot heavier than you look, or I've become a seven-stone weakling."

Noah puts his hands behind his head and I know he's about to spin a yarn. "Ooo, John, don't you think that 'strumpet' would be a good name for a toasted crumpet with butter and strawberry jam? I'd love one now, wouldn't you?"

John laughs and sits down on the bed next to him. I don't know what they're on about.

"Robert, do they have toasted crumpets in America?"

"Er, crumpets? Not that I know of..."

"They're like round spongy pieces of bread," explains John, which doesn't help my understanding, and sounds like something of an acquired taste.

Noah's face lights up. "Our dad used to take the grill off the gas fire and we'd sit round on a winter's evening and he'd have this three-pronged fork made of brass, which must have been his dad's, and he'd toast the crumpets while I was in charge of the spreading, and we'd eat them on trays with mugs of tea..."

There's a noise outside the door and it signals the end of our reminiscing and the arrival of the others, closely followed by Valery Fyodorovich Khrennikov and Vasily Yegorovich Pavlov. Noah gives me a *I told you* so look.

"Please to stand by your beds, gentlemen. I have to give you your work routine for today, which is somewhat different."

"Excuse me, Mistress, is Madam DeVeal indisposed again?" asks Noah.

"*Tovarisch* Marshall, I have no time this morning for your English japes. There is a busy day ahead for all of us..."

I decide to add my two cents' worth. "Valery, is it true that Sister Hopkins is absent from work due to an over-consumption of alcohol?"

I notice that once I had asked my question all eyes turned from me back to our Russian friend as if it were a game of slow-motion tennis.

"This question is not in order, *Tovarisch* Crittenden. If you wish to make complaints you must take it up with the appropriate authority."

"Being?"

"Professor Igor Zaronovich Rozhdestvensky is the ultimate authority in the institute."

"Who we never see any more," said John.

"Gentlemen, this is not getting us past first base, and I have more than is usual to relate."

"Oh go on then, Mistress, we know you're not the organ grinder."

I wonder sometimes how Noah gets away with half the things he says to Valery. Maybe it's because they share a similar sense of humour.

Our translator knots his brow and unfolds a sheet of paper, scanning it quickly to remind himself of what he must tell us. He seems to be in a quandary, as if he doesn't know exactly what to say, though his English is almost as good as ours. I feel sorry for him sometimes because he obviously studies hard and ought to have a proper job where his talent would be appreciated.

"I think you should be seated for this," he begins.

I notice Porky and Owen exchange hopeful glances, as if they think that the paper is about going home. I have no such expectations. Michael and Dennis Shane sidle over to Noah's bed and clamber up beside him.

"Shape up, twins," he says, and draws the duvet around all three of them. They seem to respond to Noah in a way they don't to anyone else. I figure he somehow reminds them of one of their dads.

Valery clears phlegm from his throat, which I hope won't start the twins off. "At midnight last night, the borders to the West were reopened and vehicles were allowed to enter and exit at the usual checkpoints, and civilian planes were able once more to fly through Russian airspace..."

This is in itself news to us. We look at each other, mystified.

"...Tomorrow the funeral service for the Right Reverend Joseph Akinola of the Baptist fellowship of Nigeria and his two Sisters of Charity will be held at the site of the Church of the Transfiguration. The interdenominational service will be led by Metropolitan Grigoriy of the Arkhangelsk Oblast Holy Russian Church. In attendance will be Dr Rafael Uduaghan of the Nigerian Ministry of Culture, Tourism and National Orientation, and a lay reader in the Anglican Communion. The mourners will be made up of members of the Reverend's family, and officials of the Nigerian and Russian governments and the Puksa Prison Service."

Valery pauses and says something to Vasily in Russian which makes him shrug his shoulders.

"Why are we being told this?" asks John.

"*Tovarisch* Price, I'm sure all will become clear shortly."

"Oh, twins, stop orming about!" cries Noah, and he adds with a smile, "or I'll tan your hides!"

At least I know what that phrase means and so do the boys because they grin at each other and then snuggle in closer to their 'dad'.

Valery rustles his paper. "If I may continue, gentlemen. Tomorrow, as a mark of respect for the dead and because most of the staff here will be required to attend the obsequies, this facility will be closed for the day and therefore you will be

179

confined to this dormitory for thirty-four hours from eight o'clock tonight to six o'clock on Tuesday morning."

"No food or water?" complains Porky.

"Do we piss and shit out of the window?" questions Jamie.

"Eduard Andreevitch and Galina Ivanovna Svetlanov will be on duty as usual, along with two members of the Security Service. They will cater to your toiletry needs and provide you with sufficient nutrition."

It's not often we hear Whiskers and Babooshka referred to by their proper names.

"Is that it?" asks Owen.

"No, *Tovarisch* Frost, because I haven't given you today's itinerary." Valery clears his throat again. "Your work today will consist of clearing the site of the Church of the Transfiguration and making it presentable for the service on Monday. The remains of the dead will be sorted by you under the supervision of forensic anthropologist, Professor Alexander Vasilyevich Primakov of the FSB. Members of the Security Service will be in attendance to see that the job is done to the professor's satisfaction."

"No way!" shouts Porky.

"You can't make us," exclaims Owen.

"This isn't work authorised by the Puksa authorities; this is a federal matter," explains Valery. "The Russian government has had to send its profound regrets to the president of Nigeria for the death of three of its respected citizens by a criminal act perpetrated by someone who was supposedly in the custody of the authorities."

"And we get handed the dirty work," I say.

"Surely the twins won't be made to do it?" Noah asks in an unusually sombre voice.

"All the inmates of this facility will attend," responds Valery, and carefully reads his notes before continuing. "It is now over a fortnight since the fire and therefore there will probably be little left but bones, which may be scattered. Those of the Reverend and the two Sisters will be collected and placed in coffins ready for the service on Monday and subsequent transport to their home country, whereas what remains of the two boys will be bagged up and sent for disposal at the prison. The authorities in Nigeria insist that there must be no contamination, otherwise they fear a demon might be unleashed to corrupt the souls of their departed."

A chill silence has descended on the room. If I'm not mistaken, our translator rolls his eyes, then puts the paper away and once more speaks in Russian to Vasily, who responds with a palms-up gesture and a frown.

"Thank you for listening, gentlemen. You will assemble in the courtyard at nine thirty, from where you will be transported to the site in one of our vehicles. Until then you have free time to enjoy your breakfast and maybe have an extra hour's sleep."

***

45: Monday, 14th October. 11 a.m. MSK, Arkhangelsk Oblast, Gosudarstvennyi Meditsinskii Institut (gomoseksualizm).

NOAH

So here we are, locked in our dormitory while outside in the courtyard two goons from the Russian equivalent of the FBI are looking after our welfare – if standing around, smoking and laughing can be called looking after our welfare. Their laughter is probably aimed at us, 'the Brit gays', as one of them called us earlier, which appeared to be the limit of his English. They're carrying AN-94 assault rifles, not batons. How do I happen to know that? Because Jamie Baker is a fan of the *Call of Duty* franchise and when he first caught sight of one earlier, his tongue was practically hanging out, so desperate was he to actually touch the real thing.

I asked Jamie why straight boys like to fondle something which is so obviously a penis in disguise, and he told me that a little bottom like me wouldn't understand, and to ask my top when next I see him. I guess he was referring to my Cutie Pie, who I am sure, like yours truly, has never considered his preferential position, having not had the opportunity to test same.

We've all crowded at the window, because a helicopter has just flown over so low and so loud that it rattled the tin roof. It's making its way towards the site of the Church of the Transfiguration. Oh! And there's another. I put my hands over my ears. They've both got red stars on the sides, and Mr Call of Duty decides they're Russian military helicopters. I have a sneaking hope that they'll collide in a massive fireball over the assembled guests from Puksa, including Madam DeVeal and Yurine, but I'll have to exclude Mistress Val and Vaseline from the conflag – because I've sort of got to like them.

To be honest, yesterday wasn't as bad as I had expected, and I put that down partly to Mr Clever himself, John Price. At breakfast, John who can now talk to us all without blushing, took us aside and said that we ought to treat this piece of nastiness as though we're all members of CSI. That's Crime Scene Investigation, for the uninitiated. It so happens that he's really into the programme – the Las Vegas one, that is – and owns the first ten series on Blu-ray. Although I haven't watched it, I get the idea, and was reminded of Julie Andrews singing 'A Spoonful of Sugar' in *Mary Poppins*, which if truth be told is more my style than *CSI*.

At nine thirty we were assembled in the yard. There was no sign of any of our Puksa crew, just some glum police types complete with rifles, flak jackets and helmets. Goodness knows what they thought we were going to do. The weather was dull, like our mood, but the temperature had climbed to a heady six degrees after an overnight frost. They marched us out to the Gaz-66 and we were driven through the forest to the sloping field where the church stood. It was our first view since the fire, and the skyline looked empty.

Near to the pile of ash, a grey oblong marquee had been pitched, west to east, which would be used for the service. It even looked like a little church because it had windows and a porch, and there were flags at each corner.

Among the few paramilitary types who were milling around doing very little, Porky pointed out a road roller which was flattening out the area surrounding the tent, and levelling the track up to it.

"It's a DU-54," he said in the sort of awe-inspired voice that a normal person would reserve for a beautiful sunset or something, not a dirty yellow box that looked like an oversized Lego toy.

The eight of us were taken inside the west door of the mini-church. There was already an altar affair at the east end covered in a gold and white cloth with candlesticks, and three rows of chairs that had been set out on both sides of a central aisle, which was laid with a long piece of brown carpet. A trio of open coffins had been mounted on trestles in front of the altar and there was a plastic bin, complete with bag. We all knew what that was for.

The professor was a plain and fleshy man with thinning brown hair, easily recognisable because he was the only one wearing an ordinary suit and tie. As soon as we came close, he stopped talking to this military type (with one of those ridiculous oversized peak caps) and turned to us, motioning for us to sit.

"I am Professor Primakov. You will sort through the ash for any bone or tissue that looks human and bring it to me. I shall decide if it should reside in one of the coffins or is waste material. You will place it in the receptacle that I choose. You will work methodically in pairs over one-quarter of the total site area which has been marked out for you. If you find any recognisably large portion of a human body, alert Lieutenant Gergiev here. He does not speak English and so you will signal to him. Before you begin, take a pair of polyurethane gloves from the box at the entrance. You have one hour to complete the task."

That was the theory. The practice was altogether more rough and ready, and more influenced by someone in government deciding that a bunch of schoolboys should do the work as a punishment rather than by scientific method. I took Michael as my partner in the front right sector and, between coughs, he kept asking me what we were doing. *Do your best* was my standard reply. Fortunately for his health, the ash was damp and so there wasn't much dust – but we still got filthy. Our finds were all consigned to the bin, as were Robert and Dennis's, who were working to our rear.

Owen and Porky found the chain that Dwain had used to seal the front doors, but that's about all. I think they were quite disappointed, because it was John and Jamie who came up with the real finds. The twisted remains of the examination table that I had seen through the window was their first discovery. Then they found two skulls which the professor decided were those of the Reverend Joe and one of his Sisters of Charity, followed by some whole portions of ribs and long bones, as our expert called them, which were duly consigned to their coffins. One recognisably boy- sized femur was sent to the rubbish.

By the end of the hour Professor Primakov seemed wholly satisfied and even smiled once. The only downside for John 'Gil' Price was that he took off his glasses to examine what he thought was a scapula – that's a shoulder blade to me and you – then couldn't find them until he trod on them, breaking off one of the arms and scratching the lenses. Although the scratching was mostly down to him trying to clean them then and there. Did I say he was clever?

I look at him now in our dormitory and he smiles back at me through foggy glass, the arm fastened on by wire, courtesy of Whiskers, which makes them lop-sided. And I know that if he was back at school in Swanford it would be, *Who's the speccy four-eyed geek freak with the monster zits?* But he's just a lovely sweetheart to me.

"Do you want to know a secret?" he asks.

Of course I want to know a secret; I'm gay!

"Oh; go on then, John," I reply and we sit down on my bed and suddenly all the others have gathered round us too.

Dennis and Michael smile at each other and then at me, and I see their tired little mugs because they were coughing for most of the night, and pat the bed so that they can come and snuggle up. Then I notice that every one of the seven faces about me is haggard and drawn with blue circles around the eyes, and I wonder how much longer we can keep this up.

"I found part of Ryan's skull," begins John and we all lean in to hear. "I guessed it was his because it had that chipped front tooth."

"Gruesome," says Porky.

The rest of us nod and he continues.

"I didn't show it to the professor, but kept it back until one of us found something which I was certain belonged to the Reverend Joe. Then Jamie happened on that gold medallion he wore, though the chain had mostly melted away, so I begged it off him.

"The professor was pleased when I told him what it was, and told me to put it in the coffin. That was when I slipped in Ryan's skull fragment with the Reverend's own."

"He's a smart boy," says Jamie.

I can see by Owen's expression that he doesn't get it, so I decide to put a bit more flesh on the bone, if you'll pardon the tasteless reference. "Let's hope Holy Joe's afterlife is plagued by Ryan's gay demon, then."

"Yeh!" exclaims Owen, who has finally seen the light.

Porky's face goes all mystical and I wonder what profundity he's going to come up with.

"I wish I could have had a go on that DU-54 road roller," he says.

For once words fail me.

Meanwhile, the twins have fallen asleep, leaning against me and John, and I think it would be best for their breathing if they slept in a sitting position at night instead of lying completely flat.

**

185

JACK

The school library appeared deserted when Jack entered, though he did check around all of the shelves to make sure before making his way to the bank of computer terminals that occupied the central part of the space. Shortly, a tall thin girl on platform shoes entered and made a bee-line for him.

"What are you doing here, Moseley? I'm supposed to be having a quiet liaise with Maxxy, not a fucking homo."

"Sorry; doing a little subterfuge."

"You mean all that Cluedo shite about Miss Simpkins meeting at the computer desks in the library with the candlestick was all bollocks?"

"Yes... except there was never any candlestick. I need you to do me a favour."

"Spill, Moseley, and no crap."

"The day after tomorrow I'm going to Russia to rescue Robert and Noah."

Unusually, this gave Mandy Simpkins pause, as she deliberated over the news. "So that's what your arch-enemy was talking about?"

"What?" said Jack, now bemused himself.

"If you want to play James Bond, Moseley, you've got to be up to speed, not dreaming about your lover boy."

"But no one knows about this except the people involved, and now you and Max."

"So why did I accidentally on purpose overhear Ernst 'Stavro' Masefield and his lovely new girlfriend Joanna Lively talking in the Jewel last Thursday about a queers' trip to Europe?"

Jack fell back into one of the chairs and began to think over the implications of what he had been told. "How much do you think he knows?"

Mandy parked herself on the desk and looked down at him. "As you know, Masefield is not only a homophobic cunt, he's also full of himself, especially now he's top of the class. So he'll never let truth get in the way of a good story when wanting to impress his kitten."

"You mean he doesn't know much."

"What he knows, what he thinks he knows, and what he pretends to know are three different pieces on the chessboard."

"And what do you think he knows?"

"Exactly what I said – no less and certainly no more."

"So not much, but where did he get even that amount of information from?"

"Do you want my guess?"

"Of course! Give your guesses to me."

"PC Daddy Masefield, which should make you worry more than that gob-shite knowing."

Jack felt a constriction in his throat. "It does. I wonder if they'll try to stop us?"

"If they were going to stop you, they could have already done it."

"Mum and Dad had a visit from the council about me a month ago."

"I hope they gave the neo-Nazis short shrift."

"They did, but it scared the shit out of them."

Mandy lowered herself into the chair next to Jack and spoke in what, for her, was almost a whisper. "Come on then, Tom Cruise, tell me who's going on this mission impossible and why your boyfriend has ended up in a gulag behind the Iron Curtain."

"Me, LB, Justin Walker, Alan Henderson and ... Ms Lane."

"Fuckin' Nora! That's not mission impossible, that's mission insanity." Mandy stared at Jack for several long seconds, then shook her head. "You're serious, aren't you?"

"Yup, we've been planning for two months."

"I can just about get you and the footballers, but not Alan 'thick as shit' Henderson."

"Like Stewy, there's more to Alan than meets the eye. He also happens to be Noah's boyfriend, though he won't admit it."

"'Kin' hell!" exclaimed Mandy. "This is as mad as it gets."

"We're pretending to be a school party on a cultural tour. We're travelling in a 1954 Humber Pullman limo." Jack pulled out a photograph.

The girl chortled. "This is brilliant, Moseley, a one hundred per cent nut job. And Ms Lane is driving this heap, is she?"

"Actually we have a co-driver and chief mechanic in Alan Henderson. Frankly, he's a genius when it comes to cars, otherwise he's really strange."

Mandy let out a peal of laughter. "Jesus wept, you're all bloody strange!" She wiped her eyes on a tissue pulled from the depths of her knitted handbag. "So how did your boyfriend end up in Russia?"

"His parents sent him for a 'gay cure'. Noah and a group of other boys have been sent too."

"And what part do you want me to play in this soap opera?"

"I need us to conspire to get me suspended until half-term."

"Now I know why you've been keeping your powder dry since we got back to this dump. You're obviously not as stupid as everyone thinks, Moseley."

"Thanks Mandy, I'll take that in the spirit it was meant."

***

The biology laboratory, or bio lab as it was better known, smelled of damp straw and formaldehyde. The damp straw was from a row of cages containing doomed rodents that needed fresh bedding, and the formaldehyde percolated into the air from jars of pickled animal parts which were stored out of sight, having been preserved in a bygone age when health and safety was only a gleam in a bureaucrat's eye.

Class 5S trooped in and sat on stools at their benches, waiting for their teacher Todd Crozier to enter from the door by the side of the whiteboard. Already known as Crazier or Sweeney, Todd was one of the new intake of teachers brought in to give the school a more wholesome Christian feel. Most pupils took out pens and notepads in anticipation, but Jack didn't bother. He was sitting next to Stewart four rows and two benches back, opposite Max and Mandy. All were eyeing each other silently, while the rest of the class chatted quietly.

At twenty minutes past eleven Todd entered, carrying a stack of exercise books which he deposited on his desk. "Good morning, class, will you please stand." Their teacher began to bow his head, then noticed that one pupil was still sitting. "Jack Moseley, I asked you to stand."

"Sorry sir, my legs are feeling weak today."

"It's true, sir," said Stewart. "His legs have been weak all morning."

"My legs are also weak," said Max, falling onto his stool.

At this, half the class gave out a sigh and collapsed onto their seats.

Todd was clearly uncertain about how to handle this, for Class 5S had been positively meek and mild in their first three weeks of teaching. He stroked his Van Dyke beard. "I shall pray for you all," he said and bowed his head.

The class settled and Todd picked up the exercise book on top of the pile. "I have marked your work following on from our discussion on the various theories of how the Earth was created, and the quality of essays varied quite a lot." He held the exercise book aloft. "Only one student fully appreciated the difference between creationism and the theory of intelligent design. Charles Masefield – an outstanding piece of work."

"Thank you, sir," said Charlie, who now sat on the front bench nearest the teacher.

The books were given out in order of their merit and little more was said until Todd came to the bottom four books in the pile.

"Mandy Simpkins, I could only give you a C plus. You explain the Darwin theory very well, but then you say very little about the alternative theories."

"I thought I put it quite clearly," said Mandy. "Intelligent design rests on the belief in a non-existent supreme being, just the same as Biblical creationism. It's merely pseudo-science that's been concocted by right-wing, reactionary, religious zealots in America to muddy the water of true scientific discourse."

"But it does appeal to the ignorant redneck, Mandy, so it must have merit," said Jack.

"Moseley, if you have something to say, you will show this class politeness by putting up your hand and waiting to be called," said Todd. "I gave your work a fail."

Jack put up his hand. "Why, sir?" he asked without waiting to be acknowledged.

"Because after your three pages of average work on Darwin's theory, you left two sides with no writing except for headings and the date at the bottom."

"But sir, you asked for a scientific discussion on creationism and intelligent design and so I just left the pages blank because you can't have a scientific discussion on non-science, or has that logic escaped you?"

"You're becoming impertinent, Moseley. Watch your step."

"I wish I'd thought of that, Jack," said Max. "It would have saved me writing so much clap-trap."

"The class will now be silent!" said Todd.

"Excuse me, sir," called Jack. "Did you say you had a degree from the Grace University in Nebraska... or was that the disGrace University in Narnia?"

"Nice one," murmured Max.

"Moseley, you will leave this class and report to the headmaster."

"What about my weak legs, sir?" answered Jack, "perhaps you'd like to carry me?" He winked at Todd and smiled.

***

47: Tuesday, 22nd October. 2.30 p.m. Swanford Community School.

PAM

"You're not being very cooperative, Mrs Moseley," said the headmaster. "This isn't the first time your son has been in trouble."

"When I believe my son has done something wrong then I'll be cooperative, headmaster. As it is, I don't think he's getting the quality of education he deserves."

"I admit to everything," said Jack. "The man has no right to be teaching science, or any other subject for that matter. If I have to go back to his class, I'll call him a duffer to his face."

"With that attitude, I have no alternative but to suspend your son in the first instance for the statutory five days. I'm sure the board of governors will want to review the case, and it is certain that Jack will not be allowed back in this school unless he tenders a written apology and promises to abide by the school rules in relation to respecting members of staff."

"But I don't respect him, nor that jumped-up Reverend from some backwards university in Nigeria who's supposed to be our equality counsellor but who behaves more like a demented Witchfinder General."

"I will take legal action unless you reverse your decision," said Pam. "This school has become the laughing stock of the town."

"I don't think so, Mrs Moseley, and I hope the half-term holiday will give you and your son time to reflect. Now, I suggest you both leave the premises, or I may have to call the authorities. We shall be in touch by letter."

Pam stood up. "Well, if that's your attitude, headmaster, goodbye. You will be hearing from our solicitor. Come, Jack!"

***

"Well, you got what you wanted," said Pam, changing into fourth gear for the short journey up Leighton Lane.

"Thanks Mum, an Oscar-winning performance."

"I'll post the letter from Dumbleton Boys' School at the weekend, explaining about your temporary transfer."

"At least I won't need the tie and blazer."

"What happens when all this is over, though, Jack? Come the end of your European jaunt, you'll have to go back to that school."

"Maybe other parents will have taken action by then. I know Mandy's mum and dad are looking to sue the governors for negligence in their appointment of suitable teachers."

"Hasn't anyone said anything to you about being gay since you got back?"

Jack shook his head. "Except a few comments from the likes of my ex-friend and religious convert, Charlie Masefield, and the other homophobes, not a word. But the three new teachers know; I can see it in their eyes when they look at me."

Pam came to a halt outside their house and switched off the ignition. "That must be a horrible feeling."

"Not really. If I was isolated it might, but I still sit with the same crowd in class and in the canteen. The thing is, we all accept these people are bozos and if anything, it's the likes of Charlie who have drawn away from the mainstream."

"Yet we get visits from social services about you. It doesn't make sense."

"It means the heads on the hydra aren't working together yet, which is all to the good. The worry will be if – or when – they get their act together. Talking of which, I think I'll pop along to Mr Ray's to tell him I won't be delivering newspapers after tomorrow, at least for a while."

192

"He'll have to get that idle son of his to do some extra shifts."

"Sandip! He'd be better off with Mikey."

"You've been talking to your little brother, haven't you, about your trip and about his stay with Nana Moseley?"

Jack took a sideways look at his mother. "Have you been trying to pump him for information?"

"We do not pump our children," said Pam. "I just need to know that you'll all be safe while we're away."

"Don't worry about LB and me. We are on an unbeatable team. You two go off and enjoy yourselves. I'm going to stay in touch with Mikey."

Pam frowned. "What are you up to now, Jack?"

"No need to be paranoid. I just mean that I'm giving him my old mobile so that I can ring him every day, just to see how things are..."

***

48: Wednesday, 23rd October. 7 a.m. MSK, Arkhangelsk Oblast, Gosudarstvennyi Meditsinskii Institut (gomoseksualizm).

NOAH

In a formless, grey, dawn light, flakes of snow fluttered past the dormitory window. Noah looked down into the compound. A thin layer of snow covered the ground, and beyond the corrugated iron walls the dark trees were covered in a shading of white. His eyes came to rest on a man, thickly clad in winter garments, wheeling a barrow towards the outside door. In the barrow was their delivery of foodstuffs, a delivery that seemed to be more meagre with each passing week. As he watched, another man came in through the gate with a larger barrow and began to load it with logs from their stack beneath the eaves of the building.

Clad only his boxers, he shivered, even though their stove was belching out heat. Morning inspection, which had been getting gradually later as the days grew shorter, was now an unprecedented thirty-five minutes overdue. After their showers, most of the others had got back into bed to keep warm.

"They're stealing our wood again," he announced.

"Don't worry; there are plenty more trees in the forest for us to cut down for them," answered John.

"And that comes from the worst lumberjack in the world," said Jamie.

"Can we not talk about that, please?" said Owen.

"Seconded," added Porky.

"Sorry," responded Jamie. "Thoughtless..."

"No worries," said Owen. "Where are they? We could all have had an extra half-hour's kip this morning."

"Why do we have to parade for her in our boxers, anyway?" enquired Porky.

"It's a bit late to ask that," answered John.

"Madam DeVeal loves gazing at our naked manly bodies," replied Noah, "especially mine."

"None of us is going to win Mr Universe in our current state," observed Jamie, when the hoots of derision had died away.

"Actually, Noah's body is the least changed of all of us," declared John.

"If he'd lost as much weight as the rest of us, he'd be just a little puddle of piddle on the floor," said Porky.

"Oi!" complained Noah.

"Did you notice that it was Babooshka who unlocked our room this morning and lit the lamp?" commented Jamie.

"I was asleep," said Noah.

Porky sat up in his bed. "Yeh, it's all right for you over in that corner. I'm right up against these two little blighters, who're wheezing and coughing like two old men every morning."

"Sorry," croaked Dennis, who had just returned from the kitchen with his brother after stoking up the fire.

"Perhaps Whiskers is ill," said John. "He must be about eighty."

The door opened and a flustered Valery Fyodorovich Khrennikov entered, followed by Vasily Yegorovich Pavlov, who had his baton tucked into his belt.

"Good morning, gentlemen. Please to stand by your beds..."

Reluctantly the boys emerged from their warm cocoons and presented themselves for inspection.

"Mistress Valerie, you're very late and we've been getting cold and hungry," chided Noah.

"*Tovarisch* Marshall, you should become hard and manly like Russian youth. If you pussy Brits think this is winter, think again."

"What is the temperature outside?" asked Jamie.

"According to the Ministry in Plesetsk, the mean temperature over the whole landward area of the Arkhangelsk Oblast at six o'clock this morning was a comfortable minus one degree Celsius."

"Has Madam DeVeal had an overdose of the sauce again?" asked Noah.

"No, Sister Hopkins is not suffering from intoxication. The reason we are some time late this morning is because the lady has been called into the police station in Puksa to make an identification." He let the words hang dramatically in the air while the boys exchanged puzzled looks.

"You may not know that a manhunt has been under way for nearly a month to find the culprit behind the arson attack which destroyed the holy Church of the Transfiguration, and in doing so murdered five people, including the most respected Nigerian clergyman, the Right Reverend Joseph Akinola, and his two Sisters of Charity..." He paused again for effect. "Last night the Puksa police, with the help of the Internal Security Service, found a person of African origin lying in an alley near the railway station. The suspect was taken into custody in a state of near collapse. Later he was found dead in his police cell. I am informed that the cause of death was choking on his own vomit due to an overdose of illegal drugs, though the body was already badly disfigured by homosexual sado-masochistic practices."

"In other words, the police tortured him to death," said Robert.

"This isn't Guantánamo Bay, *Tovarisch* Crittenden," responded Valery.

Noah felt a chill run up his spine, and not from the weather. "Dwain was only fourteen, like me."

"If the deceased is Dwain Matheson then I'm sure Sister Hopkins will be only too pleased to impart that information herself."

"Why are you telling us all this, Valery?" enquired Jamie.

"It is necessary that you are aware of what happens to people who flout the laws of the Russian Federation, *Tovarisch* Baker. We believe knowledge is power, as one of your Western activists once said."

"Knowledge to keep us in our place isn't quite the same," answered John.

"What's happened to Whiskers?" asked Owen.

"Eduard Andreevitch Svetlanov has been laid off as there are now only eight of you," replied Valery.

"He was too old to work anyway," said Porky. "He should have been pensioned off years ago."

"Russian men like to work hard and play hard – it makes for a meaningful life," answered their translator. "Do any of you pussies play the great Russian game of chess?"

Silence settled on the dormitory for a moment or two before John spoke tentatively. "Er, I do, but I always thought the game was invented in India or China."

"The Russian people have made the game our own because we are masters of strategic warfare, *Tovarisch* Price. Do you play well, or are you just lamb in sheep's clothing?"

"I was captain of the chess club in primary school..."

"What a typical dork!" laughed Owen.

Noah frowned. "Owen... don't be nasty to John."

"Being intelligent and thoughtful isn't a sign of weakness," added Robert.

"It's still tragic, though, isn't it?" said John

"What's tragic?" asked Owen.

"The six-foot, fifteen-year-old straight boy being verbally abused by one gay fourteen-year-old and then defended by another seven-stone-nothing, five foot two, effeminate fourteen-year-old gay boy."

"Oi, I'm eight stone!" exclaimed Noah. "Nearly..."

"Yeh, that makes all the difference," complained John.

"You come after work and we shall have a contest, *Tovarisch* Price, then we'll see whether you're a champ or a chav."

"Is John the chosen substitute for Whiskers now that he's no longer working here?" asked Jamie sardonically.

"*Tovarisch* Baker, I don't know what you mean..."

"They used to play behind the stove in the kitchen," squeaked Michael, and Dennis nodded.

"Ooo, I have an announcement to make," said Noah dramatically. He had edged towards the window, noticing some activity below. "Madam DeVeal and her consort Yurine have just entered the compound. And isn't she looking lovely today in her bloodstained furs..?"

"*Tovarisch* Marshall, one day you will overstep the mark and regret your interventions."

"Thank you for the warning, Mistress, but I already know that if I look at her directly I'll be turned to stone."

***

49: Thursday, 24th October. 11.30 a.m. 41 Westbury Avenue.

<u>ALAN</u>

The Moseley brothers have lifted the roof box into position on top of the Humber and I'm going to bolt it in place.

Justin's put the step ladder up for me and now he's holding it, like I'm an old man who can't manage on his own. The box I chose is shiny black to match the car, and it's about as aerodynamic as it can be, though it'll still have a drag factor on the engine. Most of our winter gear is inside, including our snow boots. Jack Moseley bought Justin and me a ushanka each: he said it was for fixing up the limo, but I think he just did it so we'd all have one. He probably thinks I'm ungrateful because I wasn't sure what I was supposed to say when he gave it to me, so I didn't say anything.

Justin made a last-minute suggestion that we fit an outside temperature gauge into the car, which I wasn't too happy about at first. But I had second thoughts and we chose one with an analogue display from Nassau Instruments. It has an external sensor which he fixed behind the radiator grille just above where the starting handle fits. The readings are from plus fifty to minus forty degrees Celsius, so it should work through any weather. Minus forty Celsius is minus forty in Fahrenheit as well, which is funny when you think about it.

An unmarked police car has been patrolling Westbury Avenue for most of the month. My brother, Stewart, first noticed it when he was out with his camera taking pictures of the trees in their autumn colours. He took a couple of photographs of it from the bushes, but the windows have such a dark tint that you can't make out who's inside. We think it's the same man that Jack and Justin had dealings with in Woolgrove Woods.

Ms Lane still hasn't arrived, which is why we're late starting out. She phoned to say that she was transporting her parakeets to her sister in Woolgrove because she couldn't trust her husband to look after them while she's away. I don't think Ms Lane trusts anything male. It doesn't really matter, though, because we're staying overnight in Harwich and catching the ferry tomorrow morning.

Justin keeps telling me that I'm not to get uptight about Ms Lane's handling of the car and to just go with the flow. That might be difficult for me, but I've promised to try. We have been out on several test drives and I've had to point out several weaknesses in her driving style, particularly using only the footbrake to slow down instead of the brake and gears. The trouble is, she's a teacher and doesn't like to be criticised.

I don't know what I'd have done if Justin hadn't been here to help me, probably given up. We did a bit of weight training last night, but he couldn't go to karate because he wanted to say goodbye to his girlfriend. I was a bit worried about going on my own, so Anne drove me over to the dojo and it was OK – in fact, more than OK because my Sensei said I might be ready to take the exam for my orange belt by Christmas. He asked me where my friend was this evening and I realised that he thinks Justin is my friend, which I was pleased about. I told him that we wouldn't be attending for a few weeks, and he told me to practise my katas and to learn the karate terms used off by heart because there's a written exam. That made me a bit nervous, because I'm not very good at exams. I could ask Justin to help me, I suppose, but he might say no.

I've grown a couple of inches since I've been living at number 41, and have started to get ridges in my stomach from the weight training. I'm not as defined as Justin and I'm still the shortest going on this trip. Even Ms Lane is taller than me, though only by an inch or so. Dan Moseley is nearly as tall as his brother now, though he's over a year younger. Justin says that at their posh school, they do PE in bare feet and Dan can hang upside down on the wall bars by his toes.

I could never do that. The toes on my left foot don't bend as well as my right since I was in the room with the flies. I haven't dreamed about that for ages now, but it still gives me the shivers to think about it.

For some reason, Jack Moseley told me there was a demonstration in London by the fags and their supporters on Sunday, but the police broke it up because the Christian Family Alliance had complained it was the Lord's day and the government said it was illegal. The Prime Minister threatened to call the army out if things got out of hand. I can't think why they'd need the army to control a few fags. Some people got tasered and others got tear-gassed. I'm glad I wasn't there. I expect the fag might have tried to get me to go if he'd been around, but he'd have a job because I wouldn't be seen dead at a faggy demo. I wonder what he's doing now in Russia. I can't imagine it really, though I bet that big snub nose is getting into other people's business when it shouldn't. I expect I'll have to sort him out when I get there and bring him back down to earth.

We're ready to go. Anne and Elspeth have come out onto the drive to see us off, though Elspeth said she can't stay out long. She's looking a bit frail and has a shawl wrapped round her shoulders against the cold wind. Alex is playing around in the front garden. I don't think he knows what's going on, but then he's just a kid. Stewart's at school and said goodbye earlier. He says the only good thing about that place at the moment is Barbara Carter. She's his first girlfriend, but Justin says that all his friends are worried that he's got her on the rebound from Charlie Masefield and his feelings will be hurt. I think Stewart's right to live in the moment and be happy while he can, because nothing lasts. I'm never going back to that school. The only way they'd make me go is at gunpoint.

Ms Lane has parked herself in the driver's seat. The first thing she did was gaze at herself in the mirror instead of checking what's behind her – as if any of us are bothered about what she looks like. I told her to remember that there's a lot more weight in the car and not to change up unless we've got enough revs. She gave me a look. Then she asked me where the GPS was, as if it was an essential item that I'd forgotten. I told her that we didn't need GPS; Dan had planned out the route and it was now in my head. In any case, where we're going there won't be coverage.

"I hope we don't get lost then," she said, "and I suppose you did bring a map just in case?"

It was my turn to give her a look. Typical sarky teacher. I'm sitting next to her and Justin's on my left while the Moseleys are in the back, behaving like they're royalty. Both sets of their parents are going on holiday to Gran Canaria while we're away. Jack called it 'a sexpedition by the Saga set' and Justin is betting that in nine months' time one or other of the families will be hearing the patter of tiny feet. Dan said his mum and dad had to buy a manual because it's been so long since they humped each other that they've forgotten how to do it. I don't think that can be true, can it?

I'm pretty sure I haven't forgotten anything, but it's too late now even if I have because we're moving out onto Westbury Avenue. There's no sign of that cop car, and Anne and Elspeth are at the gate, waving goodbye. Ms Lane's tooted the horn and the others are waving back, so I guess I ought to too...

**

50: Friday, 25th October. 11.30 a.m. *Stena Britannica* ferry, an hour and a half out from Harwich.

JUSTIN

I want to die! Another six hours of this to go... I managed to get to the toilet before I threw up the first time. That was my breakfast. Ms Lane told me to get up on deck as the fresh air would do me good. I think that was just an excuse to get me out of the cabin.

It's not as though the sea is particularly rough. A mild swell, I was told. The water is the same colour as me, greeny-blue, and there's hardly a cloud in the sky. One of the crew came out and asked me if I was *all right*. Of course I'm not *all right!* He said it with this snarky smile on his face, meaning another landlubber wuss hanging over the side on a completely calm day. I can still feel it though; the movement churning my insides, making me feel dizzy, turning me into a zombie. This little part of the deck is practically deserted. I guess every other passenger has heard of the pathetic creature who is throwing his guts up while everyone else is down below enjoying a full English breakfast.

Dan's just been out with a paper cup of water and two pills. You can guess where they ended up. He said he'd brought a packet of Stugeron in case any of us got travel-sick in the Humber because it had quite a roll on it. I hate my best friend! He laughed when I vomited his pills and water into the North Sea, and said, if I'd told him sooner, like when we were on dry land, he could have sorted me out. But I didn't know, did I? This is the first time I've been at sea, and the last as far as I'm concerned. I want to fly back, like any sensible person would.

It's now a quarter past twelve and it's the fifth time I've noticed him hovering. I hate my second best friend, Alan Henderson. He comes out on deck but never gets closer than ten yards away. Instead he stands there, nervously blowing air in and out of his cheeks as if he's trying to come to some momentous decision. If he'd only walk over, ask me how I'm feeling then go away, instead of loitering without any intent. I bet that he wishes I was a car, so he could put me to rights by adjusting my tappets or tightening my fan belt.

Oh God! It's taken him two hours, but he's just been and given me a hug, then he scurried away without saying a word. I know he's being kind and I know everything's difficult for him and I really do love him, but I still want to murder him!

It's just after three and I'm not feeling so bad now. Dan came out with two more pills an hour ago and I managed to keep them down. Not that I could face a bacon sandwich or anything, but I can walk up and down the deck a bit now, and my reflection no longer looks like death warmed up.

I'm near the prow of the ship – that's the front. It proves I'm feeling better because if I was going to hurl I'd prefer to be in the stern where it wouldn't come back and hit me in the face at warp factor ten. Ha! Ha!

We'll be docking soon, sideways on. It's a pity cars can't do that. We're sailing down the left-hand side of this wide channel between a breakwater of huge stone blocks and a kind of central reservation which is a narrow strip of nothingness. Holland is flat and sandy and I can see people flying kites on the beach in their anoraks, taking no notice of us. On the right are lots of oil storage tanks, more wind turbines and in the distance the proper docks with cranes for off-loading. It's not that different to England, though Harwich looks older and nicer.

The car's on main deck number three. I've joined the others now and they're all giving me sideways looks, but I'm past being sick. For one thing, there's nothing left in my stomach, not even the lining. Ha! Ha! This is the first time I've seen Jack since my first throw-up. At least he knew to keep out of my way. Alan wants to drive the car off the ferry, but Ms Lane insists she's going to do it to be on the safe side with the Dutch people. I think she's probably right, though I do feel more secure when Alan's behind the wheel. I think it's because he's so confident and enjoys it, whereas Ms Lane would prefer to be going off somewhere to have a crafty fag. Oh, yes, I've seen her. Not only that, but I now know why she used to use all that perfume at school.

***

We've been driving for an hour. It took us no time at all to get off the ferry and through customs. Everyone admires the car and smiles at us. I was told that the Dutch are a bit standoffish but I haven't noticed that. For one thing, they all seem to speak English, even the blokes on the docks. Imagine your average Brit speaking Dutch!

I'm in the front seat with Alan, who is sitting next to our driver and making disapproving noises every time she crunches the gears or rides the clutch or, worst of all, labours the engine by not changing down.

"Gears!" says Alan through gritted teeth.

I warned him not to overdo the criticisms. I don't know how high Ms Lane's tolerance threshold is, but she's doing OK so far. I think she's actually got a soft spot for the little guy. Getting used to the Humber's 1950s gear change must be a pain for someone like Ms Lane who only drives out of necessity. Still, once we were out of the Hook and got onto the A20 motorway and then the trans-European E30, everything became pretty plain sailing. Talking of which, after my wimpy performance on the ferry, I'm now starving hungry. Jack gave me a few squares of chocolate but that's not going to last me.

The sun has set behind us and we're going to stop soon so Alan can take over. We're on the outskirts of Rotterdam, which is Holland's second city. No one can explain to me the difference between Holland and the Netherlands – maybe there is no difference. I'm glad that Alan's taking the wheel; Ms Lane peers through the windscreen as though she can't see further than the end of the bonnet. What she'd be like driving in the dark is anybody's guess. I think she needs glasses; in fact, I think she's got a pair, but won't wear them for some reason.

Our communications officer, Jack, has just had a message from base, that's number 41. We're booked into the Chanterelle Hotel in Apeldoorn for one night. It's a small town to the north of the motorway and we should be there in less than an hour. One double for Ms Lane and two twin rooms with bath and shower for us boys. We don't like to talk about who's going to sleep with who, but we'll probably find the best combination during the trip. I think Alan wants to share with me, like we did in Harwich, though he won't say directly, it's just the way he looks. I'm happy to go along with mechanics in one room and brothers in the other. With breakfast it'll cost around 350 euros, which is about £270. I'm looking forward to the restaurant. Stewart says the food reviews are good, so here's hoping...

***

51: Saturday, 26th October. 9 a.m. Van Der Volk Hotel,
Chanterelle, Apeldoorn.

JACK

Ms Lane has been complaining that she has a bad back
because of the way she has to sit upright when she's driving
the Humber. You can't actually adjust the front seat, not even
backward and forward like you can in a modern car. She
claims it's really a leather bench designed for a male
chauffeur, with the emphasis on *male*. I notice that any
complaints about his 'precious' get the evil eye from Alan,
however well-founded they are. Ms Lane has excused herself
while we stuff ourselves from the breakfast buffet. Justin is of
the opinion that her breakfast consists of a cup of black coffee
and a smoke on the terrace. The Dutch seem to go big on
cheese, but I'm having pancakes with apples and whipped
cream.

Now that he's recovered from his bout of sea-sickness,
Justin is back to his usual good-humoured self, though he was
put off a bit when Alan said he snores like a walrus. LB
thought that was really funny, because he's always complained
about the snoring – not to mention the feet – when they've had
sleepovers, but was always flipped off. Justin gave Alan a
noogie for embarrassing him (that's a headlock and a knuckle
rub), but he did it so gently that our chief mechanic just smiled
through it. I hadn't realised what good friends they'd become.
I'm not sure I could tolerate Alan's attention to detail, to put it
politely, not that I'd be any good as assistant mechanic
anyway. Personally, I'll be happy to share with LB from now
on as he is a completely silent sleeper and someone snoring
close by would turn me into an axe murderer in no time.

Alan drove us over the border into Germany. Except
there is no border: blink and you'd miss the sign saying
Bundes-Republik Deutschland. Meanwhile Ms Lane is nursing
her lumbar region sprawled over the back seat. Fortunately
there's plenty of room, especially as LB decided to go up front

with Justin. It's a really comfortable quiet ride in the Humber. Dad said that Winston Churchill used to have one but his was full of cigar butts and empty brandy bottles.

It's just after one o'clock and we've driven into Hanover. Except for the language and driving on the right, you could be in a medium-sized town in England. We've parked up by Leibniz University, as directed by Ms Lane, who says we need to get a bit of culture while we're here. Justin asked her if we could go to the Choco Leibniz biscuit factory instead and Ms Lane retorted that a month at public school doesn't seem to have improved his intellectual capacity. The building is bit like a castle with a statue of a horse outside. More interesting is the electric tramway that runs by the side of the road. After much persuading and yawning, Ms Lane relented and we took a short trip up to the Herrenhausen Gardens.

What we hadn't realised was that this was her tricky teacher plan all along, and we had to spend the next hour walking round these huge grounds where all the plants are laid out in geometric patterns. It was designed in the seventeenth century by the Electress of Hanover, Sophie: a woman! announced Ms Lane proudly. She didn't say how many male peasants lost their lives in their construction, however. LB asked her what an Electress was, but she just mumbled a reply, which teachers do when they don't know the answer. Actually, I have to admit it was quite spectacular, even this late on in the year, with fountains and statues, and there was a maze which LB and Justin got lost in, on purpose I think, because it wasn't that difficult. I was glad to get inside the big old house, though, because of the café. The coffee was very tasty and hot, which was good because the temperature outside had plummeted to ten degrees.

By the end of the day's drive, Alan had got us to the outskirts of Berlin, though you wouldn't have guessed as we seemed to be still in the countryside. The E30 has changed into the E51, but essentially it's still the same road we've been on since Holland. Stewart has booked us into a little hotel in Michendorf, which is a quiet village north of the motorway.

Quite a homely place, a big bungalow and more like a bed and breakfast at home. The woman in charge is a farmer, but she can still speak enough English for us to get by on. I'm not really looking forward to being put to the test in Russia, as my linguistic abilities are pretty poor despite our training sessions.

That reminds me: Stewart said that Elspeth has gone up to London for the weekend on some high-powered visit. It was all very hush-hush, but he thinks she's been asked to speak to all the people who think the government are doing a bad job. In that case, I expect there'll be a big crowd. Overnight, she's staying at the Langham Hotel, Regent Street, which is her favourite apparently, then tomorrow she's got more meetings with her barrister or solicitor or something. Not bad for an eighty-four-year-old!

I haven't yet mentioned that it was Justin's fourteenth birthday today; he's exactly a month younger than Dan. The reason for this oversight was that we wondered if he'd remind us during the day, or maybe get annoyed that we'd forgotten. Neither happened: he just accepted that we were thoughtless, uncaring individuals and got on with it.

We booked a table at La Palma Steakhouse on the main street in Michendorf just within walking distance of our hotel. When we were all seated, Ms Lane looked disapprovingly at Justin and said: "I've only got one thing to say to you..." Then she started singing Happy Birthday. Then we all joined in, and you should have seen his expression change from one of guilt-ridden horror to blushing pleasure.

"You bastards!" he said when we'd finished.

We then showered him with cards. There was one from his parents with the promise of a present when he got back. LB gave him a small, nicely wrapped gift as well – a new tube of athlete's foot cream, which he got the finger for. But it was Alan's card which I think he liked the most. It said: *To my best friend Justin Walker from Alan* and there was a badge attached which had a crown and *Keep Calm, I'm a Mechanic* printed on it. Justin got up and plonked a kiss on the top of his boss's head, then pinned the badge to his sweatshirt and has worn it ever since. Alan didn't know where to put himself.

"Hey, you never give me a kiss," said Dan.

"That's because you buy me embarrassing foot cream," replied Justin.

Then Ms Lane bought a bottle of wine and we all toasted the birthday boy. The steaks were tops, by the way.

When we got back to the hotel, LB had his first medical emergency when Ms Lane sliced her finger open with a pen knife. Don't ask me what she was doing – peeling an apple, I think. I've learned that blood is not something she copes with easily, particularly her own, but LB soon had her fixed up with an antiseptic wipe and a plaster. However, when he asked her in a polite and professional way how her back was, she told him to mind his own business, which I thought was a bit off.

***

"Stop!" cried Alan.

Cue for Ms Lane to jam on the brakes, forgetting to press the clutch, causing the car to judder and LB and me to be thrown forward onto the floor because rather naughtily we were not wearing our seat belts; this is practically a capital offence in Germany.

Fortunately, we didn't cause a fifty-car pile-up behind us, more by luck than judgement, and once Ms Lane recovered her wits, she trundled the Humber onto the hard shoulder.

"What's up?" asked Justin, not turning a hair.

"The engine's overheating," replied Alan as though it was quite obvious.

"Is that all?" said Ms Lane testily, adjusting her back with a groan and a pained expression.

"Calm..." murmured Justin, noticing Alan's face going the colour of beetroot.

I haven't said that it's been pouring with rain since we got up this morning, which possibly explains why Ms Lane didn't notice the temperature gauge hitting the red because she was too busy peering blindly through the wet windscreen. The windscreen wipers are funny old things, each having its own motor. Alan switched off the right wiper blade and Justin did the same to the left to save the battery.

"Could you open the bonnet, please?" said Alan with a hint of ice, indicating the lever to Ms Lane's right. He handed Justin the ignition key. "Better get the can of water from the boot. Don't bother with the antifreeze."

"Good spot," said Justin, patting Alan on the arm.

So, our first delay. The radiator was practically empty, and our mechanics have to find the source of the leak. I expect if it had been dry this morning someone would have noticed water under the car before we set off. While we were holed up on the side of the autobahn, Ms Lane sweet-talked a polite *Autobahnpolizist* until we were ready to move off. Apparently they like people stopping on the hard shoulder even less than we do in England. She had to show all our documents, the first-aid kit and, for some reason, the snow chains, which made Alan rather impatient, as he had to fish them out of the spare tyre locker, interrupting his research into the water problem.

We ended up only twenty miles further on from Michendorf, limping into another small town, Ludwigsfelde, where we stayed Sunday night at the Hotel Ambassador. Everyone was very friendly and one or two of the staff said they'd like a ride in the Humber. You can imagine Alan's reaction to that.

Justin got a bit of a telling off, because he had overtightened one of the jubilee clips where the water inlet hose joined the heater. It had jumped back several teeth, and the pipe had worked its way loose, hence the source of the leak. He got down on his knees and prayed for forgiveness from the great white chief. Alan didn't know how to deal with that, which I think was the idea.

As soon as it was light on Monday morning, they were both up and out at the car, measuring the specific gravity of the water in the radiator to make sure there was exactly the right amount of antifreeze in the mixture. This meant measuring the temperature at the same time. I suspect if you'd given Alan a hygrometer and a thermometer in a physics lesson at school, he wouldn't have a clue what to do with them.

After stocking up on another cold buffet breakfast, we set off from Ludwigsfelde towards the Polish border. Ms Lane is once more in the driver's seat, and, strangely, she's wearing her glasses. Maybe this has something to do with the fact that she doesn't speak Polish and doesn't want any incidents. LB and I thought we'd show willing and began practising our Russian phrases in the back, at which Ms Contrary Lane warned us not to speak it in Poland because the locals were for a long time under the yoke of their eastern neighbours and might take against us.

***

52: Wednesday, 30th October. 1 a.m. Regent Warsaw Hotel, Warsaw, Poland.

ALAN

"Alan, I've got a nasty cough."

The fag says he's got a nasty cough, but I know that's a lie for two reasons. One, he hasn't coughed and two, he's grinning at me in that faggy way, which means he's trying to get round me.

I pull myself up from beneath the duvet and support myself on my right arm. "So, what do you want me to do about it?"

His grin's got even bigger. If I'm not careful, I'll start grinning back at him and I know that's dangerous because it means he's winning.

"I want you to kiss it better."

Does he think I'm going to give in to his faggy ways just like that? Well, he's wrong.

"I'm not going to kiss your diseases. In any case we'll wake Justin up."

Justin's snoring, but not too loudly. This is our second night in the Warsaw Regent Hotel which is in Warsaw, Poland. Ms Lane's back got so bad she couldn't move when she tried to get up yesterday morning, and Dan had to call the doctor. I don't mind, though. This hotel is a weird shape and looks like an office block from the outside but inside it's five-star with a swimming pool and a gym. Our room is enormous and the beds are like floating on air. We're on the fifth floor and the fag's looking out of the window into the courtyard below, which isn't an open courtyard because it has a glass roof and there's a bar inside.

"It's a nice view. The lights are pretty."

He says the lights are pretty! What am I supposed to say to such faggy talk?

"I thought you said you were scared of heights," I answer, which would be typical because fags are scared of everything.

"Not through glass," he says, turning back to me. "Alan, shall we have a quiet mega-Maberly?" He looks hopefully at me through his left eye, because the other one is covered by that stupid blue fringe.

"Where are your shoes?" I ask, not giving in to his brazen effrontery.

He's wearing that ridiculous multi-coloured, oversize vest and a pair of shorts, but his big flappy feet are bare.

"I took them off because the carpet's nice and thick against my toes."

He's standing beside my bed now and he's waiting for me to invite him in, like he's some True Blood vampire. I can see one of his microscopic nipples poking out from his vest and the dark hair in his armpits. I lift the covers and he jumps in and the first thing he does is pucker his pouty lips because he wants me to kiss him. I keep him waiting for at least ten seconds before I brush my lips against his, then he puts his arms around me and our bodies touch.

"Ooo, Alan, you're naked!"

That's a lie – I've got boxers and a T-shirt on. No, I haven't, I am naked! How did that happen? What's he doing now? He's trying to get his vest off.

"Alan! Help me, I'm all of a tangle..."

Typical, he's got both arms through one hole in his vest!

"Shut up! You'll wake Justin if you carry on like that."

I have to be firm with him. He half sits up and I manage to pull the vest over his head. Then we burrow down into the bed and he squeaks as he pulls his shorts and pants down but gets them stuck on the end of his toes. He kicks them off and manages to kick me on the shin at the same time, but it doesn't matter because we're in each other's arms, holding each other tight, and our skins are touching and so are our lips. It's nice, he even smells nice, and I've gone really hard. I want to see whether he has too, but I daren't.

"Alan, can I touch you?"

The fag wants to touch me *down there*. I don't know what's going to happen if he does, but I want him to, only he'd better hurry up...

It's gone dark! I'm alone and I'm wearing boxers and they're ... wet. It was a dream, wasn't it? But it was so real. I'll have to go to the bathroom and change. I hope Justin's still asleep but I can't hear him snoring. Maybe he's turned over. The curtains are so thick, it's pitch black, but if I put the light on I'm sure to wake him up. At least the bathroom's nearest my side.

So the fag wasn't looking out of the window because he wasn't really there and the curtains are drawn anyway. I should have woken up sooner. That was a real faggy dream, getting naked with him, touching each other like that. But why does the bed now seem so empty without him?

I made it to the bathroom without making any noise, and closed the door before I put the light on. The trouble is, I've got to go back out for my clean pair of boxers which I laid out on a chair ready for the morning. If I keep the light on and open the door just a crack, there should be just enough light to see by without waking Justin.

Ms Lane should be well enough to travel tomorrow. The doctor gave her some painkillers and said she had to keep moving. So, after breakfast yesterday, she managed to hobble into the spa and have a massage. Dan asked the doctor whether there was anything that could be done to the Humber to make the driving position more comfortable. The doctor spoke good English and said he would like to see the car. We went down to the car park and I showed him the driver's seat. A rolled-up towel to support the lower back, a hot water bottle and every thirty minutes a stop and stretch is what he recommended, then he asked if he could see the engine. In the end I took him and Dan for a ride round the car park. They chatted in the back while I chauffeured. He was really impressed, so much so that he waived his call-out fee.

I've cleaned myself up and am back in the bedroom now, putting on my boxers. I've still got to switch the bathroom light off, though. I look over towards Justin and I jump because I can see his eyes sparkling, which means he's watching me, though his head is still resting on the pillow.

"Good dream, was it?" he asks, deadpan, though I can see him smiling.

I don't know what to say, and can feel my cheeks going red. Hopefully he won't notice.

"It must have been a good dream by the colour of that blush," he says.

Has he guessed what's happened; does he know I was dreaming about the fag?

Justin lifts his head off the pillow and props it on his fist. "Do you miss him a lot, Alan?"

I can't say it, but I know my face has gone all faggy.

He's put the light on above his headboard and so I turn off the one in the bathroom and get back into bed. Justin's still looking at me.

"You were talking in your sleep," he says. "It won't be long before you're together again."

Talking in my sleep! "What time is it?" I ask.

"Ten past two."

213

"You won't tell anyone, will you?"

"What, about your dream?"

I nod.

"Only Ms Lane," he says. "She likes to hear stories about boys' wet dreams."

I know he's joking, but I can't help going red again.

"I'd better turn the light off, hadn't I?" Justin says and starts to chuckle, but in a nice way because that's what he's like.

***

53: Thursday, 31st October. 6.30 a.m. MSK, Arkhangelsk Oblast, Gosudarstvennyi Meditsinskii Institut (gomoseksualizm).

NOAH

Hurricane lamp in hand, John Price came stomping down the length of the dormitory to the last bed on the left under the windows.

"Marshall, get up!"

Noah screeched. "Oh, John, I was having such a lovely dream about my CP. He was just about to kiss my pouty lips! We were lying on Swanpool beach in Falmouth and it was warm and sunny and he looked so ultra-sexy in his white Speedos with a black stripe..."

"Enough! Madam's on the warpath... again."

"Why?"

"I don't know. She's been shouting and screaming at everyone."

Noah rubbed his eyes and peered at the gangly figure, clad in just his boxers and a pair of boots. "Oh John, my toes are sore..."

"Your toes will be the least of your worries if you're not up by the time she comes in. You'll be spending a day in the cage, and it's snowing again."

"But they're very poorly..."

John lifted the covers and pulled at the sock which was hanging off Noah's left foot.

"Ow! John, don't be rough."

"Hah! You've got chilblains, dummy."

"Oh!"

"That's what comes of toasting your toes too near the stove when you come in."

"Our dad got chilblains."

"There may be a genetic element as well." John said, gently sheathing Noah's toes with the sock once more.

"You see, it's not all my fault." Noah narrowed his eyes. "And I've got no one to talk to after work now, so all I can think about are my frozen little piggies."

It was John's turn to peer sceptically at Noah through his foggy glasses. "You're jealous because I go and play chess with Valery?"

"But we used to have such nice times together..."

"You mean, you've got no one to be outrageously flirty with. You don't flirt with the gay boys and Jamie doesn't respond in the same way as I do."

"He hasn't got a wedge either," smiled Noah. "I love your wedge, John. Please pull your boxers down just a little bit to wake me up."

"You see, you are outrageous! Come on, it's time for you to get moving, chilblains or no chilblains."

Noah lifted himself into a half-lying position and scanned the dark room. "Where is everybody?"

John glanced round, seeing the rows of empty beds. "The twins are coughing in the kitchen. Robert and Jamie are showering..."

"Where's Porky and Owen?"

"Probably in the rest room," John gazed suspiciously at Noah. "Why are you batting your eyelids at me now?"

"I can't help it; you're so cute."

John let out an exasperated sigh. "Why don't girls think that? They always want to run away from me."

215

Noah waved his wrist. "Teenage girls! Tush! All they're interested in is a gormless gene dispenser. They don't see what I see."

"Gene dispenser – but that's exactly what I want to be!"

"Don't worry. Once we're back home and I've given you a makeover, they won't be able to resist."

"Why is it that I like you when I know you're so good at wrapping me round your little finger?"

"But all I ever want is a bit of love and attention," whined Noah, "and now you leave me to get chilblains while you go off and have fun with the Mistress."

"All right, I may as well tell you since we're on the subject. Valery has suggested that I teach you how to play chess..."

Noah's face lit up and he smiled coyly at John. "Ooo, really, but I'm not into war games."

"Like me, he thinks you're the best strategist in the place, so you might be good competition for him. He says he'll leave the board and chess pieces with Babooshka."

Noah's eyes sparkled. "What's your score, John?"

"Humph, won three, lost seven. But it's almost worse winning because he's a very bad loser and he chain-smokes while he's playing."

"I'd better get up then... John, will you teach me with your shirt off so that if I get bored I'll have something sexy to look at?"

"Get ready for inspection, you strumpet! I'm going to roust out Owen and Porky or they'll be in trouble too."

John strode away, shaking his head, while Noah pulled himself reluctantly out of bed. Carefully he pulled off his socks to examine his feet. The middle toes were inflamed and itchy. He stood up and walked a few steps. There was no real pain, just the annoying itch.

It was dark on the landing outside the dormitory, but there was a light coming from down the corridor where Sister Hopkins had her 'suite'. Noah put his head round the corner and saw that the light was actually coming from the open doorway of the medical room, where a voluble conversation was taking place. Immediately, he recognised the voices of Sister Hopkins and Valery, but it took him a few seconds to realise that the other Russian speaker was Professor Igor Zaronovich Rozhdestvensky, Dr Death himself.

"Sister, the professor is of the opinion that the moral fibre of these boys is in your hands. Therefore, if one of them is a thief it is your responsibility."

"Tell him he's talking rubbish as usual. That stupid old goat hung up the house keys deliberately in full view of everyone when he got fired."

"The professor says the keys were there for over a week; there was plenty of time for you to rectify the situation."

"I was not aware that they would unlock every room in the place, was I? Now I demand you first of all change the lock on my door. I don't want any of these perverts going through my belongings. They would probably want to *wear* my clothes..."

Noah had difficulty not bursting out laughing at that. He had come within a few feet of the surgery and could hear every word. As usual, Valery Fyodorovich Khrennikov's voice was completely deadpan and he wondered how accurate his translations were. What did surprise him was that as the 'master strategist' he had not been aware of this bunch of keys in the kitchen, nor had any of the boys mentioned it to him.

"The professor suggests you get Yuri Semyonovich Bakaleinikoff to change the lock, Sister Hopkins, as he seems to spend considerable time in there with you."

Noah put his hand over his mouth to stop himself guffawing.

"How dare he speak to me in that facetious tone!"

"The professor says this conversation has now ended. He is expected back in Puksa for an important meeting of the prison authorities. He would like you to take charge of the situation and find the keys and the culprit post-haste."

Seeing his danger, Noah went right up to the medical room door and knocked. Immediately, three pairs of eyes held him in their gaze.

"Excuse me, Sister, I'm poorly. John says I've got chilblains..." He pointed down and wriggled his toes.

The professor said something in Russian and Valery spoke quietly to him.

"You stupid ignorant boy, you can't have been wearing suitable footwear or you've been heating up your feet too fast after coming in from the cold."

"Our dad suffered from chilblains before he died, Sister," said Noah, accusingly.

Each time he spoke, there was a to and fro between Valery and the professor, who would then eye Noah as if he were a laboratory specimen. Meanwhile, Sister Hopkins looked down her nose at him.

"Well, you'll just have to look on it as a punishment for your perverted behaviour," she said.

"Oh, Sister..." whined Noah. "Have you got any Balmosa ointment? Our dad swore by Balmosa..."

"*Tovarisch* Marshall," interrupted Valery, "the professor wants to know if you are still having these strong sexual feelings for older men?"

Noah locked eyes with their translator. "Ooo, yes... But possibly not quite as strong since we've been having all this wonderful therapy..."

"You think yourself a clever little shit, don't you?" said Sister Hopkins. "And I know you were listening at the door before you knocked. You couldn't help yourself."

"Sorry, Sister, I did hear you mention that some keys have gone missing, but I know nothing about them."

"Well, it doesn't matter if you do or don't, because the end result will be the same. The warders have already begun a search of the premises and when we do find them, as we most certainly will, I shall see to it that the ringleaders spend an interesting week in the Puksa Juvenile Prison for Boys. Now

218

get your wheedling little carcass out of here and take your rats' feet chilblains with you."

Noah scurried away, returning to the dormitory, where he was immediately confronted by Jamie.

"Where have you been?" the bigger boy demanded, though it was clear he was more concerned than angry.

Noah closed the door and made for the stove, round which all the older boys were gathered. "In the medical room. I've got chilblains, Jamie, but Madam DeVeal wouldn't give me anything for them. Our dad used to swear by Balmosa ointment. He said, *when your toes are all messed, Balmosa is best...*"

"We're trying to have an intelligent discussion here, babble-mouth!" exclaimed John.

"Oh, John, don't shout at me."

The fifteen-year-old held his forehead. "Sorry, Noah, you're right. I'm getting overwrought. It's just that I couldn't find Owen and Porky anywhere, and we'll be in deep shit now."

Dennis was sitting on his bed, panting for breath. "Something's gone missing from the kitchen as well," he wheezed. "But I don't know what."

"Yurine searched our bodies," squeaked Michael, who was hovering anxiously over his brother. "Then he and Vaseline started looking in all the cupboards."

"It's a set of keys," said Noah, warming his hands. "I overheard Madam talking."

"What keys?" enquired Robert.

"Whiskers' keys. He hung them on a hook in the hall before he left, but I didn't see them. Now Madam's afraid we're going to unlock her boudoir and prance around in her furs and camiknickers." Noah put his hand on his hip and did a swivel.

Michael giggled and John smiled despite himself. "Marshall, you are such a div!"

"Whiskers' keys would unlock the main gate," said Jamie pointedly.

"You think Owen and Porky have done a runner..." said John.

"What date is it?" questioned Robert, suddenly.

"It's the thirty-first of October," answered Jamie. "Why?"

"Ooo!" said Noah. "Hallowe'en. Madam will be out tonight on her broomstick."

"Will you shut up for a minute?" cried John. "Go on, Robert."

"Owen told me on one of our tree-felling sessions that if we were still here by the end of October, he was going to run away."

"And then there were six," said Jamie. "That explains why he and Porky were as thick as thieves recently."

"They're not going to get far in this weather," said Robert.

"That's where the loaf of bread and apples have gone," gasped Dennis, and Michael nodded. "We noticed this morning, but we didn't tell."

"Can't blame them," said John, "but it means the rest of us will pay the price."

"Whoever takes the rap, Madam's threatened to send them up the river for a long stretch, see..." said Noah, remembering his 1930s Warner Brothers dialogue.

"I didn't realise that Judy Garland had made any gangster movies," observed Robert.

"Ooo, Robert, don't be awful. Remember you're from Kansas as well!"

"I bet they'll come back," said Jamie, "as soon as the cold gets to them."

"If they get to Puksa, they might be all right," offered Noah.

"Like Dwain?" retorted Jamie.

Valery Fyodorovich Khrennikov opened the door, allowing Sister Hopkins, to enter flanked by Yuri Semyonovich Bakaleinikoff and another uniformed guard. Both had batons at the ready.

"Why aren't you standing by your beds?" she demanded. "Get into line this instant!"

Reluctantly, the boys filed to their respective stations and stood disconsolately, waiting for the axe to fall.

The nurse looked round the room, her lips pursed. "Where are Frost and Eagleton?"

"We don't know, Sister Hopkins," answered John.

She paused before speaking again. "When they come back with their tails between their legs, I shall take great pleasure in sending them for a spell in the juvenile prison. A week in the sex offenders' block for stealing and another with the violent prisoners for absconding. That should stop their little gallop."

Her eyes fixed each of them in turn. Both the twins blushed while John blinked. Only Noah, Jamie and Robert were able to hold her gaze.

"Which of you has the keys now?" she asked with quiet menace.

"None of us knew anything about what Owen and Porky were up to," said Jamie.

From somewhere deep inside her a chuckle resonated. "Get your clothes on and line up outside, all of you. You will spend a day in the forest while this place is searched from top to bottom. And woe betide you if you're caught with the keys, though if any of you speaks up beforehand, he will spend a nice warm day inside."

"But Sister, we haven't had breakfast yet!" cried Noah.

"An empty stomach might loosen tongues."

"The twins are too ill to be outside in this weather," stated Jamie.

"I'll decide that, young man," snapped the Sister, and she turned her attention to the twins. "If you had been born normally instead of sired by a surrogate with queer semen, maybe you wouldn't be so sickly."

The twins frowned at her, then looked at each other.

"We love our dads," wheezed Dennis.

"Take no notice of her," said John, quietly but firmly. "She's an inhuman bitch."

Sister Hopkins smiled, deeply satisfied to have got a reaction. "Well, the hollow-chested dweeb with the crooked teeth and pustulated face speaks. A product of the artificial insemination of a dyke with yet more queer semen. And doesn't it show. To think that England could stoop so low as to allow this sort of aberration to occur..."

"John is beautiful," murmured Noah.

The Sister signalled to the uniformed guard and pointed.

"Ooo, no!" cried Noah. "Don't hurt him..."

The guard walked over and punched John in the stomach with his baton. With barely any sound, he doubled up and sank to his knees.

Sister Hopkins looked at Valery. "Tell the guard to take him out to the cage and strip him completely. An hour naked in the cold will do him good."

Valery looked at her as if unable to comprehend.

"You heard, duffer, translate..."

Robert walked forward. "You're a disgrace to your profession, Sister Hopkins."

"You're a serial child abuser," added Jamie, coming to stand shoulder to shoulder with the American.

Yuri raised his baton, a smile of almost beatific contentment on his face, but the Sister put a restraining hand on his arm. "No, let us be subtle. Two hours in the cage for Price and if they say any more..." she nodded towards the twins, "those two will join him."

Michael made a noise of protest while Dennis's breathing became even more laboured. Jamie and Robert looked at the two frail boys and stayed their hand. Disappointed, Yuri made a face and beat his baton against the side of his leg.

"That took the wind out of their sails," said the Sister, looking at her wristwatch. "Now you have until first light, approximately fifteen minutes, to prepare yourselves for the great outdoors."

John was lifted by the scruff of the neck and his boxers forcibly removed. Then he was frogmarched out of the dormitory ahead of Sister Hopkins and her retinue. Only Valery Fyodorovich Khrennikov looked back at the five remaining figures in the dormitory, an expression of dismay on his face.

Noah covered his face with his hands and began to cry. Robert walked over and put his arms round him.

"Oh, Robert, I love John. Why does she have to be so cruel?"

"She's a hateful, hate-filled woman," he replied quietly.

"I've got to do something. He'll freeze to death out there with nothing on."

"Whatever you decide, wait five minutes until the dust has settled," the American advised.

Three and a half minutes later, fully dressed and with gritted teeth, Noah ran down the stairs and into the kitchen, where he filled a glass with hot tea from the samovar. Babooshka was sitting in her chair smoking, but she did not react except to look at him with a curious smile on her wrinkled face.

At the outside door, Robert met him, one of the thin duvets from their beds under his arm, while Jamie was at the top of the stairs to act as lookout. Though the sky was still black, the white ground reflected enough light for them to see by. Cautiously they made their way across the yard, following John's bare footprints, which were already being covered by a fresh layer of snow.

A figure loomed out of the darkness, coming from the direction of the lavatory. They stopped dead, easily recognising Vasily Yegorovich Pavlov even though he was shrouded in his winter wear. The Russian stopped for a moment, before walking past them without a second glance.

"I hope he doesn't split on us," murmured Robert.

Noah's heart seemed to turn somersaults in his chest. His gloved hand holding the glass trembled uncontrollably as they took the last few steps to the cage. The naked figure sat huddled in the corner nearest the toilet in what little shelter there was, arms wrapped around his legs, head bent.

"John!" hissed Noah.

The fifteen-year-old looked up and blinked at them through his glasses.

"Wrap this round you," said Robert, pushing the duvet as best he could through the bars.

"Put these on," said Noah, fishing some socks out of his coat pocket. "and drink this..."

John took the offerings without saying anything, but the tears streaming down his face spoke more than words.

"I love you, John," said Noah, reaching through the bars and taking John's cold hand. "We all love you. You're the best."

"Shut up," sobbed John, taking a gulp of tea. "Straight boys don't cry in front of gays."

"We better get back," said Robert. "Before we're missed."

"I think Babooshka and Vaseline are on our side." whispered Noah.

"Neutral might be a better word," corrected Robert.

"Where is she?" asked John.

"Probably being humped by Yurine in the boudoir," answered Noah. "But Jamie's going to whistle if the DeVeal rides out."

"Thanks, guys," said John, perking up. "I'm going to put you both in for sainthood."

"Ooo, no John, they'd never accept a couple of Dorothy demons. When you finally get to Oz, just think of us spending forever on the yellow brick road."

***

224

54: Friday, 1st November. 8.15 a.m. MSK, Arkhangelsk Oblast, Gosudarstvennyi Meditsinskii Institut (gomoseksualizm).

ROBERT

The snow squelched slushily under his boots as Robert made his way back across the yard towards the barracks. Dawn had not long since arrived and a damp mist hung in the trees beyond the compound. Once again, his thoughts turned to Owen and Porky, who were still missing. He reflected that no search had been organised by the adults, who were not concerned at all about their whereabouts or their welfare, and only thought about what punishment would be exacted if they did return. He blew out a vaporous breath. The temperature was poised several degrees above freezing, which made the trip to the toilet less of an ordeal than it had been on recent days.

An elderly man he didn't recognise was methodically unscrewing the brass plate by the outside door. Robert paused, curiosity overcoming his need for warmth.

"What are you doing?" he asked, but the Russian merely glanced at him and then continued working. The plate came off and slipped out of the man's gloved fingers, landing with a thud in the snow. The American bent to pick it up. It was heavier than he expected and he held it firmly in both hands, looking at the Cyrillic script and the English translation. It read: *The State Medical Institute (Homosexuality). Director: Professor Igor Zaronovich Rozhdestvensky.*

The man put the four screws and the screwdriver in the top pocket of his overalls then gave Robert a half-smile. "Goodbye to all that," he said in halting English.

The American handed over the plate, nodding as if he knew what the Russian was talking about, then went inside. Normally he would have gone straight for a shower, but he wanted to share what had just occurred with the others.

In the dormitory, Jamie was reclining on his bed rewiring John's glasses, the arm of which had come loose during the previous day's altercation.

"Can't he do that himself?" asked Robert.

Jamie looked up at him and then glanced back down the room to where John and Noah were sitting on opposite sides of the latter's bed, talking over a makeshift chess board. This consisted of a square of paper blocked in with pencil and covered in various odds and ends which acted as the pieces.

"May as well keep occupied while their majesties are engaged in their game."

"We're not playing a game, I'm teaching this young man the etiquette of chess," called John snootily.

"All the pieces have different names to what they're like. It's ridiculous," complained Noah, who had been introduced to the real thing the evening before. "There's one called a knight but it's shaped like a horse; there's another named a rook, though it's actually a tower..."

"You could call it a castle," offered John.

"You said only plebs call it a castle, even though it does this thing called castling and looks more like a castle than a rook."

"As I said, you can call it a castle," smirked John.

Noah put on an expression of disgust. "And all the pieces move in silly ways. The knight's really silly, jumping all over the place, and the king can only move one square at a time, though you say it's the most important piece on the board."

"That's because you win or lose by way of the king."

"Oh, John, it's too complicated. Can't we just have a cuddle instead?" pleaded Noah.

"He's off on a flirt," said Robert.

"They're both as bad," said Jamie.

"I don't cuddle gay boys," stated John with an air of superiority.

"Oh, spoilsport!" screeched Noah. "Why can't you be bisexual for just a minute? Then we could have a cuddle and a kiss..."

"And what would your Cutie Pie say if he knew what you were suggesting?" questioned John.

"Ooo, you want me to have a guilty conscience, don't you?" Noah grinned. "But if you seduced me, it wouldn't be so bad..."

"And pigs might fly!" answered John.

"You should take him up on it, Price," shouted Jamie. "It's the best offer you're ever likely to get."

"Whoa," said Robert, "catty."

Jamie guffawed sheepishly. "Yeh, I guess it was a bit."

"You take no notice, John," said Noah. "When you've had your makeover you can act just as shallowly as Jamie and the other straight boys."

John furrowed his brow. "Noah, are my teeth really as bad as Madam suggested yesterday?"

"Oh, shush! Your teeth are adorable, just like the rest of you," said Noah. "They're nice and gappy, which means they're easy to keep clean, as well."

John wasn't convinced. "But you'd say that about me, whatever I looked like," he said.

"They're adorable!" called Jamie, "Just like the rest of you. Convinced now, or are you fishing for more compliments?"

"Shut up, Baker," said John. "You wouldn't know beauty if it hit you in the face."

"It would have to hit you in the face before you could see it," retorted Jamie, holding up the rewired glasses.

John nodded complaisantly. "Now that is true. I'm sure I'll never be allowed to drive."

"They've taken the nameplate off the front door," announced Robert, getting to the reason for his appearance at last.

Everyone stopped what they were doing and looked at him expectantly.

"That's it," he said. "That's all I know."

"Perhaps they're going to send us—" began Noah.

"Don't say it!" exclaimed Jamie.

227

"When was this?" asked John.

"Just now, as I was walking across the yard," answered Robert. "Which reminds me, I haven't showered yet."

When he got outside to the landing, Sister Hopkins and Valery were emerging from the corridor opposite.

"Where do you think you're going?" she asked.

"Shower," he said curtly.

"If I had my way, you'd all be out in the forest by now chopping wood, like yesterday."

Robert wondered why, in that case, they weren't, and decided that Ivan the Terrible probably wouldn't allow his men to be continually at the Sister's beck and call.

"The name plate has been taken off the wall outside," he said casually.

He had hoped to elicit a reaction, but was surprised to see visible shock on both their faces.

The Sister turned to Valery. "What does this mean?" she demanded.

Valery shook his head. "I know nothing about it, Sister Hopkins. Perhaps it's been taken away for cleaning."

"Ridiculous – it's only just been put up."

Robert began to edge past the pair.

The Sister turned to Valery. "You see to it that these boys are out by nine. I'm going to make some enquiries. Something's going on behind my back, as usual."

As Robert entered the changing room, Michael was just coming out of the shower, closely followed by the similarly skeletal form of Dennis. The previous day in the forest had left the twins exhausted, yet neither of them could get enough sleep because of their constant bouts of coughing.

"You two should be in bed," said the American.

They shook their heads.

"Too chesty," coughed Michael, who was in slightly better condition than his brother.

Dennis sat on the old bench and drooped. There were dark circles around his eyes and unconsciously he began to work his bony fingers. Robert picked up one of the rough towels and began to gently dry the smaller boy's hair. Michael helped, drying his brothers legs and feet. By the time they had finished, Dennis was asleep.

"I'm going to carry him upstairs and put him to bed, and that's final," said Robert, wrapping a dry towel around him.

Michael lowered his head. "We've got to go out again later, Madame DeVeal said so..."

"Over my dead body," replied Robert, scooping up the boy and marching out of the changing room.

"Oh, twins!" cried Noah as the dormitory door was thrown open. He hurried over to Dennis's bed and pulled back the duvet so that Robert could lie him down.

"This one fell asleep while I was drying his hair," said the American.

"You still haven't had a shower, have you?" enquired Jamie.

Robert shook his head. "I'm going now. Madam's in a state about the nameplate being taken away and so Valery will be in charge of the work party today."

"What do you want us to do?" asked John, seeing the determination on the American's face.

"Make sure these two are not included." He turned to Michael. "Get into bed and rest even if you can't sleep."

The twelve-year-old nodded and yawned, his whole body shuddering with the effort.

"Come on, sleepy," said Noah. "We can prop you up a bit so you'll be more comfy and I'll tell you a lovely story until the Mistress comes and turfs us out."

***

55: Saturday, 2nd November. 11.15 a.m. Outskirts of Valga, Latvia.

DAN

Yesterday, we ended up in a small Latvian town called Valmiera. Near the centre, we crossed a bridge over the river which has parallel lines of street lights in the shape of a rib cage. Ms Lane was impressed but I thought it was a bit weird.

I suppose we've been spoilt up to now, staying in really classy hotels, so the bungalow apartment we stayed in overnight was a bit of a comedown. Jack and I had to share a double bed, Ms Lane had the single and Justin and Alan had the twin. We shared a bathroom and we had to get our own breakfast, but it was clean and friendly and as a matter of fact more like what I'm used to.

Actually, Ms Lane cooked us breakfast – sometimes she seems almost human. She's feeling better and might be getting used to me as the junior doctor because she let me change her plaster without the usual insinuations that as an adolescent male I must be up to no good. We had eggs, bacon, fried bread, tomatoes, orange juice, fresh coffee all bought at the local Maxima supermarket the previous evening. Apparently there are three of these supermarkets in Valmiera, but not so long ago the roof collapsed in one of them, killing a lot of people. Fortunately, the roof stayed up while we were there.

Ms Lane did us proud, and no sign of a cigarette hanging out of her mouth, as Justin would have us believe. Funny, I wouldn't think of touching a fried breakfast at home, but here it's different, like being on holiday with Mum and Dad, and a fry-up is just right on a cold morning.

We're coming into Valga on the E264 now which is a border town between Latvia and Estonia. We've been driving for less than an hour but the fuel gauge is almost on empty so we've taken a small detour because there was a turn-right sign with a petrol pump on it. The car has been filled up five times, once in each country we've visited, and Jack has always done the honours. He says he wants to get his time down to three and a half minutes, start to finish. A lot of the petrol stations in these parts are unmanned, so you pay at the pump with a credit or debit card. Neste is the brand and Justin's started to ask if we're filling up at the next Milkybar. You can just about work out his twisted logic if you want. So far it's all been pretty smooth running, though I think a bit of brotherly competition is in order to see if I can better Jack's time. Easy!

Since we've been in the Baltic states, as Lithuania, Latvia and Estonia are called, the roads have become mostly single carriageways, but there's so little traffic and they're so straight that progress is just as quick, especially as most drivers keep well into the right and let you pass with no trouble. It keeps raining on and off, the skies are overcast and there's a definite feel of autumn turning into winter. The last of the leaves are blowing off the trees like billy-o, and the vegetation in the fields is brown and dead. Our driving has mostly been through flat, open countryside on this part of the journey, with the occasional village or small town to relieve the monotony. I imagine areas of England were something like this a hundred years ago.

I've read that as you go further east, the motoring laws get more strictly enforced but the driving you encounter gets worse. There must be a tie-up between those two facts, surely? Fortunately, we've had no bad incidents with other drivers so far, and of course Alan is very particular that there shouldn't be. I think he's one of these people who can foresee what's going to happen a long time ahead and can take action. Ms Lane, on the other hand... No, she's fine most of the time, and it's rather a neat trick to have a right-hand-drive car so that when Alan is driving it still looks like she is.

Jack has just cheated on the time, because the pump ran dry and the tank is only a third full. I told him it had to be a complete fill to count, but he smirked at me like a big brother would and said two minutes forty-five. I know he's just ribbing me, but that doesn't stop it grating. Alan says it doesn't matter and that we'll fill up at the next town.

Well, that was another border anti-climax. At a T-junction in the middle of Valga where one narrow little street meets another it's goodbye Latvia, hello Estonia! And there's only a small blue sign with a circle of twelve stars to tell you that you're in a different country. I think there may have been a customs post here once, because there's a small one-storey building on the right-hand side which has been boarded up.

Our next stop is sixty miles to the north in the second-largest city in the country, Tartu. Put it this way, it's five times bigger than Swanford and a fifth of the size of Liverpool or Bristol. Our communications officer will be liaising shortly with Stewart at home base about our accommodation for this evening. It's not a long journey today, because we'll be starting early tomorrow for the drive up to the border with Russia. If we're lucky, we may even get to St Petersburg by dark tomorrow night.

I told Alan to watch out for a passing moose, then Justin had to show him a picture of one on his mobile and explain three times that I hadn't been talking about a giant mouse before he'd believe they existed. Estonia has the largest population of these elk, as they call them, in Europe, and when they're not being slaughtered by trigger-happy retards – I mean, hunters – they may be seen ambling along the roads. Apparently, should a car hit one, the car is more than likely to come off worst. We're all looking out for a loose moose now: such is the price of fear.

***

56: Sunday, 3rd November. 10.05 a.m. Tartu, Estonia.

JACK

The nearest Neste petrol station was only a few hundred yards from the Antonius hotel where they had spent the night. It was the usual blue-and-white liveried self-service type with a single rank of pumps and a canopy overhead.

The boys were all dressed in coats, gloves and scarves and had their ushankas ready to pull on, for it was a raw day. After an overnight frost, the temperature had only climbed to five degrees and the north wind added a significant chill.

Dan jumped out of the car even before Jack could reach for the door handle. "My turn," he said with a grin, knocking on the window and holding out his open palm.

"It's the Milkybar kid!" shouted Justin.

Jack shrugged, wound the window down and handed over their petrol card. "Two minutes forty-five," he stated.

"Three and a half minutes," corrected Dan, "for a full tank."

"If you say so," his elder brother said condescendingly.

Justin started his stopwatch. "Five past ten and thirty seconds... Go!"

"Close the window, please," requested Ms Lane. "It's like ice in here."

Obediently, Jack wound the handle.

"The engine has to warm up before the heater works," said Alan defensively.

Ms Lane, who was wearing black kid leather gloves and a thick woollen shawl, grasped the steering wheel and flexed her wrists.

"When was power steering introduced?" she asked.

The chief mechanic huffed, suspecting more criticism. "Do you want me to drive?"

"It was a question, not an accusation," answered Ms Lane. "I'm perfectly capable of handling this car or any other, thank you."

Alan rubbed his index and middle fingers on the skin above his upper lip where he thought he'd felt some downy hair growth. "Some cars had power-assisted steering in the 1950s. The Jaguar mark IX was one."

"But not this *luxury* limousine," said Ms Lane with a hint of triumphalism.

Alan set his jaw. "The drivers of these cars would have thought power steering about as necessary as a nodding dog in the back window."

Jack and Justin sniggered.

"Finished!" said Dan.

Justin pressed the button on his watch and studied the dial.

"Well?" asked Dan impatiently.

Justin took his time, as if doing the calculations in his head. "It seems that the Milkybar kid is strong and tough and only the best is good enough," he said. "Three minutes and twenty-six seconds!"

"Yes!" exclaimed Dan. "Well, brother, do you think you can better that?"

"Shall we get on?" cut in Ms Lane. "We have more important things to do than play silly adolescent games."

Dan got in the back beside his brother and gently shoulder-charged him, relishing his triumph. "Right, let's go," he said.

"Have you got your seat belts on?" questioned Ms Lane, knowing that Alan and Dan hadn't.

Two peevish clicks followed, and Ms Lane pressed the starter button. The Humber glided off the petrol station forecourt towards the exit and stopped. Alan cocked his head to listen. The engine had died. He frowned.

"No!" he snapped, putting his hand over the starter as Ms Lane was about to try again.

Alan unclipped his belt and turned, his gaze fixed on Dan.

"What have you done?" he questioned angrily.

Dan was taken aback. His mind raced, then suddenly he stiffened and a look of panic crossed his face. He released his belt and scrambled out of the car.

"What's going on?" said Jack.

"Stupid idiot," muttered Alan, and manoeuvred himself over Justin and out the front passenger door. Already, Dan was standing by the pump marked *diesel*, his hands over his face.

234

Alan ran up to him and shouted, "What a stupid, idiotic thing to do, you moron!"

Dan's shoulders began to shake and he sobbed. "Sorry!"

Jack, who had been watching through the back window, unclipped his belt. "Uh-oh, looks like it could get nasty," he said, opening the door.

Ms Lane turned to her one remaining passenger. "I want answers, Justin. Why has the car stopped, and why is Alan annoyed with Dan?"

A Peugeot 206 pulled up alongside the Humber and the driver put his head out of the window with a questioning look. Jack nodded at the man and gave him a half-smile, though his mind was on the altercation that had broken out at the pumps.

"*Moya mashina slomalas,*" he said quickly, the first time he had used a Russian phrase to a stranger, even though he was in Estonia.

Ms Lane emerged from the driver's seat to properly engage the man, allowing Jack to hurry over to deal with the outbreak of hostilities. But as he closed in on the pair his pace slowed, as it was Alan who now had his head bowed.

"Sorry, Dan. I just get so angry sometimes."

"But I fucked up big-time," admitted Dan, still holding his head. "I'm a waste of space."

"No, you're not! It doesn't matter. The car can be fixed. It's me that's all wrong. Sometimes I don't think I'm right in the head."

Dan put his arms round his much smaller friend and they hugged. "Your head is OK by me. We can't do without it, and thanks for not making me feel too much of a worm."

"Has peace broken out?" asked Jack.

"Yeh," said Dan. "I've been a jerk."

"It shouldn't be too much of a problem," said Alan guardedly.

"What can I do to help?" asked Dan.

Alan shook his head. "Justin and I will fix it."

Jack put his arm round his brother's shoulder. "Looks like you'll have to stick to doctoring us humans, LB."

Ms Lane strode up to them, Justin close behind. "The Estonian gentleman has offered to help us." She paused to wave and smile at the Peugeot owner who was now standing admiring the Humber. "When Jack spoke to him, he thought we were Russian, but I put his mind at rest. I couldn't tell him what was wrong so, Alan, could you explain to him and see what he can do for us? He speaks good English."

"206, two-litre diesel – he can tow us to the garage we were at last night," said Alan.

"How long will it take to repair?" asked Jack.

"A few hours."

"What is the actual problem?" enquired Ms Lane.

"I filled the tank with diesel," said Dan.

Ms Lane made a dismissive noise. "Is that all? Can't you just drain it off and refill it with petrol?"

"No," said Alan shortly, and walked off to speak to the Estonian.

"I'd better phone base and get them to book us another night in the hotel," said Jack.

"Who's been a naughty Milkybar kid, then?" asked Justin.

"Shut up," said Dan.

"You only got away with it because you're pretty."

Dan showed Justin his middle finger.

"I'm afraid we are going to have to mark this particular fill null and void for timing purposes," said Jack.

"Definitely," added Justin, "and for the use of illegal substances he should be banned."

"You're never going to let this go, are you?" asked Dan.

"Not as long as there's mileage in it," chuckled Jack.

Alan trotted over. "The man says his son will take the diesel out of our tank for his Nissan Bluebird."

"Won't that damage his car?" asked Ms Lane, perplexed.

"There was only a couple of pints of petrol left, and those old diesel engines are more tolerant than the new ones." Alan looked at Justin. "Are you ready?"

Justin nodded.

Ms Lane clapped her gloved hands. "Well then, I hope this teaches all of you that these silly competitive urges that you young men have need to be contained. Testosterone is not a substitute for reasoned thought. Cooperation should be the spirit of our enterprise." She smiled at them. "Now, Jack and Dan, we'll leave these two rude mechanicals to their own devices while we—"

"I'm not a rude mechanical," interrupted Justin.

"Yes, you are, with the emphasis on the *rude*," said Dan.

"It's just a figure of speech, Justin, you wouldn't understand."

"No, I wouldn't understand," mumbled Justin under his breath, "I'm just a rude mechanical boy."

Ms Lane continued, unabashed. "Now, as I was saying, while these two mend the car, it gives you two Moseley boys the opportunity to sample some of the cultural highlights that the second city of Estonia has to offer. I was looking through a magazine in the hotel last night..."

Dan looked desperately at the chief mechanic. "I'd really like to help..."

"No, you two go off and enjoy yourselves," said Alan, without a hint of irony.

"I think we should start with the 1830s house in the old part of town," enthused Ms Lane.

"You could bring us some food about one," suggested Justin. "Even rude mechanicals need food."

***

57: Tuesday, 5th November. 6.45 a.m. MSK, Arkhangelsk Oblast, Gosudarstvennyi Meditsinskii Institut (gomoseksualizm).

NOAH

The thaw at the end of October was only temporary, for on the second day of November, the temperature dipped again and continued to hover around freezing. On the third, snow fell during the night and continued all day on the fourth, replacing all that had melted and more, leaving a six-inch accumulation. During Monday night a northerly wind picked up which continued into Tuesday, blowing swirls of powdery snow across the compound which would cut into exposed skin like shards of glass.

Noah sneezed. "Oh, John, the water's not very warm and I've got such a nasty cold."

"Well, don't sneeze all your germs over me, thank you," replied John, attempting to get some lather out of the brick of hard soap.

"But my lips are cracked, my throat is sore and I've still got poorly toes..."

"And you can tell he's not very well because he hasn't got a hard-on today," observed Jamie.

"Ooo, Jamie, don't be so crude!" cried Noah.

"Huh, at least he's not wanking in the shower – like someone I could name," retorted John.

"If you sneak around like a brothel creeper, what do you expect? At least Marshall always makes a lot of noise."

"Ooo, I'll try to be quieter in future," grinned Noah, his aches and pains temporarily forgotten.

"The thing is, you continued doing it even when you knew I was there," protested John.

"If you were a normal boy, Price, instead of a crusty old fossil, you'd know that when you get to a certain point you just can't stop."

"When was this incident?" enquired Noah. "You haven't said."

"I don't wish to talk about it any more," said John sniffily, holding his glasses up to the shower nozzle to see if he could get some of the fog out. "All that grunting and groaning..."

The boys made their way out to the changing area where they dried themselves quickly and began to dress.

"Do you think we'll ever see Porky and Owen again?" enquired Noah thoughtfully, wiping his nose on a dry part of the towel. "I can't imagine them being out in weather like this."

"Funny, if two people I knew disappeared back home, I'd be thinking about them for months," answered John. "But here, it's been five days and I've already started to forget them. Same with Mark, Dwain, everyone..."

"Brandon still sticks in my mind," said Jamie. "I think he always will."

A noise outside alerted Noah and he poked his head round the changing room door. Sister Hopkins was making her way upstairs while Babooshka was holding on to the bannister at the bottom, shouting at her. Noah signalled to his two companions to join him.

"This is interesting," he said quietly.

When she got to the top of the stairs, the Sister turned as a torrent of Russian poured out from the old woman below.

"You stupid old hag!" she shouted. "He was dead weeks ago and the other one will be shortly too..."

With that she retreated out of sight along the landing, leaving Babooshka wailing after her, both arms raised and her wrinkled fists clenched in fury.

"It's the twins, isn't it?" whispered Noah. As if in answer, the pale, distraught figure of Michael appeared at the kitchen door.

"Help!" he howled. "He's dying..."

The three older boys ran the few yards down the corridor and into the kitchen, Noah putting his arm around Michael.

Dennis was lying on his back on the floor by the table where they made the bread, his head cushioned by an old coat. His eyes were half open, cheeks grey and his forehead glistening with beads of perspiration. Momentarily, his breathing stopped and Noah thought the end had come, but then it started again, growing faster and deeper. All the time there was a rattle in his throat. Then his breathing slowed and grew shallow. Babooshka entered and stood at his head,

239

crossing herself right to left with her thumb and first two fingers.

"Hold his hand, Michael," said Noah, softly, "he'll like that."

Michael knelt and took his brother's left hand.

"He's cold," he murmured.

"He knows you're with him," said Noah, "and he's quite peaceful."

Noah stepped back, joining his friends against the wall, while Babooshka fetched a cloth dipped in cold water and gently sponged Dennis's face, wetting his lips.

"Robert ought to be here," whispered John.

"I'll fetch him," said Jamie.

Dennis's breathing kept up its curious pace, deep and shallow, fast and slow. Jamie returned with Robert, who nodded respectfully at his companions, but did not speak.

Suddenly, Michael started back. Dennis had opened his eyes fully and gripped his brother's hand so tightly that it made him cry out. He seemed to be about to rise, but then his body relaxed, his hand loosened its grip and, with a little sigh, he was gone.

Babooshka knelt and closed the boy's eyes. Muttering some words in Russian, she smoothed the stubble on the top of his head. Then she gave Michael a sad smile and nodded, gently removing his hand from his brother's.

Noah had never seen anyone die before, but it was quite obvious that Dennis as he knew him was no longer in his body, and that which lay before him was just a corpse.

Michael got shakily to his feet and looked at the four older boys, bereft. Although he seemed infinitely sad, he did not cry.

An unaccustomed anger flared in Noah. He gritted his teeth. "I'm going to have words!" he said and marched out of the kitchen and up the stairs.

The corridor leading to Sister Hopkins' room was deserted, and he knew he must speak his mind before his anger evaporated. He ran up to the door and began beating on it.

"Open this door, you cowardly bitch!" he shouted.

"What do you think you're doing?" said a voice behind him.

He jumped and turned. Sister Hopkins was standing beside the open door of the medical room, her arms folded. Noah's will immediately began to evaporate.

"You killed him," he managed, but he knew that if he said any more he would start to cry.

The Sister tapped her foot.

"If you weren't such a fool," she said, "you'd have realised weeks ago that his life was over."

Noah felt his eyes sting. "You brought it on. You made them go outside and work."

"There is no point in prolonging the life of a weak degenerate."

His anger flared again. "He wasn't degenerate, he was a sweet-natured little boy. And from now on, Michael's going to stay in the warm," he stated determinedly.

"He'll be dead within a week whatever we do, you stupid queer," said the Sister, and she beheld him for a moment with an expression that was part guile and, to Noah's surprise, part disquiet. "In any case, it's over. Finished!"

Noah gaped at her, her meaning only slowly permeating his befuddled mind.

"You mean, we're going home?"

"*I* shall be leaving. What they will do with you, I don't know and I don't care."

"You're a very wicked women, Sister."

She laughed. "I am the person of the moment. The one that England needs. When I get back, with my accumulated experience, I shall be put in charge of an establishment similar to this. Only mine will be more competently run. There will be no hiding place for queers like you anywhere."

"What should we do about Dennis's body?" asked Noah quietly.

"Get it outside, you imbecile, or do you want to have a rotting corpse in the kitchen?"

"But we can't bury him – the ground's too hard."

"That's your problem. Perhaps you could get that old crone to cast a spell over him. Now get out of my way, or I'll call a guard and you will have the pleasure of a nice cold session in the cage."

Noah felt his sore throat returning. As he stood deflated and defeated before Sister Hopkins, his headache suddenly worsened and his vision blurred as if he was about to faint.

***

58: Wednesday, 6th November. 11 p.m. State Hermitage Museum Hotel, St Petersburg.

<u>JUSTIN</u>

It took us seven hours to get through the border at Narva, even though Stewart at home base had booked a place for us. According to Ms Lane, the guards were surly conscripts from Vladivostok, though she may have been joking. They looked at every one of our documents and had us unload most of our luggage, which they then picked through like we had a ton of heroin stashed away. Personally, I think they were jealous of all our designer clothes and our superb vintage Humber Pullman machine.

Earlier, Dan sent back some photographs to England of us hard at work on the car in Tartu after Brains had filled the tank with diesel. Once the fuel had been emptied into several plastic cans, courtesy of Erik the Estonian, Alan had us flush out the tank and fuel pipes, examine the pump and clean the filter. There was no damage at all. Not that we told Dan that. We kept shaking our heads and putting on very glum faces when he brought us our lunch. I tell you, there's nothing more satisfying than watching Daniel Moseley eating a shed-load of humble pie. Ha! Ha!

This is our second night in the State Hermitage Museum Hotel, which is more like a palace inside than a museum. Ms

242

Lane says it's done in the style of Catherine the Great who was apparently the brains behind the whole city, though in my opinion building a city on a swamp so there's no underground car parks isn't all that *great*. When I mentioned this fact to Ms Lane she gave me one of those looks which is meant to tell me that I'm on the same evolutionary level as an amoeba.

We had to stay here for two nights so that our visas could be ratified, which is a load of bureaucratic baloney, if you ask me. It's yet another way of collecting wheelbarrows of dosh from foreigners. God knows what it'd be like if we didn't have Ms Lane sweet-talking all the commissars, as she calls them.

I'm sharing again with Alan, who I have to say has been a bit off these last couple of nights. One of the reasons is, we've had to park on the street outside the hotel, which makes him jumpy. Even though we removed everything that could be removed from the car, including the tool kits, he's been out there three or four times a day checking for scratches, broken wing mirrors and God knows what. I think I need to talk to him, actually. There's something on his mind – or maybe more than one thing. We were down in the gym, or fitness centre as they call it, for a good hour today and he hardly said a word. As soon as he comes out of the shower I shall put him on the psychiatrist's couch.

He's out of the bathroom now with a white towel round his waist which goes down to his ankles and he's drying his hair with another. Now, I know there's something not right about him because I'm lying here on my bed in just my CKs and he hasn't checked me out once. Another thing, he's started wearing pyjamas and, let me tell you, they are like something my granddad would wear. The bottoms are fastened with a piece of cord!

"Alan, I want to talk to you."

His head is bowed and his shoulders hunched and he's kind of looking at me from under his brows.

"In a minute. I've just got to put my pyjamas on."

Mr Modesty has taken his neatly folded PJs off the bed and gone into the bathroom to put them on.

The boy's been in there for ten minutes, which means he's avoiding me, no doubt hoping I'll be asleep by the time he comes out. No way! I think I'll go in and see what he's up to. The door's ajar so he shouldn't be doing anything that I wouldn't do. Ha! Ha! But I'll make some noise anyway so he'll know I'm coming.

He's sitting on the bathroom floor in his PJs, staring at the wall. I crouch down right next to him so I can talk quietly to him.

"Alan, you're sitting on the hard floor in the bathroom, when you could be lying on your nice comfy bed talking to your best friend, Justin."

He's closed his eyes and started massaging his brow with the palm of his hand. I think he's been crying. Right! I sit next to him, put my arm round his shoulder and hug him to me, so that he knows I'm here for him.

It seems ages that we've been sitting like this, though it's probably no more than five minutes. He was tensed up like a coiled spring at first, but I just felt him relax a bit and he's put his head on my shoulder.

"Alan?"

"I'm mental, aren't I?" he says.

I give him a look.

"What makes you say that?"

"I've been back in that room with the flies again."

That needs a bit of thinking about. "My feet are going numb; let's go and talk in the bedroom. Do you want me to carry you?"

Hmm, I'm not sure I could lift him off the floor, actually. He may be small, but he's quite chunky. Good, he's given me eye contact and what passes for a smile, which means we might be in business.

We're both lying on my single bed which is almost the size of a double, propped up on this long thin thing which they call a bolster, and about thirty pillows.

"What happened to you was big-time. You can't expect to get over it just like that."

"I was doing all right."

"Yes, but if something else makes you feel down, then you're more likely to bring back those bad memories."

"I think I'm going to be a mental case all my life."

"Everyone's a bit mental, Alan. Take Ms Lane, for instance. What's the point of walking miles to the Hermitage Museum when we're already staying in the Hermitage Museum Hotel?"

Now he's given me a look as though I'm mental. Perhaps it wasn't a good example.

"I shouted at Dan for no reason, and now he hates me."

So, his very minor spat with Dan has made him depressed.

"Well, he deserved to be shouted at! Deliberately sabotaging your beautiful car..."

His eyes have gone wide and he's thinking about what I've just said. That's a relief. He's given me another half-smile which means he's got what I really meant.

"He hasn't spoken to me since."

The reason for that, if it's true, is probably the exact opposite to what he thinks. I've known DM since he was knee-high to a grasshopper and underneath his rock exterior is a sensitive soul."

I'm on my phone. "Hey, Dan, what you doing?"

"I'm asleep, arsehole."

Did I say he was sensitive?

"Well, get your butt in here. There's plenty more hours to sleep in."

"What's up?"

"We need you."

"I'm not into three-ways, especially with boys."

"OK, you can just watch, I know you couldn't take my weapon of mass eruption anyway."

"That toy pistol. All it does is fire caps... OK, on my way... It had better be good."

Dan walks into our bedroom wearing his white hotel dressing gown, like he's a junior James Bond.

"Ah! Mr Bond, nice of you to drop in. Allow me to introduce myself. I'm Walker, Justin Walker..."

He tries to frown, but underneath I can tell he's loving being called James Bond.

"Well, Mr Walker, you've stirred me now, see if you can shake me."

"You know Agent 008, Alan Henderson, don't you? Well, he's feeling like he was back in that room. He says you haven't spoken to him since he shouted at you, and thinks you hate him."

Dan pauses for a moment while he processes the information, makes a visual assessment of the situation, judges what move he should make, then executes his decision, just like a superstar footballer should. He jumps onto the bed beside Alan, takes him by the shoulders and shakes him gently. "Why do you think I hate you when I love you, you fool? Especially in your blue stripy winceyette PJs like my mum wears – only hers are pink."

Alan kind of smiles at him, then his eyes get wet and a tear run out of each of them. "You know I'm a fag, don't you?"

So that's another thing that's been going round and round in his little head.

But Dan has assumed full control of the match now, and I know we're in safe hands.

"I'm really shocked," he says, "especially as we're on our way to rescue your boyfriend. Aren't you shocked, Justin?"

"To the core. The next thing we know, your brother will tell us he's gay and then we'll be on our way to rescue his boyfriend as well."

Alan wipes his eyes with the back of his hand.

"I've decided, it's got to be me who tells him. Even if he hates me."

"You mean about his dad?" I say, and he nods.

"I think you're probably right," agrees Dan. "He'll need your support over it, however he reacts. You may have to be patient with him."

"In other words," I spell out, "if he flies off the handle at you, just play it cool."

Alan takes a deep breath and his cheeks expand as he blows it out. "Why are you two always nice to me when I'm just a little piece of shit?"

That's not just him wallowing in self-pity, I think it's what he genuinely believes when he's in one of his depressions.

"I've told you," said Dan, "you're on our team and we stick by our team-mates through hell and high water. Like you forgave me for fucking up with the diesel, because I'm your team-mate."

"I would have given him a good thrashing," I say to add to the mix.

Dan makes a noise as if he doesn't think I could, and he might be right. Then Alan yawns.

"I'm sleepy," he says, "but I've got to make one last check on the car..."

"No," I say.

"I'll check," volunteers Dan. "I can see it from my window. Just about."

Alan's head is lolling.

"You will tell me, if anything... if anything..."

"If anything, yes," agrees Dan with a chuckle.

"Looks like we're swapping for tonight," I say, getting off what was my bed.

Dan does likewise, then carefully adjusts the covers so that our little man is snug.

"If I didn't know you better, I'd say you were a nice person, DM."

"He seems OK now, don't you think?"

"Dropping off like that is a good sign." I reply.

"Better do a window check, like I promised. I don't want to fuck up again, do I?"

Ten minutes have gone by, the lights are off and I'm curled up in my nice warm bed when my phone vibrates under my pillow.

"Hey," says Dan.

"Is this revenge?" I ask.

"Not really, I've just been out to the car..."

There's a pregnant pause and my heart starts beating a little faster.

"And..." I say.

"It's freezing out there. It's covered in frost."

"And..."

"Someone's written *queers* in English on the windscreen, only it's spelled *QUeaRs*."

"Fuck! Why did you go out?"

"Because when I looked through the window, I saw three men round the car. One was on watch, another was the dick scrawling on the windscreen, and the third was doing something else, but I couldn't tell what."

"Any damage?"

"Not that I could see. I asked the doorman to keep a lookout and gave him my room number if anything else happens."

"Did you scrape it off?"

"Of course I did, but I took a couple of pictures first just to prove I'm not paranoid or dreaming."

"Shall I tell..?"

"No point, let him sleep."

"I'm going to be lying awake thinking about it."

"You and me both..."

***

59: Thursday, 7th November. 7.30 a.m. State Hermitage Museum Hotel, St Petersburg.

ALAN

I've got to get away, and fast. Justin's still asleep so if I'm quiet I can make it out without him knowing. This trip has gone to hell and it's all my fault. Why was I stupid enough to admit to them that I'm a fag? Now I can never look them in the face again.

There! I'm dressed and my overnight bag's packed. Washing stuff, two changes of socks, T-shirts and underwear. I've got my wallet with some money, but I'll need to get my passport from reception. Now, is there anything else? No time to think. Justin's stopped snoring so he'll be waking up any second...

I'm out in the corridor. The carpet's blue and gold and really posh. My dad would like it here but if he was here, I'd be a thousand miles away in the other direction. We're on the fourth floor and I've got to find the stairs. It's safer than the lift. There's no one about, except one maid with a trolley three doors down. I'm trying to look cool but I'm not succeeding.

I got past her, but I'm sure she suspects. Maybe she can tell I'm a fag. What happens if she reports me to the authorities? Russians don't like fags, so I'll get beaten up – or worse.

When I get outside I could take the car, but that would be stupid. In any case, Ms Lane's got the keys. The train station is my best bet. Can I ask for a ticket to England? No, London – that sounds better. Otherwise they'll think I'm a div. I'm shit-scared already and I'm not even out of the hotel...

I've been walking up and down these corridors, but I can't find the stairs anywhere. I don't even know where I am any more. There's a pair of lifts at the end so I'll have to take a chance. One is on its way up so I'll press the button. The doors are made of mirrors and I can see how shifty and faggy I look.

Hopefully there'll be no one in. Good, it's stopped and the doors are opening.

"Alan!"

Jesus, it's Jack Moseley! This is a disaster. I jump about a foot in the air and go red. What's going to happen now? He's looking at me with his finger on the open door button. It's a good job he's the only passenger. I could get in and maybe he'll get out, or I could run away. I don't know what to do. I'm such a stupid spaz!

"Are you getting in?" he asks.

"I'll wait..." I reply and my voice is all high-pitched, like it hasn't broken.

He's looking at me even harder now. I know he thinks there's something's wrong. If I wasn't so mental, I'd know what to do.

"Alan, why are you carrying that bag?"

Jack Moseley's come out of the lift and the doors have closed and I'm standing right next to him like I'm paralysed. He's got his phone out now and I know I'm done for.

"Justin, it's Jack. Are you out of bed?"

"Good... Yes, I know where Alan is. He's standing right next to me wearing his winter coat and carrying a holdall as if he's about to catch the Trans-Siberian Express."

"Yep! *What the fuck?* is right."

There is a pause while he listens. "At the lifts, down your corridor and to the left."

Justin Walker hasn't got any shoes or socks on, which I don't think is allowed in this hotel. He's also got on a pair of loose joggers and a tight-fitting T so that his muscles are really prominent and I've gone red, because the first thing I did when he came rushing down the corridor was to check him out.

We're back in our bedroom now and I've got on a pair of jeans, a white open-neck shirt and a pair of Vans burgundy trainers. I'm feeling a bit better and I think I look quite smart. Justin never laughs at me when I tell him what's wrong, even if I'm being a total fucktard. He put me in a headlock and gave

250

me another noogie, but he's so gentle it just feels nice, like my mum when she used to stroke my hair...

But I'm not going to think about that. Shortly we'll be meeting Ms Lane for breakfast in the Catherine the Great restaurant, but before that we've got a boys-only meeting in the lounge. Dan wants to tell me something about the car. I'm worried, but not in a mental way like just now.

The hotel lounge is plush, with wood panelling and shelves full of books. It's quiet at the moment. There's only the four of us sitting in these comfy armchairs. Just being there makes you feel important. I've been shown a photo of the car windscreen. It's got *queers* written in the frost and I know who wrote it: my brother Derek! I'd recognise that scrawl anywhere. He never knew the difference between capital and small letters, and is a complete retard when it comes to spelling. Dan says he couldn't see anything wrong with the Humber, but it means Justin and I will have to check it over before we go. Derek knows as much as me about cars, so we'll have to be thorough.

"The only thing I don't get is why he would do it," says Jack Moseley. "Why draw attention to himself?"

"Because he's a lame-brain," offers Justin.

"He wants to frighten me," I say, and they all stare in my direction, which makes me go red again, so I don't look any of them in the eye when I continue. "He wants me back in that room with the flies."

"We should have burned that house down," says Dan.

"What about the two people with him?" questions Jack.

"The copper from the woods," suggests Justin. "That's my bet."

Jack leans forward. "Detective Inspector David Rains! Good thinking, Justin, and that means things could turn really nasty."

"Pity I didn't take a picture when I first saw them," says Dan.

"Are we going to tell Ms Lane?" asks Justin.

251

"We've got to tell her something," replies Dan, "otherwise she'll be wondering why you and Alan are giving the car yet another going-over."

"Show her the pictures, but don't let on about who we think it is." says Jack. "There is a chance we could be completely wrong."

No one believes we're wrong, but they don't want to tell Ms Lane that our lives are now in danger, just in case she wants to turn round and go home. That's not going to happen while I'm at the wheel.

"You've got a pretty determined expression on, Alan," says Justin.

"I don't want Derek to win," I say, which sounds to me like the stupidest comment ever, but when I manage to look them in the eye, they're all nodding like they agree with me and they're all looking pretty determined now as well, so maybe I've said something right for once.

I'm lucky, aren't I, to have these three as my friends, particularly Justin? I know it's a really faggy thing to say, but I think he's awesome. He's not that brainy and he's not even especially good-looking, though he has a nice face and his body is really great, but I don't just mean that. It's all of him, his ways and mannerisms and how kind he is, like he's made of sunshine. If he wasn't here and I was having to manage on my own, I'd probably have topped myself by now.

***

60: Thursday, 7th November. 8 a.m. MSK, Arkhangelsk Oblast, Gosudarstvennyi Meditsinskii Institut (gomoseksualizm).

ROBERT

It was just getting light when their dormitory door was unlocked and Valery Fyodorovich Khrennikov entered with Yevgeni Borisovich Mravinsky, Ivan the Terrible at his back.

Robert stood up, but no one else moved from their beds. Jamie had kept the stove going since six o'clock with the small pile of logs that were kept in reserve, and was now fast asleep. Both Noah and John had temperatures, and their sweat had coated the windows above their beds with condensation which had turned to ice. Michael lay unmoving in a half-reclining position, his eyes open, but dim and disinterested.

"They're not well," said Robert, excusing his companions for not being ready for inspection.

Valery shrugged. "It is of no consequence now, *Tovarisch* Crittenden. We are about to evacuate the premises. You are now no longer under the care of the Russian Federation."

"Well, that's one good thing," murmured John, who was at least alert, though he lay quite still.

"What's going to happen to us?" asked Robert.

"We expect Sister Hopkins to make the arrangements for you," answered Valery in a clearly rehearsed answer.

The American nodded, wishing that Noah was able to ask his usual innocuous-sounding but probing questions.

"Where is the Sister?" he enquired.

"I think if I answer in the manner of the lady: I don't know and I don't care." Valery gave a small chuckle. "I expect she is in her boudoir, as our friend in the far bed would say."

Jamie sat up, blinking the sleep from his eyes. "What time is it?" he asked.

"Always the chronological or meteorological questions from *Tovarisch* Baker," answered Valery, looking at the watch on his left wrist. "It is five minutes past eight o'clock, Moscow standard time, and the temperature outside is minus ten degrees Celsius. The weather station in Plesetsk forecasts a cloudless day and expects the temperature by tonight to have fallen by another ten degrees with a further wind-chill factor, and so I would caution you pussy Brits against any trips outside."

"What about pussy Americans?" asked Robert.

Valery smiled. "The same, *Tovarisch* Crittenden. And now, on behalf of Yevgeni Borisovich Mravinsky, myself and Mother Russia, I bid you farewell."

Noah's head rose from his pillow. "Oh, Mistress, and we shall never get a chance to have a game."

"I am pleased you had the last word as usual, *Tovarisch* Marshall. Perhaps in another life."

With that the two Russians left, closing the door quietly behind them. Robert walked over to Noah's bed and looked down at his friend.

"Are you feeling any better after your nasty turn, yesterday?"

"A bit," Noah swallowed, still bothered by a sore throat.

Robert felt his brow.

"About one hundred, I'd say. Lie quiet and keep warm. Jamie and I had better see what's going on downstairs. For a start, we'll get you a drink. You need to keep your fluids up."

"Aren't you going to feel my fevered brow?" murmured John, who had taken up residence in the next bed.

"Don't worry, I'll look after Price," responded Jamie, sliding out from beneath his duvet.

John groaned.

Babooshka entered the dormitory carrying three glasses of a hot infusion, which may or may not have been tea. Breathing heavily after climbing the stairs, she handed one to Robert and pointed at Michael, gave another to Jamie and pointed at John, then she walked down to where Noah lay, put the glass on the cupboard and motioned for him to sit up. Robert watched with some amusement from Michael's bedside as she plumped his pillow and generally made a fuss of him.

"You good boy," she whispered huskily, handing him the glass.

Noah smiled and took a sip of tea.

"Ooo, Babooshka, are you leaving too?" he asked, knowing full well she was.

She smiled and patted his shoulder, not understanding.

"Noah, you good boy," she repeated, nodding. Then she slid her gnarled hand under his pillow.

"*Spasiba,*" she said and kissed him lightly on the forehead.

"*Spasiba,*" he replied and grinned at her.

The old woman hobbled away, head bent, looking neither left nor right as she left the dormitory for the last time.

Half an hour or so later, Robert was standing by the window watching, as below them Valery, Ivan and two guards filed across the yard towards the open gate, each carrying a cardboard box.

"Probably all the medical stuff," said Jamie, "so we don't drug ourselves."

Babooshka trailed in their wake, easing her way in the snow with the aid of a walking stick.

"And there goes Grand Jedi Master Yoda," he added.

"Oh, Jamie, don't be so rude," cried Noah. "Babooshka is a very nice old lady."

"Don't you mean, a very nice old lady, Babooshka is..." croaked John.

"Just because she likes you, Marshall, for some unknown reason," responded Jamie. "In any case, how did you know I was talking about her?"

"They've left the gate open," observed Robert.

The sound of the Gaz-66 engine being revved came to their ears and the American could just see the bottom half of the chassis as it moved off on its westward journey to Puksa.

"Shall we go and beat up Madam now?" suggested Jamie.

"She's the only one who can get us home," answered Robert. "In any case, she's just part of the rotten system."

"That's a very liberal attitude for an eye-for-an-eye, southern state American," rasped John.

"I expect she's locked herself in her boudoir waiting for Prince Yurine to come and rescue her," said Noah, clearing his throat and putting the spoon down into a half-eaten bowl of porridge.

"Don't waste food," said Jamie. "Today was supposed to be delivery day and there isn't much left of last week's supply."

"I can't eat any more," Noah replied sadly, "but it was very nice gruel..."

"At least the man with the barrow hasn't been to steal our logs today," said Robert.

"That's probably because there's hardly any left to be stolen," said Jamie. "About four days, if we're lucky."

"Plenty more in the forest," whispered John.

"Yeh, well, you get out of your sick bed and start chopping, Price. The worst woodsman in the world."

"How's Michael?" asked Noah.

"Asleep now, thank God," replied Jamie.

"Madam DeVeal thinks he will die just like Dennis."

The others went silent and Robert looked out of the window and across the compound to the small mound in the corner which was covered with a hessian sack. "I never thought in all my life I would spend time moving a dead body around."

***

It was afternoon and the sun was an orange ball, already sinking towards the trees in the south-west. The inside of the dormitory was aglow with its light when Robert entered and found all three boys asleep. Michael had crossed the room and was cuddled up against Noah in his bed. The American hesitated, uncertain whether he should wake them just to make them drink the tea he had brought.

He put the tray down on the cupboard between the beds and rubbed his eyes. Below, in the compound, Jamie was in his full winter gear, moving their remaining logs from under the eaves to where he was making a stack of them in the kitchen.

Noah opened one eye. "Robert, what's that noise?"

The American was about to ask, *what noise?* when he heard it himself. The sound of a vehicle coming at speed towards the compound from the direction of Puksa. A squeal of brakes and the sight of two giant wheels outside the gate brought back memories of the fire at the Church of the Transfiguration. This was the same pick-up truck that had once belonged to the Reverend Akinola but which had been driven away in triumph by Yuri Semyonovich Bakaleinikoff.

"It looks like Madam's taxi has arrived," said Robert, who had a grandstand view of the proceedings.

Below, Jamie was standing, hands on hips, watching, his breath emerging from his mouth in white clouds.

Three people entered the compound clad in layers of winter clothes, but none had the unmistakeable bulk of Yuri. Robert furrowed his brow. They seemed vaguely familiar.

"What's the matter, Robert?" asked Noah, looking up at him.

Two of the figures went up to Jamie and spoke in harsh Russian, then one pushed him backwards, making him stumble, while the other pulled out a baton from his pocket and went to strike him, but it was only a threat. Robert heard their laughter as Jamie ducked to avoid the blow that never came.

"Jesus!" exclaimed Robert, recognition coming at last. "It's the three boys from the prison."

"What?" said Noah.

"The three boys; the ones that shat in my bed. The ones that beat me up..."

"Oh, Robert, what will we do?"

"Stay here, don't make a sound. I'll go and see what they want and why they're in Yuri's truck."

"Be careful!" warned Noah.

Robert trembled as he made his way out of the dormitory, only to be met halfway down the stairs by Jamie, who was being followed by the three youths.

"Are you OK?" he asked.

Jamie gave him a warning look and the American gave him the merest nod in acknowledgement.

"Yankee gay, we meet again!" shouted the leader of the youths, the one with the rose tattoo.

The others laughed uproariously. It was clear that all three had been drinking.

"They've come for *the English lady*," said Jamie, realising himself now who these three were.

"Who sent them?" asked Robert without thinking.

"Take us to English lady, Yankee gay," said the leader.

More laughter. Robert climbed the stairs to the landing then, without looking at the dormitory door, walked down the corridor towards Sister Hopkins' room. Halfway along he stopped and pointed.

"That one at the end," he said.

Rose Tattoo pushed by him and rapped with his baton on the door. "English lady Hopkins, you come," he shouted.

Robert and Jamie watched, standing together with the two Russian youths just behind them. It took a good half-minute before the door opened and Sister Hopkins emerged in her furs and finery, a suitcase in one hand and a vanity case in the other.

"You no need case, your plane go now..." said the leader, making a flying motion with his hand.

"Don't be stupid," said the Sister, as belligerent as ever. "Of course I need my cases."

The two youths behind Robert sniggered.

"I wouldn't want to be driven anywhere by these three drunken dumbasses," whispered Jamie.

Sister Hopkins put the suitcase down but kept hold of her vanity case. As she pulled the door shut, Robert noticed to his chagrin, that it was fitted with a Yale-type lock. Access denied, he thought.

"Well, aren't you going to carry my suitcase?" she said to the youth, indicating with her leather gloved hand, "or are you as ignorant as you look?"

Jamie's jaw dropped and Robert had a sudden and unexpected feeling of admiration for their arch enemy, who was either totally fearless or totally unaware what sort of people she was dealing with.

Unexpectedly the youth meekly picked up the case and began to walk back down the corridor, but then he handed it to one of his accomplices and spoke some words in Russian. The Sister passed Robert and Jamie without a word or a look, but her bearing was, as ever, haughty.

Out on the landing, Rose Tattoo stopped and his predatory eyes came to rest on the dormitory door. He glanced back at Robert and a small smile crossed his face. Sister Hopkins huffed impatiently. She had covered her bonnet of golden blonde hair with a headscarf, which seemed inadequate protection against the intense cold.

Robert's heart sank as the lead youth ignored the Sister's impatience, strode up to the door and opened it. Noah and Michael were peeping out from under their duvet, expressions of alarm on their faces, while John was snoring gently in the next bed, oblivious to all that was happening. The leader began to laugh hysterically. "English gay homos!" he crowed, pointing at the two boys in the same bed. His comrades gathered by him and they began to cackle and talk excitedly in Russian.

As suddenly as it began, the laughter ceased and the leader looked at Robert with an expression of disgust. "You fly next, Yankee gay," he said, "and those two homos." Then he turned and smiled at Sister Hopkins. "We go now, English lady, fly now... yes?"

Robert and Jamie stood at the door of the barracks, watching the four figures cross the courtyard in the early twilight. On the threshold of the outside gate Rose Tattoo paused, allowing his comrades and the Sister to go before him. He gazed back at them with a smirk and made a throat-slitting gesture with his index finger. Then he too was gone.

"What did you make of that?" asked Jamie, as the noise of the big-tyred vehicle receded.

"I think we should prepare for a return visit," said Robert, closing the door and shooting the bolts.

***

61: Thursday, 7th November. Noon, McDonald's restaurant, on the outskirts of St Petersburg.

DI DAVID RAINS

The detective inspector tapped his laptop in time with the tune that was playing inside his head: 'Two little boys had two little toys...' That was as far as got because he couldn't remember any more of the words, or the tune for that matter. Meanwhile, the little green car on the screen moved jerkily, as the ten-second pulse came down from the satellite to position it a further two hundred and fifty metres along the E105. He glanced up as PC Richard Masefield emerged through the crush of people and began to unload the tray.

"What you got me then, Dickie?"

"What you asked for, David. A Big Tasty, double fries, Coke."

"Excellent! Would you like to see how our little widget is working?"

Dickie shrugged disinterestedly, but David Rains turned the laptop to face him anyway. "What a boon technology is, wouldn't you say?"

"It is when it works."

"If they do go out of range we'll just pick up their scent in the old-fashioned way. A bloody hulking great banger like that Humber isn't going to be difficult to spot."

Dickie sat down and began to pick through his chicken nuggets, making a face as he did so. The DI chuckled at his companion.

"Did you hear there's a big freeze on the way? Those bum bandits will be shivering in their ruby slippers in that draughty old car. Not like our flashy Merc, eh?"

"They seem to have managed so far."

"Not at twenty below."

Dickie dipped a chosen nugget in honey mustard sauce and took a delicate bite.

"And where has our friend Derek got to?" asked DI Rains.

Now the constable's face contorted into a deep frown. "I don't know, and I don't care. He's a wrong 'un, that one, David. Surely you can see it, councillor's son or not?"

"What's he been doing this time to get your goat?"

Dickie remained silent while he ground his teeth.

"Come on, tell Uncle David," said the DI, taking a wolfish bite out of his Big Tasty. "You're not still on about him writing queers on that windscreen, are you?"

"A bloody stupid thing to do. He could have given the whole game away."

"But it didn't, did it? It was just a bit of harmless fun to put the wind up those shirt-lifters."

"It's not proper procedure to give away your cover," insisted Dickie.

David Rains chuckled. "So, are you miffed about the young lady he brought back to the hotel last night?"

"Prostitute, you mean. I'm just an ordinary family man, David, who tries to live the Christian life. My son would never act like that and if he did he'd suffer the consequences."

DI Rains took another bite of his burger and red sauce ran down his chin.

"Don't be so serious, Dickie," he said between chews. "Derek is just a young buck. That's what normal English lads do when they're away from home. Sow a few wild oats. I tell you, he's a bit rough round the edges, that's all."

The constable handed his superior a paper napkin.

"It's not all. He's as thick as shit, got no respect for his elders and has the filthiest mouth this side of Hades."

The DI sighed. "OK, Dickie, leave it with me. I'll have a word. Stop him winding you up. We can't have dissension in the ranks now, can we?"

"It's not that he's winding me up, guv; he's a bloody loose cannon, and if we're ever stopped by the Ruskies he could get us all arrested."

David made no further comment but gazed across the restaurant.

"Ah! There he is..."

He waved, trying to draw the attention of the lean, muscular figure who was standing near the counter, a Big Mac in one hand, a Coke in the other and a long parcel under his arm. At last, Derek Henderson spotted the pair by the window and pushed his way through the throng.

"Move up, Granddad," he said to Constable Masefield, who took a deep breath to calm himself and edged along the seat.

"What you got there, Derek?" asked the DI.

"A Big Mac," smirked the youth.

"Under your arm, smart aleck."

"Bought myself a little present. Do you want to see?"

"Why not?"

Derek partially removed the brown paper wrapping, revealing a label in Cyrillic script above a picture of a Baikal IZH 61 pellet rifle.

Dickie let out a gasp of disbelief, holding his head in both hands.

"What's up, Granddad?" laughed Derek. "The barrel of this will fit nicely up the arse of that Moseley faggot. Bang! Bang!"

"Now, keep calm Dickie," said David Rains soothingly. "Derek is just having a joke."

"He's not funny," stated the constable.

The youth laughed again. "Is Granddad jealous because I got to lick a bit of Russian pussy last night?"

"You are disgusting."

"Heh, heh, heh, I know. I love it, burying my tongue deep inside all that slurpy wetness..."

The constable threw down what was left of his chicken piece.

"I'm not staying here to listen to any more of his obscenities, David. I'll be in the car..."

He climbed over the seat to avoid having to push by the youth, but he had only got a yard or two when he was called back by the DI.

"Dickie, you forgot these." David jangled the ignition keys then threw them at the constable, who failed to catch them, so that he had to scrabble for them on the floor.

"Butterfingers," sniggered Derek.

Red in the face and fuming with repressed anger, the constable retreated from the restaurant.

"Why did you bring that stupid old fucker, Davey boy?" asked Derek, tucking the remaining Chicken McNuggets into his burger.

"Less of your cheek. Because he's respectable, that's why, and we need a respectable front."

The youth made a dismissive noise. "He's not a front, he's a cunt. I'd like to cut that Brillo pad off his top lip with my knife."

Detective Inspector Rains leaned back in his seat and put his hands behind his head, replete after his Big Tasty and fries. "I'll say one thing for you, Derek. You are a chip off the old block."

"And I'll say two things to you, DI Rains. One, I hope my dad's instructions concerning that piece of shit that calls itself Stewart Henderson are being carried out..."

"Oh yes, that house of ill-repute has been condemned and the occupants are being moved into more permanent accommodation in the cemetery." David chortled at his own joke. "And what was the second thing you had on your mighty mind, Derek, old chum?"

"You may have told Dickie the Dick that I'm joking when I say I'm going to put the barrel of this gun up Moseley's faggoty arse. But I'm not, and that goes for his super-wanker brother too."

This time David gave a hearty laugh and tapped his chest. "Do you think I would come on a jaunt like this and not have suitable firepower? It's amazing what you can get through customs when you're a copper. So while you're firing your Russian pea-shooter, I'll be shoving the barrel of my Smith & Wesson 500 so far up the backside of that fairy-lover, Justin Walker, that he'll be able to lick the muzzle. I can almost hear him now, screaming for mercy as he dies oh so slowly..." He smiled and began to hum softly, 'Two little boys had two little toys...'.

***

62: Thursday, 7th November. 1 p.m. E105 motorway.

JACK

When our chief mechanic searched the Humber in St Petersburg, I think he knew what he was looking for, because it took him just ten minutes to find it, even though it was attached to one of the cross-members of the chassis, right up against the propeller shaft. A GPS tracking device, which would have taken only a few seconds to fasten on with its built-in magnets. Of course, being Alan, he didn't stop there but checked over the whole car for more devices and sabotage. Fortunately, there was nothing else.

Justin said he was shitting bricks when Alan showed it to him because he thought it was a bomb, especially as he was told not to touch it under any circumstances. The actual reason for this is that some of these trackers are fitted with motion sensors so that if they're disturbed whoever's doing the tracking is warned.

We asked Ms Lane whether she would like to get down and dirty and see what we'd discovered but she said it would ladder her tights, or something to that effect. Her teacher radar was on full alert when LB showed her the photographs, and I'm pretty sure she knows we're not telling her everything. Alan says we should keep the tracker on so as not to arouse suspicions, and he's the boss in these matters. Personally, I'd like to have attached it to one of those boats that sail up and down the Neva River in St Petersburg. That would have given them something to think about.

When we went to the hotel reception to check out and collect our documents, the man asked us where we were headed. I'm glad to say that Ms Lane must have anticipated this, because she replied without blinking.

"To Arkhangelsk. The environmentally friendly wooden architecture of the region has always fascinated me, and it's appropriate for the children to learn about sustainability in the Russian Federation."

The man nodded sagely and seemed pleased that at last he had met a genuinely mad Englishwoman. "Be sure to have your snow tyres ready, then," he smiled. "It's cold up there."

We're travelling east out of St Petersburg on a dual carriageway and we've not long since passed a couple of familiar sights – a McDonald's sign on our right and an Ikea store on our left – though it doesn't feel much like home. Now that the car's been running for a while, it's getting nice and warm inside so we've done away with our coats and *ushankas*, which are piled on the floor in front of me. With any luck, at this rate we'll get where we're going (wherever that is) by sometime on Saturday or at the very latest by Sunday dinnertime. It just seems unreal that I'm actually going to turn up on Robert's doorstep and say, "Hey, I'm here to rescue you, but first let's have a snog in front of all these homophobes."

A strange thing has happened: I can't get a reply from home base. I spoke to Stewart last night and said I'd ring just after one, which is four o'clock GMT. There appears to be a signal, so maybe another Swanford outage is to blame, because it's not even ringing. I'll try again in fifteen minutes.

The Neva River seems to be everywhere, because we crossed over it again about ten minutes ago. Now we're going over another smaller river, the Naziya. I can see ice floating on the water and there are a lot of small boats lining the banks. The dual carriageway has petered out and we're on a road *à la* Estonia – in other words, two lanes, narrow and straight, ploughing through a flat wintry landscape. The traffic has dwindled to a trickle. Alan's driving and Ms Lane is flaked out in the passenger seat. Let's hope there are no police vehicles hiding out to catch us unawares.

Two o'clock and still no contact. Everyone's tried and we've sent emails. I asked Ms Lane to phone her husband to see if he could find out what's going on, but she said he was in Scotland on business. LB suggested that she should have left her parakeets at home then we could have phoned them, but he got the evil eye for that comment.

If we're not going to spend a very cold night in the car, we'll have to find somewhere to stay ourselves shortly. LB is already looking up possible alternatives. I never thought this would happen, and I guess having everyone else we know away from home wasn't such a good idea. However, I've got one or two more irons in the fire before I get really worried.

"Hey, Mikey."

"Hi, Jack. Where are you?"

"Russia."

"Oh."

"Are you private?"

"Yeh, Nana's in the kitchen ironing her battle-axe."

"Comedian. How are things your end?"

"I had a postcard from Mummy and Daddy. They're not coming back till the fifteenth now!"

"More sexing, I expect. How was Bonfire Night?"

"Not good. Nana sent Mike packing."

"Why?"

"He let a Roman candle off in the porch."

"Oh no! He could have set the house on fire. Didn't you try to stop him?"

"There's no stopping Mike."

"That's true. Listen, Mikey, do you think you can do a special mission for me?"

"Yes, it's boring here. I want you to come home. Have you rescued Robert and Noah yet?"

"Not yet, but it shouldn't be too long now."

266

"What is the mission?"

"Well, I can't seem to be able to raise Stewy at number 41, so I'd like you to persuade Nana to take you there and see what's up. Do you get me?"

"Yep, no problemo."

"Like now."

"Jeez, très difficile, my man."

"Funny. Where did you learn that?"

"Nowhere, dude..."

"OK, let me know as soon as the mission's accomplished, or sooner. Get me?"

"Yup!"

"LB says hi and goodbye."

"Bye-bye, sweetie pies."

That was Mikey in a good mood, by the sound of it. If he doesn't come up with anything, my next port of call will be Mandy and Max. Meanwhile, LB has booked us into a hotel in a place called Lodeynoye Pole that's about an hour and a half's drive away in the middle of nowhere, though everywhere now is in the middle of nowhere. He was pleased with himself because he made the booking in Russian, though Ms Lane was by his side giving him a few prompts. I don't think I would have done so well, but I didn't say anything because his ego's big enough already.

We're heading north-east now and Ms Lane has informed us that for the last eighty miles we've been skirting this gigantic lake, Lake Ladoga, which all these rivers we've been crossing flow into. Ms Lane says it's the biggest freshwater lake in Europe and makes our Lake Windermere seem like a pond. We can't see anything of it, though, because the road on that side is bordered by pine forest. Alan has just said that the temperature outside has dropped from plus two degrees to minus five degrees Celsius in the last ten minutes. Oh joy!

***

63: Thursday, 7th November. 5 p.m. Mini Hotel Svir, Lodeynoye Pole, Leningrad Oblast.

DAN

It's been dark outside for almost three-quarters of an hour and the lighting in this room isn't up to much either. Still the old radiators are going full blast so at least I'm warm. Mikey hasn't rung back, so we still don't know what's going on at home. I doubt whether he'll call us now, because it's eight o'clock in Swanford and not far off his bed time.

This building we're in is nothing like the Hermitage Museum Hotel in St Petersburg. Ms Lane said that it's High Soviet Functional, circa 1960, and I don't think much has changed since then. It's a long two-storey affair and the rooms are like square boxes and we have to share a bathroom. Outside there are icicles hanging from the wall above the entrance as though there's a water leak somewhere, but in its favour everywhere is clean and tidy and the staff are friendly.

We're on Lenin Street and there's a statue of him just down the road which we passed when we came in. Ms Lane told us he was one of the few men in the early part of the twentieth century who had positive views on equal rights for women, but that all changed under Uncle Joe. End of lesson, I had hoped, but then Alan, who obviously hadn't been paying attention, asked her if Uncle Joe was a relative. Cue gasps of horror from the rest of us, and Ms Lane gave him the teacher's eye in case he was being sarcastic. When this wasn't found to be the case, she gave him a lecture on the deprivations of women under Stalin.

Fortunately we arrived at the hotel before she could really get into her stride, though I do remember her mentioning that Stalin introduced a medal for women who had over nine children. I might mention that to Sophie, just in passing if you know what I mean?

I can hear Justin and Alan banging around in the next room; the walls aren't exactly thick. I might pay them a call in a minute or two to see what they're up to as I'm on my lonesome. Jack and Ms Lane have gone to get some petrol and then they're going shopping to stock up on supplies as we don't know where we'll be for the next few days. Notice that they didn't invite me to go with them to the filling station. That incident still makes me feel like a complete failure.

OK, I've been sorting through the photographs I've made on this trip. One hundred and forty-three so far, now down to eighty-four because I've deleted all the blurry views of trees as we went by in the car. There's one really good shot of Justin hurling over the side of the ferry. He doesn't know I've got that one. I can't wait to show it around. Does he look green!

What are they doing next door? It sounded then as if one of them was coming through the wall. I think it's time I burst in on them.

"So this is how I find you, in a clinch, half-naked!"

Alan breaks away immediately and goes bright red, as I knew he would.

"Bollocks," says Justin, then he turns to his partner in crime. "Take no notice, he's just jealous."

"We were practising our moves because of Derek," blurts out Alan, who I notice is getting quite a bit of definition these days.

"Oh yes," I say, "it looked pretty full on kissy-kissy to me."

If he went any redder, his head would have to be sliced and pickled in a jar.

"Who invited you in here anyway, Moseley?" asks Justin, who has built up a nice sweat.

I shake my head. "Tut, tut tut, and you two sharing a bed tonight."

"I could sleep in the chair," says Alan in a small voice.

"We wouldn't have to share if you hadn't booked us into this doss house."

"Alan, you'll have to watch that he doesn't take advantage of you tonight, when you're asleep."

Justin snorts. "I never realised that's what you were after on all those sleepovers."

But I don't get the chance to give a devastatingly funny reply as Jack arrives, looking pretty shaken up. The mood darkens and we exchange worried glances.

"We need to have a talk in Ms Lane's room," he says.

"What's up?" I ask.

"Tell you when we're all together," he replies.

Justin and Alan quickly pull on socks and sweatshirts and we troop two doors down to Ms Lane's room, where we find her on the phone to her sister. She motions for us to sit down, but there are only two spare chairs so Jack and Alan sit on the bed.

Strangely, I don't really listen to what Ms Lane is saying and I only catch a few words. She presses the end call button and gives us a once-over, then she looks at Jack, who immediately focuses his attention on Alan.

"Mikey phoned while we were on our way back. There's been an explosion at number 41. Gas, according to the policeman on the gate. It happened in the early hours of this morning. Alan, we don't know anything about who may or may not have been hurt. Mikey said that as far as he could see the whole of the front of the house had been demolished."

"But..." I began, but Jack pre-empted my question.

"I know, LB, there is no gas at the front of the house. The meter's at the side where the garage is. Mikey said that looked undamaged. Stranger still, there didn't appear to have been much of a fire."

Alan has his eyes closed and he's leaning against Justin, who has his arm round his shoulder.

"Did you speak to Nan?" I ask.

"Briefly. She doesn't know very much about the place and Mikey had said it all. She asked if there was anything she could do to help, and so I told her who lives there – Stewy, Anne and Elspeth – to see if she could find out any information about them. I forgot about Alex, though. I doubt we'll hear anything before tomorrow."

"My sister knows a doctor in the cottage hospital," adds Ms Lane, "and so she's also going to make enquiries. She remembered that there was an item on the news about a gas explosion in Swanford, but she didn't take much notice."

Ms Lane scans our faces, I guess to see how we're taking the news. "It is up to you four now, to decide what you want to do."

I could see that Jack is impressed that Ms Lane hasn't tried to lay down the law. I have to give her credit for that too.

"Alan," says Jack, "what do you think?"

The boy who has taken the hardest knocks of any of us opens his eyes and straightens up, though he keeps close to Justin. "I don't know. We need to finish what we came to do," he says.

The rest of us nod in agreement.

"I think you're right," agrees Ms Lane. "But we now know the extent of the danger we face. These people will obviously stop at nothing."

"This has become personal," states Justin. "It's not just random events. Our group is being targeted."

Jack nods and then decides to tell Ms Lane all the things we haven't told her about our pursuers. Her eyebrows rise gradually at what he tells her, but otherwise she remains guardedly silent.

When Jack has finished and we've all chipped in on different points, she regards us and speaks in measured tones, just like a teacher. "I think that you should consider informing your parents of all these facts, so that they too may be forewarned of possible danger to themselves. Clearly, these ruthless people may see them as a worthwhile and relatively easy target."

"Well, at the moment mine are out of the country," says Jack, "and I've already told Nan and Mikey to be on their guard."

"It doesn't take too much nous to work out who these ruthless people are, does it?" I state.

"My dad," says Alan. "I hate him. I wish he was dead..."

271

64: Friday, 8th November. 10.30 a.m. Leningrad Oblast, P37 road.

JUSTIN

Unbeknown to everyone, Jack and Ms Lane brought back two twenty-litre jerry cans full of unleaded last night, which are sloshing about in the back of the Humber. With a full tank and a fair wind, we should get us to the coordinates we were given when Robert made his last phone call. We know filling stations are going to be few and far between from now on, and so, when we see one, we'll take advantage, however much fuel we have. My chief, Alan, is getting about sixteen miles to the gallon out of our stately vehicle, which is right on spec but really good given the extra weight we've had to carry – and I'm not saying anything mean about Ms Lane. Ha! Ha!

Talking of whom, she's been driving and we've done a creditable sixty miles since we left Lodney Pole, as I call it, because I can't pronounce it like those two Russian linguistic whiz kids we've got. But now we've come to a junction. The made road goes off to the left, but our route is straight on, and that is more or less a dirt track – a good-quality dirt track, mind you, but nevertheless tarmacadam it ain't.

Anyway, I'm rambling a bit because I haven't told you about the news that is on everyone's mind. We had a call from Ms Lane's sister, and what she had to say was pretty bad. Elspeth was killed in the explosion at number 41; Anne Waverley, Stewy's mum, died in hospital last night; and Stewy is in intensive care, critically injured, but we don't know how critical that is. Little Alex, Stewy's half-brother, got away with just a scratch and is now being looked after by social services, which doesn't fill anyone with confidence.

As you can imagine, the mood is pretty sombre, yet we're all even more determined to rescue Robert and Noah. It's what Elspeth would have wanted. She was certainly one tough lady.

Do you get the impression that I might not have taken this news in properly yet? Everyone says I'm pretty dense, but it just seems so unreal that people can be there one minute and gone the next. I guess it's just too scary for my brain to take on board all at once. Ms Lane says that if we're going to see this mission through we've got to put what's happened in England to one side, because we're facing enough dangers ourselves and need to be on full alert. Now that's something I can understand...

We've no idea where we're going to spend tonight – probably in the car. That's why we want to get this part of the journey over with as quickly as possible. Dan thinks in the next hundred miles we're going to lose our mobile signal, except for some intermittent reception when we pass through villages. It also looks like we're going to have some pretty horrendous weather, temperature-wise, as we head further north-east.

It's three o'clock in the afternoon now and two things have happened – no four. One, we've run into some lying snow for the first time. It's not deep, but me and Alan got all our gear on and went outside to attach the snow chains – a well-rehearsed procedure so it didn't take us long. That was the second thing. The third is, it's starting to get dark already, which may not be so noticeable in built-up areas, but here, it's just so total and makes driving a completely new experience, especially on stretches of the road that are shrouded by trees. Alan claims the snow will make it as good as driving in daylight, but I'm thinking, how will he know where the road ends and the verge begins? What happens if there's a dirty great ditch out there?

I've left the most worrying happening to last. We're being followed. About half a mile back, there's a big, black Mercedes Viano MPV – not as classy as our limo, of course, but possibly better for camping out in than ours. I wasn't

273

convinced at first. The road is so straight and there's so little traffic that anything on our tail may seem to be following us, but Alan is certain, simply because it has been with us for a good hour and has stayed at the same relative distance for all that time. He slowed down for a stretch just to prove it to doubting Justin, and lo! It did exactly the same.

We've arrived in a small snow-covered town called Kargopol which is easier to say than Lodney Pole, and we've found somewhere to stay – the original-sounding Hotel Kargopolochka. Ms Lane rolled her eyes and called it 'another concrete relic from the Brezhnev era', but it's reasonably clean and warm so what more do we want? Especially as it only cost 1600 roubles for a double room and breakfast.

There are nearly as many onion-domed churches in this place as there are houses. That's an exaggeration, of course. The hotel is only about a hundred and fifty yards from the Onega River, which runs out of another of those massive Russian lakes to the south and all the way up to the White Sea, nearly two hundred miles in all. One day when I'm old, like twenty – ha! ha! – it might be nice to come back here on holiday in the summer and get a real idea of what the country's like.

Alan was stressing about the car overnight and kept going on about the Mercedes and what if this, and what if that? I told him to chill. I had a bit of fun with him because the only showers here are for two people and I asked him if he'd like to share and we could wash each other's backs. Cue beetroot face. I'm not telling you if we did share in the end; I'll leave that to your imagination. One thing we did do again was to practise our moves. This time I invited Dan to watch, but he said that being present while two sweaty boys grapple with each other wasn't his idea of fun. But what else is there to do in Kargopol when it's twenty below outside?

The next morning, Alan had me out at the crack of dawn, which to be honest isn't until half past eight, to look over the car. All was well, as I expected it to be, though for the first time we had to use the starting handle to get it going. We did find a petrol station eventually, but it had run out of unleaded! Jack suggested we fill it with diesel, which got him the evil eye from both Alan and his brother. Cue more stress.

We've lost our mobile signal now. Jack got in one last call to his little pest of a brother, Mikey – though, to be fair, he has been a star and one of the team, especially since the bad news from number 41. He said that Stewy was still in intensive care and would need operations, but he wasn't sure what for. From a slow beginning, the explosion now seems to be causing something of an uproar in Swanford, and every news bulletin has some new angle on it. Mikey said that he and his friend Mike Hartley are compiling a dossier on it. I doubt I knew what a dossier was when I was seven; in fact, I'm still not sure now.

***

65: Saturday, 9th November. 2.15 p.m. MSK, Arkhangelsk Oblast, Gosudarstvennyi Meditsinskii Institut (gomoseksualizm).

<u>NOAH</u>

Noah and John tottered up the stairs to the dormitory, carrying five glasses of tea between them.

"Oh, don't spill it, John," said Noah, already gasping for breath. "I'll get the door."

Inside against the interior wall, Robert, Jamie and Michael were lined up, each in their own bed. The older boys had succumbed to the virus that had affected both John and Noah earlier in the week, only if anything it was in an even more virulent form.

A bucket lay beside Robert's bed, because he had been sick after breakfasting on a bowl of porridge. He smiled wanly up at his friend.

"Tea time," said Noah.

The American groaned in protest.

"Come on, don't be a bad patient," said Noah.

Robert dragged himself up and took the glass.

"It'll probably all end up in the bucket," he said.

"Better to have drunk and lost than not to have drunk at all," croaked John, whose literary allusion was lost on the others.

"And how are the walking wounded?" asked Jamie, who was both hot and shivering.

"We'll manage," smiled Noah.

"I've never seen anyone with such a big, red hooter as Marshall's got," wheezed John.

"It's not that big," exclaimed Noah, "it's just that the rest of me is small."

He moved over to Michael's bed.

"Come on, little angel, drink your tea for John and me. It took us ages to turn on the samovar."

The boy's dim eyes beheld Noah. "Just leave me alone," he said.

Noah took the boy's cold hand and gave it a rub. "Don't give up, Michael, please. Dennis wouldn't have wanted that..."

The boy shook his head and closed his eyes and this time tears ran out of them. Noah tucked the hand under the duvet and stroked his head. "I'm going to put the glass on the cupboard, so it will be there if you need it."

John was standing by his own bed, looking out of the window. "Strange, when everything else is going to hell, how you can still enjoy a nice sunset," he said, taking a drink of tea.

Noah came to stand by him, holding his glass in both hands to warm them. "Oh John, what a life, eh?"

The tall boy laughed mirthlessly. "Things can only get better, can't they?" He looked down at his friend and then his eyes strayed to a glint of light coming from Noah's bed. "What's that?" he said, pointing.

Noah went over and picked up a nickel-plated brass key, the bow of which was protruding from the fold in his pillow case.

"Ooo," he said, holding it out for John to peer at.

"What have you got?" asked Jamie, holding his head to shield his eyes from the sunlight.

"It's a key," said Noah. "It was under my pillow."

"It must have been given you by Babooshka," groaned Robert. "What sort of key is it?"

"Like a front door key..."

"Try Madam's door," he gasped and then he leaned over and sicked up his tea into the bucket.

"Oh, Robert!" cried Noah. "We'll have to get you tidied up first, and you'll have to try sips of water. You've got to keep something down."

Half an hour later, the two boys stood poised on the threshold of Madam's boudoir.

"Well, go on then, try it," said John impatiently...

"Oh, I don't like to. It makes me feel funny," answered Noah.

"If you don't, I will!"

"She might still be inside..."

"Don't be ridiculous!"

"Oh, all right."

Noah pushed the key into the lock, gave it a turn and pushed. The door swung open.

"That Babooshka was a bit of a revolutionary on the quiet," murmured John, who was instantly annoyed at himself for lowering his voice.

They entered what was a small sitting room with an armchair, round table and a portable gas fire.

"Ooo, chocolates," cried Noah, running to the table where a box of Cadbury's Milk Tray lay invitingly. He flipped the lid open to view the contents. "Oh, she's only left the hard ones, the silly cow!"

"They're still a treat, and we'll share them," said John.

"Oh go on, let's just have one now," grinned Noah, his mouth watering.

"All right, but only one," agreed John sternly. He picked up the book that lay by the side of the chocolates. "*The*

277

Downing Street Years by Margaret Thatcher," he read, and showed the cover to Noah. "What do you think?"

Noah was hard at work sucking the chocolate off an unforgiving caramel centre "Ugh!" he shrieked. "Put it away. It looks too much like her."

"I expect that's her bedroom," said John, putting the book down and indicating a hardboard door.

They entered a box room in the twilight. Through the small window the first stars were visible in the deep blue void. Sister Hopkins had left her bed unmade and there were magazines and sweet wrappers scattered about. The door of a wardrobe by the window hung open, revealing coat hangers and empty shelves.

"It smells of her," said John. "Lavender soap. I used to like the smell of lavender, now I'll hate it forever. Mum used to grow it in the garden and when you brushed by it on a summer's evening the scent would waft all over."

"You don't talk much about your mum and dad," remarked Noah.

"Nothing to say, really. They're just Mum and Dad. In any case, I'm not a storyteller like you."

Noah walked round the bed and peered through another open door. "It's a shower and wash basin and – oh! Come and look, John. It's a portable toilet – we could use this instead of freezing our bums off in that cubicle."

The tall boy joined his friend and nodded half-heartedly then his shoulders sagged and he sighed. "Noah, what's the point? How long can we keep going, anyway? There's hardly any food left; we're down to our last few logs; and in this cold we can't go anywhere. Maybe Michael's doing the right thing..."

"No, John, Michael's really ill. You're just feeling miserable. We can't just give up."

Noah looked round for a light to dispel the gloominess, and pulled the cord on the strip lamp overhanging the Sister's dressing table. To his surprise, it lit up.

"Ooh," he shrieked, "she's got electricity."

278

His eyes fell on a green plastic attaché case standing on the floor between the legs of the dressing table. He picked it up and put it upright on the bed. When he flicked the catch, it sprang open, revealing papers inside.

"What's in there?" asked John.

Noah held up a pair of maroon documents with gold lettering on the front. "It's our passports and things. How did she get them?"

"Jesus!" said John, and took one out at random. "Huh, this is Jamie's – doesn't he look a sight?"

"Ooo, this must be Robert's," said Noah, taking out the only blue one in the case. "Aww, what a sweetheart. All that lovely ginger hair and freckles."

The light dimmed, came back for a moment and then went out. John hit his forehead with the palm of his hand. "That's all we need. The generator on the blink. I wonder how long it is since someone put logs into the gasifier?"

"Have we got to go out and fix it, John, with my red hooter and your wheezy chest?"

"If you want boiling water to drink, hot water in the showers and light downstairs, then yes. Unless you want to give up?"

"Better go and sort it out, then."

Noah returned the passports to the case and closed it up.

"Shall I keep this under my bed?" he questioned.

"Leave the case, bring the chocolates, the book and the bottle of Aqua-Kem," said John, "and I'll carry the toilet. I bet it's still full of DeVeal's shit, but I'll put it on the landing outside the dorm in case anyone gets caught short."

"You are good, John. What's the book for?"

"Kindling for the gasifier."

Noah closed the door and pocketed the key.

"Pity it's not on wheels," he said.

John hoisted the Porta-Potti into his arms. "Yeh," the older boy answered, sarcastically, "you could skateboard on it while you shit."

When they got back to the dormitory, Michael was coughing; deep racking coughs. He looked tiredly at them, then wilted back onto his pillows. The older boys were both sleeping fitfully, Robert's duvet lying halfway off the bed.

"I'll tidy the beds, get Michael a drink, then we'll go and do that job," murmured Noah. "Then, I'll need about three months' sleep."

John yawned and swallowed painfully. "OK, but I'll need four months."

Noah set about his tasks, forcing himself up and downstairs to bring drinks and comfort to his patients. A five-minute sit-down at the end was interrupted by John, who was now wearing his full winter gear.

"Come on, Marshall, if we're going."

By the light of the hurricane lamp, Noah saw Robert moving restlessly, trying to rise, and went over to him.

"Now you lie quietly like a good boy," he grinned. "I've put an extra log in the stove and now John and I are going to mend the generator thing and then we'll be back to force you to eat something."

The American smiled listlessly back at him and nodded. "I just wanted to say thank you to you and Bigfoot over there. You're both saints."

"Oh Robert, don't be silly. We all help each other, don't we?"

It was a moonless, starlit night, the snow sparkling in the frosty air. Two or three steps outside, Noah could already feel the chill seeping up through his boots. Except for a narrow slit for his eyes, he was encased in clothing. He carried the hurricane lamp and a bag of kindling while John had a stack of small logs in his arms. When they turned the corner of the building, Noah shrank back as the north wind gripped him in its polar embrace.

The gate to the inner compound was locked but, having observed Whiskers on an earlier occasion, John put down the logs and reached up to find the key secreted on the ridge of the architrave. Once inside, Noah could see exactly why his friend had described the workings as 'a Heath Robinson affair'.

"What's that smell?" asked Noah.

"What smell?" asked John, who had lost most of his olfactory sense over the past two days.

"Stink," offered Noah.

"Probably fumes," replied John, walking up to the gasifier, which in fact was a modified forty-five-gallon oil drum with lots of poorly welded additions. He began to unscrew the raised lid from the central portion with the spanner Whiskers had kept on a shelf under the awning.

"It's still warm," he said, "so maybe we'll be lucky."

"You're very clever, John. You remind me a bit of my CP. He was good with his hands too."

The bigger boy looked askance at him, just to check whether a double entendre was intended, but it was impossible to tell.

The lid came off and smoke billowed from within. "Well, it should still be producing gas," he said, beginning to add the logs. "So there must be a blockage in one of the pipes like before."

"What do you want me to do?" asked Noah.

"Keep feeding the logs right to the brim, while I check the engine."

John picked up the hurricane lamp and strode to the little shed, finding the latch hook already out of its eye. He pulled open the door and despite his dimmed senses the stench almost knocked him backwards. Noah caught it too and gagged. John held up the lamp for just one second before turning round and running into the centre of the compound where he sank to his knees and began to retch.

Noah cast a sidelong glance at the open door before hurrying over to his friend.

"What is it, John? What's the matter?"

The older boy peered up at him through his foggy glasses, then he squeezed Noah tightly around the waist and sobbed.

"Porky and Owen are in there. Their faces... skin.... black... rotting."

Noah put his arms round his friend and they hugged. "Oh, John, what are we going to do?"

"I can't go in there again, it's too awful..."

Noah felt a helplessness the likes of which he had never felt before, even after the news of his dad. He began to shake, and everything around him seemed to recede into the far distance. Only the closeness of John seemed real.

In his head he seemed to hear a wild laughter, raucous and uncontrolled, combined with screams and a terrible wailing full of pain and visceral fear, as if a party of demons had arrived to drag their victims down to hell. Perhaps this is how it ends, he thought.

John's grip loosened, and Noah looked down to see his friend slumped on his hands and knees in the snow. Now he could hear those demonic voices again, distant but getting closer, their harsh noises resolving into speech, but speech that was unintelligible, foreign.

From deep within him, Noah found some small pocket of resolve welling up, giving him a little strength and determination to face whatever was to come. He tottered over to the gate of the inner compound and peered round it. Three figures were stumbling toward him, singing and shouting, making slow progress in his direction. The three youths from the prison in Puksa had returned, as they said they would. And each had a bottle in his hand from which they swigged, and in their other hand, one carried a baton, another an axe and their leader, a long carving knife.

"Come out gay homos!" one youth shouted, to uproarious laughter from his compatriots. "We're coming for you..."

Noah's mind suddenly became as clear as the starlit sky overhead. He knew exactly what he had to do to survive.

***

66: Saturday, 9th November. 4 p.m. Arkhangelsk Oblast, Puksa.

JACK

We've come to a halt in a place called Puksa. It's not even on the map. We're on what could loosely could be described as the main street, as it has lighting, orange sodium vapour lamps. They haven't got a snow plough, though, because there's a good six inches of snow over the ground, with a multitude of tracks going through it.

The dear old Humber is in desperate need of petrol. I guess running the heater all the time does increase consumption. Alan's been driving all day and seems indefatigable when he's at the wheel. He's also been keeping tabs on the Mercedes, which is still on our tail. It won't have been difficult for them to do the same to us either. They can, no doubt, see our lights just as easily as we can see theirs. I'm wondering when they're going to make their move, as they've stayed a constant half-mile behind us since we first spotted them. LB thinks they don't care whether we see them or not, and I'm inclined to agree. They want to frighten us as much as possible.

This place is right on top of the coordinates we were given by Rosa, and now we've driven all the way round, we can see that the real centre of the town is a juvenile prison. If Robert and Noah are in there, it's going to be difficult to extract them.

Alan is getting twitchy because we haven't found anywhere to fill up, even though there are plenty of cars in the town, most of which seem to be parked haphazardly in the road or on the pavement.

We're back on the main street.

"Stop there," orders Ms Lane, pointing to what is probably a bar because the windows are steamed up and it has fairy lights. It also has a sign on the door which says 'Open' in Russian.

She's started pulling on her outdoor gear and obviously means business. The temperature gauge is reading twenty-four below.

"I'll go with you," I say, as I consider myself to be the most useless person in the party. I haven't done anything constructive yet except to not fill the tank with diesel.

"I am perfectly capable..." begins Ms Lane and I expect a bit of a tirade, but then she obviously has second thoughts. "Good idea, Jack. It takes two to tango."

Whatever does she mean by that? I hope she doesn't expect me to dance with her! LB gives me a look as if to say *you've scored*, which to be honest is the last thing I want.

"I'll fill up from the jerry," says Alan. "That means we've got about sixty miles left."

It's funny how a well-known academic blockhead can instantly conjure accurate statistics out of the air when it relates to something he's interested in.

I follow Ms Lane into the bar, which is absolutely packed and the air is thick with cigarette smoke. My eyes are stinging already and then for the first time in my life I see Ms Lane lighting up.

"They've supposedly banned smoking in public places," she says nonchalantly. "But when in Rome..."

"Right," is all I can think to say.

We're in a narrow rectangle of a room hardly bigger than a through lounge, with the actual bar against one long wall and the seating arranged in orderly fashion along the other by the windows. It has the well-known subdued lighting of the average dive. Everyone seems to be having a jolly old time, though, and no one seems to be put off either by the smoke or the music thundering out of a loudspeaker over the bar. The only thing missing is a flat-screen TV playing endless reruns of a football match between Omsk and Tomsk.

We've come to rest in a relatively peaceful spot which, curiously, is almost in the dead centre of the bar. Ms Lane looks around with her beady teacher eye.

"Now then, Jack, when I speak, I want you to pay attention to the people down that side of the room, while I watch out this way. Are you ready?" she asks.

I nod, not knowing quite what to expect.

"English homosexuals!" she shouts.

Oh my God, I think, cowering away from her, we're going to be arrested.

Then I see him. If the other customers may or may not have been disturbed by the outburst, it was only for a moment, while in the very last seat, his back against the wall, a scruffy-looking boy of about my age is staring intently at us. He and a man, so advanced in years that my mum would say he was as old as Methuselah, are engaged in a game of chess. There are clouds of smoke from their cigarettes hanging over the board, and their ashtrays are overflowing. The older man is still intent on the game, and his nervous mannerisms would seem to indicate that they are at a critical stage.

I tap Ms Lane on an indeterminate part of her body and I guess if I'd done that at school she would have me up for serious sexual assault. But here it's different.

"In the corner," I murmur.

"Well, go on," she says, "he's your generation. See what he knows." She slips a black packet of twenty John Player Specials into my hand and I imagine I see her wink at me.

I'm doing this for Robert and Noah, and so it's no time to be the shy, retiring Brit. I walk straight up to him.

"You speak English," I say; a statement, not a question.

He says nothing but his eyes reveal that he's listening.

The old man glances at me and then says something in Russian to his chess partner which might have been, *What's the matter, knucklehead? You're not concentrating.*

"You know about the English boys," I press.

That's a stab in the dark, but even if he denies it, I'm sure he knows something.

His mouth twitches. "What do you want?" he says slowly.

"We want to take them home," I reply.

There's a sudden sadness in his expression which I don't understand. Then the old man cackles, moves a pawn one space forward and shouts in Russian. The boy looks down at the board for a few seconds then knocks his king over. "*Yebat'!*" he exclaims in anger and looks at me as though it's my fault. The old man is still cackling and already setting up the pieces for the next game.

"Fuck is right," I say, and he's surprised. "Tell me where they are," I continue and show him the pack of cigarettes.

"You think I can be bought?" he questions.

"I've lost count of the number of bribes we've given on this trip," I lie.

"What is your name?" he asks.

"Jack."

He nods slowly, then he points in the direction we came. "You go that way, turn right, follow road. In about a kilometre you cross old railway line. Except don't cross, turn left onto it. Five kilometre, you there."

"Thank you."

I put the cigarettes by his hand and the old man looks covetously at them.

"What's your name?" I ask.

He looks up at me and there's a ghost of a smile on his lips. "Mistress," he says.

I nod as if I understand, and turn away. Three steps later he calls out.

"*Tovarisch* Moseley!"

I stop dead, and wheel round.

"You hurry," he says. "There's not much time."

***

DI DAVID RAINS

Slowly, Detective Inspector David Rains drove up the main street of Puksa, passing the Humber, which was parked on the right-hand side of the road. He hadn't expected to have to drive so far into Russia, but now he was certain their journey's end was in sight.

Kneeling on his seat, Derek Henderson cocked the spring-powered air rifle and took aim at the tinted window. Through it, his sights were on Edith Lane and Jack Moseley, who were poised to enter a bar.

"How about one shot up the arse for that fag hag teacher?" he said.

"Patience, Derek," said the DI.

He turned to his front-seat passenger who was eyeing Derek as if he were Britain's most wanted. "Dickie, what do you make of that terrible explosion in Swanford. Is it worth investigating?"

"By the gas board, maybe," said the constable.

"It's a long time since there's been a gas board, my friend."

"Just a figure of speech, guv."

"I heard that only two of the occupants had their body parts rearranged, and that the oldest boy is still alive," drawled Derek. "I'm sure that will cause a stir in certain quarters."

"He was very badly injured, though," answered DI Rains, "and even if he lives, it's likely to be as a vegetable."

"Well, let's just hope for your sake it's not a talking vegetable, then," said Derek.

"Dickie, how do you assess the situation now?" asked David hurriedly.

"Er, do you mean in Swanford or here?"

"Here, Dickie. Haven't we just seen two suspected felons entering what appears to be the Russian equivalent of the Rose and Crown?"

Richard Masefield cleared his throat. "Well guv, I mean David, I guess those two have gone inside that drinking establishment to procure some beverage which is illegal for minors to consume."

Derek sniggered. "Where do you get all this stiff speak from, Granddad? Is it from the police manual for 1912?"

"Was I talking to you?" snapped the constable. "I thought Councillor Henderson's boy might have learned some manners."

"Now don't lose your rag, old man."

David Rains backed the MPV into a parking space some two hundred yards up from the bar.

"Dickie," he said patiently. "Think about it. This bunch of poofs is searching for their comrades, who were sent to Russia for corrective training. My copper's nose tells me we are very close to Camp Queer. In that drinking establishment, as you so eloquently put it, they are either consorting with the Russian homosexual underground or attempting to gather information on the fly."

"My nose tells me they're close to running out of fuel, as well," said Derek, who was observing his half-brother through the sights of his rifle, filling the Humber's petrol tank from a jerry can. "Did you know, I taught that fucking little cunt everything he knows about cars?"

"Well," said David sarcastically, "you must be very proud of yourself."

"I've never seen a thirteen-year-old handle a car like he handles that old jalopy," said Constable Masefield. "All completely illegal, of course, but you have to admire his skill."

"You sound if you're getting the hots for the little faggot, Granddad. Have you gone all paedo on us?"

"You're disgusting," declared Constable Masefield. "David, can't you do something about his dirty mouth?"

"Gentlemen, gentlemen, we are getting off the point," sighed the DI. "As the shirt-lifters are now close to their goal, we must organise ourselves so that their plan cannot be put into operation."

"But we have no concrete evidence as to what that plan actually is yet," stated the constable. "If they're going to spring the homos, shouldn't we wait to catch them at it and charge them with kidnapping?"

"Where were you when they gave brains out, Granddad?" scorned Derek. "Do you think a charge of kidnapping would stick? Faggots collaborate with one another, just like Yids and pikeys."

David Rains scratched his chin. "The evidence of their criminality will be in that car, Dickie. You realise that these adolescent benders who were flown to Russia for treatment are not here under duress. They were volunteered by their legal guardians. Though, strangely, the legal guardian for most of them is Swanford social services – or Lambda Healthcare, as it's privately known."

"Are you telling me that these inmates could just walk away from their therapy and be whisked back to our country by that group of nancy boys?"

"That is my reading of the situation, Dickie, yes." He cast a glance back over his shoulder and for a moment locked eyes with Derek.

"And we can't allow that, can we, Granddad?" said the youth.

"Therefore we need a plan to apprehend them," said the constable, ignoring the youth, who was breathing down his neck.

"That's right, a plan to happrehend them," laughed Derek, swinging the barrel of his rifle in front of him.

"Less cheek at the back there," the detective inspector said without any semblance of sincerity. "Now, my opinion is that first we need to immobilise that vehicle and draw the occupants out, but we can hardly do that in the middle of town."

"Time to show you some real skill behind the wheel," said the youth.

"Do you think you can safely put that Humber out of commission then, Derek?" asked Rains. "Given the prevailing conditions."

"Davey boy, there's nothing like going a-hunting in a cold climate. I'll show that whining, dim-witted faggot who the master driver is around here. I'll have that body-rolling rust bucket off the road before Granddad here can shout 'copper'."

"I don't want any driving histrionics," said Constable Masefield.

"You leave it to me, Dickie dear," scoffed Derek. "And if you get nervous, just shut your eyes and dream of a faggot-free England."

"All right, all right," said David. "That's enough. Now, once we've got them cornered, I want you, Dickie, to apprehend the driver, right, and get him back into the Merc. Cuff him and if he gives you any trouble, slap him down. Is that clear?"

"You mean Alan Henderson, thirteen, short blond hair, five foot tall, one hundred pounds?"

"That's right, well remembered, Dickie."

"It's because he's got the hots for him," sniggered Derek.

David Rains put his hand on his colleague's arm. "Stay calm, acting Detective Constable, it's a policeman's lot to remain unfazed under duress."

Richard Masefield gritted his teeth and tried to focus on the operational procedures.

"Yes guv, but that means you two will have four to deal with."

"A woman, a queer and two pansy-boy footballers," scorned Derek, preparing to swap places with DI Rains. "Big deal."

"Once you have the prisoner secure, I want you to get the van ready for departure. Nothing more. Are you clear on that, acting Detective Constable?"

"Yes, guv."

"Good, now you go and sit in the back, while I make sure Derek is really the driver he thinks he is."

"I don't need nannying, Davey boy," said Derek sharply.

"No, but the cheeky sod could do with a clip round the ear," suggested Constable Masefield, unbuckling his seatbelt.

As he prepared to take the wheel, Derek Henderson's eyes narrowed and he cracked his knuckles, but this time he remained silent.

***

68: Saturday, 9th November. 4.25 p.m. MSK, Arkhangelsk Oblast, Puksa.

<u>DAN</u>

After what Jack's just told us, we're all getting our outdoor kit on, though Alan's left his gloves off, I guess for better control of the Humber. He keeps peering through the windscreen towards the Mercedes and his eyes have a determined, slightly faraway look which he immediately blinks away when he sees me watching him through the driver's mirror.

We're all ready. As I sit next to Jack in these comfortable back seats, I can almost hear his heart beating, though outwardly he appears calm and resolute. Adrenalin begins to run through my veins too as Alan fronts the big machine out into the road then does a backwards three-point turn. It may be the main street, but it's only three car-widths from kerb to kerb, with two lines of haphazardly parked Russian vehicles, but somehow he avoids any mishaps and we're shortly gliding back down the snow-covered road.

"Turn first right, and then it's just over a kilometre to the old railway line," repeats Jack, probably unnecessarily, but Alan nods.

I look through the rear window and see the MPV is also executing a three-point turn, but in an even more confined space.

We leave the street lights behind as we take the south road out of town. Alan keeps our headlamps dipped. The snow glistens and overhead stars shine from the inky sky. There's no urban sprawl here and certainly no suburbs. We pass the sign for Puksa and immediately we're in the countryside, a thick pine forest on our left and snow-covered fields to our right, which stretch away unbroken to the dark horizon. As yet, there's no sign of the Mercedes, nor is there any other traffic on the road.

Jack leans forward and is about to open his mouth when Alan forestalls him.

"I got it."

Barely noticeable by the side of the road, I spot a single upright stake with a cross tacked to it. All that remains of a level crossing. As Alan makes the left turn, I glance through the side window and see a pair of headlamps on full beam coming towards us. My heart rate increases again and my breathing likewise.

We start down the completely straight track that's been cut like a knife through the forest, and I'm thinking this is one strange railway. There's not enough room for two cars to pass without scraping the tree branches on either side, never mind a train. And then, as if in answer to my unspoken question, Ms Lane offers an explanation.

"These narrow gauge railways were often built in Soviet times to use labour, and many just went nowhere," she says and her voice has an unaccustomed tremor.

"Interesting," responds Justin in that way he uses at school to denote just the opposite. I have to put my glove over my mouth. Nervousness makes me more likely to laugh when I shouldn't.

Alan slows the car to a crawl. There's something lying in the snow up ahead. It looks like a dead animal.

"Look!" says Ms Lane, pointing to the roadside. "Someone's lost a suitcase."

And that's not all we can see, for a whole wardrobe of women's clothing is scattered along the snowy verge and hanging from the trees, as though the case has been opened and thrown out of a moving vehicle.

"It's a fur coat," says Alan, referring to the 'dead animal'. "Do you want to stop?"

I look through the back window. The Mercedes has turned onto the track and is about half a mile behind, but gaining ground rapidly. "Better not," I say.

Alan glances at me through the mirror again and gives me a little smile, then he opens the throttle just a touch and I'm glad that we're picking up speed again.

"Disgusting throwing away perfectly good clothes like that," says Ms Lane, "when there's so much poverty here."

I have the feeling that there is more to that episode than meets the eye, but I keep schtum.

"Halfway," says Alan, referring to the five kilometres.

"It may be give or take," clarifies Jack.

"No problem," says our driver. "Is everyone belted in securely?"

This scares me more than anything so far, not only because of what he said, but also that someone of so few words felt the need to say it.

"Are they going to ram us?" asks Ms Lane in alarm.

"We should brace for impact," replies Justin, who is a bit of a Trekkie on the quiet, but will never admit it.

"Yes, Captain," I say, just to let him know I know, but he remains unmoved next to our driver, who for some reason is suddenly slowing down again.

Both Jack and I have the same thought and we both swivel round to check on our pursuers. The headlamps of the Mercedes are approaching at what seems to be a breakneck speed.

"Er, Alan," says Jack, tentatively, "they are coming up rather fast behind us."

He doesn't get a reply and our vehicle continues to decelerate.

I think I'm starting to hyperventilate. Ms Lane also has a glance back, then turns her head, looking across at Justin, who is the only one among us remaining quiet and untroubled in his seat.

"Alan, those men are nearly upon us!"

I think Ms Lane's words were supposed to sound authoritative and teacherly, but they came out in an unmodulated screech.

I find my sweaty gloved hands are gripping the front of my seat. The light from our pursuers' headlamps is now filling the cabin.

I feel I'm about to scream at him, when suddenly we bump against something and the front of the Humber starts to rise gently off the ground. By the time we reach the apogee, the mascot on the bonnet is almost as high as the roof. Then the back wheels touch the same obstruction. Alan revs, the tyres grip and lift, and we start to level out. Our driver gives the Humber some acceleration and we proceed somewhat less gently off the other side of what I realise is a makeshift bridge.

Meanwhile the MPV is now only four car lengths away and hurtling towards us at fifty or sixty miles per hour.

I notice Justin lean calmly towards Alan. "Brilliant, my man," he whispers into his ear. Then there is an almighty crash behind us. I look back and see the Mercedes almost suspended in the air above the bridge, its front wheels hanging off, the tyres ripped to shreds, its headlamps pointing vertically down. And then it tilts over and slams down onto its roof, crushing the windows and shattering the tinted glass. The wrecked MPV slides sideways and comes to rest, teetering on the left-hand edge of the snow-covered parapet, steam rising from the engine compartment, the open rear door still bouncing up and down.

Alan brings the Humber to a halt. We're all shaken up, but we can't let that worry us now.

"Let's get the petrol," he says, as cool as the weather outside, "before it goes over..."

"I think I'd prefer to remain in the car, if you don't mind," says Ms Lane.

***

69: Saturday, 9th November. 4.45 p.m. MSK, Arkhangelsk Oblast, a bridge over a tributary of the River Belaya.

JUSTIN

The rest of us are out of the car in seconds. It's pretty chilly out here. There's no sign of anyone moving about in the Merc – no surprise to me!

"How did you know about the bridge?" asks Dan, taking his torch from the boot.

Alan and I exchange glances.

"There's a sign, like that," he replies, pointing to the corresponding snow-topped one on this side of the bridge.

Jack comes to stand beside his brother.

"I think what LB is trying to say is that we're sorry we doubted you, unlike Mr Walker, who obviously knows better."

"Let's just say, I remain calm under fire," I smirk, annoyingly.

"We'd better see what the damage is," says Dan, deliberately shining the torch into my eyes.

"And let's try to do it in less than five minutes," Jack states.

I don't particularly want to see mangled bodies, even if they do belong to low-lifes like Derek Henderson and Detective Inspector David Rains, and so I leave that privilege to the Moseleys, particularly DM, who in my opinion has always had a ghoulish streak. I expect you have to be that way if you want to be a doctor. Poor old Elspeth certainly thought he would make a good surgeon.

He's gone round to the front of the Merc with Jack, while Alan and I are collecting jerry cans of fuel from the back. They had eight, but four of them have split and even in this cold weather it stinks of petrol. Still, we have enough now to get us back to the filling station at Lodney Pole. I'm pleased Ms Lane is still in the car and hasn't decided to come out for a fag. Boom! Boom! Ha! Ha!

Their suitcases are here too, all broken open and now swimming in fuel. Seeing them makes me sad, really, and I think how pathetic these three were to be chasing teenage boys across two continents just for revenge.

It's not as though I can't see the bodies in the front; it's just that I'm trying not to pay too much attention. One of them is still buckled into his seat – upside down. When DM wafts his torch around or takes a flash photograph – I told you he was ghoulish, didn't I? – I can't help noticing the spray of blood across the shattered windscreen, which is just held together by the plastic laminate. I'm not going to throw up or anything, and I know DM is doing the right thing, but it's just a bit too much for me. I guess I'm just a wimp who gets sea-sick and leaves the dirty work to others.

Every time we move around, the MPV creaks or another piece of glass cracks, or a chunk of metal or plastic falls off and clatters to the ground. It reminds me of the NCC-1701-D when it pitched into that planet. Oops, I'm giving away too much of my shady past there.

Three-fifths of the Merc is on the bridge and the rest is hanging over a frozen stream, or is it a river? I don't think it'll go over of its own accord, which means we're going to have to help it, because at the moment the Humber would never squeeze past.

Jack's come back round. Even though he's all wrapped up I can see how pale he's gone.

"Bad, is it?" I ask.

He looks at Alan, who's busying himself with the jerry cans and trying to look uninterested.

"Derek and the inspector weren't wearing seat belts," he says, "and only the driver's air bag inflated."

"He never wore a seat belt," comments Alan, even though he's uninterested.

"Are they…?" I ask.

"Both dead," he replies. "The inspector's head made a big dent in the windscreen."

Alan gives up trying to be uninterested.

"How did my brother die?" he questions.

"He was shot," states Jack, categorically.

"Shot!" I exclaim, too loudly.

Alan says nothing, waiting for Jack to continue.

"The gun is still in Rains' hand. I guess he thought his final act of revenge should be against the person who was about to cause his death. LB says it's best to leave it, in case there's an investigation."

"Might have come in useful," I say.

As if in answer, Jack brings out what he's been hiding behind his back. It's an air rifle.

"Jesus!" is my reaction.

"My brother was a really good shot with one of those," says Alan, and I detect a small amount of admiration in his voice. Perhaps now that Derek has got his just deserts, there's no point in hating him any more.

"Then I'm glad he didn't get the chance," answers Jack, and holds up two spare clips. "More than enough for all of us."

"Can we push the van off the bridge now?" asks Alan.

"There are two problems," answers Jack. "The first is that the deck is made of railway sleepers sandwiched together, and when the van hit, it moved the whole lot about six inches this way. The first sleeper is cracked and may give way, which will leave a gap of well over a foot…"

I watch Alan while his mechanic's brain ticks over.

"It doesn't feel as if the bridge is going to collapse, and so it shouldn't be too much of a problem. We need to find two short lengths of timber to act as rails. Depending on what we find, that'll determine how much we have to unload from the Humber."

That's my boy! I don't know how anyone can be so fucked up in one way and so totally razor-sharp in another. Though I probably can't figure out how his brain works because my own is just a wobbly jelly sloshing about inside my head.

"And the second problem?" I ask.

"Could be more difficult," he says. "The third person in the van is alive, and it's someone I know."

"Do I?" I ask.

"Not sure, Justin. It's Charlie Masefield's dad. He's a police constable. I don't know how he's involved in this, but Charlie's in my class at school and we used to be best mates before..."

"I get you," I say. "Is he the upside-down one?"

Jack nods. "He was behind the driver and was wearing a seat belt, but at some point in the impact his head got knocked. It's looks odd, and there's blood coming out of his right ear. LB thinks that being upside down is keeping him alive and that if he's moved or unclipped from his belt, it'll be the end."

"Is he conscious?"

"LB shouted at him, but there was no response, but he kind of prattles occasionally which is quite spooky. The ridiculous thing is, he's only wearing a shirt and tie, with a short-sleeved jumper over it."

"We should go," says Alan, suddenly, "the five minutes are up..."

My small buddy is back in the driver's seat again, metaphorically speaking, and I think Jack is grateful for someone to take the load off him. I call out to my big buddy, who is by the first passenger window, practically lying down in the snow, looking in at his patient with his torch.

"We gotta go, DM. You can check on him when we get back."

I know that if we're any length of time, the cold will get to him, if nothing else, but it is a let-out for the boy. I'm already feeling parky even though I've got layers of thick clothing on and I'm healthy.

Reluctantly, or at least slowly, he gets up and joins us.

"I don't like leaving him but, yeh, we've got no choice."

Jack gives his brother's arm a squeeze. "With any luck we could be back in half an hour with reinforcements."

"Are you talking about my fag?" says Alan, and although he's using it as an insult, the thought has actually made him light up.

"And mine," smiles Jack, "and he's bigger than yours."

"But not better," Alan murmurs, and hurries off to get behind the wheel.

***

70: Saturday, 9th November. 5 p.m. MSK, Arkhangelsk Oblast, Gosudarstvennyi Meditsinskii Institut (gomoseksualizm).

JACK

The Humber Pullman drew up alongside a pick-up truck with oversize tyres on a small snow-covered plot just beyond an open gate set in a corrugated iron fence. It was at the end of the old railway line, though vehicle tracks led away through the forest going south and east.

"What a dump," said Justin. "If this is it..."

"I thought it was supposed to be a clinic or sanatorium, not a prisoner-of-war camp," said Dan, pointing to the rolls of barbed wire on the top of the fence.

Jack was the first to poke his head inside the gate, torch in one hand, air rifle in the other.

"If it is a prison camp, where are the guards?" he asked, aiming the torch beam across the empty courtyard.

The four boys filed inside and clustered together.

"And no lights on anywhere, but the front door's wide open," said Jack.

"There must be someone about, or that truck wouldn't be outside," said Dan, his torch sweeping around the perimeter.

"What a dump," repeated Justin, "I bet that building would fall over if you pushed it hard enough."

"It looks like one of Ms Lane's ecologically sound wooden buildings," said Jack. "Talking of Ms Lane, where is she?"

"She'll come if she's needed," answered Alan.

"What's that?" said Dan, and strode off towards something he'd noticed by the left-hand wall. They watched as he reached his destination and knelt down, removing a piece of sacking.

"It's a body," he called out, his voice echoing very little in the freezing air.

"Who?" cried Alan in alarm.

"Don't know. A boy, not very old. No shoes or socks."

Dan's camera flashed twice.

Jack trudged over to his brother and looked down at the corpse.

"Half-starved. Sickening..."

The warning sound of raucous voices penetrating the night air gave Jack and Dan enough time to switch off their torches, a moment before three youths clad in winter furs rounded the far corner of the barracks. Each of them carried a weapon. Their singing, if that's what it was, ceased abruptly as they caught sight of Justin and Alan at the gate.

The three staggered forward several paces and, as if asserting their right to the premises, brandished their weapons.

"*Kto ty?*" the tallest of them said.

"Was that 'who are you?'" whispered Jack.

"More or less," replied his brother. "They look completely paralytic."

"They also look completely psychopathic," added Jack, "judging by the axe, the truncheon and the carving knife they're carrying."

"Shall we make ourselves known?" murmured Dan, edgily.

The tallest one pointed his knife at the two boys by the gate.

"*Shto tvorish?*"

"What are you doing? I think," breathed Dan.

"We're English," said Justin.

The demeanour of the Russians changed. Suddenly they were laughing hysterically.

"More English homo boys. You come. We show you what happen to gays in Russia, yes?"

They were now advancing as purposefully as their inebriated state would allow them towards Alan and Justin, who had a rapid exchange of words.

"Time to get involved," said Jack, switching on his torch and shining it directly at the tallest Russian as he moved swiftly to intercept the trio.

Dan followed suit. The youths were caught off guard and their laughter died.

"*Privet!*" called Jack. "You speak good English." This gave Justin and Alan time enough to put a little distance between each other.

A drunken uncoordinated attack followed. The Russian with the axe lurched at Justin, who turned swiftly and executed a high side kick into his groin.

"*Kiai!*" Justin shouted, which may not have been conventional, but obviously gave him a lot satisfaction.

On seeing this, the smallest of the three ran at him, his baton raised, but Alan, in an unorthodox karate move, stuck out his foot, tripping him up and sending him sprawling into the snow, his weapon flying from his hand. Alan jumped on the back of the boy, who looked hardly any older than himself, pinning him down. Meanwhile Justin had disarmed the axe-wielder by grabbing the weapon with his left hand and chopping his assailant's wrist with his right. The Russian stood bemused for a moment before the pains in his groin and wrist were added to by another in the throat, where Justin punched him. The youth clutched at his windpipe gasping for breath, and fell to his knees.

Simultaneously, the tallest of the three, the leader of their group and the least drunk, decided to attack Dan with his knife. Brandishing it, he came on rapidly towards the unarmed boy. What he had failed to recognise was that his companion was armed.

Without thinking or aiming, Jack raised the air rifle and fired. The tall Russian gave a small scream, more of surprise than anything. He dropped his knife and grabbed his mouth with his hand. When he removed it, blood and teeth were in the palm of his glove.

"*Sadítes'!*" ordered Jack, pointing to the ground with the barrel of his rifle.

The youth hesitated, his eyes darting this way and that, but when Jack raised the weapon again, he decided to obey and sat down in the snow, pulling his knees up to his chest.

Dan grabbed the knife off the ground and showed it to Jack. The blade was covered in blood.

By now, Justin and Alan had subdued both the other youths, who were lying face down on the ground, disarmed and defeated.

"LB, will you get the rope from the car? We'll tie them up."

Dan nodded. "Be careful, Jack," he warned. "There may be more of them inside."

"Possibly. Do you think you could persuade Ms Lane to come and interrogate them?"

"Now that sounds like a plan!"

Keeping his eye on the leader, Jack moved over to where Justin and Alan were standing over their prisoners.

"Good fighting, boys," he said. "LB's gone to get some rope."

"Jack," said Justin, sombrely, "they've got a lot of blood on their clothes, and it's also on this axe."

***

71: Saturday, 9th November. 5.15 p.m. MSK, Arkhangelsk Oblast, Gosudarstvennyi Meditsinskii Institut (gomoseksualizm).

JACK

The Russians are tied together in the middle of the yard. They're also tied individually, at their wrists and ankles. Justin did the honours, as he was taught knots in Cub Scouts. No one felt like joking about that. The youngest of the Russians tried to grapple with him, but he was given a dose of Kata, Pinan Sono Yon for his troubles. I don't really know what that is, but it caused quite a lot of pain and a bloody nose.

After that they became docile and I had Justin hold the rifle while I searched their pockets. They had nothing of any value: not a single rouble between them, but their leader had two bunches of keys on him. One for the pick-up truck and the other, having tested them on the outside gate, are the compound keys. Ms Lane said the Russians shouldn't be sat out here for too long in the cold, but that depends what LB and I find inside.

The only response Ms Lane got to her questions was *all dead*, and so I'm feeling pretty low and depressed to be honest, and I know that Alan is too. God knows what he's thinking. He's a law unto himself at the best of times. I don't know who these boys are or where they've come from, but Ms Lane seems to think they've either lived on the streets all their lives or in institutions, which in Russia can be brutal places. Soul-destroying, she says, while I'm thinking scumbags. Two of them are brothers, that's pretty clear by their looks, the youngest who's probably Justin's age and the oldest who must be getting on for eighteen, though at first glance they could be taken for ten years older.

We're about to enter the building. It's in complete darkness. I've got a torch and the rifle, while LB has a torch, axe and his camera phone. But it's not really fighting we're preparing ourselves for.

We cross the threshold into a lobby with a staircase to the left, but we're going to stick to the ground floor for the moment and we're not going to split up, like they do in ridiculous horror films. All is quiet; too quiet for my liking.

The lobby leads to a long corridor running the whole length of the building. The first door we come to is open and leads to a kitchen. It's warm in here, heat coming from an enormous brick oven. There's a grille near the bottom at the front and a pile of wood by the side. LB takes an old leather mitten off a hook, opens the grille and shoves in a couple of logs. It's glowing pretty orange in there already, so someone must have fed the fire today.

LB lights a paraffin lamp which is hanging near the stove. Now we can see properly, it's clear that this place does have electricity because there's a light bulb hanging from the ceiling and a socket in the wall, but neither of them are working. The remains of a loaf of bread lie on the big trestle table. It feels quite fresh. There's also a couple of disgusting-looking pink sausages on a metal plate, one of them half-eaten.

The next room along to the left of the lobby has no door and must be a changing area because beyond is a really old-fashioned shower with a concrete floor and half-tiled walls. There are six spray heads, three on each side. It stinks of mould and I can't imagine Robert feeling very comfortable in here.

The rooms to the right of the lobby are even less interesting. One is like a place to hang out in, full of old chairs and benches, and the other must have been a staff room, with a Formica table and ashtrays crammed with cigarette butts.

Our torches cast a light on the ceiling as we climb the stairs. At the top Dan stops and lowers the beam to the floor. There are bloody footprints leading from a door on the landing. It's standing ajar and I can almost taste the bitter iron reek of blood coming from inside.

It's a dormitory, with two rows of six old-fashioned metal beds. A stove in the centre has gone cold. The windows are to the left, but the beams of our torches are angled to the right. I freeze for a moment, but Dan walks towards the second and third beds in the row.

A naked boy lies in one, spread-eagled on his back, his wrists and ankles tied to the frame. He's been castrated and his genitals stuck into his mouth. The word 'gay' has been written with the point of a knife across his chest. He is the spitting image of the dead boy in the yard. In the bed next to him is my beloved Robert. He's lying – or, rather, been laid – on top of another youth. Both are naked; both have had their throats cut. Blood is still dripping onto the floor from the mattress.

I'm not feeling sick or heartbroken or wanting to kill myself. I'm in a rage. Pure, unadulterated, boiling, murderous rage. I notice, through the red mist that is forming before my eyes, LB wipe the back of his hand across his mouth and bend his head, dipping into his well of courage, and I think how much better a person he is than me.

I think I must have made some sort of animalistic noise. LB calls after me, but I'm not listening. It's time for action. Time to purge my feelings. I'm down the stairs and out in the yard and the Russians see me coming and I can see they're scared. I roar at them and flick off their hats, then start beating each of them about the head with the air rifle. They can't defend themselves except by throwing their bodies around, which suits me. All I can see is the red mist through which their evil, ugly faces loom. The sound of the rifle stock hitting against their skulls gives me some satisfaction, so I hit them harder.

"Jack, stop, please. Whatever they've done, this is not the way!"

It's Ms Lane's voice, but I take no notice and give the eldest thug a lovely clean blow across the back of his head. His eyes roll up so that only the whites are visible, and the others cower away like frightened vermin.

Then I'm grabbed from behind. It's Justin.

"No more, Jack," he says.

I'm panting now and have to pause anyway to catch my breath.

"Let me go, Justin," I threaten, because if he doesn't I'll hit him too.

Ms Lane appears in my field of vision.

"Jack, tell us what's happened."

"Dead," I spit out the words at her. "Murdered, killed, tortured by these..."

I go up to their leader, who is shaking uncontrollably like the coward he is.

"Big man now, aren't you?" I say.

I put the muzzle of the air rifle to his left eye. He squeezes both eyes tightly shut, and I can see his fingers with their filthy chewed nails held rigid, waiting for me to squeeze the trigger.

Dan emerges from the barracks, sees what's happening and runs over to me.

"Jack, it won't bring him back. It won't make you feel better..."

Oh, I think it will. I give my brother a look that I can see shocks him.

"Jack," he says quietly. "What would Mr Colt say?"

I look at the other two Russians as I press the rifle harder into the eye of their leader. Snot and blood are coming out of the nose of the youngest, and tears are trickling down his cheeks. "Please not, English," he says. "Please not hurt my brother..."

What would Mr Colt say? LB is trying to blackmail me because he knows what Mr Colt would say. That I should remember one of his lessons, not this year but last, where he spent the whole time on just four lines of a Shakespeare play which he said were probably the most profound words in any book or work of literature. I don't suppose many of us were taking much notice of him – after all, we were only fourteen. Probably Mandy Simpkins, and therefore Max Seddon, were paying attention. I don't know why, but I was as well. It was a lazy summer afternoon near the end of term, but something in his voice made me listen. And now the pathetic crying of this human garbage pleading for his brother has reminded me too.

The quality of mercy is not strain'd,
It droppeth as the gentle rain from heaven
Upon the place beneath: it is twice blest;
It blesseth him that gives and him that takes.

I throw the rifle down at Dan's feet, but it's Justin who picks it up.

"There, I hope you're both satisfied," I say.

"It's what I expect from my big brother," replies Dan.

"That was scary," says Justin. "You are one scary man."

***

72: Saturday, 9th November. 5.40 p.m. MSK, Arkhangelsk Oblast, Gosudarstvennyi Meditsinskii Institut (gomoseksualizm).

DAN

Dan had finished upstairs. Photographs have been taken, the other rooms explored. There was just one locked door at the end of the corridor which he couldn't open. He wasn't too bothered, guessing by the Yale lock that it was the entry to a staff room.

Of the twelve beds in the dormitory, two under the window look recently occupied, yet there was no sign of anyone else – no sign of Noah.

Dan went down to the kitchen. The Russians had been brought in and were seated fearfully near the stove, watched over by Jack. He sat unmoving in a chair, the air rifle across his knees. Ms Lane was keeping a beady eye on him, though her main task was preparing food and drink from what remained of their own supplies and the few eatables she found in the larder. They hadn't eaten in eight hours.

Justin was giving her a hand, though Dan knew his culinary skills were all but non-existent.

"Make some tea," suggested Ms Lane brightly, and he looked at her as though he'd been asked to do a manual DNA sequence of the human genome.

"I'd better take a look round the back of the building," said Dan.

No one else seemed interested, and no one volunteered to go with him.

"Be careful, then," said Ms Lane, as if it was something she had to say rather than something she meant.

He frowned and went up to the Russians.

"What's round the back?" he said loudly, making a gesture with his hand.

The youngest glanced at his brother, then up at Dan.

"All dead, English," he said, making a face. "Dead long time. Not us," he added hastily.

"How come you speak English?" Dan asked.

The boy looked away, shamefaced, and said no more.

"We should be making tracks," said Jack, looking straight at Dan.

Dan knew this meant *hurry up, there's nothing left for us here.* Did he also detect a note of blame in his brother's voice?

***

Dan plodded around the corner of the wooden barracks, bending his head against the chill wind, fearing what he was about to encounter and depressed beyond words about how their journey had ended. He also had a gnawing feeling of guilt, emphasised by his brother's tone of voice: if he hadn't been so stupid and big-headed when he had filled the petrol tank with diesel, they would have arrived a day earlier, and might now be celebrating instead of mourning.

His torch beam picked out a cubicle that looked as though it had served as a toilet, and next to it was a metal cage. Automatically he went across and snapped a picture, passing an empty vodka bottle that had been tossed carelessly aside.

He shook the torch. Its batteries were failing and its light had diminished to a yellow glow.

The foetid smell of rotting flesh came to him even before he reached the gate of the inner compound. He stopped, swallowing back bile. This was the most difficult undertaking he had faced, and he wondered if he was up to it. He looked back, seeing his and other footprints criss-crossing the yard and thinking of his companions waiting impatiently for him. Perhaps he wouldn't bother after all. There was no real point, was there?

No, if he didn't do it, he would think himself a quitter for the rest of his life. And Elspeth, or at least her memory, would be ashamed of him if he couldn't face what was, after all, just the natural process of decay. He looked up at the starlit sky, exhaled a frosty breath, then inhaled the freshest air he could find.

Dan Moseley strode into the inner compound, quickly scanning the area. The smell was coming from the shed under the barracks wall, of that there was no doubt. The door had been left half open by the Russian boys, who would have beaten a hasty retreat once they knew for certain what was inside. Next to it, beneath an awning, was an oil drum contraption with pipes leading into the shed. Strange: from the chimney in the top there came a glow, and a little smoke and flame, as if someone had recently lit a fire in the interior. Another empty vodka bottle lay in the snow nearby, but Dan doubted whether the Russians would have bothered to add fuel to the fire.

After a pause to collect himself, he walked purposefully up to the shed and pulled the door fully open, imagining himself in the role of the perfect professional. He didn't have to breathe to know of the noxious stench inside; the very air seemed to heave with the miasma. The dull beam of his torch picked out the engine and generator with the pipework coming in, and a haphazard array of electrical wiring leading out through a hole in the back wall. In the half-light, he could already make out where the focus of his search lay. The light came to rest on the swollen, blackened faces of two boys who were staring unseeingly at him. They were sitting against the back wall, legs outstretched, their shoulders touching. One had his arm around the other's shoulder. Dan felt a sting in his eyes, which he quickly blinked away. He knelt, bringing out his camera, and took two pictures in quick succession.

His job done, Dan rose quickly and ran from the shed into the centre of the inner yard, where he gulped down lungfuls of clean, frosty air. His thoughts began to coalesce. Those boys had died several days ago at least, probably from carbon monoxide poisoning, and so they hadn't lit the fire in the drum. Suddenly, he had a nagging feeling that he had missed something. It was as if he had been playing in a cup match and was heading blindly towards the goal but had become surrounded by defenders and had kicked the ball into touch, instead of taking notice of an unmarked Justin on the far side of the field. He looked back at the wide-open door of the shed and heard Coach Brennan's voice screaming at him from the touchline: *Look at the bigger picture, you pantyhose slacker, and go the extra mile.*

He took another deep breath and walked back into the shed, pointing the dim torch this way and that, until in the deepest shadows of the darkest corner its faint light picked out two pairs of eyes shining at him.

"Ooo!" said a distinctive voice.

And suddenly the smell didn't matter any more.

"Noah?" he began, a sob catching in his throat. "Is that you?"

"We thought you were those nasty Russians," replied the familiar quavery voice.

Dan reached down and all but lifted the small figure into the air.

Outside the shed, in the relative warmth near the gasifier, they held each other in a long embrace.

"You look... you're so thin! Noah, you're alive – that's the main thing!" exclaimed Dan. "We thought everyone had..."

"It hasn't been very nice," responded Noah.

The noise of someone clearing their throat came from nearby. Even Dan had to look up at the gangling figure who now stood warming himself by the oil drum.

"This is John," said Noah. "He's so lovely."

"Oh shut up, Marshall. Are those Russian ruffians still around?"

"They're all tied up at the moment," said Dan, remembering his James Bond, despite everything.

"Are you CP?" asked John tentatively.

Noah gave a snort.

"This is Dan Moseley, my hero and the most beautiful boy in Swanford, if not the world..."

"Pleased to meet you," said John, bowing slightly.

"I'm glad you didn't take what he said seriously."

"Well, he's right about the hero part, but I'm not sure about the other."

"John says he's straight," explained Noah.

"I am straight!"

Dan nodded, already aware of how close these two boys were.

"There's someone who's going to be really pleased to see you," he said, now looking down at his friend.

"Is he here?" asked Noah his eyes watering, his voice quavering, this time with excitement.

"He's here and Jack and Justin... and Ms Lane. They're in that old kitchen."

"Ooo!" said Noah, who then smiled and batted his eyelids. "Dan, will you carry me?"

"Tut! Tut!"

"Oh, John, don't tut, I'm feeling weak."

***

311

73: Saturday, 9th November. 5.55 p.m. MSK, Arkhangelsk
Oblast, Gosudarstvennyi Meditsinskii Institut
(gomoseksualizm).

ALAN

What's Dan Moseley playing at? How long does it take to get a few photographs of dead people?

I wish I'd never come now. The whole thing has been a complete waste of time. I tell you something: I'm never going to think about him again, ever! In any case, he was never my boyfriend, he was just a fag I used to know. At least I don't have to tell him about his dad now. Why does everything bad happen to me?

It's a pity Jack Moseley didn't shoot those Russians. I would have done. They've killed his boyfriend, Robert. I didn't know him all that well, but he seemed all right. Jack's standing over them with that air rifle of Derek's. He keeps looking at them as if he might beat them over the head with it like he did before. I wish he would.

They're scared shitless because the drink's out of them. They haven't said one word since Dan Moseley spoke to the youngest one, not even to each other. My brother Derek was given a cross-bred German Shepherd puppy dog once, and these three are just like it. When it was angry, it used to bare its fangs and growl at him, and then he would beat it with a broom handle until it was a puking, crying mess, grovelling on its stomach. The youngest one of these Russians was like that when Jack threatened to shoot his brother's eye out. What a wimp!

Justin Walker got fed up with trying to make tea and has gone to find some pieces of timber to lay on the bridge so that the car can cross the gap. I expect they think I'm going to drive. Well, I'm not. Ms Lane will have to do it, all the way home. No one's chasing us now, so it should be a doddle. I'm going to sit in the back and sleep. That way I won't have to remember anything.

312

I wish Dan Moseley would hurry up so we can get out of here. If I had my way I'd set light to the whole place. It's made of wood, so it would make a really good blaze. Ms Lane says we've got to leave the bodies where there are. She thinks they'll be taken back to England eventually, but I couldn't care less what they do with them because I want to forget everything that's happened.

Justin's come into the kitchen with a couple of pieces of wood.

"I broke up a couple of benches that were in one of the rooms," he says to me, and for some reason he's got this big grin on his face.

But I'm ignoring him because I don't want to talk to anyone, especially someone who is happy!

The fag must have been really scared being in a place like this so far away from home with no one to talk to. Of course, I would never get scared wherever I was. I was never scared in the room with the flies – no, never, not once!

Who am I kidding? I was pooing my pants all the time. I'm the biggest wimp of all. Why am I such a crazy, mental, fucked-up piece of shit? I've got nowhere to live, my boyfriend's dead, the only decent brother I've got is in hospital and probably dead by now as well. I might as well be dead. I wish I was dead.

Justin Walker's put down the planks and he's come up close to me.

"Did I hear you say *I wish I was dead*?" he says. I think he's angry with me.

If I try to answer him or even look at him I know I'll go all faggy on him, so I shut my eyes and keep my head down.

Justin grabs my wrist. "Right!" he says. "Come with me."

He's being a lot rougher with me than usual, pulling me out of the kitchen and into the cold passage. He must hate me now, which makes me feel worse than ever.

"OK, Henderson, look up and open your eyes, and that's an order!"

I don't know what else to do, so I open my eyes. The first thing I see is Dan Moseley grinning at me and the second thing I see is my fag, who he's carrying in his arms. And now I've gone all faggy on everybody and especially the fag, who I've got in my arms, because I love him and he's back and he's alive!

"Kiss my pouty lips," he whispers.

I have to wipe my eyes before I can look at him. I hold him at arm's length and he's smiling at me in a way that makes me think that he might love me a little bit.

"Have you got any diseases?" I say, trying to be stern like Justin Walker.

"Well, I've had a nasty cold and chilblains, and I've got a big red hooter and my lips are a bit chapped..." he goes on and on.

"Silence!" I command.

And he stops burbling and grins at me, giving me one of his faggy salutes. So I lean in and brush my lips against his and I decide I like it enough to do it again, only this time it might be a little more than a brush...

"Jesus!" I hear Justin say. "That boy's a dark horse."

"Another hidden talent," responds Dan Moseley. "Maybe he can give you a few lessons, a few pointers on your poor technique."

"Listen to it," says Justin. "Sophie tells me that being kissed by you is like being attacked by a toilet plunger."

"I've been dreaming about that for months," the fag whispers in my ear and I give him a sneer and play it really cool.

"Yeh, well, don't expect another any time soon."

Then I notice he hasn't got that stupid fringe and his hair is quite dark and when you look close it's in these tight little curls close to his fat head. I run my fingers over it and it feels quite soft and springy and I like it.

"Who cut your hair?" I ask.

"Whiskers," he says, whatever that means.

314

"Oi," calls Daniel Moseley, "you two lovebirds. We're getting cold out here and you're blocking the door."

I've just kissed a boy in public and now they're calling me a lovebird, but I don't care because I've got my fag back.

Justin Walker's come up to me now and he's looking straight into my eyes and looking very strict again. "Alan," he says, pointing at the fag. "His name is Noah, not fag."

Why is Justin Walker being all weird, as if I don't know that the fag's name is Noah? But he hasn't finished yet, and he's shouting at me again and threatening me with sanctions. "Stop calling him the fag, or else he'll be taken away from you and given to someone nice who calls him by his proper name!"

That's not going to happen.

We're back in the dingy old kitchen and we've had a drink and a snack, thanks to Ms Lane. She came up to Noah and me and started rambling on about first love being the most ardent and heartfelt of all, but I wasn't listening because she's old, and old people like to tell young people how to think.

She's given the Russians some food and drink as well, which I thought was a very bad idea. I could see that Jack Moseley didn't approve either, because he gritted his teeth and looked furious, but Ms Lane quoted something about the United Nations Declaration on the Rights of the Prisoner and the European Convention for the Prevention of Torture and Inhuman or Degrading Treatment or Punishment, which includes the withholding of food and drink, blah, blah, blah. I still think it's a bad idea, but I knew she wouldn't back down on this because she's a woman and a teacher.

Anyway, the Russians are locked in the larder now, which is a little room off the kitchen down some steps. I hope they're left to die in there.

Noah is talking to Jack Moseley over in the corner. I expect losing his own boyfriend and then seeing mine come back from the dead made him feel twenty times worse.

A boy I don't recognise is standing by me, like he knows who I am. Maybe I do know him and have forgotten, but I don't think so. He's about a foot taller than me and has zits the size of washers on his face. Maybe I should say something to him, but I don't know what.

"I'm John Price," he says with a smile. I think he's a bit shy, despite looking at least two years older than me.

I've remembered I've got to tell my boyfriend some really bad news, so I ignore John Price while I have a think.

We're both watching Noah and Jack, who are now hugging each other, and I think Jack's crying and it occurs to me that Noah's really good at making people cry.

"Those are big zits on your face," is the first thing I can think of to say to John Price.

He looks a bit shocked for some reason and gives me a curious look.

"Are you a fag?" I ask before he can say anything.

Why do I get the impression that he's now finding me funny?

"No, I'm straight," he says, "whatever Noah might like to imply."

I've got to be careful. Even though he doesn't look posh, he speaks in a posh voice.

"I've got to tell him his dad died," I say, and I hope he doesn't see how worried this makes me feel.

He looks down at me and though he's as thin as a rake beneath his gear, he reminds me of the BFG.

"He knows," he says.

"He does?" I reply and I'm sure it comes out in a squeak.

Perhaps I should be relieved that he knows, but this worries me for some reason.

"It's a long story, but no doubt he'll relate it to you at even greater length on our journey home."

I think he's being sarky about my boyfriend. Should I dis him or bop him one?

He smiles at me again, and it's a nice smile, so maybe I won't bop him, at least for now.

"I've been told a great deal about you, Alan," he says, and I'm stunned because he knows my name. "But no one," he continues, "ever mentioned the fact that you're autistic – in

316

fact, an autistic savant, if I'm not mistaken, given your talents."

An autistic savant! What's he on about? I'm nobody's servant!

He puts his arm round my shoulder and gives me a gentle hug, which is peculiar because it makes me feel quite warm towards him, even though he's just insulted me. But I don't say anything because Noah has returned with a big grin on his pouty lips.

"Watch it, Price! It'll be a duel at dawn if you try to steal my boyfriend."

"Heaven forfend," he replies, which sounds like pretty faggy language to me for a so-called straight guy. "You have a very interesting man here," he adds, giving me another hug.

I think it's going to take me a long time before I understand this John Price.

Dan and Ms Lane have just come into the kitchen, and she's carrying a green plastic case. Noah says it contains all the documents of the boys who were kept in the house.

Oh, what now? She's clapped her hands as though we're in some baby class in a primary school.

"Attention please, gentlemen," she says.

I don't see why I should have to listen to some teacher spiel, but everyone else has gone silent and turned to face her, so maybe I should too.

"For better or worse, our work here is finished and it's time to head back home."

Justin and Dan roll their eyes and smirk, but they're still paying attention.

"We've got a long journey ahead of us and we still have matters to attend to at the bridge, and so I suggest we pack up quickly and quietly and return to the car."

I hear zit boy laughing to himself behind us. "Quickly and quietly..." he chortles. I think he must be one of these eccentrics.

Noah takes my hand. "Can I sit by you all the way home?" he asks.

"Maybe," I say, because I don't want to appear too enthusiastic. "As long as you don't give me any of your diseases."

We leave the Russians tied up outside the compound. Jack locks the gate and then does the same to their pick-up. They look really fed up when he shows them their ignition keys then throws them into the forest. I hope they land in a rabbit hole. Personally, I would have punctured their tyres as well because they'll only try to hotwire the truck when they get free.

Everyone piles into the Humber. I'm in the driver's seat, of course, and my boyfriend is next to me.

"And no hanky-panky while you're driving," says Justin Walker, "or I'll have my place back." He buckles himself in next to Noah, holding the two planks of wood between his legs.

Jack and Dan unfold the occasional seats and suddenly the Pullman can easily accommodate eight people with plenty of leg room for all. That John Price looks like he's already asleep in the corner, which is a pity because I've calculated that everyone is going to have to get out at the bridge.

"Thanks, LB," I hear Jack say in a quiet voice. "You were right to stop me. I know it's what Robert would have expected of me too."

"I think it was Mr Colt who stopped you," says Dan.

"You, him and a certain W. Shakespeare."

"Jack," begins Dan. "I know I really fucked up. If I hadn't..."

"No!" interrupts his brother emphatically. "I know what you're going to say and I don't want you to feel guilty about that for the rest of your life. If you hadn't filled the tank with diesel, maybe we'd have been involved in a pile-up or Alan would have been caught by the police for driving underage. There were lots of reasons why we didn't get here earlier, and a lot of things could have made us even later. What I'm certain of is that you saved Noah and John when everyone else, including me, thought what you were doing was a complete

318

waste of time. You're the best there is, LB, and don't ever think otherwise."

I look round and I think Dan's trying not to cry. I wish my brothers, Derek and John, had been like Jack and Dan Moseley. If they had been, maybe I would have turned out better.

Noah squeezes my hand. "You're my lovely Cutie Pie and I wouldn't have you any other way," he whispers.

I must have spoken out loud again and not realised it. I'll have to watch that, or he'll start to think I'm a mentalist or something. I turn on the ignition and press the starter. The Humber's engine ticks over and I listen for any quirks, but it's running fine.

"What's an autistic servant?" I ask, releasing the handbrake.

***

74: Wednesday, 25th December. 10 a.m. Dumbleton Boys' School.

NOAH

"I'm not going to be down-hearted."

They're both looking at me sceptically.

"Our dad would never want me to be sad on Christmas Day," I insist. I'm trying not to dwell too much on the dark side – on our dad, and those cute twins, and Jamie and poor Robert and...

"At least allow yourself a degree of sadness in the Garden of Rest."

That's John Price laying down the law, and Cutie's nodding. They're sitting together on my bed. Cutie calls John the Big Friendly Giant. I'm glad they get on.

"All right, I might have a wallow then. After all, he was the best dad in Swanford, if not the world."

"That's more like it," approves John.

There's a memorial been put up to all those who died, both in Russia and England. Thirteen wasted lives. There was no government or council money for it. It was paid for by public donations, and a few charities chipped in. It's an obelisk with all the names carved on it. The stonemasons have guaranteed that it'll last at least a hundred years. That'll see us all off, won't it?

Cutie's phone's just pinged.

He looks at the text. "Justin says they'll be here in ten minutes to pick us up."

I nod. It's frosty outside, but sunny, almost like summer compared to Russia, and it's nice and warm in my comfy little room – I mean, study, as they call it here. It's even comfier because we've got some of the furniture from number 41. I'm reclining in Elspeth's armchair and my toes are nestling in a luxurious round Persian rug. She was very particular in her will about who would get what when she died. Jack Moseley says it's almost as if she knew what was going to happen. Being dumb, I hadn't realised that she had no relatives, and all of us were the nearest thing she had to a family.

"John, I've been thinking..." I say.

"That's a bad sign."

"I think we ought to write to Miss Valerie and Babooshka, asking if we can help."

"Don't be soft. We've done all we can for them. You should stop watching those English-language Russian news channels."

"It's not fair."

"Marshall, you know what we were told. Anything we say could make it worse for them"

"But—"

"No buts! Now go and get ready," he orders.

"I am ready, except for my shoes and socks."

I know he's right, but I can't help feeling bad about the two most innocent of our Russian captors being the only ones in trouble. Maybe I'll broach the subject again another day.

Cutie and I have been up since six. These days, getting up at that time is no hardship for me, especially at Christmas. We both had stockings on the end of our beds and he came into my room so we could unwrap our presents together. It was lovely, especially when he opened my special present to him, a hardback copy of *Art Deco and British Car Design: The Airline Cars of the 1930s*. You should have seen his little eyes sparkle. Of course, he had to check on his favourite first, the British Salmson 20/90, to see if the information was correct. I think it passed. The only drawback was the guilt I felt at spending over £100 on a book. That's more than our dad and me would spend on the whole of Christmas, but we both get a weekly allowance from Elspeth's estate now and it only took a few weeks to save up. Mind you, the guilt soon evaporated when Cutie gave me an extra-strength mega-Maberly for getting him such a lovely present.

Things happened so quickly when we got back from Russia. I was in a daze for days, as it were. Some of the photos Dan Moseley took were printed in the newspapers and there was a really big fuss about them. The government tried to have them banned for obscenity, they said, but it was too late. The truth was out there. John and I even got on the television news, but they wanted me to say things which I just couldn't. I'm hopeless, aren't I?

Well, it was all a ten-day wonder, of course, and by the end of November things had settled down. Then there were hours of legal talk and interviews by Elspeth's firm of solicitors. Swanford social services tried to get involved as well, but they got stamped on, fortunately, as did the police who tried to play the victims as two of their officers had died. Ten gay boys die and they're not interested. Two of their own are killed and they'll be trying till Doomsday to find someone to put away. Jack Moseley told us that his old teacher, Mr Colt, said there would have been a lot more trouble for our rescue party had it not been for our big-wig lawyers and the fact that the government hasn't yet got its dirty paws on the judges. The barrister we saw was very nice, and also very posh, but it was a bit overwhelming and I was glad when it was over. Now, here we are, Cutie and I, boarders at Dumbleton Boys' School and the only ones staying over the Christmas holidays.

We had breakfast at seven with the headmaster, Mr Forster, his wife and their two excited tiny tots. They'd been up since five with them. Mrs Forster made us feel very welcome, though I think we both went red with embarrassment several times. We had orange juice, cereal and fried egg and bacon to set us up for the day. We're going to the Moseleys' for Christmas dinner, after visiting the Garden of Rest. We have all met several times since Russia, but this'll be the first formal reunion. Ms Lane is joining us for the little ceremony in the Garden of Rest, but not for dinner – she has her own Christmas with her husband and parakeets. Justin says that Ms Lane keeps her husband locked in the cage with the parakeets. He is naughty sometimes. On Monday, Mikey and I had our hair done in memory of our dad. Let's just say Mrs Moseley did not approve of the outcome.

"What are you thinking about now, Marshall?"

"I was thinking about how much I would like to stroke your lovely wedge, John."

"Strumpet!"

"Oh go on, Cutie won't mind."

"He might not, but I would."

I bat my eyelashes at him and he whips out his new Samsung Galaxy S6 and snaps me with it.

"Can I see?" asks Alan.

John hands him the phone and he looks at the picture then at me and shakes his head as if in despair, and so I bat my eyelashes at him.

"Is this the 32?" he asks John.

"64, unlocked..."

They're going to get technical, so it's time to put my shoes on and get the bag of presents we've bought for everyone. John sneaked out of his foster carer's house early this morning and went to see his real mum and dad. That's where he got the phone from. There's a legal fund being built up to challenge the new law that says children aren't allowed to live with gay parents, and John hopes he may be part of the first wave of court cases. I heard that some of the parents – I mean the real parents of those who died in Russia – want to sue Swanford council. Mr Moseley told me that Owen and Brandon's mum tried to kill herself. I do feel sorry for them all...

Anyway, before he left, John wrote a note for his foster carers saying that he wasn't going to spend Christmas Day in church worshipping a non-existent super-being. I still have some Catholic guilt, and hope he won't get struck by lightning for saying that...

Oh, that was a car horn! I look out of the little window and see Justin standing on the gravel below, hands on hips, looking gorgeous against his dad's not-so-gorgeous van. I give him a royal wave and he smirks up at me.

"I'm going to take my book to show Justin," says Cutie.

"Well, you're not allowed to talk about cars in the Garden of Rest," I say.

He frowns, then brightens. "One day I'm going to find a 1936 or '37 British Salmson 20/90 sports saloon and Justin and I can do it up." He turns to John, quivering with excitement. "It's a six-cylinder, 2.6 litre overhead cam with independent front suspension, and only about five were made. Would you like me to show you a picture?"

"Later," says John diplomatically. "We don't want to keep Justin waiting, do we?"

I stifle a laugh, while I'm sure the BFG is stifling a yawn...

***

<u>PAM</u>

"Well, wife, what's the matter with you? Turkey not done, or are the chipolatas burned to a crisp?"

"It's not the turkey or the chipolatas, Roger, it's your mother!"

"What's she done now?"

"Prawn cocktail."

"Prawn cocktail? What's wrong with that?"

"It's common, Roger, and I don't want our children brought up to believe that prawn cocktail is the height of English cuisine."

"It was in the seventies, wasn't it?"

"The seventies is not now. She comes waltzing in here with her nose in the air and a jar full of pre-mixed Heinz mayonnaise and tomato sauce, a lettuce and a bag of defrosted prawns and, hey presto, in five minutes she's concocted ten prawn cocktails in her special cut-glass prawn cocktail dishes, while I've been slaving in this kitchen for five hours on Christmas Day getting the real dinner ready."

"Well, they do look very decorative on this tray and she has added two triangles of crustless buttered bread, a slice of lemon and a half a cherry tomato to each."

"Don't be flippant, Roger."

"Where is my mother?"

"She's upstairs in our bedroom, no doubt having a lie down after all her hard work..."

"I think I'll get you a glass of Harvey's Bristol Cream, dear. I think someone's nerves are on edge..."

"Roger, I'm not drinking, remember?"

"Surely a little one for medicinal purposes wouldn't hurt? It is Christmas, after all."

"All right, but just a taste."

Medicinal purposes! I'm surprised I'm not on crack cocaine after hearing about my two eldest sons' expedition to

Russia. And I don't expect I know the half of it. They showed some of Dan's photographs on TV when they interviewed Noah Marshall and John Price, but they said that most were too graphic for even post-watershed. They weren't allowed to broadcast anything at all on the topic before nine o'clock, in case children were watching and they heard the word 'homosexual' used in a positive light. That's what this country has become in just a few short months.

I doubt whether Dan's shown us a quarter of what he took, though the high-powered lawyers in charge of Elspeth Chamber's estate sent every MP a file on what happened, including all the photographs.

Noah came over very poorly on television; all he seemed able to say was that the conditions in their camp hadn't been very nice. John did slightly better, but hardly enough to bring down a government. Which is why Helms and his gang are still clinging on in Parliament. They lost some support and haven't been able to bring in their most extreme measures, but it still means John and his like can't go back to his parents. He's been palmed off on foster carers, though he seems to spend most of his time in the company of Noah or our Jack.

As it's Christmas Day, Rog and Simon Walker took the boys up to the Garden of Rest, where the ashes of those who died in the camp have been scattered. Ms Lane joined them there as well. There's an obelisk with the thirteen names, inscribed with the words: *Victims of prejudice at home and abroad.* The authorities wouldn't allow them to be any more specific. Even so, not a day after it was put up it had been graffitied with a cross and the words *Dead fags here: please spit on their graves* and *Good riddance, rot in hell.* It's now got a special polyurethane coating so that it's easier to clean.

There was an international outcry over the deaths in the Russian camp, though barely a whisper from our own government. Their great leader ordered the bodies of the victims to be returned to England. In a news conference, he said that he would personally take charge of the investigation into how and why so many boys died in such circumstances.

325

Roger said that was the cue for closing of files and shutting of doors. Except that a fortnight ago there was a story on the Russian news about the arrest of a couple in their seventies and a sixteen-year-old boy for alleged abuse at a psychiatric clinic for the rehabilitation of those with homosexual abnormalities in the Arkhangelsk Oblast.

When John and Noah saw it, they were fuming and sent letters off to the Russian Embassy. Rog says that these testimonies will be deemed inadmissible on the grounds that innocence or guilt are not important in a show trial.

In our parish, there have been some changes for the better. The explosion at number 41 finally got the Police Complaints Commission involved because, even after her death, Elspeth was able to pull a few strings. The Chief Constable has taken early retirement and two of the rank and file were kicked out for falsifying evidence. Detective Inspector Rains was going to be investigated for gross misconduct, but his death on a visit to Russia meant that the case was closed. PC Richard Masefield, father of Jack's friend Charlie Masefield, also died in Russia. Strange that neither Jack nor Dan has ever commented on that. Kenneth Anderson, the Police and Crime Commissioner, said he had been saddened by all the recent unfortunate events in the force, and would make certain that no stone was left unturned in finding the bad apples. Make of that what you will.

That monstrous Councillor Henderson is still at large. He seems invulnerable. There was an announcement on the radio that said: *After the sad death of his eldest son, some happiness had re-entered his life, in the form of Miss Cynthia Bizeray, a party worker and ex-model, to whom he would be getting married in February, before seeking the mayorship of the borough in the forthcoming election.*

I think someone ought to warn Swanford – and Miss Bizeray – what they're letting themselves in for.

At the beginning of the holidays, Jack, Noah and Alan went up to London to the Royal National Orthopaedic Hospital to see Stewart Henderson, who is still having treatment there and is likely to be in rehabilitation for several months. He's lost his right arm and right leg below the knee, and has a fractured skull, poor boy. Jack says he was confused when they visited and thought they had come to take him swimming. He also doesn't know – or hasn't realised – that Elspeth and his mum are both dead. I told Jack that it was a good sign that he at least recognised who they were, but I'm not sure I convinced him.

We were all indirect beneficiaries of Elspeth's estate. Apparently, not long before the explosion, she had been to see her solicitors in Chancery Lane to make a new will. In effect, it means that Stewart and Alex each own one third of number 41 Westbury Avenue and Alan and Noah the other third. From the proceeds of her estate and the income from her house in Hampstead, all four will be very wealthy when they come of age. Not that Alan seems able to appreciate it, any more than Stewart or little Alex does. He seems like a very dozy boy to me, and Roger thinks his brain lives on another planet. Despite that, Justin Walker seems to be almost as devoted to him as Noah, though Justin isn't exactly Mr Sharp himself, in my opinion.

The way we have benefited is that Dan has been offered a place at Dumbleton Boys' School, not only for this last term but right through to the end of the sixth form – and the same applies to Justin. Despite grumbling about the lack of girls at the school, they decided to accept – largely, I think, because of its sporting facilities. In addition, both Jack and Dan will have their University tuition paid for, as well as getting a generous allowance. I never really approved of their relationship with Elspeth Chambers, but I have to admit for her to have seen the potential in our boys is something I am grateful for.

Alan and Noah are now boarders at Dumbleton too. They're in adjacent rooms, but have been warned that 'sexual intimacy' is not allowed. As if that's going to stop them...

Dan said that Alan was certain at first that he was being sent back to 'juvie', as he called it. It wasn't until he realised that Noah, Justin and that huge car were going to be there that he was convinced to give it a go. Now he wants to stay there forever because, as well as having his own room and three meals a day, there's a workshop where they can work on the car and a gym where he and Justin can do weights and practise karate. The only drawback for Alan is that he has to do normal lessons as well.

"Are you feeling better, wife, with a thimbleful of HBC inside you?"

"We are not going to tell your mother today, Roger... and don't look like that."

"But if we don't tell her soon, it's going to come out anyway."

"She's in that mood where she's looking to criticise everything."

"But this is good news..."

"I can hear her now… *Roger, Pamela, how can you be so irresponsible? Isn't the world teeming with enough humanity? You're far too old to be having another child. In your dire financial straits, how can you be so reckless? I suppose you want to burden taxpayers like me with the cost of your holiday adventure?* Not today, Roger, and that's final!"

"OK, I surrender. At least the kids have been discreet about it."

"Well, that only makes up for their vulgarity when we told them."

"You mean, Mikey wanting to know if Simon Walker would now be his dad as well?"

"Obviously his brothers put those thoughts into his head."

"And Dan asking if I'd scored with Justin's mum."

"Trust you to like that."

"And Jack's question: whether we should be calling the baby Justina or Justin Junior?"

"That is something I'm not going to reveal to anyone."

"Listen! I think I hear Her Majesty descending the stairs."

"Why can't we put her in a home, Roger?"

"She's only sixty-seven."

"Well, have her sectioned then!"

"Nearly ready, are we?"

"Hello, Mum! Yes, we're about ready to dish up, aren't we, dear?"

"Yes, after five hours slogging over a hot stove."

"I'd better distribute the prawn cocktails then. A nice starter always goes down well, even if the main course proves to be something of an anti-climax."

"You go ahead, Mum, we'll be there in a minute..."

"Oh, Pamela! That turkey could do with an extra baste; it looks a bit on the dry side to me..."

***

76: Wednesday, 25th December. 1 p.m. 15 Leighton Lane.

JACK

Christmas Day. I suppose I'm enjoying it in a detached sort of way. Nana Moseley has just served up her famous prawn cocktails. Noah looks like his mouth is watering, but Justin's gone pale. I guess anything to do with the sea just doesn't agree with him. Santa brought Mikey his bike and yesterday he and Noah had their hair dyed blond with magenta spikes. He thinks he's the bee's knees – and maybe he is. Mum is determined to have it washed out by the time he goes back to school, even if it means dying it black.

I seemed to sleepwalk through the first three weeks after our return from Russia. I went through the motions of normality but I don't think I noticed very much. Then I had two weeks of mind-numbing heartache, which took everyone who hadn't been on the trip by surprise. I was off school and stayed in bed most of the time. I think if it had lasted any longer they would have sent me to a shrink.

On Sunday the eighth I got really angry and I persuaded LB to go with me to confront Robert's parents. I wanted to be there just as they got back from church and so, armed with the photographs that LB took of their dead son and some of the others, to give them an idea of what the place was like, we cycled down to the Ropewalk.

There was a 'For Rent' sign outside the cottage and when I looked through the windows, there was no furniture, no carpets, no curtains – even the gas fire had been removed. It was as if they'd never been there. So we cycled to the church on Westbury Avenue to confront the good Christians instead. As we went past number 41, we could see rebuilding work going on, even though it was a Sunday.

When we got to the church there was a handwritten notice inside a plastic wallet attached to the lychgate: *Services cancelled until further notice.*

Where did LB take me then? He took me to see Mr Colt. I was reluctant at first, so reluctant that when we got to his driveway, I turned round and rode off. You see, I'd set aside that day for being angry. But LB stayed and waited for me to come back, and when I did Mr Colt and his wife were waiting for me. It was the first time I'd seen them since the trip, and they treated me as if I was a long-lost son returned to the fold, and I suppose I got a bit emotional. But they were very patient with me. Mr Colt sat me down in the lounge and just waited until I had calmed down, saying very little, while his wife made us tea and invited us to stay for Sunday dinner.

Somehow, without me even realising it at the time, he got me to talk and I told him the whole story and how I felt deep down about Robert, something I'd never done with my parents. You see, Robert and I hardly had a chance to do anything physical together; we always seemed to be running scared of one thing or another. Except on one or two occasions, it was all in our heads and hearts, and never in our bodies. That is what I most regret now.

I wasn't going to say anything about the Russian boys and how violent I was towards them, not wanting Mr Colt to think me a psycho, but LB kind of steered me in that direction and when I told him that, in the end, what had stopped me from shooting the boy in the eye was remembering his lesson on those lines from *The Merchant of Venice*, I was surprised how deeply it affected him, possibly even more than the photographs LB showed him. We stayed for tea as well and when we left at about eight o'clock, I felt a sort of freedom – as though some great burden had been lifted from me.

I went back to school the next day, determined to get my life back on track. Mandy and Max are there to make sure I don't flag too much or start to feel too sorry for myself. Swanford Community School might be returning to something like normal. It's in special measures after getting so many complaints from parents about falling teaching standards. The board of governors resigned, the three teachers who were parachuted in at the beginning of this year have left, and the headmaster has been 'retired'. So far so good...

John Price has come to the school and is in our class. At first he was something of a celebrity, having appeared on television, but that wore off in about a week. He's a couple of months younger than me and is quite a lot like Max, being a geek, which even Noah's makeover couldn't really disguise. I've got to like him quite a lot. He doesn't mind sharing his thoughts and experiences in Russia, and will talk openly and honestly about Robert. Therapy for us both, I suppose. 'Buttoned-up' is how he described Robert: he found it difficult to believe he was gay, 'unlike someone I can name', he said, meaning Noah, of course.

When John isn't responding to Noah's endless advances with endless rebuffs; it's clear how fond they are of each other. In an unguarded moment, John told me that going to have a chat with Noah in Russia was like entering a cosy house after being in the middle of a dark miserable forest; a house where you could sit on a comfortable sofa in front of an open fire and be regaled with stories and memories that everyone was invited to share.

I wanted to find out if Robert's parents had returned to America, and so I got in touch with Rosa Miller. She seemed pleased that I'd remembered her, and we've been sending messages regularly ever since. Apparently, the Crittendens have returned to their house in Tyree and are acting as if nothing has happened. They go to the same church with the same people, and Robert has ceased to exist as far as they're concerned. It seems they behaved in exactly the same way when Robert's brother Aaron died. I sent them a Christmas card asking whether they'd like me to send them photographs of their dead son, just to see what they were responsible for. I suppose it was a bit cruel, but that's the way I feel about them. I don't expect a response.

The best thing about Rosa's communications are her scandalous stories about her sister Tammy – the one who tried to seduce Robert. I don't know how true they are, but the latest is that's she's had an abortion, though Rosa says how they managed to find anything in that Mariana Trench is a mystery.

She thinks that the sperm donor was a new recruit to the church choir, a fresh-faced thirteen-year-old by the name of Dwight Hoggins. Tammy is, of course, still a full member of the church and choir simply because she keeps all the names and addresses of the devout churchmen who've bedded her in order to blackmail them, if necessary. Meanwhile, poor Dwight isn't so fresh-faced any more, having been drummed out of the church after he was admitted to the STD clinic in Broken Arrow with a severe case of genital warts.

I had a Christmas card, a letter and a photograph that I never expected to get. It was from Tom Sanchez – Robert's Auntie Una's partner. How they got my address, I don't know. The letter was fairly standard, telling me how sorry they were to hear about Robert and 'how a young life had been wasted for no reason'. But it was the photograph that really stunned me. It showed Tom and an old lady hovering in the background, while in front was a ghostlike waif of a girl, and a little boy. His name is Barney, and he's a miniature Spanish version of Robert. When LB saw it, he did a double take and thought it must be picture of a suntanned Robert as a child. I'll write back, but I don't know whether we'll keep in touch.

Well, I've finished my part and I'm about to hand over to the person I now love more than anyone else: my magnificent, loyal and brave brother (who is, I'm afraid, as of yesterday officially half an inch taller than me).

***

77: Wednesday, 25th December. 1.10 p.m. 15 Leighton Lane.

<u>DAN</u>

We're all assembled for dinner in the lounge. We moved most of the furniture out and borrowed Nana Moseley's big table which Dad and I brought in Justin's dad's van. It's looking nice and festive with the white tablecloths, shiny cutlery and Nana's best wine glasses, the crackers, red and green serviettes and the tree in the window. A real one this year, decorated by yours truly with hindrance from a little pest.

It's a sort of reunion for the Russian six, plus Mikey, Mum, Dad and Nana Moseley herself, though the three adults have just retired to the kitchen in order to get the main course – turkey and all the trimmings – served up. I'm sitting next to Jack and opposite Justin, though most of the noise is coming from further down the table, where Noah is holding court. He's got his admirers on either side, Alan and John, and it's difficult to tell who loves him the most. No, it isn't, it's neither of them, because sitting next to Jack and opposite Noah is my little brother, hanging on Noah's every word and gesture. John says his adoration verges on idolatry, at which Noah shrieks and says he's not an idol.

Ah! At last Nana's come in with a tray to collect the remains of our first course.

"That was a really lovely prawn cocktail, Nana Moseley," says Noah.

Uh-oh! I expect he's going to get a rocket for being *too familiar.*

"Well, that's very good of you to say so, Noah."

333

What! How does he get away with it? Except for family members, no one else in my memory has dared to call her Nana Moseley.

"Some folks can be a bit snooty about my prawn cocktails these days," Nana says with a noticeable curl of the lip.

She means Mum.

"Our dad used to make a good prawn cocktail too, but I think this one was even nicer."

"I use a Webbs Wonderful," she says.

"I expect our dad's lettuce was a bit limp."

I can see John giving Noah a long hard look, suspecting gay wordplay.

"You're a good lad, Noah. A woman appreciates it when she's complimented on her comestibles."

Now, Jack's started to giggle, which is really nice to see.

"I think you would have liked our dad, Nana Moseley, he was homely and Christmassy just like you."

Now, if it was anyone else I'd say they were either sucking up or taking the mick, but Noah is nothing if not genuine.

"I'm sure, since he raised such a polite young man such as yourself single-handedly, he must have been a person of quality."

"Oh, he was, and he never drank, except for two pints on a Friday night."

"I like a man who drinks in moderation. My Walter was exactly the same."

Nana never talks about Granddad to anyone.

Then she spots Justin, who is still struggling valiantly through his prawn cocktail – shellfish are not for him. "Justin Walker, is there something wrong with my prawn cocktail?"

"No, no, Mrs Moseley, it's lovely..." He's trying not to gag.

Noah collects up his own and Alan's plate and the special cut-glass prawn cocktail dishes, both of which seem to have been licked clean, and hands them to a smiling Nana.

"Don't they feed you well at that school, Noah?" she enquires.

She's never bothered to ask *me* that.

"Oh well, not too bad, but it's not like homemade..."

"I should like to invite you and your young man over to tea at my house."

What! *You and your young man?* Since when has the rainbow flag been unfurled at the Moseley Snr household?

"Oh, that would be lovely, Nana, wouldn't it, Alan?"

"Lovely!" responds Alan on cue, much to everyone's surprise.

"How about this Sunday afternoon for high tea?"

"Ooo, crumpets please, Nana Moseley, with butter and strawberry jam."

"That's a very good idea. They're easy, and if I make us a trifle we can then watch a special Blu-ray I got from an admirer this Christmas."

"Ooo, I bet you've got hundreds of admirers, Nana Moseley."

"Oh, you're such a flatterer, Noah Marshall!"

"Do you think John could come as well?"

John shrinks back, thinking he'll be rebuffed.

"I don't see why not. He seems a nice young man, and if he's a friend of yours..."

Jack and I have never 'seemed like nice young men', and neither have our friends.

"What's the Blu-ray?" asks Mikey.

"*The Adventures of Robin Hood* – the 1938 version," says Nana, for the little pest's benefit.

Noah gasps. "Oh! Our dad loved Olivia De Havilland."

"Is it in colour?" squeaks Mikey.

Noah turns to his disciple. "It's gorgeous colour, Mikey, and on Blu-ray it should be sparkling. Our dad says that Mike had the leaves of the trees painted green to make Hollywood seem more like Sherwood Forest."

"Mike?" questions Mikey, seeing significance in a namesake.

"He means Michael Curtiz, the director," says Nana knowledgeably.

Mikey's eyes are beginning to swivel. "What's it about?"

"Ooo, it's very thrilling," says Noah. "There are sword fights and an archery tournament..."

"What's an archery tournament?"

"Well, all the best bowman in England, including Matt of Sleaford and Robin Hood, compete to see who can get the most bull's-eyes."

Mikey's practically delirious, and he hasn't even seen it yet.

"Can I come too, please? I'll be very, very good..."

I lean round the back of Jack's chair and whisper to the pest, "If you get any more excited you'll wet your pants."

The reply is a raised middle finger and a whispered *arsewipe*, also round the back of Jack's chair. 'Arse-wipe' is new for Mikey, and will call for brotherly retribution later on.

Nana squints suspiciously at her grandson.

"What do you think, Noah?"

She's asking his opinion!

"Well, Mikey does like good-quality films like *Pinocchio* and *Treasure Island*, so he'll probably enjoy *The Adventures of Robin Hood*."

I think Mum is going to be pleased when Mikey and Mad Mike Hartley are firing arrows at each other in the garden and spraying green paint on the trees.

"That's very true. At least the youngest Moseley has inherited some of the good taste of his forebears – unlike some."

Meaning Jack and me.

"I expect you're looking forward to being a grandma again..." says Noah brightly.

The cold in Russia was as nothing compared to the ice that now begins to form in our lounge. Mikey puts his hand over his mouth and goes red. So we know who let the cat out of the bag to Noah.

Oblivious to the gathering storm, Justin has managed to swallow the last of the slimy little sea creatures without being sick, and proudly hands over his plate and dish. Immediately, Nana spies my best friend as a potential barometer on the spread of this intelligence. It's my turn to go red, and I try desperately to get Justin's attention by kicking him under the table, but his feet are where they usually are, hooked around his chair.

"Thank you, Justin," she says sweetly. "Did you know that my daughter-in-law is expecting another child?"

"Oh, yes. Everybody knows. Coach Brennan says—"

"Coach Brennan!" Nana is beginning to implode. "Coach Brennan says what?" she demands.

Do you know those times when your team-mate is completely socially inept and a total embarrassment, like now…?

"Coach Brennan told Dan that the Moseleys are peculiarly fecund," he guffaws, putting emphasis on the word 'fecund'.

"I beg your pardon?" exclaims Nana.

"Yes, everyone was rolling around on the pitch. I had to look it up," he laughs. "*Peculiarly fecund!* Coach is such a laugh sometimes!"

Justin is still braying like a donkey when he spies my face across the table and realises all is not well.

"Oops," he says.

"If you'll excuse me for a moment," says Nana, "I have something I want to discuss with my son and daughter in-law."

A silence descends on the family members as we await the sound of pots and pans flying round the kitchen.

"Shall we pull a cracker while we're waiting?" suggests Noah innocently.

"I always knew you were a stirrer of the shite, Marshall," says John and he laughs and points at Justin, "and your fecund friend over there!"

And then we all begin to laugh – and once we've started we can't stop.

SATAN'S LEGIONS

The End

BOOK 3: INDEX OF CHARACTERS
(in alphabetical order by category)
(ages and status are as they were at the beginning of Book 3)

* Major character

Russia

B

Yuri Semyonovich Bakaleinikoff........guard, known as hairy man
and 'Yurine'

Jamie Baker*......................................15 yrs, kidnapped

D

Ryan Davis...13 yrs, kidnapped

E

George 'Porky' Eagleton.....................14 yrs, kidnapped

F

Brandon Frost......................................15 yrs, kidnapped

Owen Frost...13 yrs, kidnapped

G

Lieutenant Gergiev.............................. Professor Primakov's
assistant
Metropolitan Grigoriy......................... Holy Russian Church

K

M

P

R

England

R

Thomas Roberts.................................. Swanford social services

Kimberley Robinson........................... Ben Henderson's girlfriend

Louis Robinson.................................. Kimberley's younger
    brother, player Swanford Utd FC

U.S.A.

C

Roy Colt.. student, Yale University,
    son of Mr Colt

H

Dwight Hoggins.................................. one of Tammy Miller's
    conquests.

O

Shandra Oppenheim............................ Roy Colt's girlfriend